ALSO BY JUDITH FREEMAN

The Latter Days
The Long Embrace
Red Water
A Desert of Pure Feeling
Set for Life
The Chinchilla Farm
Family Attractions

MacArthur Park

MacArthur Park

JUDITH FREEMAN

Pantheon Books   New York

All rights reserved. Published in the United States by Pantheon Books,
a division of Penguin Random House LLC, New York, and distributed in Canada
by Penguin Random House Canada Limited, Toronto.

Pantheon Books and colophon are registered trademarks
of Penguin Random House LLC.

Grateful acknowledgment is made to Farrar, Straus and Giroux for permission to
reprint an excerpt from "Waking Early Sunday Morning" from *Collected Poems* by
Robert Lowell. Copyright © 2003 by Harriet Lowell and Sheridan Lowell.
Reprinted by permission of Farrar, Straus and Giroux. All Rights Reserved.

Library of Congress Cataloging-in-Publication Data
Name: Freeman, Judith, [date] author.
Title: MacArthur Park / Judith Freeman.
Description: First edition. New York : Pantheon Books, 2021.
Identifiers: LCCN 2020045179 (print). LCCN 2020045180 (ebook).
ISBN 9780593315958 (hardcover). ISBN 9780593315965 (ebook).
Classification: LCC PS3556.R3915 M33 2021 (print) |
LCC PS3556.R3915 (ebook) | DDC 813/.54—dc23
LC record available at lccn.loc.gov/2020045179
LC ebook record available at lccn.loc.gov/2020045180

www.pantheonbooks.com

Jacket image by Supawat Punnanon / EyeEm / Getty
Jacket design by Janet Hansen

Printed in the United States of America

First Edition

2 4 6 8 10 9 7 5 3 1

For it was not so much by the knowledge of words
that I came to the understandings of things,
as by my experience of things
I was able to follow
the meaning of words.

—PLUTARCH

Contents

PART ONE

The Apartment

1

I must say how I first came to this apartment where I have now lived for so long. I had been living in the small town in Utah where I was born, working as a waitress in the snack bar of a bowling alley called Wasatch Lanes. At the time I was married to a man named Leon who liked to hunt and fish and ride. When he put on a Stetson and boots he looked like the cowboy he really was, a big handsome western guy, as attractive as they come, but only if you could ignore the extra pounds he'd put on over the years. That changed the picture considerably.

Like a lot of my friends who grew up in that town, I married young, but my marriage had lasted almost twenty years, unlike those of other people I knew who'd gotten married straight out of high school. To my way of thinking Leon and I got along better than most couples, sharing interests as we did, until the day he met an ex–rodeo queen at the racetrack up in Evanston, Wyoming, and left me for her.

The day he came home and said he was leaving me I looked at him and said, Oh really? You're moving on? Does this mean I don't have to do your laundry anymore?

His news wasn't really a surprise: I had heard the rumors about him and Pinky, but I hadn't believed them. I told him it was bad enough for a husband to walk out just when you were starting to lose your looks, but to leave me for a woman named Pinky?

C'mon, I said. That's the low blow.

He didn't say anything to that. He just began making a pyramid of stuff on the living room floor, all those things he intended to take with him to start his new life with a new wife. Before it got dark that evening he was gone.

ALL THIS seems now, thirty years later, like it might have happened to a different person. Leon walking out like that, taking all his belongings and leaving me with some used furniture and an old truck and horse trailer. After that I did some hard thinking.

I had lived my entire life in one place, a small town with tall mountains on one side and the Great Salt Lake on the other. I was thirty-seven years old, and I could not see staying there any longer.

After Leon left, I had a reckoning: I saw no reason to go on living the way I was. It seemed to me there must be more interesting things for a person to do in life than refill ketchup bottles and keep a counter clean.

Growing up in that town, I'd had a friend named Jolene. I liked her because she wasn't like anyone else I knew. She was bold and talented, something of a loner, the kind of girl who didn't seem to need many friends. I felt this was because she thought of herself as an artist even then. I thought it must be the way artists behaved. They kept to themselves, as if they understood things other people didn't and this was a way of protecting their gift. She stood out even in grade school, which is when we first became friends. She could make drawings of people that looked just like them, and I found this extraordinary. It was a special gift to be able to draw like that. She came from an old family who'd made their fortune in guns and were among the richest people in town. Her parents had encouraged her art from a very young age, and whether it was the fact she came from such privilege or the way she'd always been made to feel special, the result was that she was a very confident girl, someone who always did exactly as she pleased.

The money came from her mother's side—the gun makers—but it didn't hurt that her father was a doctor, a very popular gynecologist who had delivered a lot of the babies in town, including me and my seven siblings. Jolene never flaunted the fact she lived in a way none of the rest of us did. She acted like being rich didn't mean a thing to her. This made her seem very *cool*—a word that was only beginning to come into our vocabulary, and she epitomized it. She was cool, and she was an artist—as she would gladly tell you. She had known she was going to be an artist from the time she was four years old, she said.

In truth, she was creative in everything she did. Once, I remember, she took an old pair of Levi's and cut them up and sewed the sawed-off legs together to make a miniskirt. Nobody in our school had a denim skirt like that, though in later years they became very common and were manufactured by the thousands, but this was the first any of us had seen something like this—a totally fresh idea. After she made her denim skirt everybody tried to copy her but nobody else's came out the same. In this skirt she looked so singular, so effortlessly smart, as she did in all her clothes. She was tall and thin, and she had long dark hair that she wore tousled, as if she couldn't be bothered to comb it, and the effect was very chic. Out of all the girls I knew she was the most beautiful. She could seem almost doll-like in her prettiness until you heard her speak and realized how strong she was, how outspoken and sure of herself, and then the abrupt words and sharp tongue emerging from behind those sweet looks could shock you. The fact she didn't appear to care she was so beautiful is what seemed remarkable to me. It was as if everything came effortlessly with her, including her talent and beauty.

She got into trouble in high school by acting up and dating the wrong boys, including the son of a woman who was having an affair with her own married father, and she was sent away to a Catholic boarding school in Salt Lake City, thirty miles away. When I visited her there once with friends, she sat in our car in the parking lot and showed us the condom she kept in her wallet. Just in case, she said. I couldn't imagine being so prepared for something so taboo: in that era—I'm talking about the early sixties now—sex before marriage was totally forbidden, especially in our community, where a single religion dominated everything and a strict moral code threatened serious punishment. Jolene's calm display of that condom made her seem older and wiser than the rest of us who sat with her in the car that day. I felt she acquired a masculine power by simply possessing such a thing: I think it was the first time I experienced that clear transference of power from male to female. She did not just become a girl *acting* like a boy, which many of us were capable of doing, but she assumed and inhabited a boy's thinking, his right and power to control such a complex transaction as sex. However, she made it seem unimportant and normal, as she did everything else. Now I would use the word *authentic* to describe her. She had a strange power over me. She did whatever she pleased, and if she didn't feel like doing something she didn't and she appeared to suffer no guilt for her actions: I never heard her apologize to anyone for anything she'd done or said, even when it caused offense—and it often did. It was a kind of anarchy I aspired to but couldn't afford to risk.

THAT DAY in 1984 when Leon walked out on me I started thinking about Jolene. From the time we were in junior high she had singled me out, chosen me for her confidante, made me her best friend. At the time it seemed an honor I felt completely unworthy of, and yet it thrilled me. To be chosen like that by someone so special. You're different, too, she would say to me, you just don't realize it yet. That's why I like you. And I'm going to help you: I'm going to show you who you really are.

Once, in high school, when we were in the girls' bathroom, she leaned over when we were standing next to each other in front of the mirror and kissed me on the lips. I just thought I'd try that, she said. Did you like it?

I didn't say yes or no. I just kept combing my hair and looked down into the sink and laughed. But the truth was, I did like it. It both scared and excited me. She had that kind of effect. I never knew what boundary she would cross next, or what new feeling she would arouse in me.

ANOTHER TIME, when we were still in junior high, she took a freshly soiled sanitary napkin and tied it to a wire hanger and hung it outside the open window of the girls' lavatory at school. She wanted the boys to see it when they passed by. They ought to know what we go through, she said. They're not the ones bleeding every month. Getting cramps low in the belly, going through waves of bodily leakage.

She made it sound as if menstruation were the result of some wound that couldn't be healed once opened in adolescence, like an injury girls would now always be required to tend to with things like *napkins* and *belts* and *sanitary* products.

The word *sanitary* especially offended her. She said it made us seem unclean. Even worse was the way people talked about being *on the rag,* she said, like you were just mopping up blood. It's all *unseen,* so hidden, she added, like something we're taught to be ashamed of. You're not supposed to even *talk* about it.

Well, let those guys see what we see every month, she said, climbing down from the open window where she'd left the pad, and maybe they'll be more sympathetic.

I felt shocked by her actions but also secretly pleased. I knew that what she'd done was send a message that this bright blood that came every month, demanding our ministrations, often bringing us terrible pain, was the price we paid for being girls, and at that moment it *did* seem unfair—that this was something boys escaped entirely and about which they were pretty much clueless and which, in their ignorance, they found repulsive. Later—much later, when she had become a famous artist, the sort of artist known all over the world for her performance pieces and conceptual art—I would remind her of this day in the girls' bathroom. I told her I thought it was the first of her feminist performance pieces. She didn't agree or disagree. She just laughed.

JOLENE CARVER. The name never seemed to fit her. She should have had a name like Carmen, or Isabelle, or Beatrice, something more exotic to match her strong personality and flawless beauty.

After high school we went our separate ways. She moved away, and I got married the day after we graduated. We kept in touch over the years but not with any regularity. I thought she might come to our tenth high school reunion, but she didn't. Nor did she show up for the fifteenth.

I knew she'd moved to New York City after she finished college—
she had gone to a school in the East, one of the places they call the
Seven Sisters. She sent me an invitation to her graduation. For a long
while I wondered why she'd done that. Could she really have hoped
I'd show up? Travel all the way from Utah to Bryn Mawr, Pennsylvania, if that was the name of the town, just to see her get the sort of
degree I never would?

Later, much later, she moved to California and sent me a card
inviting me to visit her if I ever came to Los Angeles, and she included
a phone number and an address. I saved that card, stashed it in a drawer,
and every once in a while, looking for something, I'd come across it
and think of her.

THE DAY Leon walked out I searched for the card in the kitchen
drawer and found it was still there. I realized that with Leon gone
there was nothing tying me anywhere anymore. I could quit my job
at the bowling alley. I was sick of waitressing anyway. I'd kept that
job only because we needed the money and it was easy work and I
liked talking with the cowboys from the nearby Golden Spike Arena,
the cattle auctioneers who regularly showed up for lunch. Still, I
understood the day Leon left I was freer than I ever imagined I'd be.
Freer than I had been since I was seventeen and married him. I was
thirty-seven and my life wasn't over yet. I could take the money left in
the checking account and the little bit of savings I'd put away and go
anywhere I pleased. Get another job. Start over. That's when I thought
of Jolene and Los Angeles.

California, though I'd never been there, sounded very good to
me. That day—the day Leon left—I spent an hour or two just sitting
on the sofa, completely immobile, as if his leaving had taken away
my physical strength. At one point I looked around the room in the
basement apartment where we'd lived for many years, and I felt the
gloom of it all. The room was dark and cold and dank: it felt empty
and eerily quiet. Leon had walked out only a few hours earlier, and it
was as if his departure had left nothing behind but dead space infected
by a preternatural silence.

For a long while I sat there, trying to fathom what had just happened. A revulsion rose up in me then, revulsion for the life lived in these rooms and for the man I'd shared them with.

On the coffee table a copy of *Western Horseman* had been left open to an ad for worming medicine. GET RID OF YOUR INFESTATION NOW, it said, WE HAVE THE SOLUTION TO YOUR WORM PROBLEM.

His leaving felt like a rejection of everything, poisoning our time together, where we'd lived and all the things we'd done together, all the friends and the places where we'd gone looking for adventures, all tainted now by his abandonment. The hunting and the fishing trips. The horses we'd trained and enjoyed riding together and all the traveling and camping and driving throughout the West. Now made meaningless by my revulsion for the person with whom I had done those things. Somebody who could go off with a person who had the ridiculous name of Pinky, a girly kind of woman who wore a rhinestone belt with a big flashy buckle and had teeth like a beaver. I could not imagine staying there any longer, living alone in those basement rooms, inheriting the abject loss and somehow accommodating it in that place where our joint lives had played out. Better to leave, I thought. Outside a storm had come in, and the wind sounded like a woman sighing, pitching her tiny granules of frozen grief in sudden bursts against the windowpanes. A bitter winter afternoon. At that moment I made up my mind.

THERE WAS no guarantee the number Jolene had given me was still good, and I felt both surprised and anxious when she answered the phone. I didn't bother with small talk. Right away I told her what had happened. That my husband had left me. I understood she didn't know what to say, couldn't fathom whether this was good news or bad. All she said was, in the old abrupt, frank manner I remembered from years ago, What does this mean?

I said it meant I was thinking of moving to L.A. and I wondered if I could stay with her when I arrived, just until I got my feet on the ground, found a job and a place to live.

I think she was surprised to hear from me and even more surprised that I asked what I did. There was a long pause before she said anything, and I began to think I'd made a mistake even calling her, let alone asking her for such a big favor. After all, it had been years since we'd seen each other.

But then she spoke. Why L.A.? she asked. Why do you want to move here?

I laughed. I don't know, I replied. It just . . . *sounds* good.

Oh dear God, she said, and I heard the judgment in her tone, you need a better reason than that. Do you have any other friends here in L.A.?

I admitted I didn't. I told her I had an ex-sister-in-law named Inez who lived down there somewhere but I hadn't seen her for years. Also an elderly aunt and uncle who lived in a place called Culver City. Was that near?

Nothing's near, she said. Her voice sounded gravelly and low, like she'd become a heavy smoker. I could hear her moving about in a room, and then after a pause she spoke again.

I still don't get how you chose L.A., she said. Do you know anything about it?

It's sunny and warm, I said, and there are oranges growing on trees.

Oh man, she said, you are still as innocent as you always were, aren't you? And then she laughed for a long time.

I WAITED until she'd stopped, and even then I didn't say anything. I didn't particularly like being called innocent, or the way she'd laughed at me. We were the same age. She may have had different experiences, seen a lot more, but I felt she was acting as if her life was somehow better than mine, more worldly and cosmopolitan, suggesting that she had grown over the years while I had remained naive, isolated in the boring atmosphere of the town where we'd both grown up. I also knew that, as much as I didn't want to admit it, what she was implying was probably true.

I understood the gulf between us must have grown enormous,

larger perhaps than I could even begin to realize, and I felt sort of embarrassed that I had even bothered to call her. To make such a request out of the blue! What was I thinking? She had been to a fancy school for smart, rich girls. She'd gotten at least one college degree, maybe more. She was a successful artist, I knew that even though I didn't understand anything about the art she made and had felt confused by a card she had once sent announcing an exhibition of her work in Europe: The card showed a picture of a sexy-looking woman wearing a bustier, with voluptuous breasts and a fake blond wig. Her lips were painted red and slightly parted, and the tip of her tongue curled against her upper lip as if she were licking something delicious. It took me a moment to realize it was Jolene. The words across the front said I'LL BE YOUR PERFECT FANTASY. On the back it announced a show of new works and a performance at a museum in Amsterdam. I kept that card in the kitchen drawer until it disappeared one day. I knew Leon had taken it though he denied it. He said I must have misplaced it, but I could just see him taking it down to the bar to show his drinking buddies. *Get this, guys!* I imagined him saying, and one of his friends talking him out of it. That card had probably ended up pinned to a wall next to a gun rack in somebody's tack room.

I figured she'd traveled a lot, seen many different countries. Maybe she was married, maybe not, I didn't even know that much. I was pretty sure that like me she'd never had children, but I don't know why I thought this with such certainty. For all I knew we'd have nothing to say to each other, and yet I was asking to come stay with her for a while.

I was about to tell her not to worry, that it was just an idea I was considering and I needed more time to think about what I wanted to do, just to let her off the hook, when she said, Of course you can stay with me, if you're sure you want to make this move. When are you thinking of coming?

I told her pretty soon. I didn't want to pay another month's rent. As soon as I could pack everything up and get rid of some stuff, I said, I'd like to leave. I added she could tell me the truth if it wasn't convenient, if she didn't have room for me. But she said, No, no, it's not that. She had a friend staying in her guest room right then, but he would be leaving soon. She said I could come anytime, the week after next if I wanted. Her friend would probably be gone by then.

There's only one thing, she added. I mean, L.A.'s a strange place. I don't want to discourage you, but it's a very weird city and it takes a long time to feel—I can't even say to feel at *home.* You'll have to excuse me but . . . it takes money to live here. Things aren't cheap like I'm sure they still are back there.

I have a little money saved to get started, I said. I could hear the defensiveness, the false assurance in my voice.

It's not just the money, she said. She paused, and I could hear a different, breathy sound as if she'd stopped to take a long drag on a cigarette, and then she went on.

L.A. is probably harder to make connections than anywhere I've ever lived, not only because things are so spread out and you have to drive so fucking much, but people are kind of goofy, you know? It can seem incredibly banal. It's a city of cliques and castes and celebrity, much more segregated than New York. People don't mix on the street in the same way, and nobody takes public transportation, so you end up seeing people who look like you all the time and spending a crazy amount of time alone in your car. It can be a really lonely place if you don't have friends, and even then nobody wants to leave their house to do anything. You are where you live—I mean the neighborhood you live in determines a lot about how easy it is to deal with the city. And the good neighborhoods are so fucking expensive.

I didn't know what to say. I felt like she was trying to talk me out of the idea of moving to L.A.

But far be it from me to discourage you, she went on. I mean if you're set on this idea. But let me just ask, how long have you been thinking about moving to L.A.?

Oh . . . a couple of hours, I guess.

Oh God, she cried, and laughed again. This is why I've always loved you. You always had guts. But what are you going to do if it doesn't work out?

Think of something else, I guess.

Think of something else, she repeated. I guess that's what we all do when life turns to shit.

I NEVER remembered her using swear words so freely. She never resorted to that kind of vulgarity in high school. It's not that I objected, times had changed: this was, after all, 1984. It's just that it didn't sound like the person I remembered from all those years ago. Even her voice had changed. A new harshness had crept in. She spoke in a different register. Low, gravelly, gruff.

After we hung up, I sat for a while thinking about L.A., whether it was a crazy idea or not. I kept looking at the piece of paper on which I'd written down her address, as if I might find some clue there in those numbers and letters. There were heavy thuds coming from the apartment above me. The Wimmer kids, jumping off their beds again. I could hear their mother, Joy Wimmer, yelling at them. *You better stop that right now,* she shouted, *or else you don't get to go to Binky's birthday party and you don't get no ice cream for a week and you don't get to go to the dump in the truck with Daddy when he gets home—GOT THAT? The fun is over. And if I hear you jumping on this bed again I'm going to spank your butts. Let me repeat,* Joy Wimmer yelled, *THE FUN IS OVER!*

How right you are, I thought. And I couldn't quite imagine when or even whether it would ever start up again, or even how that might happen, but maybe something good was waiting for me in California, I thought, if I could pull myself together and get down there.

2

Jolene lived in a very nice apartment in Beverly Hills, on a quiet side street, in a building that looked like a little château with turrets and balconies and flowers trailing down over the railings. Every building on the street was like this, more like a big beautiful house than the kind of normal apartment building I was used to seeing at home.

It all looked so much nicer than I'd imagined. That's what I thought when I first turned onto her street and saw the lovely old buildings and the big shapely trees casting dark pools of shade up and down the sidewalks. In front of every building there was a manicured garden where colorful flowers bloomed even now, in the middle of winter.

The long trip down from Utah—two days on stormy roads—had left me tired, wondering all the while if the old truck would make it. When I parked at the curb in front of her apartment building I felt happy just to have arrived. I had packed the horse trailer with all the belongings I felt I'd need to start a new life, thinking I'd sell the trailer once I got settled in the city. Even then I knew the truck and trailer stuck out in that neighborhood, but I didn't realize just what a stir my rig would cause. How shocked Jolene would be when she saw it. How the neighbors, after a day or two, would begin to complain to her, suggesting she ought to ask me to move it somewhere else. To which she had said to the elderly neighbor who had been complaining the most, *Why don't you just fuck off?*

———

SHE WAS living with a man named Vincent, a composer and musician. It took me a while to figure out they were married. In the beginning it wasn't at all clear what their relationship was. For some reason they didn't wear rings. I thought he might have been the "friend" she had spoken about who would be leaving soon. She didn't introduce him as her husband—she just said, *This is Vincent, Vincent this is Verna, my oldest friend.*

We were standing in the kitchen late on the afternoon I'd arrived when she made this introduction. A tall man carrying a bag of groceries had suddenly walked in the back door. He looked very surprised to see me. I had the feeling that whoever he was— her husband, or roommate, or friend—she hadn't told him I was coming and he was annoyed to see me standing there with her in the kitchen that afternoon. It was the way he looked at her. The glance that passed between them. And the way she shrugged and said, It's okay, Vincent, relax, Verna's just going to be staying here for a little while.

It did not seem okay, at least not with him. He nodded at me, said a curt hello, set the groceries down, adjusted his glasses and frowned, and then he nervously excused himself and in a stiffly formal way said he needed to go upstairs to take care of something.

DON'T MIND him, she said after he had gone. He's always that way.

Later she told me they were married and had been for almost fifteen years.

He was thin, like her, an angular man with a rather elongated neck so that the whole effect was of a person who had been somehow stretched upward into a stick-like presence. It was his stiff manner that also lent him this aspect. Over the next few days I came to see there was a feminine quality to his movements and gestures, though he didn't really seem effeminate at all, just very precise and careful and somehow rather delicate. He had very beautiful hands with long fingers and lovely nails polished to a smooth pinkness. Something about him made it seem as if he came from a foreign country, and the more time I spent around him the more I felt this even though his English was perfect.

Jolene told me he was working on his doctorate, finishing his dissertation on a composer named Schubert—that is what he worked on every day, upstairs in the room I'd be staying in. His study was also the guest room where I'd be sleeping on a foldout sofa.

You just have to make sure not to spread your stuff around too much, she said to me that first afternoon, and to leave the room during the day while he's working. And don't take it personally if he doesn't seem friendly. That's just the way he is.

IN TIME she told me a bit more about him. As long as she had been with him, she said, he'd never had a job. His parents had money. *Gobs* of it, she said, rolling her eyes. They owned coal mines in West Virginia, which is where he'd been born in some godforsaken little town, but his family also kept an apartment on Park Avenue in New York, and once he'd entered his teenage years he'd been shipped off to a tony boarding school in New England. He'd also spent a lot of time in Europe. The *parents,* as she called them, loading up the word with disapproval, owned a château in Gstaad—a fantastic place, she said, if you like that sort of thing. She wasn't much for skiing—or sports of any kind for that matter—but it was a nice place to spend the winter holidays if you could stand being with his mother and father, which she said she no longer could. They're dreadful people, she said. Don't get me started.

SHE WAS right about him not being very friendly. During those first few days I spent with them I found that whenever I was around him he rarely said anything. He was like a cat—a quiet, observing presence in the background, always watching what was going on. The truth was, I rarely saw him except in passing. I felt he eagerly awaited the moment when I would leave the room each morning. I would pass him on the stairs as I went down to the kitchen for coffee. He was always just standing there at the bottom of the stairs, as if waiting for me to appear. He'd offer a polite hello, but he almost never looked me in the eye. And yet whenever I was in a room with him I caught him studying me, as if I were an object of curiosity, only to glance away quickly if I gazed back at him.

JOLENE HAD a studio in another part of the city where she went every day to make her art. In the days after I arrived, I mostly hung around the apartment, checking the classifieds for work and looking for apartments for rent, making calls, taking walks in the neighborhood. Vincent tried to at least be polite to me, but those first days were pretty awkward. Jolene was away most of the time, and I could tell that Vincent, who worked all day in the room upstairs and rarely emerged, didn't really want me there. Whenever I saw them together, he often seemed upset. Sometimes I heard them arguing at night in the room next to mine, and I felt sure it was me they were arguing about.

STILL, THEY didn't exactly make me feel unwelcome. They just seemed very busy all the time. I understood. It didn't bother me to be left on my own because in truth I felt more anxious when I was with them.

I quickly discovered how little we had in common except for the fact Jolene and I had been childhood friends. They spent a lot of time reading, something I'd never done that much of. Yet it seemed to be one of their main activities. They sat around in the living room reading, not talking to each other or to me. They had a ton of books in their apartment. There were bookshelves in every room, and books stacked up on the floor everywhere, even left in piles on the stairs. When they did have conversations they ended up talking a lot about things I didn't know much about, like music and art or the lives of their friends. And food. They both liked to cook. If they were spending the evening in they often made dinner together, working side by side in the kitchen, and the meals were always incredible, featuring dishes I could never have made—sometimes using some ingredients I'd never even tasted, like the octopus they grilled one night.

I wanted to make it easy for them to have me as a guest. I tried to be my most agreeable. I helped with dishes and cleaning up, and I left the room before nine every morning so Vincent could go to work. I made sure I didn't spread my stuff around too much. If he needed to continue working in the evening I let him know that wasn't a problem, he could work as late as he wanted. What this meant was, I had a lot of time on my hands.

EACH MORNING Jolene headed out early to her studio, and often they went out together in the evening when Vincent wasn't working late. Most of the time they didn't bother asking me to come with them: if they'd been invited to a dinner party they said they were sorry but they couldn't really add another person, or sometimes they only had two tickets to whatever they were going to. Occasionally they didn't even say anything to me, they just left the apartment and said, *See you later.* Still they always asked, *Will you be okay here alone? There's lots of food in the fridge.* And I always said, *Oh yes, sure,* even though it did make me feel a bit sad.

The worst moment was always right after they left when I felt the sudden heavy silence of their big apartment and the emptiness of the long evening stretching before me. Then my aloneness descended like a sudden lurch into regret.

Had I really made the right decision, coming to L.A.?

I FOUND a lot to look at when they were out. I could roam freely around the apartment and examine everything. You can never get a good look at places people live in while they are there. I don't mind confessing I snooped a bit, looking in the bookshelves, touching objects here and there, holding things up to examine them more closely. I even peeped in their bedroom but only very quickly because I felt guilty. I just turned the light on and glanced around long enough to see how beautiful it was. I could see through French doors onto a little balcony, framed by flowering vines, with a little table and two chairs set next to the railing in the shade. Knowing Jolene and her good taste, it didn't surprise me everything was so lovely. Still I tried to imagine what it would be like to sleep in such a perfect room, and then wake up and have coffee on the lovely little balcony.

Everywhere there was artwork on the walls, in every room, all kinds of strange things, the kind of stuff that hardly looked like art to me. I spent a lot of time looking at these things, trying to figure it all out. I didn't understand most of what I was seeing. There were no pictures of landscapes or people or anything like that. One thing I kept coming back to was a neon sign, the kind you'd see above the bar at the Loading Chute back home, only instead of being an ad for Coors beer this one had neon words written in a spiral that said THE TRUE ARTIST HELPS THE WORLD BY REVEALING MYSTIC TRUTHS. I spent a long time looking at that, wondering, is this an advertising sign of some sort, or is this somebody's art?

There were a lot of magazines lying around, and sometimes when there was nothing I wanted to watch on TV I'd start looking through those to pass an evening. Most were art magazines and the articles were pretty boring or just outright over my head, but I did like to look at the pictures. It was amazing to think of all the different kinds of art people were making now—about which I was so clueless. I'd think, who knew? That this could be *art*? All the paintings with wild scribbly colors, some with things you could recognize even if they did seem so distorted, others just blobs and slashes and shapes, boxes, or stripes of color that seemed like the sort of thing anybody could do if you had a ruler and some masking tape. Sculpture that looked like stuff you'd find in a junkyard. Mostly there were a lot of ads in these magazines for artists and galleries, and it was one such ad that stopped me cold one night.

IT WAS a picture of a naked woman, half turned toward the viewer. She was wearing nothing but sunglasses—one hand perched on her hip, and the other holding a huge fake penis pressed between her legs as if it were growing right out of her crotch. She had smallish breasts and was fit and trim, you could see the little ladder of her ribs and the white bikini lines against her oiled and suntanned body. The look on her face was hard to read, but she appeared cool and rather defiant even though you couldn't see her eyes because of the sunglasses she wore.

I stared at the photo. I felt shocked and yet I couldn't turn away. What was this? What was this woman doing, and why did she look like she dared you to say she couldn't be doing it? Was this some kind of art people made now? Standing there naked with that big fake penis, so ridiculously lifelike and huge? How could this woman get away with something so outrageous? And for what *purpose*?

The opposite page was blank, with only one line of text giving her name and the gallery where she had an upcoming show of her work.

I HAD been looking at this photo for some time that night, puzzling over it, when I heard the key in the front door, and I knew they'd returned. I quickly closed the magazine and sat back against the sofa, waiting for them to walk into the room. I felt as if I'd been caught doing something naughty. It was late and they were tired, so we only said a few words and then they went to bed and I followed them upstairs, but I lay awake a long time thinking about that picture in the magazine. I wanted to understand what was going on, and I decided I would ask Jolene about it in the morning before she went off to work.

SHE LAUGHED when I brought the magazine into the kitchen the next morning while she was making coffee and showed it to her.

She said, Oh my god, so you found that, good for you. That magazine is ten years old now, but it's a collector's item and I always leave it out on the coffee table, mainly to honor Lynda. I mean that really took something for her to do that and I'm still in awe of her.

Without my even having to ask she began to explain to me that the artist was a friend of hers, someone she had met in the 1970s in New York when they were both students at the Brooklyn Museum Art School.

We were all thinking, she said, I mean the more radical women artists I knew, about how to confront this tradition of the passive female nude that male artists had represented forever, I mean we were sick of it, of feeling our bodies were being used this way as static objects for perving or decoration, religious adoration or whatever. There was a lot of talk at that time about gender and gender performativity and this idea that males, in assuming their gender identity, were responsible for a similar posturing and performativity by embodying their own guise of compensatory hypermasculinity and bravado. So Lynda got this idea that by adopting that big phallus and posing nude for an ad promoting her show she could physically and symbolically muddy the discourse and assert our right to control our own image and our sexual and cultural power in a positive way. Get it?

I looked at her blankly. I hadn't really quite understood what she'd said. What was *performativity*?

Seeing the look on my face she tried again.

Think of it this way: she was shaking things up, and believe me they needed to be shaken up—still do. She was laughing so irreverently at the art world—at the horrible sexism of the art world. And she really took heat for it. Even other feminist women artists criticized her for what she'd done. They described her ad as exploitive and brutalizing and some kind of cheap cheesecake centerfold shot. But it was a centerfold like no other, and it was made by a very brave woman. And it gave many of us courage to go on and do what we wanted to do to challenge these male artists who thought we could never be as brash or bold as they were and who basically treated us as their inferiors in every single way.

I shook my head and said, Wow. I sort of get it now. I still can't believe you can do something like that and call it art, but I guess I'm pretty out of it.

I'm glad you saw it, she said. It's iconic. Then she looked at her watch and said, Okay, sorry but I have to run now.

IT WASN'T that I exactly hated this arrangement, being left alone so much when they went out at night and didn't come home until late. It might have been harder if they'd invited me to come along. I couldn't quite imagine who their friends were, and what happened at those dinner parties and outings they were always talking about afterward. I had my own agenda, during the day anyway, looking for work, checking in with my parents at home, making it sound like I was okay even though I hadn't yet found a job or an apartment (they liked that I was staying with Jolene, someone they knew from the past). The truth was, I wasn't trying very hard to look for work. I found it easier to just hang out at their apartment or wander around the streets in Beverly Hills, looking at the people with their nice clothes and hairdos and the different things in the windows of all the fancy shops. But after a while I began to feel a bit lost. I didn't quite know what to do next. Many evenings I sat alone, thinking, why did I even come here?

I had to admit that I no longer felt Jolene was a person I really knew very well, and Vincent seemed like somebody who came from an entirely different planet. I'd never met a man like him. So quiet. So self-contained. They had an old cat who staggered around on stiff legs—a grouchy thing, as I found out early on when I'd tried to pet it and it sunk its claws into my hand, but Vincent seemed to love it. I mean, I'd never seen a man love a cat like that.

Just don't try to pet him again, he warned me after I got clawed, and you'll be fine. In fact, he added, maybe you shouldn't even look at him.

I wanted to say, what kind of cat is it that you can't even *look* at it? But instead I told him, Okay, I'll try and not look at him, though I had a hard time keeping a straight face as I said this. I felt like laughing out loud. However, by then I'd realized what a serious guy he was, and I knew he wouldn't like it if I started laughing at him.

What he did like to do was to sit on the sofa and pet this cat over and over and talk to it in a low voice, and during these times he looked happier and more relaxed than I'd seen him at any other time.

Truthfully, I found this all a bit crazy.

IT RAINED a lot that first week. Nobody had told me it rained so much in L.A. in the winter. When it wasn't raining I sometimes went outside and worked in the flower garden in front of the apartment, even though Vincent told me I didn't need to do that because they had a gardener who came every week. He must not have been a very good gardener, however, because there were weeds in the flower beds and

the roses hadn't been pruned properly. So when Vincent wasn't looking I went out in the garden and worked anyway, just to be outside
and doing something. I'd brought my gardening tools with me, and
the first thing I did was to get them out of the horse trailer and begin
pruning those roses the way they ought to be.

One day, when I was out working in the flower bed, I caught Vincent spying on me. I had been singing a favorite Patsy Cline song, "I
Go Walking After Midnight," as I worked. I knew most of the words
to all of Patsy's songs because she was my favorite singer. I'd always
been told I had a good voice, but I never really sang for any other reason than my own pleasure. After a while I began singing an old hymn
I learned in church. Even though I'd given up church a long time ago
those hymns had never left me.

That's when I looked up and saw him standing at the window
looking down at me. The apartment had two floors—their bedroom
and study were upstairs, kitchen and living room down—and he was
upstairs in his study, standing at the window, so he had a good view
of me.

The window was open, and I knew he'd not only been watching
me but listening to me sing. It seemed a bit sneaky to be spying on me
that way, and he must have thought so too because he quickly stepped
away from the window when he saw me looking up. Later, when I
went inside, he came downstairs and started talking to me.

He asked me if I'd like a cup of coffee, he was going to make
some—and that's something he'd never done before, offered to make
me coffee. Generally I found him to be about the quietest person I'd
ever met. Too quiet for my taste. I couldn't figure out what was going
on inside him. He could have been thinking almost anything, and I
wouldn't have known what it was.

After he made the coffee we sat in the kitchen and talked. He
asked me about the song I'd been singing—not the Patsy Cline song
but the other song. I told him it was an old hymn I'd first heard in
church. He said I had a lovely voice and asked if I would sing it again
for him sometime.

I shook my head and laughed. I don't know what you'd want me
to do that for, I said.

Because it's beautiful, he said, and I like beautiful music.

The way he looked at me and said this made me feel silly. His words were so direct and simple. I could see there was no artifice to what he'd said, and I knew I was acting a bit coy because I was so unsure of myself, uncomfortable sitting there across from him, the two of us having coffee when we'd hardly spoken three words since I arrived. I didn't know who he was. I was used to men who had a kind of hearty, gregarious quality, like the men I'd grown up with, the men from church I'd known when I was young who smiled whether they were happy or not, who greeted everyone with the same enthusiasm, the same happy words, a kind of male bonhomie that felt formulaic and really didn't have much substance: everything was always great with these men, they were always fine, they couldn't complain. Leon's cowboy and hunting pals weren't much different from the churchy men in this respect. They often didn't come right out and ask for what they wanted but rather wheedled and cajoled as if you had to warm the little woman up before you could get anything from her.

What's the name of that hymn? he asked. As he said this he ran his fingers slowly through the lock of hair that always flopped forward over one eye. His hair was long, not as long as a woman's, but still it came down below his ears. His eyes were an intense inky black, and when he trained them on you, you felt their penetrating force, as if he were not just looking at you but through your head at something behind it.

I wish I knew the title, I said. Something like "Down the Soft Evening Night Is Falling." But that doesn't sound right, does it? It's got one of those long titles that's hard to remember.

Would you mind terribly singing it for me?

Now? I said. Right now?

If it's not too much to ask, he replied, gazing openly at me, not showing any emotion.

Okay, I said, staring at my hands holding the coffee cup. I paused to collect myself and sang the song for him. He never took his eyes off me while I was singing.

He smiled when I'd finished and shook his head. Thank you, he said. Thank you very much. That was really beautiful. You have an amazing voice, I'm sure you know that. Then he asked if I would mind writing down the words for him sometime and I said sure, and he went back upstairs to work.

JOLENE CAME into my room that night. She brought a pile of clothes with her, things she said she didn't wear anymore—a couple of sweaters and a skirt, some trousers and a scarf, all black or gray except for the scarf, which was white with black skulls on it. She thought I might like some different clothes, she said. *City* clothes. I knew at that moment she was ashamed of the way I dressed. I took the clothes and thanked her.

That night she wanted to talk about the past. She brought a bottle of wine upstairs and poured us two glasses and settled down on the foldout sofa next to me, lighting the first of what would be the many cigarettes she smoked that evening. For the first time since I'd arrived we had what I felt was a real conversation: she began by asking me questions about some of the people we'd known back home.

Whatever happened to the two Roxies? she said.

I knew who she meant—the two friends we'd had who were both named Roxie. One had gotten pregnant during our junior year and married her boyfriend. The other had graduated and become a stewardess. Jolene wanted to know if the first Roxie had stayed married, and I said no, she hadn't.

It figures, she said. Who the hell gets married that young and stays married?

I didn't bother to tell her that I had—because I realized it wasn't true anymore.

I don't know how you stayed in that town as long as you did, she said.

She was sitting with her legs tucked up under her on the sofa, still wearing the jeans spattered with paint from the day in her studio, the cigarette held aloft between her thumb and forefinger. She was as thin as she'd been in high school—thinner even—and still just as beautiful, although looking at her now, sitting so close to me on the sofa and facing the light coming through the window, I could see all the fine lines that had begun to appear around her eyes and mouth. Thin people show facial wrinkles much more than you do, my mother once said to me. I think she meant it as a compliment.

I didn't see many options other than staying there, I replied. It's just the way it worked out. I didn't add that for the most part I'd enjoyed my life in that place where she and I had both been born and raised. I liked living near my parents and siblings: we'd all gotten along okay. I liked my nieces and nephews, watching them grow up. I couldn't imagine having lost out on being a part of their lives, not having had children myself.

I couldn't have done it, she said.

I shrugged. Probably not.

I didn't know where she was going with this line of thinking. It would be easy to feel she was being critical of me for staying while congratulating herself for leaving when really it seemed to me it was fated things should turn out as they did. It's not like I could have changed places with her even if I'd wanted to.

I felt my real life started when I left Utah, she said. My former life began to seem so strange to me, like one of life's illnesses you get over. It had passed. Or so I believed. I had managed to create something different, something comprehensible. An adult life. I never wanted to look back. But of course you can't really avoid looking back, can you? All that stuff is forever attached to you, like fingernails or hair. In some shitty way it keeps growing on you. You can try and cut it off, but it always grows back.

I didn't know what to say to this, so I said nothing. We each took a sip of wine, and in that awkward moment the conversation seemed to die. The silence stretched on, and I decided to just let it settle around us. I had the feeling the past obsessed her more than she cared to admit, though she appeared bent on convincing me otherwise. It did not seem to me that she had left it behind at all.

THE LIGHT was falling outside, evening coming on. I could see a row of tall thin palms outlined against the slowly darkening sky, all bending in the same direction, but what direction I could not have said, being clueless as to the cardinal points in this city. It was dusk, the hour between the dog and the wolf as my mother used to say, but somehow it didn't feel that way. The evening was far too gentle to betray any wolfish turn coming on. Jolene and I both continued to stare out the window until she finally broke the silence that had become rather exaggerated.

There's one incident from the past, a story I think about a lot, she said, suddenly glancing at me. I wonder if you remember it the way I do.

She hesitated as if she wasn't sure she should go on. Now, of course, I was very curious to hear what she had to say. She seemed to know this and acted as if she didn't mind keeping me waiting, or maybe she was weighing whether she wanted to continue with her story or not.

Oh, I don't know really, she said and shook her head. I don't know that I really *need* to go *there.* She sat quietly, looking at me from the other end of the couch, every once in a while taking a drag on her cigarette and then turning her head to exhale so she didn't blow the smoke right at me.

It reminded me of the days during high school when I had hung on her every word, when I'd waited for her to show me what she wanted to do next. In those days she controlled everything. She absorbed the energy from everything around her. Colored it simply by being present. She embodied a certain force in the world, and I saw that this was still the case. She could still change the feeling in a room the moment she entered. Hold everyone's attention, dominate the space. She seemed to take control of the very air. With seemingly no effort she had always been good at all that she tried, before getting bored and moving on. There was always that moment when she lost interest in what was happening. It looked as if that might be happening now. Like she'd decided to forget about the story she'd been about to relate.

Maybe I shouldn't tell you, she said.

Why not?

Because it's too much. The most difficult things to tell are those we ourselves can't understand. And I've never quite understood the meaning of this story. What we did. Why should I trouble you with my own lack of understanding?

What story are you talking about? I laughed, a little annoyed now. I felt she was testing me. Drawing it out this way. Making it all so dramatic. Controlling every moment, just like she used to do.

Come on, I said. Just tell me.

Okay, she said, okay.

She stood up and walked to the window that overlooked the street and then turned around and faced me. Her baggy jeans hung loosely on her thin frame. In the low light her face looked tired. She rarely washed her hair, I'd noticed this. It looked stringy and messy tonight, as if she'd been camping and just gotten out of a sleeping bag. Everything about her slightly disheveled and yet somehow still touched by such beauty.

Do you remember that time—it was Halloween, and we all went out trick-or-treating together?

We did that a lot, I said.

Yes, but this time was different. It was you and me and Clare Boggs—you remember Clare? Such a sad girl—so unattractive and rather mean, I think, because of it, but she could also be very sharp and funny, and I admired her for that, for that outrageous humor she liked to cultivate. We were out wandering around in the dark together that night, not much interested in ringing doorbells or getting candy or anything like that. It was really dark—you remember the area up behind the school? No streetlights yet. Just those ugly new houses with big lawns. That's where we were when we came across some other kids from school, including Jeannie Wokersein—

The moment she said this name I knew where she was going with her story. And I really wished she wouldn't.

Jeannie Wokersein, she repeated. Remember how we used to call her Weenie Wokersein because she was so square, so uptight? A classic goody-goody. The kind of girl who'd rat you out to a teacher in a second if she thought it would make her look good. That night when we saw her Clare said, *Let's get her.* Do you remember that?

Of course I remember, I said.

I remembered everything. How Clare and Jolene had stopped Jeannie and started talking with her, how the other kids had gone on ahead. And then the ugly thing happened. What I couldn't figure out was why Jolene would bring this up now.

We started talking to her, Jolene said, remember? Acting interested in her for a change. She thought we really meant it. She never saw what was coming before Clare pushed her to the ground. I sat on top of her and you held her arms down and Clare goosed her. Do you remember that?

Yes I do, I said quietly.

AT THE time I thought I was the least guilty participant. It hadn't been my idea to goose Jeannie Wokersein. I hadn't wanted to hold her down, pinning her arms out to the side while Clare did what she did, but I did go along with it. I certainly never could have jammed my fingers against her vagina, even with her clothes on, and violated her that way. Before it happened I hadn't known what Clare was going to do. And then it was over and Jeannie was crying, curled up on the grass, screaming that we'd hurt her, really hurt her, and she was going to tell her father as soon as she got home.

As it turned out, she did tell her father, who was a prominent doctor in town. He took her to another doctor, who examined her to see if she'd been seriously injured or bruised—and in fact there were some bruises from what Clare had done. The next day, while we were all sitting in class at school, someone had come from the principal's office to say the principal wanted to see some students. They were to report to his office right away. He read off Jolene and Clare's names.

I sat in that room waiting for my name to be called, feeling horribly frightened and guilty. Now I was going to be in deep trouble. My parents would be told. They would know how badly I'd acted. But my name wasn't called. Only Jolene and Clare were told to report to the principal, and they got up and left the classroom without so much as looking at me.

When they'd gone I sat there stunned, wondering why I had been spared. I felt such relief. For some reason it looked like I wasn't going to have to pay for what had happened to Jeannie Wokersein.

But Jolene and Clare did.

DR. WOKERSEIN and Jeannie and the principal were waiting in his office. Clare's and Jolene's parents had also been summoned and were sitting in the room as well. The girls were asked about the night before, and they told the truth. They said they had goosed Jeannie, but they'd only meant it as a joke. Their parents expressed shock their daughters could behave this way. Because Jolene's father was also a doctor—he knew Dr. Wokersein very well—it made it even harder to sit in the principal's office and hear a colleague talk about the bruises found on his daughter's pubis, about her *gross violation* by these girls. Jolene and Clare didn't deny they were guilty. They agreed to apologize to Jeannie, and in the end both were grounded for a month and had other privileges taken away as punishment for what they'd done.

They didn't come back to school that day or the next. When they did return and Jolene told me what had happened in the principal's office, she blew the whole thing off. She laughed about it and made it sound like she didn't give a damn she'd gotten into so much trouble. Still it wasn't long afterward that she got sent away to the Catholic boarding school in Salt Lake City.

YOU DO remember what we did that night then, right? she asked.

I nodded. Yes.

Did you ever think of that over the years?

Not much, I said. Maybe because I was never punished the way you and Clare were I don't think of it the way you do—but yes, I have thought of it. Maybe you have more reason to remember.

No, it's not that, she said. But I wonder if you remember that night the way I do.

She had been sitting on the other end of the sofa, facing me, but now she stood up and began moving around the room, turning on lights. It had begun to grow dark around us, and a murkiness had settled in. There were so many different kinds of lights, lamps sitting on bookcases and tables, and it took her some time to turn on all those lights. Then she returned to the sofa and faced me again.

She looked upset, and I felt as if she might for some reason be upset with me. She took another sip of wine and lit yet another cigarette and then began speaking again.

Tell me the way you remember it, she said.

I told her what I recalled, how dark it had been that night, the kids stumbling across lawns, flowing over curbs onto the pavement, some in costumes, all out roaming around on Halloween on a moonless night. The moment we saw the other kids. Jeannie left alone, talking to us. Clare grabbing her, pushing her down, Jolene climbing on top, sitting on her chest, the heavy dew on the grass, me kneeling at her head and holding her arms down while Clare did what she did and we looked on. And afterward Jeannie crying. Telling us we had really hurt her. The next day at school, her and Clare getting called to the principal's office.

She didn't say anything when I had finished telling her what I remembered. She just cupped her forehead in her hand and looked down for a while. I felt I needed to say something more, to underscore I knew I had been treated differently even though we had all been involved.

I never understood why Jeannie didn't tell on me, I said. It didn't make sense. Is that why you're asking me about this now?

That's the strange thing, she said. It's the way I remember it too. But it certainly doesn't matter to me now, nor did it then, that you got off. No, no, that's not it. This is what I think is important about this story.

She looked up and stopped talking, as if she needed to take a few moments to gather her thoughts, and then she began to speak again in a more passionate voice.

As an artist my work has a lot to do with the way women treat each other, and the way we've been treated by men. So that attack on Jeannie Wokersein—well, that was a very cruel thing to do—to get her to trust us and then violate her that way, by assaulting her sexually like a male rapist might. I'm interested in scraping off the niceties. In probing the wounds. Again, the most difficult things to tell, I've found, are those things we ourselves can't understand. In my work I try to construct these narratives about why we do what we do. Why I've done what I've done. Women are especially subject to break-downs, to subservience of every kind, to mean feelings and aggression toward each other, and it's this oscillation that interests me. Do you know what I mean?

I'm not sure, I said. But then I don't know that much about your art, so you'll have to forgive me.

It's like this. We have a strong female bond that has lasted, you and I—here we are, sitting together in the same room and talking intimately after not seeing each other for all these years, but we could be right back in high school, couldn't we? Our bond is made up of affection but also of disorder, instability, incoherence, feelings of infe-riority or superiority. We've known bullying and bad moods, affec-tion and intimacy, and now for many years a kind of estrangement and distance, and yet we find ourselves drawn to each other again. That is the enduring part of friendships that are established in childhood. In a certain way they're the purest—these friendships from childhood because they were formed on instinct and trust before other concerns came into play. Yet even if we're tempted to lower our guard now and attempt to establish a new intimacy, out of love, or residual affection, or weakness, or sympathy, or kindness—because we have all these shared memories or whatever—still we women shouldn't do it. We can lose from one moment to the next everything we have achieved. I brought up the story of Jeannie Wokersein because there are some experiences that are difficult to use, they're so elusive, or embarrass-ing, at times unsayable because they belong to us so intimately. I am in favor of art that is fed by these kinds of experiences. And our cruelty that night is an example of this. For years I've wondered what drove us to hurt her that way. And not just hurt her but to attack her sexu-ally? Because that is what we did. We got her to trust us, and then we set upon her and targeted her most vulnerable area—that place between her legs. Why did we do it? Where does this kind of cruelty that women inflict on each other come from?

Well, I don't know, I said. And I didn't. I could hardly even follow her line of thinking, what she was saying, let alone answer the difficult question she was asking. Why had we done what we'd done? I certainly had never asked myself that question. It just seemed like the sort of stupid stuff kids do. And what would be wrong with us letting down our guard and establishing *a new intimacy,* as she put it? I simply didn't get it, what she was saying. Unless she felt that being close to me again would be an impossibility on her part. But why? I didn't know how to ask her these questions. I was hesitant to even try. So I didn't say anything. And I could tell my silence bothered her. That she expected more of a response from me.

SHE SIGHED heavily and picked up her glass and drank the last of her wine just as Vincent opened the door and started to enter the room. Oh, he said, I didn't know you were in here, and seeing that he had interrupted us he started to leave, but Jolene called him back. Don't go, she said, we were just talking, but I think I'll start dinner now. We should have something special to bring Verna luck tomorrow. You have a job interview tomorrow, right? At a dentist's office?

I said that was right. I had an appointment the next afternoon. I had already applied for a position as a clerk in a store on Melrose that sold lotions and perfumes, and another as a salesgirl at a clothing store, but I'd had no luck with either and on a whim I decided to apply for the dental receptionist job even though I had no idea whether it was the sort of work I could really do.

Open that good bottle of Sancerre we've been saving, she said to Vincent, rising from the sofa abruptly as if she'd just thought of something important, and put some water on for pasta. Let's use those chanterelles from the farmer's market. Then she pointed to the stack of clothes and said, Why don't you try on some of these things, Verna. See if anything fits. Come downstairs when you're ready.

THAT EVENING turned out to be the nicest we spent together during the whole time I stayed with them. I felt Jolene had released something by talking to me the way she had, something that allowed her to behave now in a more relaxed manner. She touched my arm during dinner when she passed something or poured more wine, gently brushing against me and generally paying me more notice than she had before. She seemed kinder, more open, as if she actually enjoyed my company, like the friend I had once known. The past was never mentioned again during our meal.

We drank not one but two bottles of wine that evening. Jolene and Vincent made a fantastic meal. They lit candles, and Jolene asked if I would cut some flowers from the garden. She even complimented me on what I'd chosen and the way I arranged them in the vase. We worked together in the kitchen until the meal was ready. I wore the black sleeveless blouse she had given me with the skull scarf draped around my neck, rearranged by her when I came downstairs (*Let me show you how to wear this,* she'd said, and immediately began adjusting it). She kept telling me how nice I looked but how much better it would be if I cut my hair, and she knew just the right person. She said she'd even like to treat me to a haircut with Henry, her favorite stylist. It would be her gift to me, she said—a new haircut for my new life in the city. I'd be surprised, she insisted, how much better it might make me feel. It was amazing what a good haircut could do for your morale.

Later in bed, I thought about the evening, woozy as I was from all the wine, and an outsized feeling of happiness and optimism suffused me. I felt as if I had finally managed to connect with Jolene, perhaps even earn her approval (all that praise for the nice way I looked in her clothes!). Also, I felt Vincent was more present than he'd been before. He actually talked to me, asked me if I'd ever taken singing lessons, that sort of thing. It seemed the first good omen, that evening together, the first indication I might actually make a new life in this strange and impersonal city. Perhaps, I thought, it would bode well for my interview the next day.

IN THE morning, however, my luck seemed to turn: the old truck wouldn't start, and I didn't see how I could get to the interview with the dentist in MacArthur Park, way at the other end of the city, but Vincent stepped in with a suggestion: he told me about a bus I could take and helped me plan my route so I could keep the appointment. He even walked with me to the bus stop a few blocks away on Wilshire Boulevard and waited with me until the bus came to make sure I got on the right one. As we walked to the bus stop he said some encouraging things about the job interview. He said he thought I would actually make a very good receptionist because I was so friendly. He said he'd be surprised if they didn't hire me. He told me to call him from a pay phone if I had any trouble finding the dentist's office or even if I needed a ride home. He said he'd be happy to come get me if there were any problems.

It was the first time I'd taken a bus in the city, and it felt like a great relief to leave the driving to someone else. As we rolled down the wide boulevard I read all the billboards and the names on the stores and cast glances at the other riders, trying not to appear to stare even though it was such a new experience for me. I realized I was the only white person on the bus. After arriving at my stop and wandering around for a while I finally found the dental office in a corner shopping mall, beneath a sign in Spanish that said DENTISTA FAMILIAR.

Dr. Marvin Lovestedt was a tiny man with pointy yellow teeth— not a good advertisement for his work, I thought. After we talked awhile he said he thought I might be just what he was looking for in a receptionist. He said some of his patients were from Mexico or Central America and he wanted to know if I spoke Spanish, and I told him I did not. He appeared to warm to me in spite of this. When the interview was over he told me he thought I was a pip and said he'd call me within a few days and let me know if I'd gotten the job.

I had no idea what a *pip* was, but I assumed it wasn't a bad thing.

I HAD a good feeling when I left his office, and I decided to walk around the neighborhood a bit before heading back to catch the bus, just to check out the area. I walked up Rampart Boulevard, a wide street with large leafy trees and older apartment houses painted pretty colors. It seemed like most of the people I saw were Mexican. I decided to make a loop around the block, and that's when I saw the "Apartment for Rent" sign stuck on a metal pole in front of an older building on a street called Carondelet.

It had the look of a little Spanish villa, something out of an old movie, a two-story pale-pink stucco building with a roof made of red clay tiles. Ornate metal scrollwork covered the windows, and a plaster coat of arms crowned the arch above the main entryway.

The building sat at the top of a series of steep steps, high above the street, surrounded by an overgrown garden. It wasn't so big compared to some of the other buildings on the street, and somehow its smaller size made it look friendly, even though I could see that it was a bit run-down. There were a few cracks in the stucco, and the plaster coat of arms above the entry was so worn you could barely make out the figures of the shield and two lions. Still, I liked the place. It called to me. I could almost hear it saying, *Come on up!*

I climbed the steps and knocked on the manager's door, and a middle-aged man with very white skin and almost colorless eyes opened it. I asked about the apartment, and he gave me an application to fill out. He told me what the rent was, and it surprised me it was so low. I thought it was something I could afford, especially if I got the receptionist's job at the dental office around the corner.

It's difficult to explain how certain I felt at that moment that I had found the place where I was meant to live in this city in order to begin my new life. I thought of Jolene's words—that she had found her *adult life* when she left Utah. I wondered if I could find my adult life here, if it wouldn't begin in this place that looked so welcoming.

I NEVER got over the feeling I was imposing during the time I stayed with them. There was so much tension between them already. It's one of the first things I had noticed when I arrived, how they did not seem right with each other, or for that matter right *for* each other. They appeared badly mismatched to me—one so gregarious and confident and brash, the other so quiet and uncommunicative and subtle. It did not appear to me they had much fun. There was no lightness to their life. The atmosphere in their apartment was always so serious. They often openly sniped at each other over some little thing. Or rather she sniped at him: she got upset easily, and then she would begin complaining while he simply retreated into silence and waited for her anger to pass. I felt my unwanted presence was making the situation worse, and the day I moved out I felt relieved and I imagined they did as well.

WHAT I couldn't have known was that I had arrived just as their relationship was ending. Jolene had already begun having an affair with a younger artist who had a studio in the same building as hers. As I later learned it had been going on for some time, and during the days I spent there with the two of them she and Vincent had been discussing the terms of their separation and eventual divorce. All the arguing I had heard at night in the room next door wasn't about me at all. It was the sound of a deeply unhappy couple.

I ended up getting the receptionist job with the dentist in MacArthur Park and also the apartment in the building I had looked at that day of the interview. It was the beginning of the great change in my life, the moment when I left behind the world that had fashioned me and instead began to fashion a new one of my own.

The apartment I rented was located behind the main two-story building in a separate little duplex. From the beginning I felt tucked away, sequestered from view, and even though the apartment overlooked a noisy alley I instantly felt at home in those rooms. There was a large kitchen with a dining nook, a bedroom, and a very big living room with tall windows, as well as a spacious bathroom decorated with beautiful old Spanish tiles. More room really than I needed. Even the closet was huge, like a little second bedroom. A strip of dirt beside my front porch seemed like a place where I could plant some vegetables or flowers, a spot where I could put a chair and sit outside in the sun. There was even an orange tree growing in the wild garden that surrounded the building, as well as giant cacti and palms and avocado trees, all mingling in a kind of neglected profusion. As I soon came to realize, no one ever sat in that garden except me. In fact I rarely saw any of the other tenants. The building seemed to be inhabited by elderly recluses who rarely showed themselves. This was fine by me. I had found my own private place in the churning city. And from the very beginning it felt exactly right.

3

It would be a long time before I learned what had happened with Vincent and Jolene and what had led to their divorce—meaning the fact she was having an affair, even though there must have been other problems before that.

One day, several months after I'd moved into my apartment, Vincent came into the dental office late in the afternoon around closing time. I was surprised to see him—I didn't even realize he knew where I worked, but of course he had remembered the dentist's name and had looked up the address, as he later told me. He asked if he could take me out for a drink when I got off work. He said he wanted to talk to me.

We went to an older restaurant on Wilshire Boulevard called the H.M.S. Bounty and sat in a red leather booth in the darkened bar. That was when he told me that Jolene had left him. She had been having an affair for some time, he said. Her boyfriend, a sculptor, was much younger. He said she had moved out not long after I left. She was now living with her lover. They had moved back to New York, where he was originally from. She was no longer even in L.A.

The news surprised me, of course, and yet it also explained why she hadn't returned my phone calls. Why I hadn't found anyone home the one time I'd driven over to see her unannounced. For weeks I had tried calling her, but no one answered. And then I got a message her number had been disconnected.

I WASN'T sure why Vincent had come to see me with this news, but I assumed he wanted me to know what had happened because Jolene and I were old friends. However, it wasn't just that. Because gradually, more and more frequently, he began coming over to spend an evening with me.

It became clear to me he was lonely. Often he brought a bottle of wine and picked up something to eat, and we sat around in my sparsely furnished living room and listened to the music he'd brought along, sometimes not really even talking much. But then he never talked much. I knew that already from the time I'd spent with him. Silence seemed to suit him. He was a very different sort of person, that much had been clear to me from the very beginning, but I couldn't put my finger on exactly what that difference was: he seemed so singular in his seriousness, so self-contained. I cannot say I would have ever imagined us together as a couple, even in those early days when I first began to realize he might be interested in me. For a while he had simply felt like a friend . . . a very unusual friend . . . until one day he didn't.

I understood he was falling in love with me, and gradually I admitted to myself I was attracted to him, though for a long while I wasn't sure of what I felt. I found him to be such a mystery. I didn't understand who he was. It was often awkward to be with him, he could be so quiet, but he also had a very quirky sense of humor and delighted in making puns and little jokes. He could be very witty, just as he could be startlingly blunt, as if indifferent to how his honesty affected others. He was like Jolene in that way. He couldn't be bothered with trying to be friendly to people he didn't really like, and he didn't seem to like that many. I felt he was a natural loner—just as she had always been. I saw that he lived close to his nature in a rather unfiltered way. At unexpected moments he might become distant, almost rude, but this mostly happened when he found himself in a situation that didn't interest him or where he didn't feel comfortable. Then he simply checked out and disappeared into his own world. Still, he was very polite, almost formal with me. I continued to find it hard to know what he was thinking.

One thing did become clear to me almost immediately: he was obsessed with a single subject and that subject was music. He had never played sports, had no idea how games were scored, and showed no interest in the kinds of activities I was used to men pursuing. The idea of hunting horrified him—he refused to even eat what he called *dead flesh* and had been a vegetarian for many years. Football was barbaric—in fact all sports, he once told me, seemed like thinly veiled excuses for manly aggression or boyishly immature competition. Neither did nature or the outdoors exert any pull on him. He had no interests except music. And books. He was passionate about books, all kinds of books, on all kinds of subjects. He told me he had created a large library over the years, starting when he was in his teens. It now contained only the books, he said, that had been most important to him, those he wished to keep and reread. He said he'd been an obsessive reader since childhood—*it's how I survived that dreadful period of my life,* he added. Music and books. Those were his only true interests. And it seemed to me they absorbed him to the point where they left little room for anything else.

I KNEW from the beginning there was something impenetrable about him. A way of showing little or no emotion, and yet I saw what a good, honest person he was. There was nothing artificial about him. Nothing forced or false. He seemed to be one of those rare people who lived what he believed to a very pure degree. I saw how he kept things very simple. He never seemed to get upset. There was an evenness to him, a way of moving through the world with a certain untouchability that I had never encountered in another human being. He seemed protected, somehow, from ordinary concerns.

The more time we spent together, the more I came to feel his strong moral center: he was a person who could be trusted. In the wake of Leon's infidelity and the breakup of my marriage this seemed incredibly important. Yet I never quite understood what he saw in me, untutored as I was in the things of the world he valued so much—the symphonies and operas he loved, the composers and books he often mentioned, his travels and his knowledge of art—that world Jolene had inhabited and which, she once told me, she had brought him into through her singular devotion to her work. Later I would understand this is what had likely brought them together—the thing they had shared—this obsession they each had with their work, which took precedence over all else. And yet it had also perhaps been the thing that finally drove them apart, the fact each was so absorbed with something outside their relationship.

ONE DAY, after he'd been coming to visit me for several months, often arriving unannounced in the evenings, knowing of course that he'd always find me at home, we had driven to the beach together. It was a beautiful morning, sunny and warm—one of those perfect days in L.A. when the city lives up to its reputation as a kind of Shangri-La. This was our first real outing together. He had a little sports car, a Mercedes convertible, and he took the top down and we headed up the coast to Malibu and climbed down a steep cliff to a secluded little cove. It had once been a nude beach, he said, but now it was mixed, and still not many people knew about it or were willing to make the effort to walk the distance it took to get there.

When we finally arrived at the beach he spread out a blanket on the sand and undressed and stretched out in the sun. I was relieved to see he was wearing swimming trunks under his clothes—I had been afraid he might think it would be okay to be naked, like a few other people were, and I couldn't have done that. As it was, I'd worn my bathing suit beneath my clothes and was shy about undressing and exposing my winter-white skin, but he was so pale himself it didn't seem to matter.

The red bathing suit I wore that day elicited the first real compliment I ever received from him, aside from my singing. You look great in that, he said when I finally undressed and lay down beside him. You should always wear red, he said, it's your color.

He talked about himself that day. More than he ever had before. He told me he'd never gotten along with his father, who resented the fact he hadn't wanted to enter the family business. His mother had also been a difficult person. My father kept her under his thumb, he said. It was hard for me to watch the way he treated her. She became a very nervous and insecure person. I think it was her fear of him. And her desire to please. She grew very unhappy over the years, and she couldn't hide it. She spent a lot of time in bed, suffering from ailments no one could ever name.

They used to go to Switzerland every winter, to their château in Gstaad, he said, and these stays had been very unpleasant for him. He hated skiing, he said, and he'd never been able to stand the cold. He hated winter and the whole atmosphere of the ski resort. He found it all so stupid. The way everyone talked about their great runs that day, the perfect snow, the fabulous instructor they'd hired. The women in their heavy furs, the men in their Alpine outfits, the fondue everyone made such a big fuss over. Furs and fondue and ski instructors. He hated all the fake festivity, the way people made so much of the holidays. All he wanted to do was stay in his room and read.

One winter, when he was about ten, his mother had insisted on him going to a children's Christmas party he really didn't want to attend, and because he looked so pale she had put makeup on him. Rouge, and a little color on his lips. The other kids noticed he was wearing makeup, and they'd been cruel to him. He'd ended up fleeing the party and walking home alone. When his parents arrived to pick him up they panicked when he wasn't there. They found him trudging along a mountain road through a terrible snowstorm, not dressed for such weather. He'd gotten very sick, and he'd also been punished. Once he was well he'd been forced to leave his room every day and join them on their stupid outings. He'd had to take dreaded ski lessons. He'd had to eat the stupid fondue, which he felt sure was germ-ridden from everyone sticking their long forks into the same pot and then right into their mouths, and doing it over again. He could no longer stay home alone, which had been all he'd wanted to do.

So you see I got it from both ends, he said. Ridiculed by the kids at the party, then punished by my parents. If I had to describe what my childhood was like that's the story that says it all. I've never really fit in anywhere . . . but the good news is, I don't have to even try to fit in anymore. I can be the way I want to be now.

———

HE'D COAXED me into the ocean that day even though the waves had frightened me. I had never ever seen the ocean before. We walked along the edge of the surf until the water no longer felt so cold. He led me out beyond where the gentle, rolling waves were breaking, showed me how to duck beneath them and emerge farther out where the ocean was calm and flat. He told me I should try floating and looking up at the sky. He put his arms beneath my back and held me while I drifted faceup in the water. I felt so light and safe in his hands, and I experienced an exquisite sense of being suspended between water and sky, with him cradling me as if I were a weightless child. It was the closest we'd been to each other—physically the closest and I suppose in every other way—but the moment didn't last long. Later, when we'd returned to the apartment and he was standing in the kitchen looking over my shoulder as I opened a bottle of canned pears I'd brought from home, I had turned to face him and put my arms around him. I held him, placing my head on his chest, but he had gently pulled away. I'm sorry, he said, but I just don't—I just can't—I don't have those feelings.

Then he'd turned and left the apartment abruptly, leaving me standing there, feeling very confused.

I THOUGHT perhaps that was the end of it. But he'd come back a few days later and brought me a gift. A book by someone named Goethe. I didn't want to accept it. I didn't know what he wanted from me, and he'd hurt my feelings by refusing my embrace. I was cool to him that evening, and I knew he felt it. But when he left he stood in the doorway for a moment, and then he put his arms around me and pressed his face against the top of my head and said, So sorry, Verna, I have difficulty showing my feelings but I really do care for you.

After that he began coming to see me regularly again. What was it that had drawn him to finally propose one evening? He was so much more worldly and sophisticated. But maybe that was part of it. Maybe he, too, needed to be able to trust someone with his feelings and he understood he could trust me. Perhaps that was the most important thing after all. To really be able to *trust* somebody. To know one is safe. In me he had found a rather uncomplicated companion—certainly less complicated than Jolene. What I understood was that he cared for me deeply. I could feel his caring in his kindness, his gentle if serious manner, in the way he cooked for me and brought me little gifts of books and music. Even if he continued to seem so reserved, I sensed how much he cared, and gradually I began to care more and more for him. In this way we fell in love, if that's what a feeling so slow and subtle can be called, and when he asked if I would marry him I didn't even think about it that long. I smiled and shrugged, and said, Yes, okay.

HE EVENTUALLY moved out of the apartment in Beverly Hills that he'd shared with Jolene and we began to make a life together in my place on Carondelet. There had been no question of me moving in with him. He said he no longer wished to live in that apartment, even though it was much larger and nicer than mine. He gave away much of the stuff she didn't take with her, bringing only the few pieces of good furniture and the china and silver that had come from his family, and his books and the kitchen things he liked and felt we could really use. Anything that reminded him of their life together he didn't want to keep. Much of the art they had collected was divided between them or sold. He ended up with very little. Of course he brought his piano with him when he moved in. He figured out how to get it inside by temporarily removing a big window and hiring professional movers, and it took its place at one end of the large living room and instantly transformed the space. He seemed very happy as he settled in with me. He said he had come to like the MacArthur Park neighborhood. It suited him much better than Beverly Hills. It was a *real* place, he said, for real people, and that's how he wanted to live.

And thus our life together began.

I NEVER did get over the feeling there was something different about him. Something inaccessible, closed off, the part that had to do with his emotions. If I raised a subject or expressed a feeling he didn't like or that upset him, he simply fell silent and refused to look me in the eye. There were so many things about him that struck me as rather odd. His obsession about various things. For instance, if I left anything out on the kitchen counter—an apple or a box of crackers—I'd return and find it put away. He needed precision and order, everything always in its place. He kept his few clothes organized by color, spaced evenly on the rack. He was very particular about what he would eat, and he always ate the same things. He didn't like to vary his routine. He couldn't be flexible. Or very sociable. The little niceties often perplexed him. If someone called me on the phone—my mother, say—and he answered he would never talk to her, he'd simply say, *Here she is,* and hand me the receiver. Why don't you say a few words to her? I would later ask. Why not chat with my mother for a minute? He would look at me then as if he didn't understand what I meant. It was as if he simply didn't understand what it meant to *chat.*

I just didn't think of that, he'd reply. And I saw that what he said was true.

But there were so many things he simply didn't think of. The kinds of things that would come naturally to most other people. It must be the way he was raised, I kept thinking. That must be it. The strictness of his parents, their unvarying routines, his mother's sad retreat into a kind of perpetual bedridden state. His father's remoteness.

I told myself it was due to the differences in our backgrounds. A problem of class, I thought, and education, a difference in how we'd been brought up. Like Jolene, he'd been raised in a world of privilege: he had gone to private schools, traveled widely, earned a doctorate in music theory. Geographically we'd come from opposite ends of the country. I thought perhaps people behaved differently in the East, not to mention the South, where he'd spent so much time. I was a fifth-generation westerner, a woman who had never been to college, with a narrow experience of the world. Obviously differences were to be expected. But not for many years would I begin to comprehend just how deep those differences were, let alone the cause of his often inexplicable behavior.

———

SIX MONTHS after Jolene left the city Vincent moved in with me, and we were married shortly thereafter. At the time we were both thirty-seven.

Now we were sixty-seven. Thirty years had passed. Thirty years of marriage and of living in the apartment in MacArthur Park—the same apartment on Carondelet that I had rented all those years ago.

I always believed we'd move one day, get a larger place in a nicer part of the city, but that had never happened mostly because Vincent couldn't stand change. He was happiest when everything stayed the same, when each day had a recognizable shape and the background of life didn't shift. He required everything to flow around him in a predictably satisfying pattern in order to keep his attention focused on his work. And I had come to understand over the years how important this was. How his work *was* his life. I saw that clearly, and I think I always had.

That morning, however, two letters had arrived that threatened to change everything. When I read them I knew at once our lives were going to soon be disrupted. I saw no way out of it. The change he'd always feared was coming, perhaps in more ways than one.

4

The first letter I opened came from something called the Ingenious Capital Asset Management Group and was addressed to both of us. It said our apartment complex was being put on the market and their firm had been appointed by the probate court to oversee the sale of the building once owned by our recently deceased landlord, Billy Ray Williams.

As soon as a buyer could be found, the letter continued, we would be given three months to leave. Since the apartment was rent controlled and because of our age and how long we'd resided in the building we'd be entitled to a buyout. There would be no possibility of staying on since it was likely, given the condition of the building and the value of the attached extra lot, any buyer would choose to tear down the existing structure so a larger complex could be built.

I stared at the letter from Ingenious for a while, hardly able to comprehend this news. It was a teaching day for Vincent. The letter had arrived on a Tuesday, when he tutored students at the Colburn School of Music, and I knew there was no possibility of talking to him right then no matter how much I would have liked to. I couldn't imagine moving out of this apartment that had been our home for so many years, but it was Vincent I was really thinking of. I knew how upsetting this news would be to him.

After a while I got around to opening the second letter. It was addressed only to me, one of those old-fashioned thin blue airmail envelopes that could be folded and sealed in such a way so that it had to be opened carefully to avoid tearing up the message inside. It had no return address but appeared to have been mailed from overseas. Not until I opened it did I realize who the sender was. I didn't even have to look at the signature at the bottom. Jolene's handwriting was unmistakable.

I had heard from her only intermittently over the years, and it had been some time since we were last in touch. She had written then to congratulate me on my most recent book, a nonfiction work on the mystery writer Raymond Chandler and his marriage to a much older woman named Cissy. Jolene was full of praise for what I'd done as well as for the fact that I had even become a writer, as she put it, *against all odds. You can imagine my surprise,* she wrote, *when I saw your book, translated into French, in the window of the Village Voice, my favorite bookstore in Paris.*

In this letter she said very little about herself except to note that she had been living in Paris for the last ten years, but she had recently left a relationship and she intended to now move back to Los Angeles and she wanted to see me. Of course, she said, she knew Vincent and I had gotten married, and she hoped we were happy, that things had worked out for us. She asked me not to tell him she was returning— *not just yet,* she wrote. This was very important, she stressed. She had decided to keep her plans private for the moment. She didn't want anyone to know she was coming back to L.A. There were reasons for this which she would later explain. She reminded me that once, when I had found myself in difficult circumstances, I had asked her for a favor, and she was hoping I would help her now by keeping her return, as she put it, *entre nous.*

At the end of her letter she asked if I would meet her for lunch. She named a day and time, two weeks away, as well as a restaurant, and gave me a number where I could text my response. I shouldn't try calling her, she said, as she no longer cared to speak on the phone. The letter ended with a plea:

> *Again, I must ask you not to tell Vincent or anyone else I'm coming back to L.A., at least until we've talked. I'm counting on you to do this for me. Don't let me down.*

———

ALL DAY long I'd been thinking about these two letters.

It was hard to say which was more disturbing—the fact we'd be forced to move or the idea of Jolene reentering our lives—but of course it was the news that we'd have to leave our apartment. We had hung on here so long that I found it ironic we might now be paid to leave. These rooms had held us for so many years. I felt we were tethered here in every way. I couldn't quite see how we could possibly think of leaving.

Thirty years was a very long time.

How long we'd lived here on Carondelet.

How long we'd been married.

How long since we'd seen Jolene.

And now she was returning to the city, and presumably to our lives. What did this mean? I had no idea. But of course I'd do as she requested, just as I always had. I'd meet her. And I wouldn't tell Vincent.

I HAD gotten up earlier than usual that morning. I couldn't sleep past five o'clock. Mornings were actually the best time for me in the apartment. I enjoyed the hours alone, with just the cats for company. I usually woke up early, long before Vincent did. I made the coffee, as usual, saving some in a thermos for him. Then I turned on the heater in the living room and lifted our old cat Barney from his place on the sofa so I could stretch out, but before I did this I plugged in the little white lights draped around the windows and front door. The room had come to feel lifeless to me without these faerie lights we put up for Christmas one year and never took down. Now we simply replaced them whenever a string burned out.

I began thinking of the first night I slept in this room. I had not yet unpacked the horse trailer, and there was no furniture in the apartment. I slept in the down sleeping bag I'd brought from home, here in the living room because I wanted to be where I could see the front door. I needed to feel safe on my first night alone in the city.

For much of that night a police helicopter had circled low overhead, its blades beating the air noisily as a slanted cone of intensely bright light bore down on the neighborhood, sweeping across the houses and apartments, the alleys and streets. It felt so menacing to me, the light raking across the windows, invading the room over and over again. Who were they looking for out in that black night? I thought of what Vincent had said the day I told him and Jolene I had rented an apartment in MacArthur Park. *That's not such a good neighborhood,* he'd said, frowning. *I'm not sure you'll feel safe there.*

But Jolene had only shrugged and said, *Lucky you, finding something you can afford.*

That first morning I was awakened by birdsong. So many birds, singing from the tall eucalyptus trees in the garden next door just as the dawn was breaking. I hadn't expected that. More birdsong in the city than I had ever heard in that basement apartment at home.

The birds were singing again this morning. Such a sweet sound to greet the uncertainty I felt hanging over the day.

LAST NIGHT, when Vincent saw the letter from Ingenious Capital Asset, he said, How can they be selling the building? The probate case isn't even settled.

I watched him from across the room as he slumped in his chair, staring at the letter. He was still a very handsome man, even as age continued to change his appearance. But at the moment he looked distraught and his face sagged and he seemed suddenly older. I told him I thought the letter meant that the probate case involving our landlord's estate had, in fact, probably now been settled.

I imagine that they have to sell the building in order to pay off the heirs, I said. We'll have to move. I don't see any way out of it.

Vincent didn't look at me when I said this. He sat staring at the letter in his hands and then he said, so softly I could hardly hear him, I guess there isn't.

I HAD a dream about Jeannie Wokersein last night, perhaps because of the letter from Jolene. The dream was vague. I did remember one part, however: Jeannie had appeared to me suddenly, in what seemed like my old backyard, and said, *I trusted you.*

That's all. Just, I trusted you.

Over the years I came to believe the incident with Jeannie Wokersein had much more importance for Jolene than it did for me. I even imagined it had somehow affected the kind of art she went on to make. I had no way of understanding if this was true, but I had seen a good deal of her work and I had come to know much more about these things than I once did.

Early on in our relationship Vincent began taking me to museums and galleries. Talking to me quietly and patiently in an effort to help me understand what I was seeing. He also began suggesting books for me to read. In this way he became the instrument of my education on many subjects—not just art, but literature and, of course, music. He did this in the most subtle of ways, never forcing any idea upon me but rather quietly suggesting I might look at a painting this way or that. He played music for me that he loved and told me why he loved it, or brought me a novel he thought I might like. Because of him I became a reader. I have him to thank for that. He opened up my mind. And then he furnished it with such wonderful ideas.

DURING THE course of our marriage we'd had had ample opportunity to see Jolene's work even though we had never again seen her in person. We had followed her career, not because we made any particular effort to do so but because she had become so famous it was impossible not to be aware of her success—at least for anyone with any interest at all in the art world. She had emerged as one of the pioneering figures in the feminist body art movement of the 1970s and '80s, and then gone on to have a robust career as a performance and conceptual artist though she had never given up painting, and in more recent years it was her paintings that were so sought after, especially the early work. What was she up to now? I wondered. And why was she coming back to L.A.?

I let several days pass before I texted her to say I had received her letter. I agreed to meet her on the date she'd suggested, in the restaurant she'd named in Beverly Hills. What I did not say was that this suggestion to meet on Rodeo Drive struck me as rather sentimental. We were going back to Beverly Hills, the place where we had last seen each other, and I had the feeling she'd chosen this place on purpose.

She got back to me immediately: *Thank you so much,* she texted, *I'll see you then. Looking forward to it.*

I FELT nervous about meeting her, but it was keeping the news from Vincent that felt especially unsettling. In general I had a habit of telling Vincent everything—what I was thinking, how I felt about my writing, any future plans for my work as well as the ordinary events of the day—to the point where this often seemed like a small fault. I seemed compelled to tell him *everything,* even the little things that I knew could make me look foolish. This had come to seem to me a particularly female weakness—this inability to keep certain things to ourselves—and I had recently begun trying to change this habit of spilling everything. Now I carried the secret of Jolene's return, and in some way it felt as if I were cheating on him.

As it was, the days following the arrival of the letter from Ingenious were difficult enough. We talked frequently now about what it would mean for us to move from this apartment where we had lived for so long but—maybe because it still seemed so far off (Wouldn't it take longer than they thought to sell the building? Couldn't we somehow end up staying here longer?)—we did nothing to prepare for such a big change. Instead a kind of low-level anxiety began to affect our daily lives.

I felt his nervousness in his silence and the way he appeared so somber much of the time. It was as if we had just discovered a much-loved friend had been diagnosed with a terminal illness, only the friend was the old building that had been so kind to us. Particularly upsetting was the idea set forth in the letter from Ingenious that a new owner would likely want to tear the building down. The thought of it being destroyed made us particularly sad.

———

WE BOTH became rather distracted, unmoored by the idea of such a big change. I kept thinking of the apartment building and how we would soon have to move. I had no idea where we would go. It upset me to think of our lovely old building being destroyed, but L.A. was notorious for trashing its own history, as I had discovered while working on my Raymond Chandler book. Chandler and his wife had lived in over thirty-five different places in and around L.A., and I had tracked down every place where they had ever lived and photographed what I found. It was a bit like detective work. I discovered that at least half of the places had been destroyed and replaced by something else—most often by something uglier and more poorly constructed than what had been there before. I hated the idea our building might become another victim of this kind of casual effacing of the city's architectural history. And for what? So the kind of cheap new struc-ture I saw going up everywhere these days could be erected in its place.

WE'D HAD a pleasant evening the night before, managing to avoid dis-cussing the impending move. During dinner a package had arrived—the door to the front porch was open, and from our place at the kitchen table we could see through the screen as the mailman dropped the package on the porch and then hurried away.

It's Robert Lowell! I cried. Robert Lowell has arrived.

The week before, I had asked my editor to send me the new biog-raphy of Lowell that had just come out from my publisher, and I could tell from the size and shape of the package that it was probably this book.

Great, Vincent said. Can't wait to look at it later. He was the one who had wanted the Lowell, and it was for him I had requested it.

After dinner we lit candles in the bedroom and put on music and made love. I often felt surprised at how much we continued to desire each other. It seemed to me that a willingness to indulge fantasies, the crafting of erotic narratives, was what enhanced the act and kept it exciting. It didn't hurt that I still found him so attractive. When he walked across the room naked, as he did last night, I looked at his slim, taut body and found the sight to be exceedingly beautiful.

After we made love we sat in the living room. He wanted to read me a passage from *Madame Bovary,* in a new translation by Lydia Davis.

He took up his place in the Eames chair, wearing his silk dressing gown, while I lay on the sofa in my long white robe, eyes closed, listening to his melodious voice:

> At the unexpected shock of that sentence falling upon her thoughts like a lead ball on a silver plate, Emma, with a shudder, lifted her head to try to understand what he meant; and they looked at each other in silence, almost dumbfounded to see each other there, so far apart had their thoughts taken them. Charles was contemplating her with the clouded gaze of a drunken man, even as he listened, motionless, to the amputee's last cries, which followed one another in lingering modulations punctuated by sharp shrieks, like the howling of some animal whose throat is being cut in the distance. Emma was biting her pale lips, and, as she rolled in her fingers one of the fragments of coral she had broken off, she fastened on Charles the burning points of her eyes, like two arrows of fire about to be loosed. Everything about him irritated her now— his face, his clothes, what he was not saying, his entire person, his very existence.

WHEN HE had finished reading, I didn't say anything. I wanted to let the words hang in the air and reverberate. His voice had lilted me into a brief trance.

By this point she hates Charles, Vincent said.

Yes, I replied, though I had read the book so long ago I couldn't remember this passage or what exactly had prompted this scene of revulsion—except now of course I was reminded that an amputation was taking place in the next room. A nice echo of the severing of the Bovarys' marital bond.

I love that opening, he said, about the sentence falling like a lead ball on a silver plate.

And her eyes, I added, the burning points of her eyes fixed on him that way. There it is, the whole story.

There's another passage I want to read to you, he said. Let me look for it.

I LAY still, with my eyes closed. I could hear him ruffling the pages, searching the book for the sentences that had captured him. *Bovary* was one of his favorite books. Every few years he read it again. Earlier he had said to me that he found Flaubert to be a very beautiful writer, in terms of his prose style, but every once in a while he produced a paragraph that was so dazzling you had to stop and go over it again, like the one he'd just read to me.

I'd never stopped admiring how well read Vincent was. What would I have become if he hadn't introduced me to books? There had been no books in the house where I grew up, except the religious tomes with names like *Answers to Gospel Questions* or *A Marvelous Work and a Wonder*. My parents hadn't been readers. As a child I'd never owned a library card. I was also a rather indifferent student, more interested in the outdoors and the animals I'd owned in my youth—the horses and dogs I'd so loved—than in book learning. Leon certainly hadn't been a reader. Books had never figured into our life together.

NOW IT was a different story. When Vincent moved in with me he brought his library with him, lining the walls of the rooms with the bookshelves he built himself, and my life underwent a great change. I discovered *literature*. All those books he discussed so patiently with me. At the time I thought, who knew what worlds awaited between those covers?

You must find something for yourself, he had said back then, something you wish to do that really engages you. There's no point in living a life without knowing that.

And slowly, as if reading stories could naturally lead to wanting to tell them, I had begun to write some stories down. Stories about the years I worked in a canning factory, the day the boilers exploded and sent boiling plums and peaches and cherries spewing into the air. Stories about my great-grandfather, a horse trader and polygamist who had settled a town in Arizona named after him. I wrote about the Indian School where I had once worked as a housekeeper—how the Ute kids always fought with the Navajo kids and nobody ever figured out how to keep them apart. I told stories about the past. Baptisms for the dead. Missionaries in Mexico. A brother who had died young. Stories that had been in my head for years and came out of the way I had been raised.

Vincent read my stories and encouraged me, so I continued to write them down. And in that way I saw a first book of stories published. Stories, that as one critic pointed out, came from a culture and religion that hadn't produced many writers. It still astonished me that such a thing could have happened. Even now, many books later.

AS HE continued to look for the passage, I thought about Jolene's letter. It was the unspoken thing between us now, the secret I was keeping from him, and it made me increasingly uneasy. I knew something he didn't—that Jolene had returned to the city, or would soon be returning. I had agreed to meet her without telling him. I carried this secret in his presence, and it dangled in my consciousness like a tangible dark lie I hadn't yet told. A lie of omission, but nonetheless a lie. Already, even before she had turned up again in our lives, she was confirming my deepest fear, that somehow she might return and come between us. She had already come between us by forcing me to keep a secret from him. I felt annoyed with her for putting me in this place where it seemed to me I was committing a small betrayal. And yet until I saw her—until I knew what was going on in her life—I couldn't violate her request. I'd given her my word.

I can't find it, Vincent said after searching awhile for the other passage. I'll look for it later. I think I'll go to bed now. He stood up and crossed the room and bent over and kissed me lightly, and then he lifted his head and looked at me for a moment, his face only inches away. I saw the age and tiredness on his face, and also the clarity and beauty, and I felt a little tug of feeling—love, affection, familiarity, all the tender intimacy of our years. Good night, he said, smiling, and ruffled my hair before he turned and left the room.

5

The next evening I went outside and sat on the porch steps for a while, listening to Vincent playing the piano in the living room. There was no light coming from the apartment opposite ours, on the second floor of the main building, where a horrible old woman named Shirley lived. We deeply disliked this neighbor. She had been the bane of our existence for many years. I had never used the word *sociopath* to describe any other human being, but it fit her perfectly.

Her bedroom and bathroom windows were both dark, as they usually were these days. She'd had a stroke some months ago and survived, though she now walked with great difficulty and one side of her face drooped. Did she stay in bed most of the time now? Lying in her darkened room, on her soiled mattress? We knew from people who had gone into her apartment that it was a filthy place, crammed with decades of accumulated junk—the detritus of a hoarder who lived alone and had once had five cats and three dogs before our landlord Billy Ray had demanded she scale back her menagerie. Her place was trashed after years of neglect. She was over ninety now and rarely left her apartment. And yet she was still here, alive and living above us in those rooms she'd inhabited for so many years, and just as mean as ever. We'd often dreamed of the day when she'd be gone and we could live in peace. But she appeared indestructible. She'll be the last one standing, we said. She'll be here after everybody else is gone. It was hard to imagine how she was surviving, as old and frail and impaired as she was, with a nurse's aide coming by only once a day for a few hours to help her with basic chores. But she had an iron will. I'd observed this for years. How she could will herself to keep going against all odds, as if driven by some kind of superhuman strength fed by malice.

Her windows looked down on the porch where I was sitting. A narrow walkway and little strip of garden separated the main building from the duplex where we lived. Because she was on the second floor opposite us, she could easily look down into the windows of our living room. For years it felt as if we were living in the shadow of an evil presence that took the form of an elderly gray-haired crone whose face reflected such deep inner ugliness. A face so etched with meanness it was horrifying to look at. We hesitated to even use her name, often referring to her simply (and of course very uncharitably) as The Pig. She was more of a force of nature at this point than a mere neighbor, a power of elemental negativity lodged within the heart of our building. Our loathing of her was so pure it had almost passed back again into affection, or at least familiarity. She was, in a way, like a horrible aging parent, crouched in sinister malevolence in the psyche of the building, the living vessel into which we could heap all our mistrust and dislike, the enemy I hadn't even known I required.

LOOKING UP at her darkened bedroom window I remembered an evening many years earlier when we had been barbecuing on the grill we'd set up on the walkway between the buildings that served as a kind of patio for us, even though there was no privacy—everyone in the rear apartments could see what we were doing from their windows. It wasn't a particularly welcoming space, but at least it allowed us to be outside on hot summer nights. That night Shirley stood above us at her bedroom window, looking down at us, spying as she was wont to do. We knew she was there and tried to ignore her. But soon she began tormenting us, as she always did.

Oh, it's the intelligentsia, she said, hurling the word down at us. She made it sound like intelligentsia was the worst thing you could possibly be. They're having a little barbecue tonight, she said. The intelligentsia, throwing their own little party, isn't that nice?

It was summer, one of those evenings in L.A. when the air feels so sensuous as it begins to cool down it's as if you're simply glad to have survived another hot day. On such evenings you only want to emerge, having been trapped all day in air-conditioned rooms, and now, as the day begins to wind down, you're drawn to the sultry outdoors. In any case it was far too hot to cook inside, and we were enjoying the evening, sitting outside with a drink, with the smell of barbecue wafting on the air, feeling happy—until, that is, Shirley started with her ugly business.

As she continued to torment us, Vincent suddenly snapped: He simply couldn't take it anymore. He stood and picked up a rock from the garden and hurled it at her window. There was the sound of glass breaking, then Shirley shrieking. The rock had broken the window and hit the air conditioner sitting inside on the ledge, which was lucky because it helped deflect the flying glass, and she ended up not being hurt. Still it had caused a big ruckus. Our landlord Billy Ray, who lived in the adjoining duplex, appeared on our porch later that evening, shaking with anger. We knew he didn't like Shirley any more than we did, but we had damaged his property by breaking the window and we could have caused serious injury to one of his tenants, he said, perhaps making him liable. Vincent apologized and agreed to pay for the damage. It all eventually blew over, and Billy Ray forgave us. We never attempted to barbecue outside again. And we never said another word to Shirley after that evening. For the past twenty-five years we had continued to pass her coming or going, in the alley or on the stairs or walkway, while pretending she simply didn't exist.

All the good and the bad that had happened had created the kind of attachments and memories with the power to bind Vincent and me emotionally and psychologically as surely as if we had been attached by physical tethers. Our stories were here. Our history. It was here we had written books, composed music, formed our life together as a couple. We felt safe here, in spite of the fact the MacArthur Park area had long been regarded as one of the most crime-ridden neighborhoods in the city. As for Shirley, she had long ago become the visible evil, the incarnation of all that was foul in human nature, and perhaps such an enemy eventually ends up being useful in focusing one on the good. In any case old age had finally arrived to more or less limit the amount of damage she could inflict on us. Or so we hoped.

———

JOLENE WOULD ask about our lives when I saw her. I figured she'd want to know everything. She was never shy about probing one's life. Asking the pointed questions you'd prefer no one brought up. Why had we never moved? she might want to know. How could we have stayed in such a place for so long? In such a poor neighborhood? Didn't we think we deserved something better, given the success we'd both enjoyed? I could hear her saying, *Surely it can't have been a matter of money, considering Vincent's wealth,* and I would have to tell her that his family cut him off long ago. That he no longer had access to the money that had once kept him enjoying the good life. I could imagine that this would sound like some sort of failure to her.

She'd surely have other questions as well. About Vincent, our marriage. What could I tell her about that? What do you say to your oldest friend whom you haven't seen for many years when she asks about your marriage to her former husband? The marriage that had lasted while her own had failed?

IT WASN'T as though we hadn't had contact with her over the years. Even before she sent the letter about my Chandler book, she had written a note when Vincent's volume on Schubert was published. And even before that, when my first novel had come out, she had written me a congratulatory letter in which she expressed the same sort of amazement over the fact I had become a writer as she would later do when congratulating me on my Chandler book. She said she had been very surprised to receive the copy of the book I had sent her—how had *that* happened, she wondered? How had I managed to become a writer? She said she had read my novel with great interest, aware of how much of my own life I had used to create the main character. She found the story of a woman moving to L.A. from a small town in Utah and reinventing herself an interesting one. She thought I had done a rather brilliant job of it. Of course she had seen herself in my story, even though she had been nothing more than a minor character in the book, appearing at the beginning in a few scenes, but still she had no trouble recognizing herself, especially since I had used her real name, but she said she found nothing objectionable about that or in the portrait I'd drawn of her. She had read the reviews of my book and had felt very proud of me. That I had been able to do what I had, with no education, coming from such a modest background. Well, that was something to be proud of, wasn't it? she said. That was something unusual. She said in many ways she felt I had surpassed her own achievements, because after all she'd had so many more advantages.

And then, at the very end of her letter, she delivered several criticisms. She said she had been disappointed by the ending of my book. She felt that by having my protagonist get married and have a baby, it suggested I had never thrown off the ideas I had been raised with. This sort of traditional resolution of a woman's story culminating in a husband and children, it *just wasn't on,* as she put it. She suggested the book would have been stronger had I avoided such an ending. She found the toxicity of familial relationships in reality often canceled out such happy endings. *What is taken from you to fit yourself into these intimacies is something you can never reclaim,* she had written. She wondered if I regretted not having children and that's why I'd given my narrator a baby at the end of the story.

And that brought her to her other point, she said. Why had I chosen to portray the Vincent character in my novel as such an eccentric, fragile person? Did I imagine it might make him more attractive to a reader? Why not a more honest description of him as he really was— a pampered mama's boy with an almost maniacal sense of entitlement, a self-involved narcissist, raised by an unloving and strict father who had made his fortune from strip-mining coal in poor Appalachian communities, exploiting his disadvantaged workers and fouling the landscape. Vincent's father, she said, was a man who had constantly berated his son and bullied him into submission, then sent him off to an expensive boarding school just to be rid of him, with the result of creating a mortally wounded adult. She did not find my portrayal of Vincent to be sympathetic—he hadn't come off as terribly likable, had he?— but then, she added, he is a complex man, not an easy person to get close to.

At the end of her letter she wrote, *But again, just to say I am full of admiration for what you have done with this novel. But then I always knew you were different. I could see possibilities in you I felt others couldn't. Still I have to admit you've surprised me. And that is not an easy thing to do.*

SHORTLY AFTER that time she staged one of the art performances for which she'd become famous. It had gotten a good deal of attention, and of course we heard about it—I can remember turning on the evening news and seeing her being interviewed shortly after she had posted bail and been released from jail. She had been a visiting professor at San Diego State University at the time and she'd fallen in with a group of artists known for their political performances. She and another artist friend had gone to a store and stolen meat—steaks and chops and roasts, packages of hamburger and hotdogs. They'd taken this meat from not just one store but several in the San Diego area until they had quite a cache. And then she and her friend had driven the freeway, throwing the meat out the window of their car, where it was run over and smashed by passing vehicles, all the while photographing what they were doing. They had taken close-ups of the bloodied smashed packages of meat, slowing down to do so, and eventually they'd been spotted by a state trooper who pulled them over and arrested them, charging them with inattentive driving, littering, and creating a public nuisance. They were also later charged with theft when it was discovered they had stolen the meat. This was more or less the outcome the artists had hoped for. It allowed them to publicize their performance as a protest against war—all wars, any war, but especially the Gulf War known as Desert Storm. All that bloodied desecrated meat was intended to remind people of the deaths that were occurring in such an immoral and unnecessary aggression. Stealing the meat was important to the performance, suggesting how we were also stealing the lives of innocent people killed in these horrible wars.

She looked strong and clear that night when I saw her on the news. I remember staring at the TV screen and thinking she was as beautiful as ever, even if a certain harshness was more evident in her looks. She wore no makeup. Her hair was cut very short, so short it looked as if she had shaved her head and it was just growing out. She was even thin-

ner than I remembered, her face a bit more lined—after all we were
no longer so young. Her angularity and the lack of hair and makeup
gave her a certain androgynous look that was very much in vogue. She
spoke well during the interview, full of passion and anger, denouncing
the war as morally indefensible, the work, she said, of men unable to
control their aggression and a capitalist system that profited from war
in deeply obscene ways. She was sick, she said, of seeing rooms full of
men making all the decisions for the rest of us. Every day she turned
on the news and all she saw was men—men running corporations,
running governments, running the world. Nothing but rooms full of
men, *white* men, and mostly *old* white men, acting like they belonged
there, like it was their *right* to control everything. Where were the
women? she wanted to know. Why were women largely still shut out
of making decisions that affected all of humankind?

From that point on, her work took on even stronger feminist and
political overtones. She moved back to New York and continued to
feature her own body in the pieces she made just as she had done from
the beginning of her career. One work in particular had startled me.
We had stumbled upon it in a museum in Paris, not realizing her art
was included in the group exhibition we were touring. We had simply
entered a room in the Pompidou and there it was, a large black-and-
white photograph of Jolene, sitting outside on a bench against a wall in
bright sunlight, wearing jeans with the crotch cut out. Her legs were
spread, her pubis exposed. The dark hair looked like a small furry
animal crouched on her lap. She stared directly at the camera, no
expression showing on her face, but her eyes nevertheless seemed to
challenge the viewer, as if to say, *Go ahead and look, that's why I'm here,
exposed this way, for you to look at.*

Oh for God's sake, Vincent said when he saw the picture.

I laughed. I didn't know what else to do. He turned and walked
away, but I stood there for a long time, gazing into her eyes. Secretly
I approved of the picture even if I didn't really quite get what she was
doing. It was enough I could intuit the emotion that produced it: *You
think you can objectify women, isolate their sexual parts for your own private
pleasure—well, isolate this then. Have a good look.*

I also realized, just before turning and walking away to join Vincent in the next room, that this was a view he must have seen many times for himself, and not just in a photograph.

VINCENT STOPPED playing the piano and came out onto the porch, interrupting my flow of thought, and asked me what I was doing.

Just sitting here thinking, I said.

About . . . ?

Oh . . . nothing much. I felt flustered. What if I were to say to him, *I'm thinking about Jolene and that picture of her in the Pompidou we saw and the fact I've arranged to meet her next week because she's moved back to the city and wants to see me?* I was tempted to tell him about her letter. But I didn't. Because I had promised I wouldn't. And I liked to believe I was a woman of my word.

Instead I said, Are you hungry?

As a matter of fact, he said, I am.

I went inside with him and we made dinner together. I caramelized some parsnips and sweet potatoes, and he made a salad with fennel and red onion and blood oranges. We worked beside each other in the kitchen, and when the meal was ready we lit candles and opened a bottle of wine and sat down at the table to eat.

At one point he said, We should probably take the air conditioner with us when we leave. It's a good one. He meant the air conditioner sitting in the window that a friend had given us many years ago.

Yes we should, I answered, but I was thinking, *if we leave*. I still could not accept the idea of moving as a reality. There was something surreal about the whole thing. Was I in denial? Yes, I certainly was.

And of course the bed, he added, smiling knowingly.

Ah, the bed, I said. He knew I really didn't like our bed. It felt like an institutional hospital bed even though it was an antique that he had salvaged from an old hotel. I had been trying to talk him into getting another bed for some time.

Remember, there were a lot of them from that old hotel downtown? he said. They were all painted white. I stripped it, remember? To get it down to the raw metal. It was a lot of work. He shook his head. A *lot* of work.

The bed. The air conditioner. Already he was mentally beginning to pack up our things, trying to prepare himself for the inevitable. Knowing him as I did, I knew he was attempting to be brave even though the idea of change was so obviously disturbing to him, as it was to me. We were doing that thing where each of us was trying to appear strong for the other.

I said, I guess we're going to have to start looking for another place soon.

Yes, he said quietly. And then, after a long pause, he added, Very soon, I think.

After that neither of us said anything for a long while.

DURING DINNER the cats entertained us. Max lay outside on the porch, sticking his paws through the rubber flaps of the cat door. His white paws with their black tips looked like little characters in a vaudeville show that kept popping out of the curtain and ducking back in. Barney crouched just inside the door and took little swipes at Max's paws every time they appeared. It was like a Punch and Judy puppet show, and each time Max stuck his paws out and Barney attacked them we broke out in laughter. Then Max came inside, and he and Barney began wrestling under the kitchen table.

WE WERE crazy for cats, that was a fact. Until I met Vincent I was more of a dog person while he was already devoted to cats to an almost irrational degree—I should have realized that, and in a way I did when I saw him with the old cat he and Jolene had, the one that had attacked me and he advised me not to even look at. The one he used to spend evenings stroking as it lay on the back of the sofa in the apartment in Beverly Hills. That cat had developed kidney issues, and he'd had to put it to sleep not long after Jolene moved out. I think it was part of what made him appear so terribly unhappy and lonely during those months when he first began visiting me. He missed his cat so much. He talked about it in a way he never spoke about Jolene.

After dinner Vincent wadded up a little ball of paper and threw it for Max, who skidded across the kitchen floor, batting it around like a hockey puck. This went on for quite a while, long after I'd lost interest in watching their game.

Vincent's love for animals was so deep and intense that at times it seemed to eclipse any feeling for humans. For many years it had confused me. He had difficulty expressing his feelings, and yet he could spontaneously exhibit the most profound affection for almost any animal—but especially an animal in need. When ads for the Humane Society came on the television tears came to his eyes as he looked at the pictures of the woefully sad or abused creatures, and yet he couldn't look away, which was always my first instinct.

Vincent had rescued both our cats from the street. The first, Barney, had been a kitten—so small its eyes were barely open—who had been left behind by its feral mother when some workers cut the weeds in a nearby empty lot. He'd heard it mewing from beneath a stack of branches. I had not believed something so small would survive, but we bottle-fed it and somehow it made it. The second kitten, Max, was not much older when he rescued him: he had been run over by a car just ahead of Vincent's on a busy street but had somehow managed to avoid being crushed, and Vincent had immediately stopped and jumped out in busy traffic and grabbed him, and then called me once he had the kitten safely with him in his car and said, *You won't believe what I'm bringing home.*

But I did believe it. Max and Barney. They had given us such happiness. And we had given them a safe home.

WE SAT in the living room and had some chocolate. Just one square each, as we did every night. Vincent said he had found the other passage in *Madame Bovary* that he'd been looking for. Did I want him to read it to me? Yes, please, I said, and settled down onto my place on the sofa and closed my eyes:

> Deep in her soul, however, she was waiting for something to
> happen. Like a sailor in distress, she would gaze out over the
> solitude of her life with desperate eyes, seeking some white

sail in the mists of the far-off horizon. She did not know what this chance event would be, what wind would drive it to her, what shore it would carry her to, whether it was a longboat or a three-decked vessel, loaded with anguish or filled with happiness up to the portholes. But each morning, when she awoke, she hoped it would arrive that day, and she would listen to every sound, spring to her feet, feel surprised that it did not come; then, at sunset, always more sorrowful, she would wish the next day were already there.

He closed the book, waiting, I knew, for me to say something. But I didn't feel like saying anything. The idea of a woman waiting each day for something to happen struck a very personal note. I felt that I, too, was waiting for something. For the move that was now inevitable, for the meeting with Jolene, which had begun to feel like an assignation with a past full of complication as well as affection, competition, and unease, a kind of unresolved story in which Jolene and I—and perhaps also Vincent—each had had a part to play. I was a little afraid to see her: I was made as I was made. She was stronger, more confident by nature. I didn't want to feel colonized again, as I had in the past, by her dominating presence: I had no way of knowing on what sort of terms we would meet again all these years later.

IT SEEMED to me the world was and would forever remain the place that had formed me. That small town we had both come from but which had ended up playing such different roles in our lives. The religious culture where everyone had believed in the same things but which she had largely escaped, as the daughter of a nonbelieving Mormon mother and a lapsed Catholic father, parents who loved to party and drink, who had affairs and lived carefree lives so tinged with hedonism. The devout, sober parents who had nurtured me had felt the importance of everyday niceties rather than the need to scrape them from the surface of life. But what was that place we had come from except an artificially delineated patch of earth, as she had once suggested, given an arbitrarily chosen name? *Utah.* So vowelly and breathy. A tiny fragment of the world.

Jolene had considered the institutions of family and church suffocating and couldn't get away from home fast enough. But only belatedly, in those first months in L.A., had I felt what she had always known. I came to understand such a feeling of release. Freed from the restraints I had accumulated over the years—those of my sober origins—I had felt myself slowly evolving. I had been energized by the largeness and diversity of the city and the feeling anything could happen here, and yet I had never lost my feeling for home or my love for the family and friends who continued to live there.

Jolene was like a person who had lost not only her home, but also her homesickness, her nostalgia and feeling for that home. *Stick a finger in the wound that is still infected,* she had said that night when we were discussing Jeannie Wokersein, quoting a writer Jolene admired. *That's what an artist must do. Attempt to lift layer by layer the gauze that binds the wound so as to reach the story of the wound.*

The story of the wound. These were the kinds of stories that she liked. Even when we were young she'd had an obsession with sad tales. Stories that often showed up the dark side of human beings.

Another thing she had said came back to haunt me: *Once you've been noticed,* she said, *you won't ever fit back in your box. You have to walk around naked for the rest of your life.*

We had both been noticed now. By making the work we had, I suppose we each stood naked, though I felt she was much more exposed than I—*literally* exposed—not only by her greater fame but by the nature of her art.

VINCENT SAID, Have you fallen asleep over there?

No, no, I said. Just thinking. Thank you for reading that passage from *Bovary.* It's wonderful.

Isn't it, though? he replied.

He closed the book and stood up slowly and carried it with him into the bedroom, holding it against his chest as if pressing it to his heart.

6

In the morning Vincent said he'd like to mop the floors in the kitchen and living room and he wondered if I had something to do to get me out of the apartment for a few hours while he cleaned. I said I could go to the coffee shop up on Sunset where I sometimes went to write. This was our routine: he liked to clean house and he preferred to be alone in the apartment so he wouldn't be interrupted and could move the furniture around as he wished. I didn't know where his love of mopping floors and cleaning house had come from, but I valued it. He also did the laundry each week, and since there was no room for a washer and dryer in the apartment, it meant he had to go to a laundromat. He had done this once a week for thirty years and never complained. He always refused my offer to share this chore with him. The truth was I think he liked these jobs. He liked neatness. He liked clean floors. He liked his T-shirts and pants folded in a certain way when they came out of the dryer. I, of course, liked that he did all this so I didn't have to, though once in a while I felt a little pang of embarrassment: here we were in our sixties and still going to a laundromat as if we were college students. He, on the other hand, never felt put upon. Life, for him, was lived on very direct and uncomplicated terms.

I PUT a few notebooks in a bag and headed up to the coffee shop on Sunset. The morning was shrouded in fog, and it gave the world a subdued feeling. Lately I had been thinking about what sort of book I

wanted to write next—another nonfiction book, like my volume on
Raymond Chandler? Or a sequel to the memoir I had recently pub-
lished? Perhaps even another novel. And yet I kept coming back to
Chandler.

I had several ideas for another book on him. I thought there was
an interesting story to be told about the three women who had played
such a large part in Chandler's final years. All three women were fas-
cinating. There was Natasha Spender, the English pianist and wife of
the poet Stephen Spender, who had befriended Chandler after meeting him at a dinner party in London, where he'd begun spending more
and more time after his elderly wife, Cissy, died in 1954. And Helga
Greene, a wealthy English heiress once married to Graham Greene's
brother Hugh, who started a literary agency in London and became
Chandler's agent—and part-time companion—during his final years.
And then there was Jean Fracasse, a divorced Australian woman living in La Jolla who worked briefly as Chandler's secretary after Cissy's
death and with whom he later became romantically involved for a
short time until she became a nuisance. Each woman had a significant
part to play in the last few years of Chandler's life, and all had ended
up distrusting each other.

This was a story that had never really been properly told—the
story of these three women, Natasha, Helga, and Jean, and their
involvement with Chandler during the last years of his life—and yet,
as I sat in the coffee shop on Sunset, mulling over the possibility of
writing another book on Raymond Chandler and looking at my notes,
I felt it was in truth a rather tawdry story. Chandler's final years were
so sad, as were his relationships with women by that point. Why tell
this story now? I thought. Why not leave the poor writer in peace?

I came across my notes from Chandler's interview with a London
journalist who had asked him about his suicide attempt in the wake
of Cissy's death. I had never been convinced that Chandler had really
wanted to kill himself when he took that revolver into the shower
stall of his house in La Jolla in 1954 and fired two shots, both of which
managed to miss him, as did the bullets ricocheting off the tile. Before
heading to the bathroom with the gun, he had called the local police

and told them he was about to kill himself and gave his address. This seemed to me the act of a man who wished to be saved rather than one intent on dying. What was incontestable was his despair.

In the interview Chandler had told the journalist that Cissy had been his "home," and given the fact that they had moved so often— sometimes two or three times a year—and had no children and few friends or family connections, thus creating a symbiotically self-contained and peripatetic life, it was easy to see how he could conflate a *person* with a *dwelling.* For him home was not a place but an irrevocable condition, a connection to his beloved wife. His home was Cissy, wherever she was. *I loved her very much,* he told the journalist, and added, *When you lose a home you've loved for thirty years it takes courage to start another.*

Reading this sentence now, years after copying it down, I felt a small shock of recognition. I, too, was being asked to start another home after thirty years. But Vincent and I still had a full life. Most importantly, we had each other. Surely we could sustain that life under another roof, couldn't we?

Why, then, was I so nervous about what felt like such an impossibly disruptive move?

I GAZED up from the notebook at the scene unfolding in the coffee shop. I was surrounded by attractive people, most much younger than me, and with the exception of a couple talking quietly at a table set against the wall, all were looking at phones or computer screens that cast a bluish glow, like radioactive light, against their skin. I felt these devices were conditioning our brains to respond to a continuous desire, but for what? A kind of affirmation of our physical existence and importance? Neither Vincent nor I had ever been involved with social media, making us an anomalous couple within our circle of family and friends. It contributed to our feeling of leading cloistered lives. If anyone ever asked why we'd made this choice Vincent would reply, *I'm a private person,* and leave it at that. I usually said, *I prefer not to,* though I knew something other than a simple preference was driving my reticence, and that something was a fear of finding myself engulfed by sycophantic and obsessive worlds. We were loath to cede our time to these activities. And so we existed largely in ignorance of many of the things that occupied other people around us. And we didn't mind. Only occasionally, as now, gazing around the coffee shop, did I feel the odd person out as I sat looking at my worn spiral notebooks covered with my writing in longhand.

FOR SEVERAL years I had been thinking of another possible book that focused on Chandler. While conducting research at the Bodleian I had come across Cissy's old recipe box. Chandler had considered his wife a very good cook, and since he regarded most American restaurant food as inedible they had mostly dined at home. After her death he had set about teaching himself to cook using her recipes. He became very interested in cooking, so much so that the last book he had been working on in the months before he died wasn't a mystery novel at all but rather a cookbook with the title *Cookbook for Idiots*. He intended to collaborate with Helga Greene on this project and use the recipes Cissy had perfected during their marriage. She had kept her recipes in the black-and-white recipe box he had saved after her death, which I discovered at the Bodleian.

I had spent an entire afternoon perusing that recipe box, and I am sure I was the first researcher into his life to ever take an interest in such an ordinary object. I was of course looking for traces of Cissy. Most of the recipes were written in her hand, in the turquoise ink she favored, but some had been clipped from ladies' magazines in the 1930s and '40s and pasted on cards. They revealed a quintessentially middle-class American sensibility. There was a recipe for Cissy's Ham Goodbye and Cissy's Lemon Cream Pie, canapés made of liverwurst, a frankfurter pickle spread, and a cocktail made of canned pineapple, rum, and frozen lemonade. There was a recipe for her mother's soup, and one for Lobster Thermidor from Town Lyne House in Massachusetts, others for Cheese Roll-Em-Ups, and something called Mystery Chef's Steamed Raisin Pudding, as well as a Palace Court Salad that had come from a woman named Clementine Paddleford. There were also recipes for My Pet Mayonnaise and Apple Dumplings à la

Rouen, as well as Applesauce for Gallibeoth—one of her nicknames for Chandler, chosen to reflect his aura of being her White Knight.

I had been fascinated by how very American the recipes were, how they called for canned goods—tomato soup and pineapple chunks and tinned mushrooms—dishes not so different from the ones my mother had prepared for our family when I was growing up. There was nothing sophisticated about the food Cissy had cooked, or the recipes that Chandler had wanted to include in *Cookbook for Idiots*. In pure Chandlerian fashion, the first recipe he had chosen for his cookbook was called "How to Grill a Steak" with a one-word instruction: *Don't.* Steaks, Chandler wrote, should always be pan-fried in order to properly sear the meat and retain a juicy inner pinkness.

Sitting there in the coffee shop I thought how I would like to put together a Raymond Chandler cookbook. I could use his title for the book, *Cookbook for Idiots*. In a way I would be finishing the book he had abandoned at the time of his death. I imagined trying out Cissy's recipes, actually cooking the food she'd made for her husband, and gathering quotes from his novels and stories relating to food—and there were many, most of them very witty and amusing. One-off comments about food and American dining habits that his detective Philip Marlowe had delivered in his wisecrack mode. Why shouldn't I write something like this?

I checked my watch again. Another ten minutes and I could return to the apartment without the worry of disturbing Vincent.

I TURNED to the back of the notebook where I had made notes on Helga Greene, Chandler's English agent. From everything I had read about her, I had always felt she had to be the most marvelous person. A bit eccentric, perhaps, as the very rich often are. She had grown up in one of the great houses in London, attended to by a servant named Proudfoot who had a passion for embroidery. Her father had made a fortune in the oil business. In the 1930s she had lived in Germany with her first husband, Hugh Greene, brother of the novelist Graham Greene, before they returned to England and later divorced.

One story about Helga had stayed with me, this one from the

1930s, when she had lived in Germany during the years when the Nazi movement was gathering force, and ugliness had begun to pervade everyday life. According to an account by a friend, he hadn't realized quite how dangerous life was becoming until one day he went for a walk with Helga in what he described as a little semideserted public garden near her home in Berlin. Suddenly they realized they were being dogged by a couple of hulking bully boys in plain clothes who eventually accosted them, using threatening language. He hadn't spoken any German, and he felt particularly helpless and ineffective as the boys continued to verbally abuse them in a very aggressive way. He realized it was Helga who was really the target of their abuse, and he gathered they were objecting to her appearance. Later he was to learn that they were rebuking her for wearing red lipstick. Whatever she may have felt, she remained outwardly cold, calm, and collected. She answered them precisely and severely in her perfect German, and they retreated with only a little face-saving bluster. Characteristically she made little of the episode afterward and would not tell her friend exactly how she refuted the attackers. Nor did she reveal to him at the time how she was even then actively helping her Jewish friends to escape to Britain to avoid the wrath that was to come. That day in the park, her friend said, was the first time he fully appreciated Helga's most notable quality—the stoic courage with which she was able to confront any situation, no matter how threatening.

On the drive back to the apartment, I continued to think about Helga Greene. Of all the women Chandler had been involved with at the end of his life, only Helga had really had his best interests at heart. She was the selfless one, the true friend. I knew there was little point in imagining I might write another book about Raymond Chandler, whether it be *Cookbook for Idiots* or a book about the various women who had played such a part in his later life. I had covered that territory, hadn't I? And yet I found I didn't want to let go of these stories. And I didn't want to leave Chandler just yet.

THE ALLEY behind our apartment was crowded on my return from the coffee shop, as it usually was, blocked by illegally parked cars and

an old mattress someone had thrown out, as well the gaggle of loitering men who hung out in front of an open garage lined with nude
girly pictures. Every day, coming and going, I passed this group of
men who always stared at me, watching me with blank looks as if
they didn't know who I was or hadn't seen me practically every day
for years. I never acknowledged these men with a friendly wave or
smile, and they never acknowledged me. I never even met their eyes
anymore. They were too threatening. Some were young gang members and dope dealers. Some were older, maybe the uncles or fathers
or other relatives of the gang kids, and often there were a couple of
homeless men who stored their carts nearby and hung out with them.
I never knew who they really were. Just guys from the neighborhood.
For years I had driven or walked past them as if they didn't exist or I
didn't exist for them, and I'd always felt strange doing this. It felt so
unnatural to me. Being *neighborly* was one of the fundamental ideas
I'd grown up with. But I had learned early on that it was better not to
engage with these men: once I had said hi to one of them as I walked
by and he had followed me all the way up the block, whispering men-
acingly, *You are so beautiful you are so beautiful, I would like to know you
baby . . .*

   He'd scared me. He had been following me so closely that I could
feel his breath on my neck and smell the rank odor of beer.

   After that I never spoke to any of the men again, not even a hello.
And they'd gotten the message. We ignored each other and had for
years. Yet I had never stopped feeling how weird it was that these
neighbors who I saw every day were not the kind of people I felt I
could even speak to.

I PARKED in the garage and unlocked the door in the alley and headed
upstairs to the apartment, only to find Vincent sitting outside on the
porch playing with Max.

   All done, he said. The apartment's clean. Boy were those floors
dirty.

   He gazed up at me and smiled. He was wearing the plaid shirt he
wore almost every day over a clean white T-shirt. His hair, so neatly

cut, looked silvery and shiny in the sun. His face was tan, and his deep black eyes shone with points of light behind the lenses of his round black glasses. He appeared calm and peaceful and handsome, sitting there with Max curled up on the step next to him. He stroked the cat slowly, lovingly. I thought of Chandler's words about Cissy that I had just come across in my notebook: *I don't know how I managed to get her.*

I felt my own good fortune at that moment. He was strong, that was the great thing. He was sure—sure of himself always. He had a taste for the rare and true. What stood out beyond anything was that he was a great and deep and high man—so immensely talented—and to love him with tenderness was not to be distinguished from loving him with pride. Though it had taken me many years, I had come to this place of acceptance and peace. Of *acquaintance* with him. Like Chandler and his Cissy, I could not imagine life without him.

The letter from Jolene, the knowledge I would soon see her, had somehow drawn me toward him more fiercely, this man to whom she had once been married. Was it that I felt more protective of him? She had left him. But I had stayed. Just as she had left that small undistinguished place where we were both born while I had stayed on. Yes, it was true: I felt protective of him, as if I must keep her from him. I don't know why I felt this way, but I did. I felt she was a threat not just to him but to our happiness.

The truth was, I had never known much about their relationship. He'd never spoken of it in any detail. I had never really known how much he'd loved her, or she him, or why they had married in the first place, what had attracted them to each other. And I couldn't ask him about that now. I couldn't have asked him about it before, because those were exactly the sorts of questions he was loath to answer, the subjects he avoided. Those were the areas of danger for him, the realms of emotion, of causation and self-examination. I had no idea how he would feel about seeing her again, if it came to that, and it seemed likely it would if she intended to stay in the city. I felt certain that her opening to me was only the beginning. That she would attempt to come back into our lives. She wanted something from me, but what was that thing? Perhaps she imagined it would be okay now for all of us to come back together, now that we were all safely ensconced in our own lives after thirty years of separation. But were we really safe? Would he ever forget the injury she had inflicted by leaving him? Would I have no reason to feel threatened by her? None of this seemed exactly true to me.

I REMEMBERED now something he said to me long ago, when he had first begun coming to see me in the evenings, not long after she had left him. It was one of the very few times he'd spoken about Jolene and their history.

He told me that when he met her he was twenty-four. He had never had a girlfriend. She was the first. Yes, he said, I was twenty-four and I'd never been with a woman.

I remember how he looked at me when he told me this. He stared straight ahead, not making eye contact, as if to do so would be more than he could bear. What does that tell you? he asked.

He said they had met in a park in Brooklyn on a day when funds were being raised for a new arts complex. Musicians were performing in an outdoor bandstand. Jolene had been wearing black ankle boots with sharp toes and high heels and studs and buckles everywhere, even though it was the middle of summer and everyone else was wearing sandals. Other women wore sundresses or shorts: she had on black leather. Her boots looked so dangerous, he said, with the silver studs and spikes and sharp toes, and after she had left him he kept thinking of that day and those crazy boots. She seemed so wild, he said, and so worldly. He thought she knew so much more about everything than he did.

Only later did he realize she must have thought he was as wild as she was—another creative person with radical ideas. But that wasn't true at all, and it was only over time that she began to understand how conservative he really was, how normal and a bit dull. In the beginning he believed she saw him as some shy case that needed her help. A musical scholar who'd never had a girlfriend. And she was going to help him come out, overcome his shyness. But, he said, she didn't understand how hard it is to change someone, to become something other than what you are.

That night—the first and only night he ever spoke to me at any length about their relationship—he told me it had been unbearable when she left him. He'd fallen into a black funk. He didn't know what to do. And then it had gotten so much worse when he'd had to put Ursa down—that had been the old cat's name. Ursa. That's when he began coming to visit me because he found me easy to be with. Not just easy, he said, but comforting. I didn't try to talk to him about the breakup with Jolene. He appreciated that. In time he was able to begin working again, and not simply working but composing music that really pleased him. He began to consider me as his muse. He said he felt he could not have survived those bitter months after Jolene's departure had I not been there to help him. It was as close as he came in those early days to telling me that he loved me.

The memory of that evening when he opened up about Jolene both comforted and disturbed me. I knew that he did love me. But he had loved her too, or he wouldn't have been plunged into such a terrible depression when she left. Perhaps, in the end, I had been the muse, the one who had calmed him and helped him survive his loss, but his love for me might have been different from his love for her. She could have been a different sort of muse, a more passionate love. This is something I couldn't know. Something, I felt, I would never know.

WE WENT inside and fixed a late lunch and talked about our upcoming trip to New York. A piece of Vincent's was to be performed at Carnegie Hall as part of a program celebrating new works for strings and soprano. I had written the text for the piece, inspired by a drawing by Edvard Munch that I had seen in a museum one day. A drawing of a bear and a woman, the first woman to emerge in the world who meets her animal lover. The image moved me with its beauty and simplicity—the woman and the bear embracing so tenderly. After seeing it I wrote a poem, something I rarely did and then only for my own amusement. But Vincent had liked the poem, and immediately he'd taken it and set it to music, composing a piece for strings and soprano. This is how *Song of Elos* came to be.

We had never collaborated before, and even now it seemed wonderfully unique to us that this had happened, something born naturally out of the intersection of our separate perceptions and interests that might never occur again. We couldn't have planned such a collaboration, it would have to have arisen naturally, quixotically, as *Song of Elos* had. The idea that we were now going to New York to hear this piece performed by an accomplished soprano in such a great setting—this is what we were looking forward to. We had booked our flights months earlier and reserved a room in a hotel near Carnegie Hall where we'd stayed on previous visits.

We were to leave the day after my lunch date with Jolene, which of course Vincent still knew nothing about. Just as I had no idea what would happen when I finally saw her again. I had already made up my mind that once I *had* seen her I would not keep it a secret from him any longer. I didn't care if she didn't want him to know she was moving back to the city—that could be her story to tell—but she must understand I couldn't keep it from him that we'd met. He had to know.

I'd already thought it out. I'd wait until we were on the plane to tell him I'd seen her. Discuss it with him during our long flight when he would be my captive, as my seatmate, unable to avoid talking about her with me. I understood now better than ever that he did not, that he *could* not, easily confide his feelings or thoughts about her. In truth, any subject that generated intense feeling was off-limits. Anything that produced deeply uncomfortable emotion. He fell silent. He was especially silent, however, whenever Jolene's name came up.

WE TALKED about going to a movie that night, but instead we spent the evening at home and ate a simple dinner of fruit and cheese. Again Vincent wanted to read something to me when we later retired to the living room and he'd settled into his Eames chair, which really was *his* chair, the only one he ever sat in and which I knew better than to occupy.

He'd almost finished the Robert Lowell biography, and he'd talked about it obsessively over dinner, in the manner he often did when something absorbed him. He did this without really being able to measure the effect on other people of such a singular focus or absorption. He seemed unaware of passing time, how he might end up talking about something for a very long while and in great detail, but I understood this now and often indulged him rather than trying to change the subject as I had once done. Thus the whole dinner had been taken up by him relating the story of Robert Lowell.

HE EXPLAINED what a difficult but rich life Lowell had had, the number of times he'd suffered mental breakdowns due to his severe bipolar condition and been confined for months in upscale mental institutions, the nearly twenty electric shock treatments he'd received after his mother's death, and the experiment with Thorazine that left him feeling both the mania *and* the depression more acutely, as if, Lowell said, he were carrying 150 pounds of concrete in a race. He recalled for me the names Lowell had formulated for his depression— that "blind mole's time," that "dust in the blood." He talked about the women who'd been attracted to Lowell's good looks and brilliance, how devoted Elizabeth Hardwick had been during their twenty-three years of marriage in spite of his multiple affairs with younger women, and how disastrous the next marriage with the English-Irish writer Caroline Blackwood had been. He spoke of Lowell's deep friendship with Elizabeth Bishop, a poet with her own demons, which had endured for so many years and resulted in such a profusion of remarkable letters. He went over so many facets of Lowell's life as we sat at the table, repeatedly slicing off pieces of cheese and plucking grapes from their stems, pouring a second, and then a third, glass of wine, that I felt a bit dismayed that I might not now have the pleasure of discovering all these facts and details for myself should I choose to read the book, and I wondered if I would even bother doing so. He went on and on, talking about Lowell, unaware of the time passing, until half an hour, then almost an hour had gone by. But I said nothing about this. I simply nodded when he told me he had just ordered a book of Lowell's poems after reading the last poem he had ever written, called "Day by Day," which appeared at the very end of the biography—the book he had just read. That was the poem he was preparing to read to me now in the living room.

———

HE WAITED until I had gotten comfortable on the couch. The little white lights around the windows and front door were the only lights on in the room, aside from the reading lamp next to his chair. He held the book open under the lamp, with a cone of pure white halogen light shining down on his beautiful hands like a bright benediction, and began reading the poem, his voice steady, sonorous, and deep as it pronounced the lines, which rolled over me, only half understood, though certain phrases I captured whole, their shapes as bright and perfect as passing birds bursting with vivid color: *I want to make something imagined, not recalled. . . . I hear the noise of my own voice. . . . all's misalliance, yet why not say what happened? Pray for the grace of accuracy. . . . his girl solid with yearning. . . . we are poor passing facts. . . .*

When he had finished, I was quiet for a moment, and then I said, Read the beginning again, would you? And he did, pronouncing the lines carefully: *Those blessed structures, plot and rhyme / why are they no help to me now / I want to make / something imagined, not recalled.*

I knew better than to take the words literally, but how could I escape their personal call, the way I made their meaning mine at that moment of hearing? I couldn't resist doing so. I felt Lowell was speaking to me, telling me something important. About *making something imagined, not just recalled.*

THE NEXT afternoon, as I was packing for New York, I got a text from Jolene. She said she was going to have to reschedule our lunch. She was sorry, she wrote. Could we postpone our meeting for a few weeks? She would explain later and get back to me with a date. She added an emoji, a yellow smiley face, with one eye winking at me.

In a way I felt relieved. Her message let me off the hook. Gave me a reason to back away and not have to go through with a meeting that felt fraught and complicated. My first instinct was to text her back immediately and say I didn't really think it was such a good idea for us to meet after all, not even at a future date. But how could I do that without sounding churlish? Without it seeming like I was punishing her for postponing? It would make it appear I was closing the door on her. What a waste it would be, I said to myself, to ruin our story—the story of our long, if interrupted, friendship—by leaving too much space for ill feelings. The feelings might be inevitable, but why not keep them in check? That was the thing, to keep them in check.

I wrote her back and said, *No problem. Let me know when you'd like to reschedule.*

Just ten words. Keep it short, I thought. And keep your feelings in check.

THE NEXT morning I took my coffee outside and sat in the sun. The cats had dragged the little blue cushion off my favorite chair, and I shook it out and put it back before settling down in the shade.

I found myself thinking of Jolene, of our childhood. I could see her clearly as she was then, a beautiful girl—perfect in every way, and so unaffected. So talented and sure of herself always. I recalled the way she managed to make even the braces she wore in junior high look like jewelry for the mouth. Everyone hated those things, anyone who had to wear them. But braces were neither pretty nor ugly to her, not a hindrance or hassle, just an unremarkable fact that she could effortlessly turn into an asset. It's how she dealt with so many things.

Her mother had been a difficult person—vapid and spoiled and ruined, made indolent by the money she'd inherited from her family's gun manufacturing fortune and the fact she was an awful drunk. That's how people spoke of her. As a drunk and a harpy. And people did talk about her in that town—in part because she was married to Dr. Carver, a very popular gynecologist, a man so handsome and revered by his female patients that most of the women who went to him for their pregnancies or female problems couldn't help getting crushes on him. His charm matched his extraordinary good looks. He was friendly and warm, and he made the women who came to see him feel special, as if each and every one was worthy of his complete attention and kindness. I know because my mother went to Dr. Carver,

who delivered every one of her eight babies, and she regarded him as
a kind of godlike figure. But Mrs. Carver was another story. Nobody
much liked her. They pitied Dr. Carver for having such a wife.

There were rumors Dr. Carver had affairs, but nobody could
blame him given the floozy he was married to. There were rumors
Mrs. Carver also had affairs, just to get back at him. Everyone understood they were a very unhappy couple, but people didn't get divorced
so easily in those days, not in that small town.

None of this gossip about Dr. Carver and his wife was a secret to
anyone, including Jolene. Jolene talked about her parents' infidelities
openly, as if she didn't care what they did. It had nothing to do with
her, she said. She would tell us who her father was supposed to be
sleeping with before other people heard about it. Still even she was
shocked when it came out her father was seeing the mother of her
boyfriend Scott. *Can you believe it,* she said. She and Scott had even
caught them making out in her father's car in the driveway one night.

It seemed so embarrassing and weird to us, but to her it was just
another amazing story, the sort of thing people constantly gossiped
about in that small incestuous place. She laughed about it. But when
her parents finally broke up it wasn't so funny. It got ugly, and she
couldn't deny it. I remember being at her house one night, toward
the end of their marriage when her parents were arguing rather
viciously. We were studying in her room with the door shut, but still
we could hear everything. They shouted at each other at full volume,
her mother broke things, they threatened each other and ended up
screaming terrible abuse. The completely raw and unfiltered rage
of her parents—her mother's violent and hateful speech—was inescapable, and we were forced to listen to everything from behind the
closed bedroom door. Jolene made no excuses for them. But I could
tell she had reached her limit. Finally she just stood up and without
saying anything ran down the stairs and out of the house, leaving me
to trail behind.

I SAT outside so long I lost track of time and had to rush to make my
appointment with my hairdresser in Beverly Hills, the same stylist

Jolene had sent me to when I first arrived in L.A. *You'll look a lot better if you cut your hair,* she'd said to me that night when we'd had been discussing Jeannie Wokersein. *Let me make an appointment with Henry. You'll be surprised how good the right haircut can make you feel.*

She'd been right, of course, as she was about so many things. The haircut *had* made me feel different. It was part of the transformation I began to feel myself undergo all those years ago and that even today still surprised me.

In truth, I did not really feel so different from the woman I had been then. All that had happened in the intervening years—my life in this large and varied city, the learning and exposure to ideas, the traveling, the art I had seen and the music I had listened to with Vincent, the books I had read and those I had written—it often seemed all this had only changed the outer circumstances of my life, like the good haircut, and that inside, in the most essential way, I remained the same provincial woman I had been when I first arrived in the city.

7

The situation with the apartment steadily worsened.

A "For Sale" sign had gone up in the garden at the front of the building where it sloped down to the sidewalk. An ugly thing that appeared overnight. It brought home the reality of our situation in a new and concrete way and upset us both terribly, just the sight of this sign, but it was particularly hard for Vincent. He'd grown ever more quiet and withdrawn in the last weeks. It was as if we could no longer escape the reality that sign announced: we would soon be forced out.

The "For Sale" sign appeared a few days before we were to leave for the concert in New York, and as we sat in the kitchen having coffee the morning before our departure, discussing the new sign, Vincent suddenly said, We should just pull that thing down.

Yes, I said. We should. Why I agreed to this I don't quite know because even then it seemed like a bad idea.

We'll do it tonight, he said, after it gets dark.

But we didn't wait until it was dark.

The sign was stuck in the earth on a steep slope above the sidewalk, and we agreed it would be too dangerous to flounder around on the loose dirt at night when we couldn't see anything. The ground dropped steeply, and the footing would be unsure. Better to do it during daylight, we decided.

It was late afternoon when we crept quietly down the front steps, carefully checking to see that none of the other tenants were around. I stood on the sidewalk, looking up and down the street, keeping watch while Vincent worked his way down the steep slope and began pushing the signpost back and forth, loosening it from the earth. It toppled over rather easily, a heavy wooden cross with Ingenious Capital Asset's metal sign hanging from one arm. The whole thing was too heavy to move in one piece, so he pried the metal sign off the post first, using the hammer and screwdriver he'd brought. This took a long time, and meanwhile I stood on the sidewalk, calling out to him when I saw someone walking down the street so he could step behind a tree. Finally he managed to free the sign, leaving the heavy post tipped over on the ground.

We need to get rid of this, he said, indicating the sign. I waited while he pulled the car around and helped him load it up. He drove it a few blocks away and dumped it in an empty lot where there was already a lot of trash.

AS SOON as he returned to the apartment I began to worry. What had we done? I knew we'd committed the sort of vandalism that could have repercussions if it were ever traced back to us. I felt we were stirring up a hornet's nest and almost immediately I began to regret our actions. But I said nothing to Vincent. I tried to pretend I still thought it was a good idea to have destroyed the sign, that it constituted some sort of vigilante justice.

Before going to sleep we agreed we would tell no one about what we'd done. We wouldn't even speak of it again, as if it had never happened.

In the night, however, I awoke with a terrible thought. What if the security cameras attached to the front of the apartment building next door had caught us in the act of destroying the sign? Was that a possibility? I had forgotten this fact, that in the world we lived in now cameras were everywhere and our every move was being recorded. I seemed to remember the cameras next door were fastened above the entrance to the underground garage, right next to the edge of our property where the sign had stood. Could the cameras have a wide enough angle to have recorded our illicit activities?

In the morning, over breakfast, I mentioned this concern to Vincent.

I hadn't thought of that, he said. You forget about those cameras being everywhere.

I know, I admitted. You just don't think about how you're always being watched.

We tried to reassure each other that it was very unlikely such a minor act of vandalism would ever result in the sort of investigation where neighborhood security camera footage would be reviewed. But how could we be sure?

LATER THAT morning something else happened. Our cat Max became locked inside Shirley's apartment. I heard him meowing and went outside to see him pressed up against the screen covering Shirley's bathroom window, looking down at me and crying. I felt furious. Shirley had trapped him in her apartment! Perhaps he had wandered in when she left her back door open. She fed several strays who lived in the neighborhood, sometimes coaxing them inside. This must have been how Max found himself trapped. She had lured him inside, then shut the door. Even in her diminished state she was capable of plotting such devious schemes simply to disrupt the lives of others. She adored seeing the reaction she caused, the injury or offense, the sight of the anger or suffering she engendered.

I began calling up to her, telling her she needed to let Max out.

Please get up, Shirley! I yelled. If you're in bed you need to get up and go downstairs and open the door and let Max out! Can't you hear him crying? Let him out now please!

But there was no response. I had no idea if Shirley was even there. Perhaps her caretaker had come and taken her shopping or to a doctor's appointment and somehow as they were leaving Max had slipped inside and gotten trapped without her knowing it. Or perhaps she had intentionally lured him inside and shut the door, locking him in, just to demonstrate that even now she was capable of making our lives miserable, as she had done for so many years.

I went back inside and tried calling Vincent, but it was a teaching day, he was at school and I knew he wouldn't answer. I waited awhile, considering what I should do, and then called him again, but still he didn't answer. Max continued to cry, and the sound began to drive me crazy. A shy cat, he avoided other people, and clearly he was now under duress, finding himself trapped in a strange apartment.

An hour went by, and then two. Max began frantically scratching Shirley's window screen, standing on his hind legs and pressing his full body against it, yowling even louder. I was afraid now that the screen might give way under pressure and Max would be catapulted to the ground from two stories up, tumbling into the spiny cactus that grew below the window. I called out to Shirley again and again, but still there was no answer. It occurred to me she might have had another stroke, even died in her bed, and that's why she wasn't responding.

Finally Vincent returned, and as we were debating getting a ladder from the garage and trying to rescue Max, Shirley suddenly appeared with her caretaker, who held on to her as she slowly began climbing the back steps, using her canes and stopping to rest after each step.

We waited until she had reached the top of the stairway before confronting her. Did she know she had locked Max inside her apartment? we asked. He had been crying for hours.

Heh heh heh, she said, fixing us with her crazed stare. Too bad.

She gave us one of her wolfish grins. Clearly she was pleased she had caused us such distress.

I felt so angry I could barely stand to look at her. That ruined face, the flesh so gray and ashy now, her cheeks sunken over missing teeth, a face etched into a horrific ugly countenance by the years of meanness, like a witch from a fairy tale. At the snail's pace at which she now walked, I knew that it would take her many minutes to make it to her back door, even with the help of her caretaker, and I couldn't stand it any longer.

Give me your keys right now, I said to her. I need to let Max out.

Heh heh heh, she said again, and shook her head.

I felt like striking her. I had an impulse to push her over and jump on her and pummel her with my fists, releasing all the hostility that had built up over the years and that had now reached a level of fury after hours of listening to Max's frantic crying. I saw that within me there was the capacity for such violence. I could have beaten her. This person who clearly took delight in disrupting the lives of others for her own twisted amusement, by tormenting them with small aggressive acts of insanity. Intentionally breaking off the flowers in my garden. Hiding bits of trash on our porch. Singing to herself off-key in a loud voice at night as she walked around the building in the dark. I understood now that she had trapped Max on purpose. How had we managed to put up with her all these years? How had we been able to accommodate this horror show? This hulking evil presence lodged within the heart of the building, always peering down on us?

Give me the keys! I yelled again, and stepped closer to her, now on the verge of losing it.

Vincent reached out and took hold of my arm and drew me against his side and held me there. He turned to her caretaker, a heavyset Mexican woman, and calmly asked her if she had the keys to the apartment, and she nodded. He told her she needed to give them to us now, and she did. And then he simply unlocked the back door and called Max, who came rushing out, and we went inside our apartment, leaving the keys dangling in the lock of her door as Shirley, leaning over her canes like a hunchbacked crone, looked up at us, still laughing under her breath.

WE LEFT early the next morning for New York, no longer thinking about the sign, or Shirley, or the future of the apartment building, but focused entirely now on the pleasure of setting off for a much-anticipated trip. From the moment we arrived in the city, however, everything felt wrong.

The hotel we had booked, just around the corner from Carnegie Hall, was a place where we had stayed before though not in recent years. We discovered it had grown shabbier since we'd last been there. The room wasn't quite clean. The lobby, too, had a rather dingy feel, and the restaurant offered a mediocre and overpriced breakfast. We found the bar empty when we went down for a drink, and the bartender dull and rude. The hotel, we discovered, was not a place where we really cared to spend much time.

Much worse, the concert itself was disappointing. *Song of Elos* had been buried far back in the program, and the soprano wasn't impressive. Vincent felt she rushed the tempo of the piece, and this immediately upset him. I caught him covering his eyes at one point during the performance, and I think he might have covered his ears as well if he thought he could have gotten away with it. The text I had written, based on the Munch drawing—that mythological rendering of the first woman to emerge from underground to meet her animal lover— became almost undecipherable as sung by the soprano. The music and words rolled out fast, too bright and brittle and brassy, and all the subtleties of the piece were lost. I could not even decipher my lyrics, blurred as they were by her marbly voice. And then it was over, and the song on which we had collaborated with such pride and pleasure felt as if it had been given a poor outing.

The dinner afterward was no less dismaying. Held in a large, noisy restaurant across the street from Carnegie Hall, a group of around twenty people, all connected in one way or another with the evening's performance, had been seated (following a very chaotic consultation with organizers) at two long tables. We didn't know any of the people at our table, and as usual Vincent grew quiet and withdrawn in the presence of so many strangers who, as it turned out, wished to talk politics all night. Nothing new was said about the wretchedness of what was happening in the country—no intelligent or original insights offered, just a litany of complaints and outrages recounted, again and again, in long and angry back-and-forths. Words like *resist* and *fascism* and *revolution* were repeated with increasing vehemence. But what was there really left to say? We remained largely silent throughout the meal, quietly eating our vegetables and polenta while around us people happily forked the roasted flesh of dead animals into their mouths. Vincent could hardly look, he felt so disturbed by the sight of the rare steak oozing blood on the plates. He instead gazed out the window for much of the dinner, watching the parade of New

Yorkers, pedestrians walking by in the dark. It ended up being a distinctly depressing and awkward evening. We returned to the hotel dispirited by the experience.

TO MAKE matters worse it rained the whole time we were in the city—a cold rain, accompanied by fierce winds. I'd always enjoyed New York, but this time the city felt hard to me. It wasn't just the bad weather. Construction was under way everywhere, and the noise and congestion, the dirt and dust, the constant commotion, made even a short walk feel tiring. Only in the serene calm of Central Park did I feel the old affection I'd long had for the city, as we strolled the wet pathways among the wintry-bare trees dripping with rain.

The day after the concert Vincent came down with a bad cold and took to bed. I felt the concert had depressed him to the point of sickness. For the next two days he didn't leave the hotel room, and I took care of him, bringing him medicine and takeout vegetarian meals. Then I caught his cold, and the last days of our trip were spent entirely in the hotel, lying in bed next to one another, watching movies on TV and ordering whatever we could find to eat from room service. By the time we boarded the plane to return to L.A., we were both anxious to get home.

VINCENT RECOVERED quickly, but my cold worsened and then turned into bronchitis. My doctor prescribed antibiotics, and I spent the next week in bed, coughing and feeling miserable. It did not help to discover, on the first morning after our return, that a new "For Sale" sign had been erected in front of the building in our absence— this one even larger and more prominently placed than the old one had been. The bigger sign was now impossible to ignore. It stood in the middle of the property, right next to the front steps. It looked even more solid and intimidating than the old one. An ugly reminder of our failed attempt to get rid of it.

We had to admit that by removing the smaller sign we had only made matters worse.

———

THE BRONCHITIS hit me hard. I felt my age, my vulnerability—what I often thought of now as the *eternally impending ending.* The idea of death was not so foreign as it had once been. Even though I knew I was being overly dramatic in thinking this way—after all, I simply had a serious case of bronchitis, not some fatal disease—still I felt the advancing years more acutely during the time of my sickness. When I mentioned these feelings to Vincent he chided me for being morbid. I envied him his unconcern. I don't believe he ever thought about death. He lived immediately in the present, and for the most part gave little thought to the future. Not for the first time did I find myself wishing I could do the same.

During the time I spent recovering, I decided to read *The Golden Bowl,* Henry James's last novel, which my friend Ruth Jhabvala had once recommended as her favorite of all his novels. It seemed like the sort of book that would be perfect for passing long hours in bed. Yet I found the novel so difficult, the prose so dense and convoluted, that reading it soon began to feel like a task rather than a pleasure. I was determined not to give up, however, especially as I was drawn further and further into the account of the love triangle at the heart of the story, involving a charming Italian prince who reconnects with his former lover, Charlotte, on the eve of his marriage to a wealthy American named Maggie, who is also Charlotte's best friend.

All too soon the plot had me thinking of my own situation, as I faced the possibility of reconnecting with my former best friend and Vincent's ex-wife. Were we not also an entangled triangle? The intense complication of the feelings James was describing began to echo my own anxieties. This idea of a "predestined phenomenon," as he put it—but what was that? The question James asks is, why has Charlotte come back now? Will she spoil the prince's happiness with his new wife, Maggie? Charlotte is such a handsome creature: she wants to be "magnificent," James says. She wants to be thoroughly superior, and she is capable of that. She *knows* the prince well, knows how to appeal to his weaknesses, his desires, how to insinuate herself within his new life with the more innocent Maggie. And of course she does disturb things. Charlotte is clever and courageous, not afraid of anything. And then there is the fact that she is so *interesting,* as James puts it. Against such a woman, Maggie feels herself *a small creeping thing* who lives in terror and trembles for her life. Until, that is, she discovers the secret Charlotte and her husband have kept from her—that they are still in love and are having an affair! Then she becomes fierce and cunning in an effort to save her marriage.

The more I read, the more Charlotte began to become inter-changeable with Jolene in my mind. Charlotte, with her great imagi-nation, her great attitude, and her great conscience. Maggie, at first unaware that her old friend has been her husband's lover, attempts to forge a new bond with Charlotte. She decides to invite her to come and stay with them at their beautiful house in the country. *I'm going to like her better than ever,* Maggie thinks. *I've lived more myself, I'm older, and one judges better.* Yes, she thinks, and vows to see in Charlotte more than she's ever seen. This woman who has something about her that "carries things off." For Maggie, Charlotte is the "real thing"—the exact phrase I had often used to describe Jolene. Because I believed she was beyond any need for pretense or falsification. She was stron-ger than me. She had always been so directly and immediately real to me—so *superior*—that it was hard for me to see her in any other way. Her immense clarity—her decisiveness and surety, her sophistication and her great talent at making art—all these things had surely caused the imbalance in our friendship that I had felt from the very beginning. And yet hadn't I, like Maggie, *lived more* now myself? Wasn't I older, more worldly and experienced, better able to judge things? Didn't the books I had written amount to a measurable accomplishment, even when placed next to Jolene's enormous achievement and fame?

AT SOME point during my illness, when I was still confined to bed, Vincent decided to defrost the refrigerator using the ancient contrap-tion we kept on a shelf in the kitchen for just this purpose. The fridge was old and very small, the freezer compartment could only hold a few items, and the flap that covered the opening didn't shut completely, and thus the ice and frost built up to a point where the freezer could hardly be opened anymore and then it had to be defrosted manually. It had now reached this point, as it did every few months, and just as the laundry and the housecleaning were Vincent's domains, so was the archaic task of defrosting the ancient little fridge. Even if I had felt up to it, I knew better than to offer my help.

He began by taking everything out of the fridge and placing the items on the kitchen counter—the eggs and block of parmesan, mayonnaise and a container of yogurt, sunflower seeds and salsa. He removed all the vegetables from the lower bins. He set pans in the fridge to catch the falling ice and dripping water, and then he placed the old-fashioned coil, which plugged into an outlet on the wall, directly into the freezer compartment with the black cord snaking out and waited for the melt to begin.

All afternoon I could hear the ice chunks falling into the metal pans he'd set on the wire shelves and the sound of water dripping slowly. While the ice thawed, he amused himself in the living room by reading and playing with the cats and occasionally checking in with me to ask if there was anything I needed.

READING THE final passages of *The Golden Bowl* that day, with the sounds of ice breaking up coming from the kitchen, I began to feel that everything in the world was Jamesian. All human interactions, in all their labyrinthine layers and intensities. That's what my friend Ruth had recognized and loved about the novel. James took apart every little feeling, every nuance of word and deed, and examined the causes and ramifications in passages that went on for pages. I felt now more than ever that all our human interactions were driven by the desire to be loved, and I saw what small power over this outcome we really had. I thought of the friends I trusted and those I hadn't, and I wondered which category Jolene fell into now: What would I feel for her when I saw her again? *If* I saw her? Friendship, as someone said—who, I couldn't remember—was a crucible of positive and negative feelings in a permanent state of ebullition, and this seemed true: strong affections could harbor rancor, trickery, betrayal, not only kindness and love.

I was thinking of Charlotte, how she *liked the past,* as James puts it: it's the charm, she says, of *trying again the old feelings. They come back— they come back. Everything comes back.*

What about Jolene's feelings for Vincent? Or his for her? Would they also come back? Once again I felt disturbed by how little I knew about what their marriage had been like. I was jealous to know. I wanted to understand what she had had with him so I might measure my own life with him against hers.

Yes, I was jealous. It was quite simple. But what did I imagine I had to lose by seeing her?

I resolved that I should tell Vincent everything. How Jolene had contacted me by letter a few weeks earlier. How she invited me for lunch and told me she was moving back to L.A. How that lunch had been postponed indefinitely. I would tell him I was having second thoughts about meeting her and see what he said, if he had any advice to offer. Why should I keep this secret from him any longer?

I DECIDED I would wait until we sat down to dinner to raise the subject of Jolene. For the first time in several days I got up to eat at the kitchen table rather than having food brought to me in bed. The dinner was simple—soup and bread from our favorite bakery. Jazz was playing on the radio in the kitchen as I sat down at the table, and as often happened a particular song sparked memories for Vincent of all the hours he'd spent listening to jazz as a teenager. Jazz had been his passion during those years—jazz and books—his way of escaping, and inevitably whenever a song came on the radio and he recognized it, he could usually not only name the artist and the song but also the backup musicians.

What is that? he said now, as we settled down to eat and a song came on. For a change he seemed uncertain of the musician. Not Tito Puente. I think it's Carlos Santamaria. Maybe Barbieri Gato?

He was mixing up his words, as he often did, transposing names.

When I think of jazz, he said, I think of light. That landscape of light goes so well with jazz. This song's like that. Full of light. But who is this? He looked frustrated, upset, as if his failure to recall the name of this artist had temporarily unbalanced him.

I don't know, I said. My mind was drifting. I was thinking of how to bring up the subject of Jolene.

But when the song ended he suddenly began discussing something else. He wanted to tell me about a conversation he'd had that afternoon with a colleague at the music school about a new opera by John Adams. I barely listened. It didn't interest me. My illness contributed to the difficulty I was having in focusing. But Vincent didn't pick up on my obvious signs of detachment. He never did. He wasn't adept at reading those kinds of messages, which is why he could go on and on about a subject, discussing it at such length without realizing others simply weren't interested.

I felt suddenly tired and was overcome with a fit of coughing.

I should go back to bed now, I said.

Yes, he replied. I'll bring you your pills and a glass of water.

I got back in bed, feeling tired. I realized I couldn't discuss Jolene with him then. Not while I still felt so sick. I felt too unprepared to ask the sorts of questions I wanted to ask. I wanted the story. Of how they'd fallen in love after they first met. How long they'd known each other before they got married. Whose idea it had been. Whether they'd been happy together. Whether he'd deeply loved her, if it had been a passionate marriage. If he thought she'd been unfaithful to him before the affair that caused her to leave him, or whether he himself had ever had affairs.

I wanted to know *everything*. If he might have wanted to stay with her if she hadn't left him for another man, if he thought the marriage could have lasted. Could he have forgiven her if she'd come back to him? I wanted to know how he felt about the idea of seeing her again or having her return to the city. Every one of these questions I knew he'd be loath to answer, and even if I'd felt stronger I might have felt it was territory I shouldn't enter, that it would be asking too much of him to try and discuss such things, but I wasn't well and it made it easy to forget about bringing up Jolene at the moment. Perhaps it was all a mistake.

I didn't need him to tell me whether I should or shouldn't see her. Why couldn't I make up my own mind? Even in high school Jolene used to say that girls suffered from the male colonization of our imaginations and that women were rewarded for thinking like a man but the reverse was never true. Men were more decisive, she said, and women needed to learn to do this, to inhabit their own minds, make their own decisions based on their deepest desires instead of predicating everything on what others needed or wanted, especially men. This is what we are trained to do, she said, to think always of others, and this is what we must resist, this inclination to think of others first. It made for falseness, including false generosity and affection. I'd known she was right. The phrase stuck: *the male colonization of our imaginations.* Early on she had developed the ability to think like a man, as she'd demonstrated when she showed us that condom in her wallet while we sat in the parking lot of the Catholic girls' school. I possessed a woman's uncertainties. In other words, I wasn't her. I was made as I was made, and this was something I had not been able to significantly alter over the years.

I could hear Vincent humming to himself in the kitchen.

And then there was the sound of the table being cleared, and he began doing the dishes and I dozed off to the gentle clinking of plates and silverware.

OVER THE next few days I began to feel better. I could sit up for a while in the living room, and I spent hours reading while stretched out on the sofa with the windows open. I read a book on Flaubert and *Madame Bovary,* written by Francis Steegmuller and published in 1946. Vincent brought me the book as I lay in bed one morning and said, This will make you feel better, you should read this. I didn't know much about Flaubert, and the book was a revelation. I saw how cold, arid, and selfish he was, how attached to his mother, whom he addressed as "my darling" in his letters to her. He reminded me of Raymond Chandler in this way. Chandler had also had a deep attachment to his mother, and like his character Marlowe, he harbored a similar mistrust of women. Flaubert professes desire when he writes to his mistress, Louise Colet, but he also insists that their relations be conducted entirely on his terms—he will not leave the country house he shares with his mother and niece to join her in Paris for any length of time. He must have his freedom. When Flaubert's mother asks when he is going to get married, Flaubert replies, *Never! For me, marriage would be an apostasy which it appalls me to think of.* He tells his mother she will never have a rival. *I shall never love another as I do you,* he says. Louise accuses him of having a monstrous personality and he doesn't deny it, though he dryly insists he *is* still capable of human feeling. Still, for him the sight of a nude woman makes him think of her skeleton. He confesses a "strange thing" by admitting he has violent sensual appetites but cannot give a kiss that is not ironic. So jaded is he on the subject of love that he dreams of hiring a prostitute to take back to places of his youth when he *had* believed in love in an effort to purge the last vestiges of romantic feeling.

I LEARNED that the story of Madame Bovary was based on a true story of a "fallen" woman named Madame Delamare who had lived in a nearby village and who committed suicide in the aftermath of a scandalous affair. Initially, when his friend Louis Bouilhet proposed the idea of writing a novel loosely based on Madame Delamare's story, Flaubert felt disgusted. To write about such provincial characters, with their bourgeois manners and scandals, was beneath his lofty literary aims. How could he write such a novel? Madame Delamare's husband did not pose a problem—the medical background and the mediocrity he could describe. But the lady! A woman unbalanced, as he put it, not in any mythical way but in regard to the matters of daily life, a woman who was pretentious, nervous, discontented, burdened by a dullard of a husband, a woman without a shred of nobility? How could he write *that* story?

Louis eventually convinced him he could write it, and write it he did. He spent many hours gathering his material, visiting local agricultural fairs, describing the countryside, acquainting himself with provincial manners—he devoted the better part of four years to writing the book. *Madame Bovary* was immediately hailed as a new kind of realistic novel, based on nonmaterial bourgeois themes that detailed ordinary life. Flaubert could even admit that the pretentious, nervous, and discontented woman he had created was actually him. *Madame Bovary—c'est moi!* he announced, even as he continued to regard the novel as a vulgar book. The real tragedy was her disgust with the surroundings in which she found herself and beyond which she could no longer look with indifference. This is why she killed herself.

ONE PASSAGE in the book struck me with particular force, something Flaubert had written in a letter to Louise Colet, who had accused him of no longer having any feelings for her: *Observe yourself carefully,* he wrote. *Of all the feelings you have ever had has a single one disappeared? No—every one of them is preserved, is it not? Every one. The mummies in one's heart never fall into dust, and when you peer down the shaft there they are below, looking at you with their open unmoving eyes.*

This was an idea that felt true. That our feelings remain intact and never go away but simply lie dormant, ready to peer back at us unchanged should we offer our sincere gaze. And the thing that I wondered was, what sort of mummified feelings, unblinking and preserved, were still lurking in Jolene's heart, or Vincent's for that matter, lying in wait and ready to gaze back at them in forceful silence?

LATER, WHEN I had finished the book about Flaubert, Vincent asked if I had liked it.

I said I did. But, I added, it wasn't necessarily a book that had made me *feel better,* as he said it would. I found something very cold in Flaubert, in the way he treated his mistress Louise Colbert. His selfishness. How he withheld himself from her and forced her to accept everything on his own terms.

Ask me to do nothing and I'll do everything, that's what he told her, Vincent said.

Maybe that's what I mean.

But that was just Flaubert. You can't blame him for that. And when you think about it, it makes sense. If you let people be who they are, then they *can* do everything for you.

I smiled at him and said I would have to think about that, it seemed rather complicated what he was saying, but I had liked reading the book, I'd learned so much about Flaubert, and I was glad he'd given it to me.

THE MEETING with Jolene, now postponed indefinitely, had taken on an outsized importance in my mind. I wished I didn't have such a long time to think about it. The anticipation had been intensified by the delay, and also by my desire to see her, a feeling that surprised and confused me and that I felt was really based more on curiosity than any sense of mummified affection. I could come away from our encounter feeling defeated by her in some way. I would not be able to withstand the strength of her personality, or know how to deflect her curiosity about the current state of my life and my marriage. I wanted to delay making a decision about whether I would see her or not. But I didn't have to think about that because something else happened to occupy my thoughts.

THE NEXT morning there was a knock on the door as we were having breakfast. Vincent went to see who it was, and I could hear him speaking in a low voice with someone. When he came back he handed me a letter from Ingenious Capital Asset that had just been delivered.

The letter informed us that the property we resided in had been listed for sale and was currently being marketed according to guidelines issued by the probate court. Two open houses were going to be held in the near future in order to show the units to prospective buyers. We were asked to cooperate and make sure our apartment was open and available for touring on those dates in order to avoid multiple inspections. The process of selling the building could take approximately three months. We were assured we would be kept advised, as necessary, about the results.

So that's it, I murmured, after I'd read the letter. It's real now. Open houses. We have to let people into our apartment.

Complete strangers, I added. I don't know that I can bear it.

I folded the letter and laid it on the table and stared at Vincent.

He said nothing. He just looked at me and shook his head. And then he stood up suddenly and said he needed to meet a student at school, changing the subject abruptly as he was wont to do. He said he wouldn't be back until late afternoon. He told me not to worry, we'd figure out what to do.

But worry I did.

I HAD hoped to get some work done that morning. Instead I spent the morning on the sofa, thinking about the past and all the years we had lived in this apartment, how it had provided a refuge for us and how impossible it now seemed that we were being forced to leave. The apartment was alive with stories—*our* stories—all the things that had happened here, both the good and the bad.

I remembered the night Billy Ray, our sweet elderly landlord who had lived in the duplex next to us, had confronted a group of gang kids in the alley. They had backed a boy up against a wall and were kicking him and beating him viciously. We heard the noise and went to the window to see what was happening, and at that moment Billy Ray, a small gay man, then in his eighties and leaning heavily on a cane, had come out into the alley and walked up to the gang kids.

It was a hot night and he was wearing a thin white undershirt and somehow it made him look more vulnerable—he appeared so frail and rather feminine standing there in front of the beefed-up boys. He positioned himself in front of the gang kids and told them to stop what they were doing. What they were doing, he said, was wrong. He just stood there, immobile and seemingly unafraid although we were very afraid for him. But he shamed the kids with his courage, and they backed off. They simply left. And then he went up to the injured boy and helped him stand up. The kid limped away without even thanking Billy Ray.

The gangs. For years they had been a menace in the neighborhood. Shooting guns at night, racing their cars up and down the alley with tires squealing. Playing loud music at two a.m. while parked beneath our bedroom window. Always hanging around, casting menacing looks. Loitering on the street or in the alley, drinking and doing dope. Scrawling ugly graffiti over every surface they could find. There had been frightening incidents over the years. On New Year's Eve we always heard gunfire in the alley, and we often didn't dare stand up in the bedroom for fear a stray bullet might come through the window, but one year the shooting had gotten out of control, there was the sound of repeating semiautomatic gunfire, and we awoke the next morning to find bullet holes riddling the stucco beneath our bedroom window.

WHY HAD we stayed here in this neighborhood for so long? That was the question. Why hadn't we left MacArthur Park before now, given all that had gone on? That's what I found myself wondering as I lay on the sofa listening to the birds with the light making a delicate pattern on the worn wooden floor and the polished surface of the piano. What were we thinking, putting up with Crazy Shirley and the gangs, the gun violence, the noise at night, the discarded junk and old furniture piled up on curbs, the homeless sleeping by the door to the alley with the smell of their piss rising from the corner. Why hadn't we left? Moved to a safer, quieter neighborhood, found a house with a yard and privacy, a place of our own?

I did and did not know the answers to these questions.

ONCE VINCENT had moved in with me all those years ago it was as though he had made some sort of irrevocable commitment—not just to me but to this apartment we came to share, and it had resulted in the arrangement taking on an air of unquestioned permanence. Of course I didn't see it at the time, that this place would be our home in perpetuity because it met his needs. I always felt we would eventually move. Several times during our years together I had pointed out to Vincent that the one-bedroom apartment was really too small to contain us, especially once I had begun writing and needed a room of my own instead of working at a desk in the bedroom. I offered to begin a search for a bigger place. But he had always let it be known he didn't want to move. For him the thing that mattered was that everything should remain the same. Patterns were *not* to be altered. I remember thinking not long after he'd moved in that it was strange that whenever we went to our favorite movie theater we always had to turn left in order to find our seats. If I turned right he would take hold of my arm and steer me firmly in the other direction and say, *It's this way.*

The problem, I realized over the years, was that everything had ended up being *this way,* which was really *his way,* the only way it could be. Literally and metaphorically, we could only turn left, not right. Routines mattered deeply to him. It was as if he was driven by necessity to maintain such strict order not by choice but by some urgent primal need, and I couldn't understand why this was so, at least not for a very long while. And then the time came when I finally did get it. And the knowledge so disoriented me I felt lost not only to him for a while, but to my own self.

8

Over time, the idea that everything must be *his way* had become more and more disturbing, a barrier disrupting the flow of my life, as if everything about our communal existence had been forced into a narrow channel whose high banks prevented me from seeing anything beyond.

His self-absorption, his focus on his work, his tendency to dominate our waking hours with his singular vision had grown tiresome. Worse, I had begun to feel a kind of erasure of my being, as if day by day I knew less and less about who I was and what I really felt.

During the first years of our marriage there had been no question that he was the educated, worldly one, and it seemed natural he was the more dominant. He had, by default, begun to introduce me to things about which I had been clueless. Books, art, music. I gave him that without question. I had not yet discovered what I might possibly be capable of doing, and I was happy to assume this was a good thing, his guidance, that he would always take the lead. And then I began writing. I published a collection of stories and several novels. It grew more difficult to accept the feeling of being so dominated, overwhelmed by his self-involvement and his overweening confidence.

I had not understood him when I married him, but I thought in time I would. The day arrived, however, well into our marriage, when I awoke one morning and admitted that not only did I not understand him, but I was unhappy.

———

YEAR BY year it had become more difficult to remain the pliable woman I had been when he met me. The woman so well conditioned to think of others that it seemed the natural order of things.

It became harder for me to accommodate his oddities and obsessions, especially his self-involvement, without feeling I was giving away parts of myself, slice by slice, reducing my sense of relevance until I wondered what might eventually be left of me. I realized so many decisions were made by him because his needs were so absolute—and I could no longer hide my feelings that day by day I was being suffocated. I had always *turned left* with him, but now I wanted to separate myself and turn right.

I had accommodated his often strange behavior, as if this were my purpose as the partner of a gifted man—but as time passed I began to feel not simply more confused but more uncertain about almost everything. I felt as if I were in the grip of his personality. He was so effortlessly sure of himself, and so rigid in his preferences and his desires, that he had no difficulty setting the rhythm of our lives.

During this period, I spent a lot of time looking for my true self in an effort to determine what I really felt or thought, suffering from the delusion that such a *true self* existed, unable to see that I had in fact become a collection of selves, that I had always been thus, beginning with the child who had been so heavily indoctrinated by a closed system of religious thinking that I was often required to hide what I thought or felt.

In many ways my upbringing had prepared me to accept Vincent's domination and the absoluteness of his preferences. He knew who he was. There was no question of this. I saw that I did not, I was not quite sure of myself: I had only a floating idea. I had not questioned this state of things for a very long time.

Now, however, I did. I did question things. I questioned his rigidity. His self-involvement. His inability to show his feelings, or respond to mine. I questioned my complicity in this situation. Increasingly I felt occluded, scattered, disguised, drawn into a thinness of being. I saw that in trying to conceal my secondary status from myself I had been guilty of consenting to it.

———

DURING THIS period we began to argue, perhaps inevitably since arguing is often a form of self-assertion. I should say *I* argued while he fell silent . . . and then, frustrated, I would push my argument further until I saw how pointless it was.

I was trying to define myself, but mostly (as it turned out) in opposition to him. To clear out a space in this regimented existence of ours for a life of my own. He felt confused by my sudden change in behavior, and now, being so willfully engaged in my own project of self-discovery, I didn't care that my unhappiness disconcerted him. I didn't really like what I thought my project required of me—the pushing back, the more aggressive and confrontational stance I began to take, the attempt to state my own wishes when they were contrary to his, sometimes even intentionally taking an oppositional stance just for the hell of it. But as a friend had said to me long ago when discussing her troubled marriage, all romances must mature or die. This seemed true to me. Hers had died. I didn't want mine to suffer the same fate. I felt as if I were engaged not only in an attempt to balance our lives but salvage our love for each other.

But rather than moving forward as a result of my questioning, the gears of our relationship began to feel like they were running in reverse. I worried that I was dismantling much of the solid armature we'd constructed for ourselves. The relationship we had created had served a purpose for many years, but what was that purpose now?

I had cultivated a gift for storytelling, it was true, but I didn't appear to know what the ending of this story would be.

AS MY unhappiness deepened, I began seeing a therapist recommended by a friend. The therapist lived on a narrow, windy street in the Hollywood hills, in a large handsome house surrounded by tall sycamore trees. The small study where she saw her clients was attached to the back of the house and had a view of a lovely garden that climbed up a steep hill. She had a large dog that occasionally wandered out into the garden, often appearing suddenly—an old white dog that ambled along slowly on stiff legs, as if in pain. Sometimes during our sessions I would look up and see it emerge as it set off slowly along a diagonal path before disappearing again out of sight. Often the dog would stop on the path and look down at me through the window, casting a mournful look my way. It seemed to me that the dog would appear at just those moments in a session when I felt most upset. It would look down at me, peering into the study through the window, as if to say, *I see you and I share your sadness.* I know it's ridiculous, but I began to believe the dog showed up at certain times simply in order to comfort me.

DURING OUR first session, I sat on a couch, and the therapist, whose name was Deborah, positioned herself close by, in a chair opposite me. There was a glass of water on the table between us, and a box of Kleenex, the sight of which for some reason always discomfited me. A candle burned on a windowsill, and the sound of a fountain in the garden just outside created a soothing white noise. From that first day I understood Deborah was a very wise woman who could likely help me, if I could tell her the truth.

But how to find the truth amidst the pile of complaints and miseries beginning to stack up in my mind that I was only beginning to admit to myself? How to make a coherent story of *that?*

During those first sessions I struggled to find the right words to explain my frustration and unhappiness. She listened carefully, as therapists of course are trained to do, trying to parse the essence of what I was telling her.

She was an attractive woman—trim and stylish, always well dressed—perhaps a dozen years younger than me. Her face had an angular beauty, accented by her very short hair. A calm woman, with great warmth. Her kindness and intelligence were palpable, as if an incandescent capacity for empathy extended deep beneath her flawless skin.

Sometimes I arrived early for my appointment and let myself into her study, and through an adjoining door she'd left open that connected to her house, I could hear her speaking to someone and laughing—her husband, perhaps, who I later learned was a screen-writer, or her daughter, who had recently had a baby and occasion-ally visited. It was as if the therapist were taking a little break from listening to the woes of her patients, stopping to take the measure of her own domestic bliss so that she might be fortified in order to go on ministering to the suffering of others.

And then she would enter her study to greet me. Her smile nei-ther effusive nor forced but somehow just right, as if she were actually happy to see me again.

IN OUR first few sessions I talked about my marriage. I described many details of our lives together. The strictness of the routines imposed by Vincent, the suffocating regularity that had taken hold. He had rules for everything, I said. I mentioned his mania for order, how even a lone apple left out on a kitchen counter must be put away, and cof-fee made in the French press timed for exactly four minutes—not three or five but four—with a timer set to make sure. I described how our lives were dominated by his penchant for neatness. How he hated change of any kind. I mentioned his seriousness. The unwaver-ing regulation of our routines and habits. The lack of spontaneity in our lives. The detachment from him I'd begun to feel.

As I spoke, these things sounded so petty to me. Yet I pressed on. I tried to describe his *difference* in a way she might understand. I described his strange fixation with numbers. His extreme reserve. I said that whenever I tried to discuss my feelings with him, or ask about his, he simply withdrew, and if I persisted or grew upset he shut his eyes and tilted his head back, retreating to a place where I couldn't reach him.

I mentioned his inordinate affection for animals, especially cats, and his deep feeling for plants and trees, especially those that had been neglected, and yet his difficulty in showing spontaneous affection for other human beings. I said he didn't like to be touched without warn-ing but that he was a very considerate lover and that I knew that he loved me deeply and wished me to be happy.

The therapist stopped me then and asked, And do you love him?

Yes, I do, I said. I wouldn't want you to think he's anything other than a very good man. I do love him. I just don't understand him. Why he acts as he does.

She told me to go on.

I told her that by and large he preferred his own company to that of others. He enjoyed spending time alone. He never acted lonely or bored. It had always seemed to me that he had little need for an active social life, and yet he was devoted to his few friends.

It bothered me, I said, that he was often the most silent person in a room. As if he weren't actually really there, communing with others in the present, connecting with what was going on around him. If we were invited to a dinner party, for instance, he often sat quietly through the meal, hardly speaking to anyone—unless they should happen to ask him about his work, and then he could become rather garrulous. I said that sometimes he would seek out the hosts' cat when we first arrived, if they had one, and play with it for a while, or sit off by himself looking at a book he'd taken down off a shelf while the other guests were gathered around a table talking to each other. At these times I felt acutely aware of his separateness, and I would try to bridge the gaps between what was happening—what I perceived as his antisocial behavior—and what I felt was expected of a guest. In such situations I had often appointed myself a sort of interface—the intermediary attempting to smooth over his isolating behavior, and in truth I hated doing this, the awkwardness of these moments. I always felt my efforts were at best unsuccessful, and they often made the situation even worse.

I can understand why that might be uncomfortable for you, Deborah said. But have you ever asked yourself why you feel you must do this? Why you feel so responsible for his behavior?

It's what women do, I said. We try to make things okay in the world when it feels like they're not. It's what my mother did.

I see, she said. Still, I'm not sure yet I understand what accounts for the unhappiness you've described feeling. What's really troubling you the most about your relationship at the moment?

The isolation I feel, I said.

Isolation?

His self-absorption. The fact I can't discuss anything with him that might upset him. He simply goes silent, or changes the subject. Sometimes he just leaves the room. He acts as if these moments cause him terrible anguish.

Has he always been this way? she asked.

Yes, I said.

And how long have you been married?

Twenty-two years, I replied.

She seemed surprised. Twenty-two years is a long time. Have you felt such unhappiness before?

No. I looked the other way. I made excuses. I don't want to do that anymore.

Why? Why now?

Because I've become very lonely, and I don't wish to live this way.

I see, she said.

I SAW her a few more times before she suggested that I needed to bring Vincent with me to a session. She wanted to meet him. If he was agreeable, she would like to see us together.

He came with me to the next few sessions. But it was difficult for Deborah to get him to talk, as I knew it would be, even with all her skills. His answers to her questions were often monosyllabic. I knew he didn't want to be there. He'd agreed to come only to please me because he knew that, for whatever reason, I was struggling.

In the sessions with Deborah, whenever the conversation wandered into an area that produced any upwelling of emotion in me— and I did cry at times as I attempted to explain my feelings—he would simply lean back and shut his eyes, as if he could not bear to witness my tears. Deborah would wait for him to speak, to come back to us, but often he didn't. He just sat silently, head back, eyes closed, until she intervened and tried to draw him forth once more.

And yet I understood, sitting in that room with him—with Deborah watching us from the comfort of her overstuffed chair and the old white dog occasionally wandering by outside—that she not only seemed to really like him but had formed an obvious admiration for him, especially after she discovered he was the composer whose works she knew and loved. She always spoke to him so gently, never pushing him too hard to answer a question he didn't feel he could. They seemed to be on the same wavelength somehow. I felt a kind of respectful intimacy growing between them. I could understand why she felt this way. He was so clear and calm—and like her, so truthful and frank—how could she not react favorably to him? And yet in some way her evident admiration for him unwittingly caused me to feel once again reduced in his presence, as if our imbalance were magnified by these therapy sessions instead of lessened. I knew it was foolish to think this way, that she was doing her best to help us both, but my depression began to deepen anyway over the course of the time that we saw her together.

EVENTUALLY THE therapist said she'd like to see me alone again, and as I sat across from her one afternoon I asked her the question that had been on my mind for a long time.

Now that you have had the chance to get to know him, I said, do you think he is simply a narcissistic personality? Is that why from morning till night he talks about himself and his own work and almost never asks about mine? Why he thinks it's okay to dominate every aspect of our life? And I saw her shake her head.

No, she said. And then she gave me her diagnosis.

He has Asperger's, she said. He's on the autism spectrum. Very high functioning, but nevertheless all the indicators are there. I'm only surprised that no one has ever diagnosed him before.

SHE EXPLAINED to me that day that his brain was wired very differently, and that was why he behaved the way he did. Everything he did was normal to him, if not to me. He came from a different neurotribe, she said. He saw the world in a unique way.

There were a number of indicators that had caused her to make this diagnosis, based on her observations and interaction with him. She had noted a lack of empathy—his inability to feel what others might in certain situations, or even recognize those feelings and respond to them. He failed to read certain social cues. There was the transposition of letters and names, the spatial difficulties, the inability to detect irony or other nuances of language. She had, of course, noticed his difficulty in making eye contact whenever an emotional issue came up. The tendency to simply shut his eyes was another indicator, as was his preoccupation with one subject—music—and his great giftedness in this area. This was often the case with Asperger's, that a person might have elevated awareness or competence in a certain area. They might show exceptional creativity. She explained to me that his self-absorption was not the result of a lack of interest in me but the natural workings of his mind.

I can't tell you what to do, she said at the end of this session. There is no cure, of course, for autism. But one can try to help him increase his consciousness, his awareness of what other people feel, even if he's not feeling the same things. He can be taught to read cues. But these things will never come naturally to him. You'll have to accept him the way he is, if you choose to remain in your marriage. And that will mean accepting you will always be with a partner who does not naturally feel empathy, which of course is the most difficult aspect of all. He won't want to discuss his feelings—or for that matter yours. He will always spend a good portion of time in his own private world. He simply won't have the same responses to things that you or I do. Or similar capacities. But—and she stopped here and smiled warmly at me—you might find that it's not so difficult to accept these things, if you are able to think about them in a certain way—not as behavior that intentionally *excludes* you, not as rudeness or carelessness with your feelings, but as a different way of moving through the world. In other words, you are going to have to do most of the heavy emotional lifting in this relationship, and I'm afraid to say this is not so abnormal. I think women, in the end, have always had to do this.

She suggested I go online and read about Asperger's syndrome, although it was a term professionals no longer cared to use. Now people preferred to speak of Asperger's as being on the autism spectrum. The term *Asperger's* was so loose and overused it had lost much of its meaning as a diagnosis.

She asked if I would like to bring Vincent with me to the next session and she would explain to him the diagnosis she had come to believe was correct, or if I would prefer to tell him myself when the time was right. It would then be up to him, and to me, to decide what we wanted to do. What we were *capable* of doing together. Unfortunately, she said, she didn't have another appointment open for several weeks. I could decide what I'd like to do—wait, or talk to him myself.

I LEFT her that day feeling stunned. I went to a coffee shop and looked up Asperger's syndrome on the Internet. I spent several hours reading various articles on the subject. One site listed fifteen common symptoms. Another nineteen. Vincent had every one.

OVER THE next few days I existed in a privately agitated state. In a way I felt relieved. I finally understood what had been so mystifying for so many years.

But I also felt deeply troubled by the thought I had lived in darkness for so long. I had been clueless as to why things were the way they were. I began to feel deeply upset. I convinced myself I had suffered. I felt tricked. I had paid a price for his "difference." And I had done so in total ignorance.

I went back over our time together, picking at various wounds. Events that had been so difficult. The embarrassing times. The messy times that were painful and confusing. And there were many that swam back into my consciousness.

I had suffered in darkness. I'd felt emotionally marooned. I had been cut off, left holding the bag, over and over again. I saw how naive I'd been: A more worldly person would have surely seen the light. Would have suspected that something was *actually wrong.* Perhaps even guessed the cause. Not just suffered. Not just *waited* for twenty-two years to see how things would go.

But I was not that person. I was made as I was made. A woman raised in a narrow world who had stupidly married young thinking it would be some kind of ticket to somewhere. A woman who'd later found herself transported to a much more complex and sophisticated realm where people did and said things in very different ways. From the beginning Vincent's *otherness* had seemed proof of the truth of this. That's how I'd seen it. It wasn't he who was *off* but me, as the newcomer to this world. This is the way I'd felt for a long time. As if I simply needed to somehow catch up.

I THOUGHT of Jolene. Hadn't she suspected anything during her time with him? Hadn't she noticed his quirks? *Don't pay any attention to him,* she had said to me that day when she introduced us in the kitchen and he'd simply turned and walked off. *He's always that way.* She had never said anything during the time I spent with them, but why would she? She hadn't discussed her marriage to Vincent at all. Except for a few comments, including something she'd said at lunch one day. *He's not really a very good lover,* she confessed to me, a thing I'd never forgotten and that I later recalled with unseemly relish. Because with me he had been a very good lover, and I liked to think it was perhaps her, not him, who had been the problem.

The truth should be told here: Right or wrong, I decided to reveal to Vincent what Deborah had said because I couldn't keep it to myself any longer. I couldn't wait for an appointment weeks away. Besides, weren't we the ones who were going to have to work this thing out?

One morning, as we were having coffee in the living room, I said I needed to talk to him.

We were sitting in our usual places—he in his chair, me on the sofa, with the cats sunning themselves on the rug in between us.

Straight out I began by telling him what Deborah had said, the conclusion she had come to, that he had Asperger's syndrome, that he was on the autism spectrum. I read him a list of symptoms, which Deborah suggested I might want to do. From the years of living with him, I said I felt he had every one, including the inability to empathize, something Deborah had recognized during our joint sessions and that led her to make the diagnosis she had.

I told him I had struggled to understand what this diagnosis might mean—for him, for me, for us, and especially for our future. It explained so much, but I also found it so disturbing.

I paused for a moment, feeling I must proceed with caution in order not to frighten him. To give him time to absorb what I had just said.

But he simply stared straight ahead, without looking at me or showing any emotion. I couldn't tell how he felt. But it was clear he wasn't ready to say anything.

So I began speaking again. I entered much more emotional territory. I could feel the anxiety building in me. *Be honest,* I thought, *just tell him the truth.*

I told him I was relieved Deborah had been able to make such a clear diagnosis because it had caused the scales to drop from my eyes—that's how I put it, *the scales had dropped from my eyes,* I said— and because of this I could see him quite differently and understand so much that I couldn't before. But it had also made me very sad, even angry, when I thought about the years I had spent in the dark. I felt damage had been done. Damage to me.

I stopped again to see if I might be frightening him, but still he was affectless, he sat quietly, as he always did when I tried to talk about something serious, and so I simply continued but I felt my heart racing.

I mentioned a few incidents to show him how intractable he'd been, how rigid and oblivious to my feelings, how I had felt so embarrassed at times, and hurt, unable to know what to do. I said I felt he had never been a *player,* a person who could join in what was going on around him. He'd often isolated himself, and this too had been difficult. I recalled times when friends had visited and he had been the only one who wouldn't go out with us, who wished to stay home alone. I knew my friends had often felt sorry for me. *It's too bad Vincent can't join us,* a friend had once said, *it must be hard for you.*

I told him I'd hated it when people said things like this to me. Over the years I had made excuses for him at such moments, and then felt ashamed afterward that I felt the need to do this.

I said he was like Bartleby the Scrivener, who had been so fond of saying *I prefer not to*. But what about what I had preferred? But of course I now understood. He shouldn't be blamed. Still it had been so hard, I said. So terribly painful at times.

I told him that over the years I had begun to feel increasingly lonely. This was not a good thing to feel when you were sharing a life.

I began crying then. I couldn't help it. And I saw how much distress this caused him.

He closed his eyes, and I watched him recede from me as he tilted his head back against his chair and refused now to look at me.

Please don't do that, I said. Please open your eyes and stay with me.

I saw what a struggle it took for him to do this, and I gained control of my feelings once more in order not to frighten him away, and yet I continued to go over the past, I couldn't help it. Some great sense of injustice was driving me forward. I wanted him to understand the cost of living this way all these years. I wanted him to acknowledge just how difficult it might have been. I had suffered such confusion, I said, such disappointment and shame, leading to self-doubt. I'd become a contortionist in order to adapt to life with him. Could he see this? How this might have happened?

Still he said nothing. Which didn't surprise me.

So I pushed on.

I pointed out how he constantly talked about his own work while rarely asking about mine. This had been one of the hardest things— his self-absorption. Could he see how difficult this might have been for me?

I said even though I was very grateful for Deborah's diagnosis— very very grateful—I did not yet know what to do about what she had revealed. I felt unable to go on without some hope that things might change, and yet I had been told by Deborah it was unrealistic to expect change. What should I do then? I asked him. What can I do?

Of course he didn't answer. These were rhetorical questions, as we both knew.

———

WAS I frightening him? Yes, I'm sure I was. Should I have expressed more concern for him, been more sensitive about what he might be feeling having just received this news about himself? Yes, I should have. But intuitively I felt the news was much less disturbing to him than it was to me.

I began to feel foolish, self-conscious, as if I were talking to myself, engaged in some painful rambling soliloquy. My words seemed to drop into that space yawning between us where the cats slept on, oblivious to our distress. I felt I had just been making noise, like a wounded animal. Quacking angrily, mewling in distress, trying so hard to be understood, but weren't my feelings just one big soupy mess? What should he make of them—he who resisted feeling? I wanted so badly for him to say something, to lift the lid off his silence and show me what was beneath. And so suddenly I stopped speaking. I just sat there, gazing at him.

The room grew quiet. I heard only the sound of the wind chime clanging on the porch. Inside nothing stirred.

I waited. But still he said nothing, and finally, very gently, I asked him what he thought.

I could see him mulling over what to say, sitting quietly, showing no emotion. And then finally he did speak. Just one sentence.

He said, I wonder if my mother had this too . . .

AND THAT was it. That was his only reaction to all that I had revealed, everything I had attempted to explain to him.

I wanted to laugh. It was the perfect Asperger's response. I knew that. Just as I knew at that moment that this was my future. I understood then how difficult it would be. I would always be confronted with a variation of this distant, detached response: *I wonder if my mother had this too.*

OVER THE next few months we visited the therapist regularly. We saw her separately and together. In our joint sessions I came to see how frightened he was, how confused—not because of the diagnosis, which didn't really appear to faze him much, but because he couldn't bear any emotional display on my part. It only caused him to drift further away. I had to give up settling old scores. I saw the reckoning needed to end. The more I insisted he try and understand the difficulty I'd experienced living with someone with his condition, the more I felt him slipping away.

DURING THIS period I spent a lot of time walking around the neighborhood by myself. I wanted to be alone, out in the the world, away from the apartment. Walking was a good way of thinking about my life and the different turns it had taken.

I'd walk down Rampart Boulevard, past the dental office where I'd worked when I first arrived in the city. It was still there in the corner shopping plaza, along with a storefront Korean church, a hair salon, and a payday loan place. Dr. Lovestedt no longer practiced dentistry, but the DENTISTA FAMILIAR sign still bore his name.

I headed down to Sixth Street, past the Superet Light Church and the billboard for *Wonder Magazine,* past the life-sized Christ in a glass box, and then on to Wilshire Boulevard, passing through the throngs of Latino children playing on the sidewalks and the women selling tamales and menudo from little carts. Clusters of old men standing around parted to let me pass, and the odor of their cigars lingered on the air as did their lilting Spanish.

I walked by the blanketed cardboard shacks of the homeless, their crumpled bodies spread out on the grass as they napped next to shopping carts overflowing with junk. The busy bus stops, the streets thick with traffic, the distracted pedestrians and noisy exuberant children—I moved through this clamorous world, caught up by my own clamorous feelings. I passed restaurants where people were eating *pupusas* outdoors on shaded patios, and the doughnut shops and *panaderias,* the check-cashing joints, places where lives ground forward, and I felt the violence, the grotesque cruelty, the filth in this pitching and heaving world, the poverty and displacement writhing under the semblance of order in the neighborhoods around MacArthur Park. I felt the air crackling with the unacknowledged harshness of life, and I would feel acutely the small, stupid betrayals I had committed against myself and others, and by "others" I really meant Vincent, who often had to suffer my emotional outbursts during this period.

In those days because I was roiling inside, the outer world roiled too.

I BEGAN swimming at the old Ambassador Hotel, which had suffered a fall from grace since its glory days when the elite of Hollywood had gathered there to dine and dance at the Coconut Grove or stroll through manicured gardens and sun themselves around the beautiful pool, but still it was a grand old place where for a modest sum I could swim every day surrounded by such faded glory.

I started carrying a camera and taking pictures on the street as I walked back and forth between the apartment and the Ambassador. On these walks I often cut through the park. I made friends with an older homeless man named Tommy. He had once been a short-order cook in Canada, but he'd been on the street for many years. I took him to the county hospital when he developed bad skin sores and occasionally I brought him food. I helped him find homes for the puppies his dog Lady had after she got pregnant by a stray. He was such a kind man—an alcoholic, yes, but his drinking never made him mean or scary. And later, when a Black woman named Sharon who worked in the neighborhood agreed to take him in if he stopped drinking, letting him live with her in her house in Watts in exchange for cooking for her, I visited him and Lady there, happy to think he was no longer on the street.

I took photographs of prostitutes in the park, the mothers and children in the playground, the ladies in white dresses banging tambourines at the religious revivals, the thin young men washing car windows at intersections, the old men playing checkers. I carried a camera with me everywhere I went, day after day, and no one seemed to mind that I took their picture except for a young Black woman who'd been sitting on a bus-stop bench one day and who, when she saw me raise my camera to my eye, rushed over and grabbed me by the

neck and shook me and yelled, MAYBE I DON'T WANT NOBODY
TAKING MY PICTURE WHEN I JUST GOT OUT OF PRISON,
SO PUT THAT FUCKING THING AWAY!

I didn't bother trying to write during this time. I didn't want to
attempt to tell stories. I just wanted to walk and think, stroll through
the park, take pictures on the street, swim in the beautiful old pool
and go home when I finally got tired, and then the next day do the
same thing.

Wandering through the area around MacArthur Park, I felt all the
sadness and struggle in this immigrant neighborhood, the predation
and cruelty, the fear, the crushing effort to find a way to earn a living
and make a new life in this new country, one that might be safe for
the women and children who depended on their men to take care of
them. Life often appeared unspeakably hard for these poor people.

Something was working out of me during this time, snakes writhing to the surface, and I let them rise, hoping one day I would be free
of their venom.

I OFTEN thought of something Jolene had said to me when I first
arrived in L.A. *What do you want to do with your life,* she had asked, *now
that you have a chance to start over?*

Oh, I don't know, I replied. *I'd just like to live alone for a while, see how
that feels until I figure out what I want to do.* I had never known what it
was like to live alone since I'd gone straight from living with my parents to getting married.

But I hadn't stayed alone very long. Vincent had found me. Within
a few months of my moving to Carondelet he'd inserted himself into
my new life, cutting off any chance of the sort of independence I'd
imagined. No one had held a gun to my head and said, Marry him or
else. We had fallen in love. That's all. And I was still in love. I knew
now that he couldn't be held to the codes of behavior that applied to
other people, but it wasn't much help, knowing that he wasn't just
another troubled male genius making an exception of himself. The
problem I faced was mine, not his.

———

I ENDED up spending more time than I ever had in the park during this period. I knew the history of MacArthur Park very well from the research I'd done on Raymond Chandler, who had moved to this area in 1912 when he first arrived in the city. He had often walked in this park, first with his mother and then with Cissy, whom his mother had disapproved of because she knew Cissy was much older than she claimed to be, and this was true—when Chandler had married her, two weeks after his mother's death, he was thirty-five and Cissy was fifty-three, but she had listed her age on the marriage certificate as forty-three, knocking a cool decade off her years.

I felt L.A.'s history when I walked in this park—the history so many people claimed the city didn't have. But it did. A short history, true, but still if you knew where to look you could sense it, and I felt it everywhere in this neighborhood.

When Chandler had lived in this area the park was known as Westlake Park. It had been a lovely place, featuring palm-lined paths and a large lake with a charming two-story boathouse where one could rent a wooden canoe and paddle out onto the water. Many of the city's wealthiest families had built houses in the area. But in the 1930s the park had been cut in two by a wide new street constructed to accommodate the burgeoning automobile culture. Wilshire Boulevard had been dubbed the "Champs-Élysées of L.A.," but of course it was no such thing, and instead it had marked the beginning of the park's decline. Wealthy families had already begun to leave the area for neighborhoods farther west, and the big old houses that were left behind were divided up into ramshackle apartments as the area grew poorer.

During World War II the park had been renamed MacArthur Park in honor of General MacArthur, and a large statue of him had been erected on the south side of the park in front of a reflecting pool, with little islands made of concrete meant to replicate the Philippines. By that time the swans that had once been such a feature of the lake had begun dying off. No longer were new cygnets hatched on the little island. The boathouse closed. The canoes were retired. The lake grew

fetid and gave off a brackish odor. A feeling of decay and neglect began
to infect the whole area.

Gangs moved in. Prostitution and drug dealing and gun violence
became common. For a while after I had first moved to the neighborhood I stopped walking in the park because it felt too dangerous, but
during the time I am speaking about now—in the months following
Vincent's diagnosis—I was drawn there again. I think the darkness I
felt during this period propelled me to take my chances, as if I imagined my internal disquiet somehow made me immune to danger.

OFTEN ON my loop around the lake I would stop in front of the statue
of General MacArthur. The reflecting pool was dry now, the concrete cracked and broken, the monument itself defaced by graffiti.
The statue of the general portrayed him in military uniform, standing
erect with his arms pinned to his sides. On either side of the statue
two large walls featured brass plaques with quotes from the general.

The left-hand wall, under the heading "Soldier," celebrated
MacArthur's life as a military man and bore these words: *Battles are
not won by arms alone. There must exist above all else a spiritual impulse, a
will to Victory. In war there can be no substitute for Victory.*

On the right, under the heading of "Statesman," was another
quote: *Could I have but a line a century hence crediting a contribution to the
advance of peace, I would gladly yield every honor that has been accorded by
war.*

Each time I read those words I felt perplexed, and I wondered,
was there really no substitute for victory in war? Wasn't retreat, as
in the case of Vietnam, a more noble choice than the continuation
of an immoral and unjustified conflict? And what did a "spiritual
impulse" mean in the context of war? Would the famous general really
have given up all his medals for one single line crediting him as a
peacemaker?

I knew nothing about General MacArthur, so I couldn't judge the
truth of his words. I knew only that the sad, desecrated monument
dedicated to him stood in the most degraded part of the park, the area
where the hard-core homeless congregated, so that the nobly posed

general looked out over the human detritus of society, the scorned and forgotten, the mentally ill and the deranged, the poorest of the poor, those who wore tattered and filthy rags, their buttocks and privates sometimes exposed, men and women who slept in the rough, defecating and urinating openly, ranting wildly and swinging their fists at imaginary opponents or sitting in catatonic stillness staring out over the fetid lake.

This is what MacArthur Park had become, an outdoor camp for the ravaged souls of society, a place for jobless immigrants to spend their days, watched over by a forgotten and desecrated monument to its warrior namesake. A sad place to which I was drawn, day after day.

FOR WHAT seemed like a long time life went on this way. Visits to the therapist, alone or together. Solitary swims and walks in the neighborhood, taking photographs on the street. We maintained a sinuous and respectful attitude toward each other. A tendency to speak carefully in order to avoid injury.

Even during this period we continued to desire each other. We made love. We made dinner. We saw our close friends regularly. In other words, we continued to form a couple that at least outwardly appeared no different.

We made an effort to understand what previously had been unfathomable to us, and yet I speak here for myself. I knew that Vincent had no interest in his condition. He never once spoke the word *Asperger's* or mentioned the autism spectrum. Never asked a question about the signs or prognosis. Never showed any inclination to discuss the subject outside the therapist's office, and if he could have avoided it there he would have. He never showed the slightest curiosity about how his brain might work differently from other people's. Because he really didn't care to know, it didn't matter one way or the other to him. As Deborah kept reminding me, *He only wants you to be happy, that's all. If you're happy, he's happy. That's what he understands. And that's what he cares about.*

But how to be happy? I felt such disappointment. How could I live without empathy, with a partner who couldn't express his feelings or make an effort to understand mine? Whose boundaries kept our world so strictly delineated? Who focused so heavily on himself?

I could sense how hard he was trying to put into practice the behaviors Deborah had recommended. The small adjustments in attitude. The way he attempted to be less obsessed about his work. I could see him catching himself at various moments. Uncertain, he would suddenly think, I should ask about *her*. But there was always a slightly feigned feeling to these efforts, as if he were practicing for a role that might someday feel real. I felt moved he would try these things that did not come easily to him. I saw how deeply he cared for me. Sometimes he left me messages that said things like *I am always with you.* Or *I am trying because I love you.*

SLOWLY OVER a period of many months my sadness began to dissipate. My sense of disappointment and concern for the future. I had worn myself thin . . . and, to my surprise, I began to see everything in a different light

What did it mean to have a "normal" brain anyway? There was no normal anymore. I could see that what I had formerly regarded as normal might be less preferable than "abnormal" in certain ways. In time I not only began to understand Vincent's difference but to admire it. And then I began to envy him.

I found myself wishing that I, too, could be made differently so that I might be more like him. A private, subtle person, restrained in personality, who marched to his own drummer and cared more about pleasing himself than others.

I began to think of his silences in an altogether different way. I wanted this ability to be silent. I saw silence as power. Not a greater power than words, but a concurrent one. I began to view silence as a positive force. I saw that one could actually *make silence,* as Vincent often did, by temporarily withdrawing from a world that clamored for attention.

To be silent was to be in control of an extraordinary faculty.

Why, I wondered, should I feel compelled to make conversation at a dinner party? What would happen if I embraced periods of silence as Vincent often did? What about simply listening? There was never a shortage of people who wished to speak. It was the listener who was rare.

And why not look at a book, or play with a host's cat, if that's what you felt like doing, even if it meant you took your time joining others? Why always have to be *on*? I realized Vincent lived close to his impulses and feelings in a way I did not. For me there were always filters. Considerations. Multiple competing scenarios. There was always *history*. The training to be a *dutiful woman*. Like many women, but perhaps especially those from deeply religious or patriarchal cultures, I had been taught to think of others. To engage in acts of self-sacrifice. I'd been conditioned to be conciliatory, encouraged above all to *accommodate*. Could you ever really know yourself if you were always busy thinking of others this way? And what about the authenticity of your responses?

Vincent, by his very nature, thought of himself first, and primarily. Not really in the selfish way I had imagined, but because this was the way his brain worked. It was what came naturally to him. Thus he was always able to know what he thought before other considerations flooded in and swamped him, and he could act accordingly in an authentic fashion.

He had never been able to fake anything. He could not say something or affect an emotion that wasn't true. I saw how at times I said things to make others feel better. Things I perhaps didn't fully believe or that reeked of the easy sentiment. I said these things looking for love, for acceptance and safety. Trying to balance the world around me, as I had seen women forever do. I saw what a horrible amount of work this was. But what, I wondered, would happen if I learned to wait—to test my feelings first, and value them, so that I could know what I wanted to do before the need arose to act in some circumscribed way? What if I were, in other words, to acquire the art of *silence*?

This is much of what I spent my time thinking about during those days, on my long strolls through MacArthur Park and the neighborhood. I saw how Vincent's calm, serene nature resulted from the fact he wasn't moving through the world distracted by clamorous thoughts, always seeking love and acceptance, constantly trying to make the pieces fit together. Because he already fit into the only picture that mattered to him, and that was the picture of himself.

I thought a lot about how he had never been one to apologize or admit he was wrong—he was like Jolene in this way. For years this had confused and upset me. But he seemed not to know how to apologize, or what it would mean to say he was sorry for something. He acted as if it would be too much. As if it would disrupt some primary vision he couldn't afford to disturb.

This, too, I began to think about differently.

I discovered I wanted to be the person who didn't need to apologize. I wished to be able to withhold the impulse to confess a wrong, to say *I'm so sorry.*

I SAW that we lived in a world where feelings were everything. How prone we were to revealing the intimate details of our lives! Feelings had been elevated above thought, and nowhere, perhaps, was this truer than here in America where the looseness of social mores and an absence of older traditions encouraged such things.

On my walks I found myself going over Vincent's many attractive qualities—all the reasons I had fallen in love with him in the first place—and the list grew quite long.

Whatever feelings Vincent had they did not *occupy* him at any length. They came and went like the passing wind, leaving very little disturbance in their wake. As a consequence he held no grudges. No pent-up or unexpressed feelings roiled inside him. Nor was he troubled by painful memories. Anything too disturbing was rather quickly swept from his mind because it found no ready home there.

Whatever his emotional limitations, I had to admit again and again what I had always known, that he was the kindest of men, even if he could appear austere and abrupt, remote and withdrawn at times. I saw how things never troubled him the way they did most people. He stayed focused on his work: it was where he lived. He possessed great confidence about his music, none of it feigned. He was patient, much more so than I. Whenever he spoke to someone on the phone, to settle a dispute over a bill, for instance, or book a reservation, he made genuine contact with the person on the other end through his quiet, direct manner, his clarity and calmness. He treated everyone with the same cool respect.

He rarely raised his voice. He almost never got angry.

And then there was his dry wit.

Nothing I had read about Asperger's suggested this was a common trait.

But he could be brilliantly amusing, and his humor came fast, arising quickly as if erupting from some rapidly firing space in his mind, and all this would happen before anyone else could even think of something to say.

He never let things get him down. He didn't obsess about bad news. He could shut out anything he found unpleasant. If I happened to inform him of some new political outrage, he might shake his head and say, *Wow, incredible,* and then in the next breath mention he hadn't realized it was going to rain.

He didn't fret over things he couldn't do anything about. He moved on. Immediate life is what interested him. The composition he was working on. A current museum exhibition. A concert. A new biography of Henry James.

I came to understand he was a private person by nature rather than choice. He would always be that way. I knew I could only open the door so far before it closed again. But did I really need to barge in?

He didn't keep his feelings from me for devious reasons. Self-revelation was simply foreign to him, as was, for the most part, self-reflection. It contributed to his aura of calm, his natural inclination to be discreet. He was good at keeping secrets. He rarely gossiped. He was deeply loyal to his friends.

Over time I began to see all the beauty and advantages of his "abnormality." I realized that perhaps I didn't really want him to change but rather wished to make some changes myself. It was as if a symbiotic swap began to take place during this time, and I entered his mind as he made his labored attempts to understand mine.

I felt myself falling in love with him all over again. But falling in love with the person I now understood him to be. I no longer thought of the past with regret. It was what it was. It was *gone*. He had shown me how I might live closer to my own nature, and in the end a new harmony arose between us, and an even deeper intimacy. I felt a kind of grace enter our lives, the thing of which we are all made in our finest moments.

It turned out the therapist was right. Vincent only wanted me to be happy. If I was happy, he was happy. It really was that simple. I came out of this difficult period understanding how to be happier, how life could be lived differently, in greater harmony not just with him but most importantly with myself.

But now, with the apartment being sold and the first open house looming, that harmony seemed threatened by a change neither of us wanted. We both were thrown off our game. Day by day we grew more anxious, and that anxiety made us sometimes sharp with each other, as if we'd forgotten what we had learned all those years earlier.

9

We couldn't bear the idea of an open house. People roaming through our apartment. Looking at our belongings, inspecting the evidence of our lives. It was terribly upsetting to both of us. Yet what could we do?

I worried about Vincent. I saw him growing more withdrawn every day, anxious and upset by the prospect of what such a large change might mean, he to whom even small changes could be so unsettling.

The apartment had come to mean much more than a place to live: it was a refuge, a *routine* we could not bear to think of changing. And so we pretended we didn't have to do anything. Not yet anyway. But of course the time came when the unwanted invasion of the outsiders began.

THE FIRST open house was held on a day when a light rain was falling and a fierce wind whipped through the branches of the trees next door: little heaps of twigs and leaves littered our porch and blew into the corners where they lay in soggy heaps as people came and went, leaving soiled footprints on the wooden floor.

We didn't have to be present for the open house. We could have gone somewhere else, avoided the trauma altogether. But we couldn't imagine allowing strangers to wander through our apartment alone, even though an Ingenious employee named Oscar had promised to be present. Still, how could we trust Oscar, whom we didn't even know? How could we leave strangers to rummage through our lives?

———

THE OPEN house lasted for several hours. We sat in the living room, pretending to read but unable to avoid looking up at whoever came through the door. There were young couples and lady realtors, older Chinese businessmen, Korean developers, men who wore expensive suits and watches, women with puffed-up lips and clipboards. They waved to us. They said hello. Sometimes they ignored us, strolling through our rooms as if we were mannequins propped up there. Occasionally a question was asked.

Who plays? a woman inquired, pointing to the piano. We continued reading as if we hadn't heard her.

Love the old metal bed, her companion said after touring the bedroom. Where'd you find that?

Another admired our "distressed" kitchen floor, which had once been painted red, then green, and was now a worn mixture of the colors.

They looked at our books and record collection, our CDs and the pictures on the walls, our few pieces of good furniture that were well cared for. They strolled across our handsome rugs, oblivious to the dirt they left behind, they glanced at our Berber pillows, and the copper pans hanging above the stove. They stopped to admire the old silver stored in a glass-fronted cabinet that had come from Vincent's family. They ogled our belongings with interest—when they weren't ogling us.

The questions kept coming. One woman inquired, Where's the washer and dryer?

There was none, we explained, due to the lack of space and plumbing. The woman looked at us as if she didn't believe this was possible.

I don't understand how you could have lived here without laundry facilities, she said. Who could do that these days?

A well-dressed Chinese man asked if we'd be willing to accept a buyout.

Twenty thousand? he said. Maybe twenty-five?

Two young developers thought the place was a teardown. Look

here, one said, you can see where the termites have been at the wood floor. Place is riddled with bugs.

Someone else thought the building was worth saving. You could put some money into a remodel, she said, turn these apartments into upscale condos. The building has such good bones.

Tough neighborhood for upscale, her companion replied.

But the neighborhood, she insisted, was bound to change given the high demand for housing. MacArthur Park was ripe for gentrification. And wasn't a lovely old building like this one worth saving? It's classic L.A., she said. Lovely 1930s L.A.

Two women stood in the kitchen puzzling over the little metal door with the lightning bolts cut out. We could hear them discussing it, and then we heard them laugh when they opened the door and discovered the metal shelf in the shape of an iron. Oh my god, a woman said, it's a little cupboard for the old irons that were once heated on the stove.

They opened the tall cupboard next to it, designed to hold an ironing board.

Ancient artifacts, the woman said. Who even irons anymore?

SOMEONE ELSE marveled over the tin-lined cupboard once used to store ice blocks and now turned into a liquor cabinet.

Can we take photographs? a woman asked. It's so charming. You've made such a charming place here.

No, we said. No photographs? No pictures, please. And still we saw them snapping away with their phones when they thought we weren't looking.

A YOUNG couple said they loved the bathroom with its original Spanish tiles. It's nice you haven't changed anything, they added. How long have you lived here?

They were not the only people to ask this question that day.

To this couple we refused an answer. Because by then we had

grown weary of saying, Thirty years. We have lived here for thirty years.

When the last people left we both felt a heavy exhaustion. We locked the door and drew the blinds. Then we put on Mozart, poured ourselves a drink, and stretched out on the bed. For a long time we were silent, as if overtaken by a stupor that rendered us speechless.

IT WAS the uncertainty that began to wear us down. That and the way things began to go downhill.

Luis, the gardener, no longer came every Friday. He said Ingenious had stopped paying him and he could no longer take care of things. The garden had already suffered a steady deterioration over the years. Where there had once been grass there was now bare dirt surrounded by untended plants and trees. Now more plants began drying up, and the walkways were soon littered with yellowed leaves.

It began to look like no one lived in the building anymore. The remaining tenants, all of whom were older, rarely left their apartments, and when they did they used the back steps that led to the alley. At night, from the street, the building appeared dark, and the kids who had always used the front steps to hang out and smoke dope could now be found there at all hours. They left behind their beer bottles and cigarette butts, their candy wrappers and trash—and occasionally a used condom. I realized the little flat area where the steps jogged to the left was a place where the teenagers were now having sex, hidden from view by the overgrown lantana.

Trash began to appear on the dirt between the sidewalk and curb in front of the building, as if the property had become a convenient neighborhood dumping ground. Old mattresses and broken cabinets showed up. Chairs with missing legs, discarded coffee tables, and soiled sofas. Large items difficult to remove. Once there had been tall artichoke plants growing in that area. And jacaranda trees. But the artichokes had died long ago, and the jacarandas had also finally succumbed for lack of water. Now they were nothing but stick trees, their dead branches spreading out from dry trunks.

It depressed us terribly to see this happening. We took to trying to keep things up ourselves. Every day or two I swept the walkways and picked up trash. We called the city to request removal of the discarded furniture. In the evenings Vincent watered—it deeply disturbed him to see how the plants and trees were dying. He stood at the lip of the steep hill that sloped down toward the street, hose in hand, spraying the thirsty plants. And still everything continued to deteriorate. One day Vincent returned from teaching to find someone had defecated on the front steps. The gang kids perhaps. Or the homeless men who slept down the street. He was shaking when he told me about this. I'm not cleaning it up, he said. I'll pick up the beer bottles and trash but not that. He called Ingenious and demanded that Oscar send someone to deal with the mess.

WHAT WERE we to do? We made halfhearted attempts to scan online ads for rental possibilities, searching for another apartment, but there was always something about a prospective place that didn't work. Pets were banned from many places, and of course there were Barney and Max to think of. Barney would be fine with a change: in his advanced years he now slept most of the time and was happy indoors, but Max was another story. He was young and full of energy, and he went crazy if he couldn't go outside. The wild untended garden had always been such a safe haven for the cats. How could we find another place like this for them? We couldn't see ourselves living without a garden. A spot where we could sit in the sun. Something with a little privacy. Away from a busy street so the cats would be safe. In the end nothing we saw listed felt right to us. And after a spate of searching we'd give up and not think about it for days.

THERE WAS a second open house. And a third. People checked out our closets, looked at our clothes, drifted through the bedroom, commented on our belongings. And always they tried to take photographs and questioned us about our lives. They mentioned the terrible state of many of the other apartments they'd looked at in the building. Shirley's was the worst. A real pigsty, someone said. Totally disgusting. Ours was the exception. The one that had really been kept up. And then we usually got the inevitable questions: How long *have* you lived here? Or, how did you get that piano into the living room? And then, always, Which one of you plays?

Oscar kept reminding us we didn't have to be present for these open houses, but somehow we couldn't not be. We didn't trust what might happen in our absence.

I CAME to see our lives in a different way against the background of these invasions. It was as if I suddenly began viewing us from the perspective of other people—these strangers who had barged into our lives. We were an insular couple who had grown a bit eccentric, perhaps, with age, rather like Chandler and his wife, Cissy. We lived quietly, just the two of us. We were devoted to our work and to our cats, just as the Chandlers had been devoted to their black Persian named Taki. Rarely did we ask anyone to dinner anymore—it had been some time since we had done so—and like the Chandlers it was something of an occasion for us to accept an invitation to go out.

We had grown more isolated over the years, even in the midst of this chaotic city. We didn't seem to have the same interests that other people did. We rarely watched TV, didn't have a clue about the programs other people were constantly referring to. We didn't connect with friends on social media. We listened to music each evening, just as the Chandlers had done, only instead of tuning into the *Gas Company Radio Hour* as they had we played our favorite CDs and records, or sometimes Vincent sat at the piano, playing something, and occasionally—just occasionally—he would ask me to sing. I had memorized a number of Schubert's songs. His favorite composer. And it always felt good to me when my singing pleased him, as it usually did, as his playing always pleased me.

We doted on each other, just as the Chandlers had done. We had private jokes, pet names, even a collection of objects not so dissimilar from the Chandlers' collection of little glass animals, which they called their *amuels,* each one of which they had given a name—all forty-four of them.

Our collection was perhaps even quirkier: over the years we had accumulated odd little figures and doll parts, gleaned from second-hand or antique stores. The headless nurse, in her white dress with a red cross on her chest, was the first we had acquired. The rustic doll made out of a travel-size toothpaste box and pipe cleaners was the second. Then came the single bisque arm, the severed limbs, delicate in their perfect pinkness. There was a hairless porcelain head with eyes that rolled open and shut that we'd found in a thrift store in San Bernardino. And a bisque boy, his arms and legs articulated. There was a pink crystal figure of a woman holding a lamb, whose naked body reminded Vincent of mine. The collection had grown over the years. The wooden hand once used for displaying rings. A primitive figure from Guatemala with a tin hat. A Hopi kachina, and a crude homemade cloth doll that had been carried across the plains in the nineteenth century, so minimal and bizarre it resembled a space alien. In all there were several dozen figures, or partial figures, in our collection, items displayed in an old glass-fronted lawyers' bookcase in the living room. I saw how people stopped during the open houses and glanced at these objects and then looked at us, as if to say, *What the hell . . . ?*

One great difference between us and the Chandlers was that Chandler and his wife had moved so often, more than thirty-five times during the years they spent in L.A. They were constantly changing residences, rarely staying so much as a year in one place and always renting furnished apartments, fussy, restless people who were forever finding an excuse to leave a place and move on, whereas Vincent and I had attached ourselves so firmly to one spot it had now become unthinkable we could leave it.

I saw how strange we'd actually become. A bit old-fashioned. Outmoded—like the cupboards in the kitchen for holding the iron and the ironing board.

Over the years, I had adopted many of Vincent's ways. His capacity for solitariness. His silences. His particularity about so many things, his inflexibility when it came to trying anything new. I saw more clearly than ever how his multiple obsessions and rules and peculiarities had in certain ways now become mine. I had to admit there had been an absorption of his personality into my own. We had, perhaps unwittingly, subscribed to the idea, put forward by someone whose name I no longer recalled, that the highest task for a bond between two people was this: that each protects the solitude of the other.

Yes, it was true: I had conformed to his habits and whims rather than him conforming to mine, which I understood was largely impossible for him to do. Long ago I stopped cooking foods he didn't care for even if I longed for them myself. I stopped buying a certain kind of cracker, for instance, because he didn't like the way they made his teeth feel. Only now did I realize how odd many of our habits and inclinations had become. How isolating. It was as if by opening up our lives to the inspection of strangers I had been able to see how I had grown more inward and detached, less capable of navigating the complexities of the world. It could now appear that my brain was also wired differently. Only it wasn't.

I realized that if I didn't take matters in hand—if I didn't manage to find us another place to live—it wouldn't happen. Because he couldn't face it. We would continue to be stuck in the netherworld of indecision in which we found ourselves. I needed to return to that sense of being the strong and capable person I had been when I met him. Then I had been a woman who'd had the resourcefulness to leave the only home I'd ever known and start over in a completely new place. Surely I could do that again. Couldn't I?

And still I did nothing.

I made no effort to find us a new place to live because, as I told myself, the guillotine had not yet dropped. We had not yet been given a firm date for when we had to leave.

I began to feel my health suffer. I developed pains in my feet (plantar fasciitis, according to the doctor). An old knee injury flared up (same doctor: You'll likely need a replacement). Worst of all, two root canals needed retreatment, and I spent long tortuous hours in the dental chair. On one of the visits to the dentist, while sitting in the waiting room watching TV, I saw a report about another school shooting. A twelve-year-old girl had taken a gun to her elementary school and shot two of her fellow students. Twelve years old! I thought. A little girl. How had this happened? But of course I knew how it had happened. Something like this now occurred almost every day.

And then driving home, as I approached our street, I saw the police cars and realized the shooting had taken place at a school just a block from our apartment.

We needed to leave MacArthur Park.

We needed to move on. And we needed to do it soon.

Why was it so difficult for us to do this?

ANOTHER NIGHT, a week or so later, we returned in the evening to find our street blocked off. There were dozens of police cars in the area. An officer stopped us, and when we told him where we lived he informed us we couldn't go home. A situation was unfolding, he said, in the building next to ours. A man with a gun was holding a woman hostage and threatening to kill her. The whole area had been cordoned off. The officer had no idea when we'd be allowed to return to our apartment and suggested we contact friends or family to see if we might spend the night with them, just in case the incident dragged on.

Friends or family? We had no family in L.A. But we called our friends Laurie and Tom, who lived not far away, and they said to come right over.

We sat in their living room, watching the news and the regular updates on the ongoing hostage situation on Carondelet. A number of shootings were getting attention that night. One at a beauty parlor in Van Nuys: a jealous husband had gunned down his estranged wife and the woman whose hair she'd been cutting. Another woman sitting in her car had been randomly shot while waiting at a traffic light on Ventura Boulevard. She was expected to live. But the gunman had driven away, and they had no leads.

It was shocking, the idea of such random violence. But what had Chandler said about America? That it was at heart a mobster culture. Nathanael West once remarked that in this country we don't have to prepare for violence. Violence is our birthright. This is the way we kill each other: randomly, while sitting at a traffic light or while getting a haircut.

Our friends offered wine and kept us entertained while we waited and watched the news, and finally around midnight we heard a report saying the hostage situation on Carondelet had ended with no one getting hurt and we drove home, past the garish red flares still burning at the end of our street and the enormous white trailer—*the incident command center*—that was slowly being dismantled in the floodlit darkness.

IN SPITE of these disruptions and the worries about the apartment, our lives went on much as before. The days when Vincent saw students, he left in the morning and came home in the early afternoon. I worked, consulting my notes, typing out Cissy's recipes, paging through Chandler's novels and stories in search of passages about food, still imagining I might write the book he had started before he died. *Cookbook for Idiots.* It often felt like I was the idiot for imagining the idea had any worth.

We often took a walk in Echo Park late in the day—a lovely graceful little park, well maintained, so very different from MacArthur Park. And then it was time for dinner. Reading. Music. Bed. Or perhaps a concert downtown if a program attracted us.

And yet, as we waited for news from Ingenious about when we'd be forced to leave, nothing really felt the same. Except the things that never changed. Like Shirley's insidious presence.

ONE NIGHT I went outside to cut some rosemary from the bush beneath her window and I heard her calling down to me. *I see everything,* she hissed. *I hear everything too. I know everything that's going on in your lives because I can hear everything. You don't know what I know about you. Heh! Heh! Heh! But I do.*

I refused to look up. I went on with the business of gathering rosemary, pretending not to hear her, wondering how not even a stroke and invalidism and the prospect of imminent death had been able to temper her horrible personality, but she continued to torment me.

What are you, deaf? she hissed. *Are you deaf, is that it?*

She was still calling to me as I turned and went back inside.

Are you deaf? Are you deaf? Are you deaf?

FOR YEARS she had been up there in her bedroom with the window open, listening to everything we said. We knew this. She had no other life. Long ago she had retired from her job as a bookkeeper. Eavesdropping had become her full-time work. Eavesdropping and harassing her neighbors. Leaving bits of trash in our garden, breaking off flowers, scuffing heavily down the walkway in the middle of the night calling loudly for her little dog Pookie. Hurling vile words from her window.

In the past she would emerge from her apartment, dressed in her big hats and festive sweaters, and walk down the alley to the bus stop and return with heavy shopping bags, a burly woman in big brown shoes. She seemed to have no friends. Not even acquaintances. No one ever came to visit her. She was the aging succubus drawing energy from our lives, turning the details of our existence into her own modest entertainments. For years I had tried to keep my voice low if the windows were open in an attempt to deny her material. I knew how freely the sound traveled between our apartments because I could hear her so clearly. The raspy coughs at night. The slobbery hum of her TV. The scrape of a spoon against a bowl as she ate her cereal or ice cream at two in the morning. We had tried to protect our privacy by speaking softly, but now I didn't care what she overheard, and in truth Vincent had never cared. I wished for her to hear us. I wanted her to know that we were alive, still vigorous. We spoke normally now and played music at any volume we wished, and at night Vincent stood on the porch calling the cats in his loud voice, using his nickname for Max: *Monkey! Monkey! Monkey! Where are you, Monkey? Come home right now!* And all the time I imagined her up in her bedroom, confined to her bed, listening to our every word.

———

OUR UNHAPPINESS grew during this period of waiting, of anticipating the now inevitable move. We had several bad arguments. The first was over the broken glass in the alley. Someone had begun breaking bottles against our garage door every night, pitching them, perhaps, from the balcony of the apartment building across the way—at least that's where I suspected they came from. Bottles that exploded into tiny pieces, as if tossed from some height. Every morning we found broken glass in front of the garage. We had to sweep it up before we could take the car out or risk a flat tire. Day after day broken beer bottles and cheap wine bottles, shattered and strewn in front of our garage. It was all so disturbing. So mysterious. Why was this happening?

Who was doing this?

One day as we were sweeping up the glass I looked up the alley and saw the group of men and boys loitering in front of the open garage. The gang members and elderly men who always hung out in the same spot. The ones who had made driving or walking past them feel like running a gauntlet.

They know, I said. They know who is doing this. We should ask them.

They won't tell us, Vincent said. No point in asking them about it.

It upset me that he dismissed the idea so quickly. I kept at it, insisting they might know, and if we asked them politely—if *he* asked them politely (it would be better coming from him, I said)—and told them how much it was disrupting our lives, making everything so difficult for us, maybe they'd tell us something.

I hadn't even finished the sentence before Vincent turned and marched up the alley. He approached the gang kids, many of whom were really gang *men*—heavily tattooed guys with wifebeaters pulled up over their big bellies. I could smell the odor of pot wafting down the alley. I stood watching apprehensively as Vincent approached them. He was wearing his khaki shorts and plaid shirt. His legs looked so thin in contrast to those of the large boys and men. I saw how they scowled at him as he stood in front of them, speaking words I couldn't hear. Still it was clear what was happening. They were blowing him off. They shrugged and looked bored and passed a joint, and then they simply turned away from him and began laughing.

Are you happy now? he said angrily when he came back to the garage. Satisfied? Now that I've humiliated myself in front of those guys? I told you it wouldn't do any good. They wouldn't even talk to me. And why should they?

I'm sorry, I said, and tried to touch his arm and explain I hadn't meant he should talk to them right *then,* only think about it, but he pulled away. It was one of the few times I could remember seeing him so angry. But by evening he'd forgotten all about it.

THERE WAS a second incident, prompted by an email I'd gotten from someone named James Smithson, who reached me through my website. He informed me he'd bought a used book at a local library sale. It turned out to be a book signed by Raymond Chandler for his wife, Cissy. The dedication was very touching, he said. There had also been a letter inside that fell out when he picked up the book. The letter was addressed to Jean Fracasse, Chandler's former secretary and one-time paramour, and it was from Somerset Maugham. A short letter expressing sadness at the news of Chandler's death, saying what a fan he had been of Chandler's work, and thanking Jean for writing to him. James Smithson said he wouldn't have even thought of acquiring the book if the letter from Somerset Maugham hadn't fallen out. That's when he put the pieces together and realized the book had been a gift from Raymond Chandler to his wife. He thought it might have value. That he might make money off it. The book was called *Masters of the Keyboard: A Brief Survey of Pianoforte Music.* That Chandler would have given his wife this book made sense to me, given that she was an accomplished pianist. Mr. Smithson was a musician himself, he said, and that's why he'd picked up the book in the first place. But the book was really rather dreadful, he said. A collection of essays by someone named Willi Appel. Quite unreadable, he added. Its only value lay in the dedication. He said he would send an email and attach photos of the dedication page, as well as a screenshot of the cover of the book, and added that he'd done some research online and when he learned I had written a book about Chandler and his wife, he thought I might be interested in acquiring it. He did not name a price, but I told him I'd be eager to see it and get back to him.

THE DEDICATION moved me:

For My Darling, because God meant her to be one of them (see title) but her heart was too big to let her live for herself.

It was signed "Raymio," her nickname for him, and dated December 25, 1947.

A Christmas gift for Cissy, the talented pianist who had once hoped for a concert career, who by then was a semi-invalid, suffering from the lung condition to which she would eventually succumb just a few years later. At the time Chandler give her this book Cissy was seventy-seven; he was fifty-eight.

I WANTED this book. I wanted it very badly. I didn't feel there was anyone who deserved to own it more than I. I, who had spent so much time looking into the marriage of the Chandlers. Who understood their devotion, their happiness, as well as the difficult times they had endured when Chandler was drinking and having affairs. I understood the pain this had caused his much older wife. Who nevertheless always took him back and helped to ground him and keep him sane. It was she who had enabled him to continue writing during his bouts of alcoholism and depression.

I wrote to James Smithson saying I was interested in buying the book. How much was he asking? He quoted me what I thought was an outrageously high price, and later, over dinner, I told Vincent what had transpired that day. How Smithson had contacted me, the great find he'd made, the beautiful dedication, and the price he was asking for the book. I thought, I said, that perhaps I could make a counter-offer, but Vincent immediately felt this wasn't wise. He thought I should forget about the book. It was too much money, he said, and for what? A book on piano music, by a famous musicologist it's true, he knew who Willi Appel was and even with the dedication it wasn't worth the outrageous asking price.

Now it was I who got upset. I accused him of never wanting me to have what I wanted, while I almost always wished for him to have what he desired and helped to see that he got it. I reminded him of an expensive book on Schubert I had recently encouraged him to buy because he'd longed for it. I became unreasonably upset. Because now the argument wasn't just about a book, or money. It was about the double standard in our marriage. His insensitivity. The way I felt he always got what he needed or wanted while he refused to think of me and my desires. None of this was exactly true. But it didn't matter. I was blinded by my anger. I felt swept back to the moment Deborah had told me about his difference. How his insensitivity wasn't *willed* but somehow inevitable

I got up and left the table. I went into the bedroom and closed the door. I could hear him doing the dishes, just as he always did. Then he went into the living room, and all was silent.

I texted him from the bedroom:

IF I THOUGHT FOR ONE SECOND YOU UNDERSTOOD WHAT I'M SAYING TO YOU AND RECOGNIZED THAT IT'S TRUE I WOULDN'T GET SO ANGRY BUT THERE'S AN OBTUSENESS, A REFUSAL IN YOU TO SEE THE INEQUALITY AND UNFAIRNESS THAT EXISTS IN OUR MARRIAGE THAT I CAN'T PUT UP WITH. IT COMES DOWN TO THIS: I AM USUALLY EAGER FOR YOU TO HAVE WHAT YOU WANT, AND YOU ARE NIGGARDLY WITH ME. AND IT HURTS.

I then sent a second text defining the word *niggardly* because, perhaps foolishly, I wasn't sure he would know what it meant ("reluctant to give or spend; stingy; miserly; ungenerously small"). I thought the word perfectly appropriate. But I immediately felt sorry I had been so arrogant as to think he wouldn't know the meaning of the word.

After a while he texted back one sentence: *I will try not to be so niggardly.*

But I knew there was only so much he could do. It was like saying *I wonder if my mother had this?* It wouldn't sink in. He might try to change, but it was much more likely the idea would simply disappear from his beautifully self-involved brain.

I decided I would act on my own. But by the time I got back to James Smithson with a counteroffer, the book had already been sold.

I was disappointed. I could not stop thinking of Chandler's dedication. The truth as well as the fiction it revealed—an imbalance I was acutely aware of in my own life. The preposterous notion that God might have meant for Cissy to be one of those "masters of the keyboard" if only her heart hadn't been so big and prevented her from living for herself. It made me laugh. The whole idea. It made me sad as well. It wasn't a big heart that had prevented me from living for myself but an upbringing in a culture that had been so completely devoted to training women to think mainly of others. How to be if you wanted to be wanted. I was again reminded that I had ended up with a partner who struggled to find within the recesses of his gifted mind any consciousness of what others might be feeling. And by others, of course, I meant *me*.

GRAFFITI APPEARED on all the garages again, just a day after the city truck had gone down the alley spraying out the old graffiti. The garages had been sprayed so many times, the layers of paint had built up to a heavy sheeny thickness.

I was so tired of seeing graffiti everywhere. On every possible surface. I had been walking to the market recently when two teenage boys passed me on the sidewalk and began spraying a tree trunk just ahead of me. It upset me very much to see this, yet I dared not walk past them, let alone say anything. So I hung back. I watched from up the street. They knew I was watching them, and they didn't care. I hated the feeling that I had been intimidated into silence while they desecrated this tree. But no one dared confront these boys and their

spray cans. I was sick of seeing this meaningless ugly scrawl everywhere but for some reason it especially upset me to see them spraying
living things—a tree, agave spikes, cactus, even a wall covered in ivy.

I mentioned this to our neighbor Hector, the retired nurse who
lived across the walkway from us, whom I met walking back from the
market that day. What are we to do? Hector said, everything is going
downhill. You know, a while ago I caught two boys who were having sex with a girl in the bushes below my window. You know, right
where the stairs jog to the right. The girl was very young, he said.
Maybe only eleven or twelve. He said he had gone out and confronted
the boys and told them to stop what they were doing. What they were
doing, he said, was wrong, it was nasty and he was going to call the
police if they didn't stop. But the boys told him to shut up. We know
where you live, they said. Leave us alone or you'll be sorry.

Imagine, Hector said. A little girl like that. What they were doing
to her! It was wrong. So nasty, he said. And yet she laughed. She told
me it was none of my business. Go away, she said. What could I do?
What can we do? It's not nice, he said, but what can we do? My sister
came to visit me last week. She said, Hector, what is going on here?
This place is going to hell! Isn't anybody taking care of things anymore? How can you live like this? It's fine for her. She lives in a big
apartment complex in Balboa Park. Very expensive apartments. I told
her, Listen sister, we do what we can do.

Hector said, This building is in very bad shape, you know? I think
whoever buys it is just going to tear it down. They have let things get
too bad. But until we hear something, we don't know, do we? We just
have to wait. And meanwhile, look what is happening? Nobody cares
about this place anymore.

All afternoon I couldn't get his words out of my head. The way
he'd said *nasty*. So nasty, he said, what those boys were doing with that
little girl.

Once again I wondered how we had lived for so many years in a
place where such things could go on. But when I mentioned these feelings to Vincent he only said, What do you mean? This is our home. He
used that word often now. He no longer referred to this place as just

our apartment. But our *home.* As if it were an irrevocable condition. And as we had begun to realize, one does not leave a home so easily.

A GAS leak erupted in a line running beneath the building. It was Hector who first smelled the gas and pointed out the place where the odor was coming from. We called the gas company, who sent someone over immediately. He said the situation was very dangerous. He had to shut off the gas to the apartments until the line could be repaired by a professional licensed plumber.

But when we called Ingenious and told them about the problem, they didn't send a licensed professional plumber but instead two young Mexican workers, who after several hours said they had fixed things. But when the gas company worker returned to turn the gas back on, he found there was still a leak. The work had been shoddily done, he said. He couldn't restore service until it was properly fixed. We should understand the situation was dangerous.

On it went. Ingenious sending the Mexican workers back. Refusing to hire a licensed plumber. Trying to do things on the cheap, resulting in still more delays. And meanwhile the problem remained unsolved.

FOR ALMOST a week we had no hot water or heat, or gas for cooking or taking showers. Vincent could not begin a day without a shower—he found such an idea unthinkable. And yet he was forced to do so. We had to consider what we could eat without cooking. I began to wonder if perhaps there was some sort of conspiracy on the part of Ingenious to make our lives so miserable we'd simply want to leave. I'd heard of other instances where renters were forced out by such methods. And yet Vincent insisted I shouldn't worry. He was not worried, he said. He did not think I was right about there being an attempt to force us out. I saw how we had suddenly managed to switch roles: he was now trying to comfort me, and I was the worrier.

Finally a licensed repairman was sent to fix the leak. The gas was safely turned back on, and it seemed we would not succumb to carbon monoxide poisoning or an explosion after all.

But how, I wondered, could we go on this way?

And yet still we did nothing about looking for an apartment. I saw what strangely frozen people we'd become. We seemed to believe if we did nothing, something would happen on its own.

WE WERE told we must clean out the extra garage we had used for storage for many years and given only a few weeks to do so. The garage was packed with stuff we hadn't looked at for ages. There were boxes of photos and other things I'd hauled down in the horse trailer and never used—an old tennis racket and ski clothes. Ice skates and a badminton set. Items that reminded me of my past and suggested I must have long ago imagined a sporting life for myself in L.A. though it had never materialized.

I found scrapbooks I'd made in the classes the church held for teens, stuffed with handouts extolling chastity and prayer and obedience. I discovered certificates of awards for public speaking, and ribbons from horse shows I'd competed in. Detritus from my past. Stuff my parents had saved and passed on to me. Old report cards attesting to what an indifferent student I'd been. Mostly things I could discard or give away to a thrift store, except a sealed cardboard carton marked "family" and a large box of photographs, both of which I carried upstairs.

I SAT down on the living room floor and began looking through the box of photographs. There were a lot of pictures I remembered as well as others I hadn't expected to come across that seemed fresh to me, including snapshots of Jolene that I hadn't seen in many years.

There were photos of us in high school, on a field trip to a planetarium in Salt Lake City, and eating at Uncle Leo's Noodle Parlor, a favorite place of ours. There were pictures of us in swimsuits, stretched out on a beach at Pine View Dam looking tanned and lean, at ease in our firm and youthful bodies. Photographs of us standing with our arms around each other wearing the matching bikinis Jolene had made for us. We laugh for the camera. Hold each other close. We seem almost like lovers acting out our affectionate poses.

There were a number of pictures taken at her house, in the large garden and around the swimming pool in her backyard. The house was very imposing, built at the turn of the century by an early railroad baron. It was meant to resemble a gabled English country house, constructed of stone and white stucco and rising up three stories. The street on which it stood was lined with the houses of the town's wealthiest residents. A small pocket park filled with flowering bushes ran down the middle of the street, and the beautiful old trees on either side created a leafy canopy.

I remembered the house as being so elegant and impressive, and the pictures confirmed my memory. Some showed the interior, revealing the polished wood wainscoting and heavy beams, the large kitchen, a living room with a massive stone fireplace, velvet draperies, and oversized furniture with ornately carved legs. A house so different in every way from the modest white frame house where my own family had lived. The walls were painted blood red in one room, forest green in another, and the moldings and details had been enhanced with gold leafing. Rooms gay with glossy color and a shiny patina that caught the light from the chandeliers that hung from the ceilings. Little etchings and framed paintings covered the walls, depicting hunting and pastoral scenes. Everything so rosy, so polished, so precious. I recalled how I had spent many hours in that house. From Jolene's bedroom on the third floor one could glimpse the spire of the tabernacle rising above the treetops.

To me this was a magical place, but Jolene had hated that house. She called it the Tomb. *I guess I have to go back to the Tomb now,* she'd say whenever we parted. It made her mother very happy to live in such an imposing house where she could indulge the sort of social life she relished—the cocktail hours and special parties she regularly threw to benefit the charities and institutions on whose boards she served. The lovely garden that was always featured in the annual home and garden tour.

As teenagers we had lived in that garden during the long hot summers, sunbathing on the grass near the fountain or swimming in the pool and lying in the shade of the pergola covered in wisteria. The family's maid, Constance, would bring us lemonade and little sandwiches with the crusts cut off. We held sleepovers on the lawn and played croquet with the boys we invited over. Mainly we tried to avoid spending too much time around Jolene's mother, who often seemed ready to pick a fight. Her mother knew Jolene found the house pretentious because she often ridiculed it, calling it the Tomb in front of her, and I don't think her father much cared for it either. It was one of the things her parents regularly argued about. Dr. Carver had wanted to build a modern house in a new subdivision up in the foothills, one he could help design, with large windows offering sweeping views of the valley and the Great Salt Lake, while Mrs. Carver had refused to leave the old house in the established neighborhood on the flats.

I finished looking through the box, put the photos back, and taped it shut. I considered showing some of the pictures to Vincent, but then I thought better of it. The truth was, he'd barely be interested. I knew that. My past was mine, nothing he'd ever really cared to hear that much about. Not even the pictures of Jolene would interest him, or maybe especially not those. In fact they would likely unsettle him were I to simply spring them on him. So why bother?

I'D HARDLY thought of her at all since she had sent the text canceling our lunch the day before Vincent and I left for New York. It had come as a relief. It wouldn't be necessary to see her after all, I thought, and I wouldn't have to keep anything from Vincent. Now that the silence had gone on for so long I believed it was over. Whatever impulse had caused her to reach out must have faded away. Perhaps she'd had a change of heart. Maybe she hadn't returned to L.A. after all. Or she might have decided she didn't really want to resurrect the past and had given up on the idea of getting together.

So it came as a great surprise to hear from her a few days after I'd looked through the box of photos from the garage. It was as if I had conjured her. I woke up one morning to find she had sent a text during the night: *Forgive me for such a long silence. I'll explain when I see you. Can you meet me for lunch next Tuesday? Same place, Beverly Hills, one o'clock?*

I did not see how I could refuse her. So I said yes, I would meet her, just as she'd requested.

THE WEEK went by quickly. She had not insisted, in this recent text, that I keep our lunch date a secret from Vincent, as she had done earlier, but nevertheless I felt it was a good idea. Why I thought this I'm not quite sure. I didn't know what she wanted or why she'd decided to reach out to me, and until I knew that, there really wasn't much to say to him.

And so I said nothing. I let the days slide by. I tried not to feel anxious about seeing her. Nevertheless I did. So many thoughts crossed my mind. So many memories surfaced, images from the past, freshly seeded by the photographs I'd just seen. I began wondering how she had changed, and this led me to various recollections of her artwork and performances I'd discovered over the years and the fact she had become so famous. Wouldn't she feel even more like a stranger to me?

I KEPT going back to a moment, just a few years earlier, when Vincent and I had seen one of her performance videos at the Hammer Museum. This was some time after we had come across the photo of her in the Pompidou, sitting on a bench with the crotch of her pants cut out. Her video at the Hammer was part of a retrospective show called "Radical Feminist Art: 1979–1999." Her video piece, titled *Sanitary Products,* had been made a number of years earlier. It was projected in a continuous loop in a small darkened room. The video showed her in a gallery space with the walls painted white and nothing hanging on them, shot at some sort of opening—her opening, obviously, for which she had devised a special performance piece: in the video she is nude and walking around the gallery where people have gathered to watch. She has taped a number of sanitary napkin pads to her body in various places, except the one place where they were meant to be. She is menstruating. Blood has run down her legs and is spotting the floor as she walks around. She approaches a wall and rubs her body against it so that the menstrual blood leaves its mark against the whiteness. She walks to another wall and makes more marks with her blood. Then she strolls around the gallery some more, making additional red smears on the walls while people stand at the edge of the room and look on, sometimes parting to let her naked and bloodstained body pass by. The video lasted for perhaps five or six minutes, and then it started all over again.

When we saw the piece at the Hammer and realized it was Jolene, we both had a startled reaction.

Wow, I said, as we stood watching. And that's all I said for a while.

I was looking at her naked body, which did not seem to have changed that much. She was still remarkably lithe, and she looked very attractive, with her long dark hair and large eyes. She moved about very gracefully on her long slim legs, like a trained dancer. Watching her was a mesmerizing experience. I was thinking of the guts, or the courage, whatever you might call it, that it would take to pull off such a thing. I felt I was watching a powerful taboo being broken. The audaciousness of it all! I wondered where you got that kind of fearlessness, the ability to expose yourself so completely—down to the inner workings of your female body. Few things were more generally repulsive to people than menstrual blood, and in this performance she had made it her medium. Of course I thought of her in high school, how she had tied that sanitary napkin to a hanger in the girls' bathroom one day and dangled it outside the window. Then I had been shocked but also secretly admiring of her audacity. I had the same feeling watching the video at the Hammer.

Vincent had glanced at the video only briefly, and then he simply shook his head and moved on to another gallery. Later, driving home, I said to him, Where do you think an artist gets the kind of courage it takes to make that kind of work?

You have to be born that way, he said.

And I knew he was right.

She was born that way. And I definitely was not.

PART TWO

The Great Basin

10

When I arrived in L.A. all those years ago, at that moment I suppose you could say I started my life alone in earnest. And even if I didn't stay alone that long it felt to me like I had in many ways become a more solitary person from that point on.

I often wondered about this—that in the midst of a great crowded city I had grown so much more solitary. Was this due primarily to the fact I had left the place that had formed me and with it all my familiars, the intimacy of being surrounded by family and old friends and a landscape that would forever bind me—things that could never be replaced—or was it perhaps the case that Vincent's quiet and largely solitary nature had rubbed off and left me feeling more isolated than I might have otherwise? I occasionally returned to that moment, shortly after Leon walked out on me, when I had first called Jolene to see if I might stay with her for a while in L.A. She had tried to warn me off the city. *It's not an easy place,* she had said. And I had come anyway.

That day—the morning I left for L.A.—it had been snowing hard all night. When I awoke there was a foot of new snow covering the truck and horse trailer. I remember standing in the driveway, getting ready to start my journey, and brushing the snow away with a broom, full of anxiety and anticipation. Was I doing the right thing by leaving home so abruptly? Would California work out? Make me any happier than if I stayed put? I had stopped by my parents' house to say goodbye to them, but they were doing temple work that morning, performing baptisms for the dead, and I found only my ninety-year-old Aunt Fannie at home. She had lived with my parents for many years. Hard of hearing and suffering from multiple other little infirmaries, she was nevertheless still the kind and uncomplaining person she had always been. She had asked me to thread some needles for her that morning, and I'd taken the time to do that. For some reason I felt compelled to confess to her I was getting a divorce. Oh that's nice, she said. A new horse. You've always loved horses, haven't you?

WHO HAD I been then? And who was I now? It was the latter me I often found perplexing, as if I had emerged from a younger and stronger self to become someone much more unknowable. I had come to understand that none of us can entirely maintain our identity as time flows past. But in many ways I felt closer to my earlier self. As Joan Didion once wrote, *It's a good idea to keep on nodding terms with the people we used to be . . . we forget all too soon the things we thought we could never forget.*

There was so much I had not forgotten over the years, and the idea of seeing Jolene had opened the gates to the past. Certain memories had begun flooding back unbidden. Shifting and sometimes confusing gusts of recollection that lasted only a few seconds. Little bags of detached and dissimilar fragments, dropped on my mental doorstep. The aggregate of these moments is what we call our *selves,* but it remains an aggregate, not a whole. The whole, I've discovered, escapes us; perhaps it does not exist. Perhaps it never has.

Wasn't it Proust who theorized that the quality of direct experience always eluded one and that only in recollection could we grasp its real flavor? I have Jolene to thank for reminding me of that, in a letter she wrote long ago.

My own upbringing had been so modest, so tempered compared to hers. She had grown up with wealth and privilege, in a liberal atmosphere, as the daughter of one of the town's leading doctors and his notoriously hard-drinking wife. In her youth Jolene had never once stepped inside a church, as she was always happy to tell you, and this in a town where a single religion dominated everyday life. She considered this fact a point of pride. Aren't all religions simply schemes? she'd say. Fantasies devised by men to keep control of societies and regulate women?

When we first met I had been deeply attracted to the ribald atmosphere in her house, which sparkled with forbidden excess. The drinking that went on, the cigarettes her mother smoked one after another, the strapless summer dresses and formal gowns she wore that bared the tops of her fulsome white breasts. All things forbidden in the realm in which I was raised. Excuse my potty mouth, her mother used to say after letting fly with some obscenity. And then she would laugh, her red-lipsticked mouth opening wide as if she were trying to stuff the vulgarity back in. I discovered an infectious liveliness whenever I visited Jolene, so different from the staid sobriety in my own household. In the evenings, when I sometimes went over to Jolene's to study with her, I often found a living room filled with people talking and laughing and drinking, women glittering with jewels, and men with gin. Something always seemed about to happen, if not something good at least something exciting. Loud conversations running atop each other, naughty jokes being told, and a hazy erotic current coursing through the room. The festive, jovial, boozy moods that made up life in the shiny, colorful rooms of the old mansion.

My father sold shoes for a living. He had eight children to support. It was not an easy thing for him to do. But I never felt I went without. My mother occasionally took in boarders as a way of making ends meet—a farm boy attending the local college, a returned missionary taking up his studies again—and she made a point of canning our food and sewing our clothes. She was skilled at the home arts. Often, coming home from school, I would find her sitting around a quilting frame with a few other ladies from church while the gamy smell of a venison roast wafted from the kitchen. Hi honey, she would say, come over here and say hi to Velma and Annalee. And I would cross the room of unreconciled furnishings—the gleaming gold fireplace insert, the sectional couch with a faded pink bouclé, the brown Naugahyde Barcalounger, and the spool rocker with homemade denim cushions—to find myself engulfed in an embrace from each of the church ladies, encircled by their fleshy arms. Every night we prayed as a family, kneeling before the sofa, each child taking his turn: as soon as we learned to speak we learned to pray. Every meal started with a blessing and then the great bowls of pinto beans would be passed, and the platters of deer meat from animals my brothers had shot, accompanied by slices of homemade bread still fragrant from the oven.

My father would have never said that he simply *sold shoes* for a living. He would have put it another way, given things a little spin. He was a manager, he'd say—the manager of one of the largest shoe stores in town. Sometimes he made it sound like he actually owned the store. *At my store,* he would say, when describing some event or transaction. *At my store we do things this way.* He didn't mind leaving one with the impression that he owned the place, even though it was a Thom McAn store that everyone knew was part of a national chain.

HOW AM I supposed to have a normal childhood, Jolene would sometimes say, with my parents always screwing other people? And then she would laugh to let you know that none of this really bothered her. It only became an issue when her father started sleeping with her boyfriend Scott's mother and word of it got around school. That genuinely annoyed her. What sort of example does that set for us? she'd say. I guess it means Scott and I should be doing exactly what they're doing, don't you think? And then she'd get that wicked look on her face.

Her father was tall, with a refined countenance and eyes so startlingly blue they took you by surprise when he trained them on you. There was no denying he was an exceedingly handsome man. Her mother on the other hand was a ruined beauty, and I think she knew it, which often made her behavior seem more desperate than it otherwise might have appeared. I've had my share of fun, she would often say, to which Jolene would reply, I bet, in her best monotone, and then add, It certainly looks like it.

Her mother fancied herself an expert on interior decorating and liked to show off her house as proof of her excellent taste, the rooms picked out with golden moldings and the walls painted teal or crimson or butter yellow. More than once I heard her extol the virtues of painting a ceiling pink in order to soften the light and create a pleasing overhead glow.

One of the first times Jolene came to my house my father looked at her feet and said, Come on over here, gal, and let me take a look at those shoes you're wearing. He was sitting in the Barcalounger, pushed back so far that his own feet appeared slightly higher than his head. She threw me a funny look, as if to say, *What's all this about?* But she didn't resist. She allowed herself to stand quietly before him as he flipped a lever and launched himself out of the chair and knelt down by her feet, subjecting herself to his patient analysis. He pushed down the front of her shoe to see if the shoes were too short. He felt for her big toe. She was wearing a pair of what looked like ballet slippers with thin leather soles. He ran his fingers along the sides of the shoe, and then he asked her to push her foot slightly forward and attempted to fit a finger between her heel and the back of the shoe. He told her to take the shoe off and felt inside, and then he put it back on the floor and she slipped her foot again inside. Finally he stood up and shook his head. I don't know where you got those crappy things, he said, but those shoes are doing you no good. They're too short and too wide, and there's no arch support. You'll end up a crippled old lady if you keep wearing shoes like that. Jolene looked at him and nodded sagely. Well, thank you very much, Mr. Flake, for that advice, she said, and we beat a retreat to my room.

Later, as we lounged on my bed with the door to my room closed, she looked genuinely amused as she asked me if my father went through that routine with everyone who came to the house.

Pretty much, I replied. He's got a thing about shoes. I had never talked to her about what my father did for a living.

Well, I bet he's a rather nice person, she said, when he isn't fiddling with people's feet.

In truth, he was a nice person. And so was my mother. But at that moment I felt so deeply embarrassed I couldn't help blushing. When she saw the color rising to my face she said, Oh for God's sake, Verna, don't be silly. Don't you realize how much better it is to have a parent with a nice little foot fetish rather than a dedicated ditch-bank drunk?

She waited a moment and then added, Don't you know that we can be anything we want to be? We don't have to be like our parents. Our parents have nothing to do with who we are or what we can do.

She reached over and touched my face with the back of her hand. We were no more than fourteen years old then. In that touch I felt a consolation and a tenderness I had never experienced outside my mother's loving touch, except Jolene's touch was accompanied by an entirely different feeling. I experienced a sudden electric buzz, a feeling of almost frightening excitement as she caressed my face, and it was so disturbing and unfamiliar that I immediately stood up and pretended I had to go to the bathroom. From the beginning she had produced these sorts of feelings and sensations in me that I simply didn't know what to do with.

WE BEGAN spending much more time together, and under her influence I experienced a sea change in behavior. I started to believe what she had said was true, that we could be whatever we wanted to be. Rules that had once seemed so unbreakable I now violated with much greater ease. I experimented with smoking, sharing cigarettes from the packs she stole from her mother. Sometimes I found myself in her room, on the top floor of the Tomb, drinking bourbon straight from the bottle during a sleepover, and in the morning I couldn't quite remember what we'd done the night before.

I began wearing odd clothes, things I fashioned myself in a largely unsuccessful attempt to emulate her creativity. I cut the heels and toes out of a pair of sneakers, leaving only the laces and a saddle of canvas over my arch, and then I painted the canvas with red and green circles and dots and squares. What is this? my mother said the first time she saw me leaving for school wearing my modified sneakers. What have you done to your good gym shoes? Do you know what your father will do if he sees you wearing those things? Do you think new sneakers grow on trees?

I HAD always had a great capacity for solitude, ever since I was a small child, but it increased during these years. Yet I still joined my family in their group activities, including the drives to southern Idaho to visit relatives on their farm outside the small town of Driggs, where we spent long summer days picking huckleberries on the steep slopes beneath the massive peaks of the Grand Tetons.

My aunt and uncle were an interesting couple—or at least an unusual one—in the sense that my Aunt Marie was responsible for running the farm, managing the animals and plowing the fields and harvesting crops with an old John Deere tractor, occasionally even using a team of magnificent draft horses she was exceptionally proud of, while my Uncle Wilbur wore an apron and did the inside chores, including all the cooking. It was Wilbur who turned the huckleberries into delicious pies and jams and purple-tinged pancakes. He was a very small man, with tiny hands and a widow's peak that made his hair stand up straight in front, as if he'd just gotten a little electric shock. Marie, on the other hand, was a big woman, and somehow the shapeless denim overalls she always wore made her seem even larger. Wilbur was soft and feminine, and Marie was gruff and masculine and pear-shaped. She kept her hair so short that looking at her from the back you would swear she was a man. Her hands were like great brown cracked claws, with calluses as thick as oven pads. I admired her very much. Her great strength impressed me, and I understood early on that her gruffness was nothing more than an easily penetrated front. She had always taken a special interest in me, maybe because she knew I shared her love of horses.

ONE TIME my parents said I could invite Jolene to come to Idaho with us on a huckleberry-picking trip, and to my surprise she loved the idea. Obviously it wasn't the sort of thing she'd ever done with her own family, whose notion of a vacation was a trip to Paris or Rome. She took to the huckleberry picking right away, tying the handle of the tin bucket to her jeans with a rope. She was thrilled when my father pointed out some fresh bear scat, heavily pebbled with huckleberry seeds. The bear had been working the same bushes not long before us, harvesting one of its favorite foods. Oh man, she said, I'd love to see a bear. But my father knew the bear might be a sow with cubs, in which case there'd be no defending ourselves from her if we crossed paths or somehow surprised her, and he insisted we leave the area immediately and try another spot. Who knew huckleberry picking could be so dangerous and *thrilling,* Jolene said to him, rolling her eyes dramatically. By then she had won my father over completely with her bantering and enthusiasm for the picking, and it didn't hurt that she was so attractive. She wasn't shy about using her charms on anyone, but she seemed to particularly enjoy netting an unsuspecting adult just for fun. I couldn't help noticing, however, how my mother regarded her with suspicion. She was a much better judge of character than my father and immune to Jolene's charms. It was on this trip that I began to think my mother knew much more about Jolene's morally loosening effect on me than she had yet let on.

The few days we spent with Wilbur and Marie on their farm, picking berries during the day and eating the delicious food Wilbur prepared in the evening, were altogether idyllic until something happened to mar our visit.

IT OCCURRED late one day when we were out in the barn. We often hung out there, lounging before dinner, sitting on the hay bales in the lofty and cool central chamber near the wooden stalls where Marie kept her milk cow and the big gray Percheron stallion she used for ploughing and lent out to neighbors for a small stud fee. It was a beautiful animal, a true workhorse, almost nineteen hands high, with a great thick arched neck and hooves the size of manhole covers. It had a gentle nature, especially for a stallion, and sometimes in the afternoon we took it a carrot or two and stood admiring it. Even Jolene, who had no true feeling for horses, was amazed by this stunningly beautiful animal.

That afternoon, as we stood feeding the stallion carrots, it let its penis down out of the sheath that normally kept it hidden. For anyone used to being around horses this was no big deal. Stallions, as well as geldings, often let their penises hang loose for a while before drawing them back in, and it meant nothing other than they were having a relaxing moment. But Jolene's eyes grew wide when she saw it. Dear lord, she said, look at that thing. He could do some real damage with that.

Oh stop it, I said.

No, I'm serious. Does that mean he likes me?

Do you have to be so silly? It bothered me that she was making such a big deal out of it. I still hadn't gotten used to how often she turned our conversations toward sex, but I felt this was ridiculous. It didn't seem funny to me, what she'd said. For some reason I felt embarrassed for the stallion. As if his dignity were being compromised by her.

Have you ever seen horses have sex? she asked.

Horses don't *have sex,* I replied sharply. They mate. They *breed.*

She frowned at me. Why are you so upset?

It seems infantile, I said. Those kinds of comments. Just really stupid.

I walked away and sat down on the hay bales. When I looked back at her I saw she had taken two cigarettes out of her shirt pocket. She was preparing to light one with a book of matches and holding the other awkwardly between her fingers.

Oh no! I said. No, no, no, you can't do that!

Why? Nobody can smell it out here if that's what you're afraid of. And I've got some mints for our breath so no one will even be able to tell—

No! I said, and this time I raised my voice and really yelled at her. Don't light that match!

All of my life I had been taught that the one thing you must never never do is smoke in a barn. The dry hay. The old wooden stalls. The fine dust everywhere. One small spark from a cigarette, and a barn could ignite so fast you'd never have time to get the animals out.

You can't smoke in this barn, I said. You just can't do that.

I can't believe you, she said. So uptight today. And she began to strike the match against the cover.

At that point Marie appeared in the doorway, her large body framed against the light.

Don't you dare do that, she said to Jolene in a voice so menacing it froze her.

Oh, okay, Jolene said cheerfully, and put the cigarette and matches back into her shirt pocket.

Marie strode into the barn, and now that she wasn't backlit I could see her face, which had a look that could kill. She walked right up to

Jolene and stood in front of her, her great size dwarfing Jolene's wiry thinness.

What sort of stupid little city shit are you? Marie said to her.

Really, I didn't know—

Don't lie to me. I heard Verna tell you not to do it, and you were about to go ahead anyway.

Well, I mean—

As the lord is my savior, Marie said, if I ever find you in my barn again I'll whup your ass so hard you won't be able to sit down for weeks. I'll beat the living daylights out of you. Do you understand?

Yes, of course. She shrugged. She was trying to act nonchalant, and she came off as haughty. She was still making the mistake of thinking Marie was someone she could manipulate. But Marie wasn't having any of it.

You're a little piece of work, aren't you? Marie said. I knew that when I first laid eyes on you. The thing I can't understand is why Verna would have you for a friend. I always thought she was a sensible girl. A girl with a good head on her shoulders. And then she goes and drags you up here to my farm. Some little vixen always playing with her hair. Putting lipstick on for breakfast. How come you're so stupid, Verna, to even associate with a girl like this?

I could hardly look at her, but I knew it would be worse if I couldn't meet her gaze.

I'm sorry, Marie, I said. And the way she looked at me I knew she understood how much I meant it. I felt sick inside. I knew how close we'd come to doing something that could have ended so badly. I was also afraid that Marie would now go straight to my parents and tell them what had happened. They would know I had started smoking.

Jolene tried again to mollify Marie.

It's true, she said, once more adopting her casual tone, that I don't know the first thing about barns or country life. Of course, if I did I wouldn't have even considered smoking in here, I hope you believe that.

I don't believe a thing coming out of your rotten little mouth, Marie said, and she sounded weary now. All the anger gone from her voice. Her face was so big and round and tanned, lined and worn from a lifetime of physical labor, and the deep wrinkles and rolls of flesh on her neck were fat and shiny with sweat. Her short brown hair was dry and dulled from the sun. She stood in such stark contrast to Jolene, who with her lean white arms and youthful, pretty face appeared so doll-like next to her. They might have been entirely different species of female.

Marie turned away from Jolene as if she could no longer stand the sight of her. For her part Jolene now looked truly shaken. She had more than met her match in Marie, and she knew it.

Really, I . . . Jolene began to say something, and I felt she was about to apologize, but she didn't. She just fell silent. It was as close as I'd ever heard her come to offering an apology to anyone. Ever. And in the end she just couldn't do it.

Come on outside for a minute, Verna, I want to talk to you, Marie said. And don't you even move a muscle while we're gone, she called back to Jolene without even bothering to turn and look at her.

I followed her outside, the anxiety boiling in me.

We stood in the shade of the barn, and she spoke quietly to me.

You know what could have happened in there, she said.

Yes, I know.

I know you know. Just as I know you tried to stop her. I heard what you said. And I also heard what she said about the horse. You're not a stupid girl. But I want you to promise me you won't take that arrogant little shit into my barn again. It's off-limits to you both for the rest of your stay. Understood?

I nodded. I had not been able to stop the tears, and they were now flowing. I was crying from shame. Shame and fear, and the feeling I had disappointed someone I loved and respected.

Something's wrong with that girl, Marie said. It doesn't take a genius to see it. I don't think she's right in the head.

I looked at my feet, and the tears, which were coming harder now, fell onto the tips of my boots. I didn't know what to say.

You're probably nervous as hell thinking I'm going to tell your parents about this. But I'm not. I've always despised snitches. I don't give a damn if you've started smoking. I tried a few stupid things like that when I was young. But it does bother me that you would associate with someone like her. Now stop your blubbering and wash up for dinner.

FAULKNER BELIEVED that human beings could never fully know their past, that the highest level of understanding remained fleeting and speculative. This was a profound and disturbing truth. "We dimly see people . . . performing their acts of passion and simple violence," he wrote. They were there, along with the letters from that forgotten chest, but so shadowy, he claimed, so inscrutable and serene, against that turgid background of a horrible and bloody mischancing of human affairs as to remain largely unreadable. In the coils and crucibles of memory, he wrote, we find only the cold ashes.

Mischance: a mishap or misfortune. What happened that day was certainly a mischance. It wasn't bloody, but it was horrible. Though Jolene and I continued to be friends, something changed between us after that experience in the barn. I could not rid myself of Marie's words: *Something's wrong with that girl.* We returned to our normal lives with our friendship slightly altered—so slightly that it was easy to pretend nothing was really different. Anything I might say about it after all these years would certainly remain fleeting and speculative, as Faulkner suggested, but I cannot help thinking that Jolene began to separate herself from me at that moment because she understood I had seen her at her most defeated, when the aggregate of her self had been pulled apart by a rustic old farm woman and she'd been left exposed to some truth she couldn't bear to face. What was that truth? I don't know. I wouldn't pretend to say. But I believe no one had ever made her feel so vulnerable before. Or so *seen.*

She never spoke to me about what had happened in the barn with Marie. And I never brought it up with her. The next day we rode home in silence, each of us, I'm sure, wondering what the other was thinking. Our huckleberry-picking outing had ended on a decidedly sour note.

It wasn't long after this time that the incident with Jeannie Wok-ersein had occurred, when we had held her down on the grass on Hal-loween night and, as Jolene would later put it to me, sexually attacked her. Of course I hadn't thought of it that way at the time. I considered it a childish prank. We had simply *goosed* her. That was the term we used for something that wasn't so uncommon, the sort of thing kids occasionally did as a joke. But our attack on Jeannie had been savage, in the sense that a trio of girls had set upon a classmate they didn't like and had actually injured her by bruising her genitals. Now I wonder, were those two *mischances* connected somehow? Had something brutish and rash been brought forward and found its way to the surface? When Marie had called her rotten, when she had referred to her as an arrogant little shit, had she set loose the furies inside Jolene that would propel her forward and cause her to act with even less inhibition or regard for what others thought?

ALL THIS happened during our junior year of high school, the year that Jolene's parents decided to send her away to the Catholic boarding school in Salt Lake City, in part as punishment for what had happened on Halloween night. We saw each other much less often after that, although when we did get together I could feel how the old affection we possessed for each other was still there. In some ways it became more intense because we'd saved our feelings up for the moment when we could be together again: it was as if the separation caused our attraction to become concentrated into a kind of emotional urgency.

And then we graduated, and she had gone away to college in the East, and I had gotten married, and we might never have seen each other again if I had not made that phone call the day that Leon left me. If I hadn't imagined that something better might await me in Los Angeles. Had I never shown up in Beverly Hills with my truck and horse trailer in tow, asking for that favor of a place to stay, I doubt very much she would have ever contacted me again. But that's not the way it turned out, or I would not be telling this story. And perhaps things would never have come to the mischancing end that they did.

11

The day I was to meet Jolene for lunch a turgid afternoon lay stalled over the city. I took my time dressing, finally choosing jeans and a black shirt, the simplest outfit I could think of. And then, responding to some nostalgic impulse, I found the black-and-white scarf with skulls on it that she had given me long ago and tied it the way she'd shown me. I was curious to know whether she would even notice this little nod to the past.

I arrived early at the restaurant and chose a table outside where a little patio area had been created next to the sidewalk. It was a bright day in spite of the thin layer of clouds skimming the sky. I wore sunglasses against the glare. There is a pressure on the eyes from the light in L.A. that one doesn't feel in other places, a little hallucinatory interval between the air and light and solid things, and over the years I had, like almost everyone else in the city, taken to wearing dark glasses as a means of dealing with the persistent glare. I was rarely without them now, though I often felt they had become less a protection than a way of cloaking oneself, for what would we be without our eyes for others to read? I was not averse to concealing myself on this particular day: I had to admit I felt nervous about seeing her again after all these years.

She was late. Ten, fifteen minutes passed and still she didn't show, and I began to think I had mistaken the time—perhaps even the day—that we were supposed to meet. The longer I waited, the more I felt things going wrong. The waiter threw me frequent glances, as if annoyed: people were waiting for tables, and a small line had formed not far from where I was sitting. More than once he asked if I

wanted anything, and I had to assure him I was fine, my friend should
be arriving soon, but my assurances hardly dented his disapproval.
I texted her to let her know I was at the restaurant, but there was
no response. Another ten minutes went by: she was now twenty-five
minutes late. I told myself I would give her five more minutes, and if
she hadn't shown up by then I would leave.

I FOUND plenty to look at while I waited, in the scenes unfolding
around me. The expensive cars navigating the traffic on Rodeo Drive
with music booming from open windows. The continuous parade of
locals and tourists. I took pleasure in observing the ladies of Beverly
Hills—not the plastic surgery freaks although there were plenty of
those, but the trim, pampered, handsome matrons who could afford
to outfit themselves in some of the world's most beautiful luxury
goods. Women for whom style and money had made an excellent
match, right down to their lovely shoes.

There was no shortage of vulgarity of course. The plump American girls in skimpy, garish clothing, out for a day of shopping on
Rodeo Drive, such a contrast to the Japanese tourist girls with their
understated taste and lithe little bodies. Celebrity tour buses rolled
by, their open upper decks filled with gawkers, and couples strolled
the street holding hands and grinning at the world as if it held nothing but good news. There were fluffed-up little dogs with rhinestone
collars and leashes. Men looking sartorial in red bow ties and pink
shirts. Couples with babies, and couples without babies. Babies wearing outsized sunglasses, looking like little arthropodal creatures. Girls
in long dresses, and girls in short ones. The families speaking Chinese,
the families speaking Farsi, and Spanish. Overweight women in tight
dresses and crippling high heels. The dyed blondes and the hennaed
ladies with gray roots and bald patches. All the pampered shopping
creatures. A German shepherd wearing sun goggles was being photographed on a nearby corner, and a couple in matching plaid shorts
had stopped to watch. The same couple who later stood hesitantly
before the glittering stores—Dolce & Gabbana, Chanel, Gucci—too
intimidated to enter such fabled places. Another tour bus rolled by,

this one promoting "Dearly Departed Tours: The Tragical Histories of Celebrities." Must be many of those, I thought, and such a beautiful day to be out trolling the dead.

I WAS about to stand up and leave, making my apologies to the waiter, when suddenly I saw her.

A car pulled up at the curb in front of the restaurant, and the driver, a slim woman with closely cropped hair, came around to the passenger side and held the door for her. Jolene emerged slowly, setting her feet carefully on the curb and rising with what appeared to be some effort. The young woman steadied her for a moment as they exchanged words. And then the woman got back in the car and left, and Jolene, having spotted me sitting outside, began to slowly make her way down the sidewalk toward me. She walked with a cane. When she was only a few feet away she said, Well, my god, it's awfully good to see you. And then she put her hand on the back of the chair facing me, and I could tell she was catching her breath.

Do you mind if we sit inside? she said. The light's a little much for me out here.

She turned abruptly, and I followed her into the restaurant, where she spoke briefly to the maître d', who showed us to a table that had just been vacated toward the back of the room. There was a moment when I might have hugged her in greeting, but she'd turned away, as if sensing this, and I remembered how she'd never been a hugger. Her attitude was businesslike as she stepped out ahead of me, leaving me to trail behind, feeling a tiny painful void inside where a gesture of affection had arisen and then abruptly died when she'd turned away.

Much better, she said, indicating the table that had been chosen for us, I'll sit here if you don't mind, and she took hold of the chair that faced away from the windows. All that light hurts my eyes these days.

I told her that was fine. It did not escape me that she hadn't bothered to apologize for being so late. No hug. No apology. Some things had not changed. And yet looking at her I felt that so much had.

Obviously she was not well.

It took her a while to remove her jacket and arrange it on the back of her chair, and she did all of this very slowly and deliberately, then she laid her cane on the floor and sat down and looked across the table at me.

That scarf becomes you, she said. Still.

I smiled. I wondered if you'd notice.

My eyesight, she said, is perhaps the one part of me that continues to function just fine. As you can see, I am—if not a shadow of my former self a poor reflection. A sort of hologram growing dimmer and dimmer. I remember the first hologram I ever saw. At Disneyland on a trip with some friends when we'd taken acid. All I remember is this wonderful display of a couple dancing through a ballroom. Everything life-sized, blue and ethereal, like in a dream. You could see through the figures, and yet they seemed so real. Little did I know I'd become that sort of figure.

I didn't know what to say to this. Of course I could tell something was wrong. I knew that the instant she emerged from the car. She was shockingly thin. She wore a gray cashmere hoodie, unzipped partway, and the bare expanse of chest above the line of her white T-shirt appeared sunken. Her breastbone stuck out, and the skin that stretched across it was pale and translucent. I could see the webbing of blue veins. On her head she wore a cashmere cap, a sort of stocking hat that hung down in back like a loose sock. It was gray and patterned with black spots, like a leopard print. There seemed to be so little flesh on her body. Her hands, her wrists. Her long fingers. So bony. Her face, too, was so thin that when she smiled the skin stretched like parchment over her jawbone.

And yet she was still beautiful. My immediate thought was that she looked like an actress from the 1930s. It was the hat that gave her that look of another era. Like an old-fashioned snood. And the large sunglasses that hid her eyes.

You're staring at me, she said.

It's just good to see you, I replied. It's been so long.

That it has, she said, opening the menu and again adopting a businesslike attitude. The first thing we're going to do is order a bottle of wine. If you don't mind I prefer white. I'm hoping for a long lunch, and the wine will make it easier.

She studied the wine list for some time and then called the waiter over and consulted with him and finally chose an expensive bottle of Sancerre.

Now I can ask you how you are, although I can see for myself that you're fine. A little heavier perhaps.

I laughed. There's not a woman in the world who would welcome that comment. But it's true. I am a bit fatter, aren't I?

And I'm thinner. But we won't discuss that now. No, not yet. There's so much else to talk about first.

When did you get back to L.A.? I asked.

January. I'd planned on coming back even earlier, but it didn't work out that way. Too much going on, she said, and shrugged.

I could see that she had lost her hair. The cap was pushed back far enough to reveal that there was nothing but a kind of pale fuzz covering her scalp.

The city has changed so much. That's what I can't get over, she said. I've been back a number of times over the years, but this time it's much more intense. It's like Randall Jarrell said: *Back in Los Angeles, we missed Los Angeles.* I feel I'm missing the city I knew, but then I doubt that place ever existed. There are so many more people and cars. But it's all the homeless I find shocking. They're fucking everywhere. That's really what's so different, the thing I'm most startled by. It's unbelievable, isn't it? How did this happen? You simply don't see it in Europe. Nowhere close to this extent. Tents lining the streets, people living in filth.

SHE EXPLAINED she'd been living in Paris for the last decade or so. She had married a Frenchman, an art collector whom she'd met at an opening, but she'd finally left him. She should have done it sooner, she said. It had gotten very messy toward the end. The men we choose say so much about what kind of women we are, don't they? She said she had really fallen for him, believed herself to finally be with the *right person* (she put air quotes around these words) and in the *right place* (more air quotes). But strong love disfigures you, doesn't it? She

said she had come away from the relationship disfigured in more ways
than one.

She launched off on a long explanation of what had gone wrong.
Her husband came from a very wealthy old French family who had
never accepted her. You can live for years in France, and no matter
how you try you'll never really be accepted by such people, she said.
They had humiliated her, over and over, with their coldness and rejection of her. But that was only the beginning. Her husband turned out
to have a nasty drug habit. Heroin. Cocaine. Pills. Whatever he could
find. He loved being high, not because it offered an escape from everyday life, as she had first thought, but because—as he had explained to
her—it made everyday life seem less everyday. When he was high, for
a brief while the world was splendid and unknown and exciting, and
when he wasn't he often took his unhappiness out on her. Of course
this made things very complicated. On the one hand she hated that he
got high all the time; on the other, he was so much nicer to her when
he did.

He ridiculed her for not learning to speak French better, and so
she began taking lessons. But she came home from these lessons with a
headache, even though over time her French improved greatly. Still he
spoke to his Jack Russell terrier more than he spoke to her, and always
in such rapid French that she couldn't understand what he was saying.
She began to believe he was talking to the dog about her. And the
more her French improved, the faster he spoke, making it ever more
difficult to understand what he was saying. It was a sort of gaslighting, don't you see, she said. She had gotten used to being happy and
unhappy at the same time, because even if her domestic life often felt
like a war zone, her work continued to get a lot of attention in Europe.
She found herself becoming much more famous in Europe than she'd
ever been in the States. She went around recognizing herself in an
idea that suggested general disintegration and, at the same time, new
composition.

Finally, after a number of years with Lucien—that was his name,
Lucien—she had realized the limitations of her marriage. The toxicity
of it—what is taken from you when you attempt to fit yourself into

such a relationship. It becomes horrible, she said. Still, she had come
to believe more and more in the virtues of passivity and of living a life
as unmarked by self-will as possible. One could make almost anything
happen if one tried hard enough, she said, but the trying, it seemed
to her, was almost always a sign that one was crossing the currents,
forcing events in a direction they did not really want to go. There was
a great difference, she said, between the things she wanted and the
things she could apparently have, especially when it came to relationships with men, and until she finally made her peace with that fact, she
had decided to want nothing at all. Sensing her retreat from him into a
kind of indifference, her husband had become ever more abusive—not
physically, of course, he was too refined for that. But emotionally he
brutalized her, and the gaslighting got worse. It was at this point she
remembered something that Faulkner once said, about how the heart
is a very tough and durable substance—however, when it came to his
tortured marriage he said he didn't have enough time left to spend it
like this. That was when she had decided to leave Lucien. She realized
she didn't have enough time to live that way any longer either.

The repeated failure of her relationships over the years had left her
convinced she wasn't cut out for the sort of commitment it takes to
make something work over the long haul. You think it's going to solve
so much, she said, when you fall in love, but really it's the beginning
of another set of problems, isn't it? Or maybe this hasn't been the case
for you?

I said nothing. No way was I going to reveal anything at this point
about my life with Vincent. And she seemed to understand this. She
changed subjects and returned to talking about L.A.

In any case I'm here now. Back in this non-city. I'm regarding the
change with a pleasurable apprehension. Flying in from New York,
there was a terrible blizzard when I left, and I realized there's something truly seductive about stepping off a plane in L.A. and feeling
the gorgeous quality of the air here, especially in winter, and experi-
encing this amazing light. No wonder half of the Midwest moved to
Southern California. But it is an odd place. You can't deny that. I think
of what Brecht said about this city.

I didn't know what Brecht said about L.A., and I didn't ask. Why encourage her to keep disparaging the city I had come to like? Which of course could only seem like a comedown after her time in Paris.

Brecht said L.A. doesn't give a shit. Yet he thought it was a much more interesting city than New York. An unpoetic city, not very cultural but very real. I think he was right.

No doubt, I said, and smiled at her, then added, I find it to be very real. I tried not to sound defensive as I said this but I knew that was what I was feeling.

THE WAITER brought the wine and poured it.

I took off my sunglasses and lifted my glass, and she did the same, and without attempting to say anything we toasted each other with our eyes. I felt a tremendous emotion in that moment, as we looked across the table at each other, and I believed she did too. We drank and held our silence. And then she spoke, breaking our connection, as if it were a lovely gown that had to be rapidly stepped out of in order to preserve it.

I must tell you something, she said looking away, at the risk of upsetting you. It's not something I feel I can keep from you. Or at least I don't want to.

I looked at her and shook my head, as if to say, *What is this about?* I felt apprehensive in terms of what might be coming.

I've been spying on you and Vincent, she said. It's nothing I intended to do. It happened quite accidentally.

She had returned to the city, as she mentioned, a few months ago. Her longtime assistant, Ina, who was from Germany and who had been with her now for many years, had come with her to L.A., and together they had rented a house in Silver Lake. She wanted to be near MacArthur Park. That was where she intended to stage her next performance piece, which she felt would be her final one.

She took another drink of wine and looked directly at me. Obviously, she said, you must have noticed that I'm sick. I'm living in the world of cancer.

———

THERE WAS no point in going into it, she said, all the stage-three stuff, and the stage-four, the rounds of chemo, the radiation, the relapse, the spread, a hasty emergency surgery—the terrible choices left to her. She had spent most of the last year in treatment. That was over now. There would be no more treatments after the final round of chemo that she was now receiving here in L.A., unless by chance she might qualify for an experimental immunotherapy trial. She was waiting to hear about that but she didn't have high hopes. She had adjusted her horizon line. What she wanted now, she said, was to look at art, see some people she really cared for, and visit a few landscapes that she had loved. And make one final performance piece, which she hoped could be staged in MacArthur Park within the next few months. She couldn't say much about it yet because she was still trying to figure it out, but she hoped to deal with the subject of war and what she called the bestial and imbecile rabble intent on fighting and promulgating what had become endless conflicts, taking their toll in country after country, killing children and ordinary citizens and causing such suffering. She knew it was crazy to try and address something so big, but why not? She had done it before with her "Meat" piece, and that had gotten a lot of attention. She wanted the new work to be her most political performance. She had chosen MacArthur Park for various reasons. There was the Jimmy Webb song, for one thing, such a part of her old art-school hippie days. A song so strange, so wonderful, and so cryptic. All the sweet green icing flowing down. The cake left out in the rain, when it took so long to bake it, and *I'll never have that recipe again*. You think the song is about lost love, she said, but it could as easily be the song for the end of the world as we know it.

There was another reason for choosing MacArthur Park, she said, and it had to do with General MacArthur himself. She'd been researching him. The great American warrior, and the great American blowhard. The brilliant general, and the bunco man. So emblematic of this country. There was a statue of him in the park—that's where she thought she would stage her performance, right in front of the statue of one of America's most famous warriors—

Wait a minute, I said, interrupting her. I was feeling annoyed. I know that statue, I said. I know it very well. I walk a lot in MacArthur Park. But tell me, Jolene—what does all this have to do with you *spying* on us? I find that very disturbing.

I'm coming to that, she said. Just hang on.

She and Ina, once they'd gotten settled, started going to MacArthur Park often, and they had done this now for over two months. Sometimes they took their lunch and ate in the park, and sometimes they went to Langer's Deli on Seventh Street, just across from the park, and ordered the amazing pastrami sandwiches, but the point was that several times a week, ever since arriving in the city, she'd gone to MacArthur Park. She just wanted to get a feel for it, see whether it could work for what she had in mind, and the more time she spent there the more she came to think it was the perfect place for her final performance. Also, in terms of how she felt, it helped to get out and sit in the sun. She had begun to feel better just being outdoors in such idyllic weather, relaxing on the benches overlooking the little lake with the spray erupting from the tall fountain in the middle. Feeding the ducks and seagulls and geese. Watching the Mexican kids play soccer on the big field on the north side of the park. Strolling around the water on the concrete path. Of course it was disturbing as well. The number of homeless people camped everywhere, even in the old bandshell. The garbage floating in the lake. The overflowing trash bins, the terrible smell. Even though the park was rather derelict and run-down, she liked it—in fact that was a big part of what she liked about it, how distressed it was, how it served the poor, the neglected, the newly arrived emigrants, many of whom had not only fled poverty but ongoing violence in their native lands. In spite of this decayed atmosphere, she had felt less depressed during her visits to the park than she had in a long time. Part of this, of course, was the excitement of thinking about the new work she wanted to make, trying to imagine how it would fit in a particular place near the statue of MacArthur—

And . . . the spying . . . ? I said, interrupting her again.

I'm getting to that, she replied, just be patient. She smiled at me. I did not smile back. She's enjoying this, I thought. She's testing me.

————

ONE DAY, she said, when she and Ina had been driving back to Silver Lake after an afternoon in the park they passed Carondelet, and she recalled that was the name of our street. Before moving back to the city she had asked around and discovered that we still lived in the same apartment I'd rented when I first came to L.A. She knew it was on this street. She even remembered the address from the few letters we'd exchanged over the years.

She said that when she saw the name of our street that day she'd abruptly and spontaneously asked Ina to turn and drive past our building. She said she just wanted to see where we lived. And that's when she'd spotted us.

You were outside, she said, in front of the building. Both of you, and that really caught me by surprise. I hadn't expected to actually *see* you, I thought we'd just drive by.

I told Ina to slow down as we crawled past. You were standing on the sidewalk, and Vincent was up on the hillside above you, doing something with a big "For Sale" sign. You weren't looking at me, and I realized I didn't want you to turn around and suddenly see me, it would feel too awkward, so I told Ina to drive up the street a bit and I asked her to park. I just wanted to keep watching you. I sat there and watched you for a long while. It seemed so strange, what you were doing. I couldn't figure it out. But then I realized you were taking the sign down. It took a long time for you to actually do that, and then Vincent came with the car and took the sign away and you went back up the steps and disappeared. What was most strange was simply seeing the two of you together. Knowing that you'd been married all these years. Before, it had been an abstract idea, the fact you two had gotten together, but now it became suddenly real. I'd never before seen you as a couple. How could I not want to stare at you as long as possible, especially knowing you wouldn't see me?

From that point on, she said, she and Ina had often taken Carondelet when heading home from the park, though Ina had objected to what she called her *naked voyeurism*. She had to admit she hoped she'd see us again. Ina was okay with driving past the apartment on the way home, but she had refused to *park and spy,* as she put it. It did not feel right to her.

Then Ina went back to Germany for two weeks, leaving her on her own. During this time, she began stopping on our street for a while whenever she visited the park, now that Ina wasn't around to judge her behavior. Not all the time, just now and then, she said. Occasionally she ate her lunch in her car, sitting across from our apartment building or wherever she could find parking on the street. Sometimes she sat there at the end of the day, just resting and thinking. Several times she had seen Vincent come down the steps and get in his car and drive away. She'd also seen him returning. But she had never seen me again.

EVERYTHING SHE was saying was so startling to me. It also rang true. She had seen us taking the sign down. Watched Vincent coming and going. I parked my car in our garage in the alley and rarely used the front steps. That's why she'd never seen me again.

You never thought of getting out of your car and speaking to Vincent? I said. Or just coming up the steps and visiting us?

I couldn't bring myself to speak to Vincent. It would be like ambushing him. To walk up to him unannounced on the street. How would I explain my being in his neighborhood? No, I could never do that. But one day I did talk myself into seeing if you were home. I decided to climb the steps and knock on your door and surprise you. But when I started up the steps I stopped. Up close, the place looked so run-down. It disturbed me. The cracked sidewalks and overgrown garden, the trash left out. The building looked almost uninhabited, and when I realized that the steps jogged left and I'd have to climb another set of stairs and go around to the back of the building to find your apartment—well, that's when I lost my nerve. I don't know why. I just didn't want to go any farther, and I turned around and went home.

That was the last time she had spied on us, she said. She never took our street again. She had talked about it with Ina when she came back from Europe, and she realized how skanky it was to spy on us. That was the word she used: *skanky.* An ugly word, I thought, for an ugly business.

Ina told me that she thought all art was a kind of voyeurism, she said, and wondered if that had figured into what I'd been doing while she was away. But I knew this wasn't about art. This was simply spying. Naked voyeurism, as she had rightly called it. If that was the case, Ina said she didn't think I should be doing that—parking on the street and watching for you and Vincent—that it amounted to a moral violation. Or at least an ethical lapse. That's when I stopped.

It was Ina who said I should write to you if I really wanted to see you and arrange a meeting. So that's what I did. But then I felt nervous. As you know, I canceled our first meeting. I was trying to understand what I'd done. Why I'd felt so compelled to sit there across from your building day after day. But I'll tell you why I spied on you because I finally figured it out. It was an act of love. I missed you. And I missed him. It felt like a safe way to see you two, after all these years, and discover what you looked like, what it meant for you to be together, how you were with each other. But it did give me the advantage. And I knew at some point I'd need to tell you what I'd done. To be fair.

THE WAITER had been angling for a moment when he could approach us, and during the silence that fell between us at that moment, he moved in and asked if we'd decided what we'd like. Jolene ordered a steak and pommes frites. I ordered a salade Niçoise. The waiter poured more wine and, sensing the tension at the table, quickly left.

I need protein, was all that Jolene said in the renewed quiet that followed his departure.

I WAS thinking about her spying on us. Why would she tell me about it? I didn't know what to say. She had seen us taking the sign down. Watched Vincent come and go. And all the time we'd never suspected she was even in the neighborhood.

Are you angry with me?

It does seem creepy you were watching us. I don't really know what to think of that. I could see doing it once, by accident. But *parking* across from our building? Intentionally *spying* on us? And then coming back and doing it *again*? And *again*? What should I think of that?

Don't think anything. Or if you must, think this: I'm jealous. Jealous of everyone at the moment. All that life spreading out before everybody, the fulsome futures. It's been hard to think of you and Vincent over the years. Of you two together. And I suppose I just couldn't refuse the desire to *look*. As I told you, whether you believe it or not—it was an act of *love*.

FOR REASONS I couldn't quite understand, I felt embarrassed by her confession, as if I had been the one to commit a violation. I felt hesitant to speak. Instead I gazed around the restaurant. It had been crowded when we first arrived, but now tables were beginning to empty and the room had grown quieter. The walls were covered with mirrors patterned with gold leaf. Bottles of rosé wine were lined up on shelves, and the pretty pink liquid caught the light from the heavy crystal chandeliers. A small vase of white roses sat on the table between us. Only now did I notice how the flowers had already started to turn, just a faint trace of rust at the edge of the petals. I continued to say nothing. I decided to let her fill the silence.

Are you angry with me? she asked.

I shrugged. I would say it's more complicated than that.

We fell silent again. She played with her wineglass, turning the base on its edge and rolling the wine around in the goblet while staring at the liquid.

Strange to be back, she said after a while, then lifted the glass and took a drink. I never felt at home in L.A., and it still feels like a cultural vacuum to me. A non-city, endless burg. I don't how it makes me feel. Out of my element, especially after Paris and New York, but still I'm glad to be here. Today I'm definitely feeling tired more than anything. I feel rather . . . dislocated, I guess. Uneasy in my body, uneasy in the world. But I've felt that way ever since leaving Paris. I felt at home in Europe in a way I've never felt at home here in this country.

———

SHE HAD been talking since we sat down, and she now looked quite exhausted. I felt that she must have needed to talk, and I didn't mind listening. I had become a good listener, thanks to Vincent. Somehow I could understand her spying on us. And I decided it didn't really bother me terribly much, especially since she'd been honest enough to confess. It only felt sad, that she would be driven to do this. She was sick, obviously very sick, and under the circumstances how could I blame her for anything? I didn't know how to tell her how sorry I was that she was so sick. I felt myself struggling to find the right words, but then she spoke up again.

Vincent looks wonderful, by the way, she said. He's aged very well.

You probably don't remember saying this to me many years ago, when I first came to L.A. and was staying with you in Beverly Hills, but you told me then that you thought that would be true. You said you felt Vincent was one of those men who would age very well.

Really? I don't remember saying that.

I didn't mention that during the same conversation she'd told me she'd never had very good sex with him.

Are you happy? she asked suddenly. Is that something I can ask?

I told her it had been a stressful time. I explained the situation with the apartment, how uncertain everything felt, how neither one of us really wished to move, and how the prospect of such a big change had turned our lives upside down for the last little while.

But why not just move on? she said. If you don't mind my saying so, that place where you live looks half abandoned already. It can't be a matter of money. Vincent's never had to worry about that.

But no more, I said. His family cut him off years ago. I thought you knew that.

No, I didn't.

He had an argument with his parents. I shrugged, as if to say, *Isn't that always the case?* They stopped speaking to him. When his father died not long after their falling-out, he discovered he'd been cut out of the will. This was maybe fifteen years ago. Since that time we've had to make our own money. Not easy to do, especially for Vincent, who'd never had to worry about that before.

But you've had success! And so has he.

Yes. No complaints. We've done all right. However, it's been a big help to have an apartment where the rent is low. I don't know how we could have done it without that once Vincent's family cut him off.

Funny, she said, but I think it's one of the things that drew us together, Vincent and I, the fact that we came from wealthy families who'd made their money doing things we deeply despised—strip-mining coal in his case, and manufacturing guns in mine.

It's what finally caused the break with his father, I said. Vincent grew more and more upset over the environmental consequences of what his father's company was doing. The disastrous effects of removing whole mountaintops, the degradation of streams, strip-mining on such a huge scale, the horrible damage it caused—all the stuff you hear about. It deeply upset him, and yet he didn't want to rock the boat, so he said nothing for a long time. We continued to take their money, because, you know, we needed it. It's not that easy to survive doing what we do. But then there was an accident at one of the mines, and a number of miners died. It turned out the mine had been cited several times for safety violations that had never been corrected. His father had intentionally failed to fix things in order to save money, and he'd lied about it. Anyway it resulted in a big lawsuit, and his father was taken to court. Vincent couldn't be supportive. For years he had been openly critical of the family business, but after the miners' deaths, well, that was the last straw. His father felt betrayed. If you don't like the way I make my money, he said, I'm not giving you any more.

I remember what an unpleasant man his father was—a real asshole, Jolene said, aggressive, rude, unprincipled. I knew he was morally corrupt the first time I met him. It doesn't surprise me he would act that way. But I'm sorry. It must have been very difficult for Vincent, who of course hates any sort of emotional scene, as you must know. I think that's why he put up with his parents' abusive behavior for so long. And look where that got him.

———

THE WAITER brought our food. Jolene began eating, slowly cutting her steak into small pieces and chewing carefully.

I can eat okay, I still have an appetite, she said. It's afterward that's the problem. The digestion. Everything was so badly damaged by the radiation, and then the surgery later didn't quite go as planned. My intestinal tract . . . She let her voice trail off.

I'm just so sorry, I said, about . . . the cancer.

It was a hard word for me to say, and as I spoke it I felt how terrible it sounded. A frightening, difficult word. I wished I could have put it another way. It always sounded like a death sentence falling out of my mouth to even utter that word. But it also felt foolish to avoid it.

Ah yes, the cancer. What a bitch. I think all the stress I went through with Lucien contributed to my becoming ill. But how could you know, she added, why anyone gets sick? She said she hated it when people tried to blame you for getting cancer. That was the killer.

I couldn't bring myself to ask her what kind of cancer she had— colon, stomach, liver? What difference did it make anyway? I felt she really didn't want to talk about it right then. So instead I asked about where she was living, exactly what part of Silver Lake, and we talked about that for a while as we ate. How the neighborhood had changed from what she remembered. The obscenely high rents in L.A. had shocked her, she said. Not even Paris seemed that expensive, though it was probably worse.

SHE ASKED if I was working on a new book, and she mentioned again how much she had liked my book on Raymond Chandler. I told her he had drawn my interest once more, that I was hoping to write a short book based on his wife's recipes, called *Cookbook for Idiots,* which was the title of the book he'd been working on when he died.

Cookbook for Idiots? she said, interrupting me. You think that's the book the world needs now? At this particular moment, in this age of planetary civil war and environmental disasters?

You make it sound perfectly idiotic, I said, laughing. And it probably is.

We really are in the end phase of something, you realize that. We are living in an era of hypercirculation of digital images that threaten to replace reality, in a culture ruled by kleptocrats and shitty rich people, with accelerating inequality, precarious employment and debt bondage, uncompensated labor, the trivialization of truth and the shaky evidentiary status of documents and images, where the prevalence of surveillance and the datafication of everything has erased all privacy, and permanent wars, lethal weather, and the slaughter of innocents have resulted in copious waves of refugees . . . not to mention the threat to humanity posed by artificial intelligence and some of the most despotic rulers the world has seen in many years . . . plus the planet is melting and we're on the verge of civilization collapsing . . . and you're turning your talents toward producing a cookbook for idiots? How perfect!

I wasn't going to be baited, though I did feel she was right.

You were always so much more serious than I was, I said, so I guess it makes sense that you're thinking about global civil war as a subject and I'm thinking about canapés with Vienna sausage.

Hysterical, she said, but she didn't laugh.

OVER COFFEE, she said, There's something I want you to do for me.

She let that statement hang there for a moment, and I thought, *Ah, what's coming now?*

It's not a small thing I'm going to ask, I must warn you.

I raised my eyebrows and tilted my head, as if to say, *Really? What is it?* But I stayed silent, wondering where she was going with this.

I want you to make a drive home to Utah with me. Of course you'd have to do most of the driving—actually *all* of it since I no longer even have a valid license. We don't have to be gone that long. I just want to go back one more time. And I want to drive through the western landscape again. To see it all once more.

Are your parents still alive? Is that why you want to go back?

No. Well, my father died some years ago. But if you can believe it, my mother is still around at ninety-three though she has Alzheimer's and is apparently quite gaga and lives in a sort of upscale care facility for people with dementia. She sold the house long ago to my cousin's daughter, Aimee. Still I'd like to see it again. I don't care so much about seeing my mother, though of course I will. I know that sounds brutal. But you know what our relationship was like. Also, she likely won't even recognize me. I just want to go home, and I can't fly right now. I can't face airports, my immune system is so vulnerable to crowds, and the air on those planes would kill me—I've decided that last flight I took from New York to L.A. would be my final plane trip. Besides, I want to drive through the West, not look at it from thirty thousand feet up in the air. You're the only person I could ask to do this favor for me. You're the only person it makes sense to do it with, because of our history with each other. It wouldn't be the same trip with Ina. I'd like to go home with you. It's been so many years since I've been back. And the time to do it is now.

She drained the last of her coffee and then spoke again.

Someone said to me not long ago, *A woman without love for her origins is lost.* And I realized—almost too late—that there's more affection there for my past than I thought.

I saw something in her face, a look forming—the already petrified distress the knowledge of her seemingly certain demise was causing her, how it was fighting its way from the inside, and she was trying to hold it back. Her countenance resembled a visual howl. I could feel the cry, *Please do this for me.*

Can I think about it? I said. It seems very possible it could work. But I need to talk it over with Vincent.

Ah, Vincent, she said, and there was a terrible sadness in her voice. I don't imagine he'd care to see me, would he?

Oh, I don't know, I said. You know Vincent. He really doesn't hold grudges.

No, he doesn't, does he? Still, I did walk out on him. I was unfaithful. I cheated. And then I left him. That's a lot to forgive.

He doesn't know I'm meeting you today. But of course I'll tell him. And I'll talk to him about the possibility of making the trip with you and let you know.

It has to happen soon, you understand that, I'm sure. I have one more round of chemo, but then I'll have a break so we can see where I am. I can't qualify for the experimental trial until the doctors are sure the chemo isn't working—but even with the chemo there's not much chance of remission. I can only hope to hold the line, stop the spread, until my bone marrow can't take it anymore. The first few days after treatment are hard. But by the third or fourth day I'm usually feeling better. What I'm saying is, we could leave next week. If that could work for you.

SHE LOOKED terribly tired, so I wasn't surprised when she suddenly said, I need to text Ina to come get me. She retrieved her purse and got out her phone. I'm at the end of my energy for the day, she added.

I could drive you home, I said, I'm going in the same direction.

It's all right. Ina's been waiting for me at the library. She'll come right away.

She stood up slowly and steadied herself with one hand on the back of her chair as she reached for her cane, and then she spoke, smiling at me.

Who was it who said that the only thing wrong with the present is the future?

I think that was Flaubert, I said.

Flaubert. Of course. It would be him. If I don't think about the future, well . . . I don't have to finish that sentence. Leaving the airport in Paris I saw a sign in the departing lounge, written in pink neon above the coffee bar. It said BE POSITIVE, BE ZEN, BE HAPPY. Isn't that fine? It really just about covers it. Except for those of us who've always thought happiness was overrated. Just another unrealistic expectation in a sea of manufactured human responses.

WE WALKED out into the harsh light of midafternoon. I put my sunglasses on, and she put on hers—the large round very dark glasses that stood out so starkly against her thin white face and gave her a somewhat glamorous aura. We stood together at the curb, looking up the street, waiting for Ina to arrive with the car. It was one of those awkward moments between things, when something seems over and yet you're left standing there, waiting for the actual end.

She turned to me and suddenly grew serious. What I want to say to you is how amazing—and how wonderful—I feel it is that you've done what you've done with your life. How you have made yourself into a writer—I would not have foreseen this.

It was Vincent, I said. He should get the credit, for giving me the love of books. Who knew they would stimulate my own appetite for telling stories? Without him I wouldn't have made this discovery.

We aggrandize the men in our lives to our own detriment, she said, and in doing so undercut our own accomplishments, and then she reached over and laid the back of her hand against my cheek. Her hand was so cold it shocked me.

Let me know about the trip, she said.

INA PULLED up to the curb just then and got out and came around to open the passenger door. Jolene briefly introduced her, and we shook hands and said we were pleased to meet each other. I could not help thinking of how she had seen me before, while spying on us, and I imagined she might be thinking of this as well. She helped Jolene into the car, and I noticed how gentle she was with her. As they pulled away Jolene pressed her long thin hand against the glass and mouthed the words *thank you.*

I waved goodbye.

And then I walked slowly back to my car in a parking lot a few blocks away, feeling such emotion. *She's dying,* I thought. That seemed clear. Having just found her again, my oldest childhood friend, I had to accept that I was bound to lose her to her illness. By the time I reached the car I had begun quietly weeping.

12

I said nothing to Vincent about my lunch with Jolene when I returned home that afternoon. He'd been absorbed with his work in any case. I found him sitting in his Eames chair with a score spread out before him on the hassock. He broke his concentration long enough to say hello when I walked in, but he showed no curiosity about where I'd been. This wasn't surprising. He often forgot to ask the kind of basic questions one might expect, secure as he was in his own engaging affairs. I believe his attitude was that I would tell him whatever he needed to know, but it often came off as a profound lack of curiosity about the most basic questions, such as "Where have you been?" or "What have you done today?" In any case there would have been no point in speaking to him about Jolene right then when his mind was elsewhere. I had come to understand the need to choose very carefully the moments when I could bring up something important with him. Even the smallest modicum of success depended on the right timing.

THAT NIGHT we sat in the living room and listened to a Thelonious Monk CD that he'd been playing over and over for several nights in a row, as he was wont to do with music he loved. I was waiting for the moment when it might feel right to bring up the subject of Jolene, and was about to speak when he stood up and started playing with Max, dangling a fake fur tail attached to a stick in front of him.

Oh look, Monkey, he said. Look what I have for you. He flipped the tail in the air, and Max jumped up after it. And then he flipped it again. This went on for some time—Max jumping and Vincent laughing and me sitting on the sofa, attempting to seem amused by the happy antics but really thinking about how free and fun-loving he was with cats, as opposed to humans.

When Max grew tired of the game Vincent sat back down, and I saw my chance.

There's something I need to tell you, I said. I had lunch with Jolene today.

Jolene? He looked confused.

She's moved back to the city.

He didn't say anything. He continued to stare at me. And wait.

I got a text from her a few weeks ago, saying she was back and asking if I'd meet her. I didn't mention it to you because I wanted to wait and see her first, to try and figure out what was going on.

I knew he wouldn't question why I hadn't told him beforehand that I was meeting her. He wouldn't care about this. He never bothered to cast blame or question why something had happened one way and not another. He was laser focused on the present, the immediate news that I had seen her, wondering what this meant.

She's living here now, you mean? Full time? In L.A.?

Yeah. In Silver Lake. In a house she's renting with her German assistant, Ina.

Wow, he said. And shook his head. And she plans on staying here?

Yes, I said. I think so.

Why did she come back? He asked this with a deeply puzzled look on his face. The kind of look he'd had when he said, *I wonder if my mother had this too.*

She's sick, Vincent. She has cancer. The prognosis isn't good, I don't think. I really don't know why she came back.

It seemed odd to me now that I hadn't asked her this question. It was so obvious, and yet it was the one thing I hadn't inquired about. Why L.A.? Why now?

She's getting another round of treatment here, I said. She's hoping to get into an experimental immunotherapy trial. Maybe that has something to do with it. But why she came back now I don't really know. She wants to do some kind of performance piece in MacArthur Park this summer. Maybe that's the main reason. She thinks it will be her final work. That's all I know.

Not in a million years would I have revealed to Vincent that she'd been spying on us. I knew how it would have upset him, and I didn't want to tip the scales against her. It was clear he felt agitated as it was, just knowing she was back.

I explained to him what she had told me that afternoon, about how she'd been living in Paris for a number of years, married to a wealthy Frenchman named Lucien, but her marriage had ended badly and she had moved back to New York, and that's where she'd been diagnosed with cancer and treated over the last year. I told him how thin she was, how fragile, how hard it had been to see her looking this way. Her eyes, I said, were what you noticed now. Her big dark eyes. How huge they seemed in proportion to the rest of her face. I told him she moved very slowly, gliding along in a kind of tentative shuffle, relying on a cane to steady her. She seemed to have very little energy.

He didn't say anything for a while and then he asked, What kind of cancer does she have?

I don't know. I didn't ask. Maybe colon. She has a hard time digesting food. That's why she's so thin.

He closed his eyes and tilted his head back. I waited for him to open his eyes again and come back to me, but he just sat there, eyes closed, as if he could shut out the bad news by simply lowering his eyelids and thus retreat into some deeply quiet inner space where nothing could touch him.

There's something else, I said. She's asked me to do something for her.

Now I had his attention. His head jerked up, and he opened his eyes and looked at me.

What? What did she ask you to do? He sounded alarmed.

Don't worry, Vincent. It has nothing to do with you. She asked if I would drive her back to Utah so she could go home one more time.

But why? She's never cared about where she came from. Why would she want to go back there now?

You'd have to ask her, I said.

I'm not asking her anything, he replied. There was an edge to his voice.

Does that mean you won't see her? She asked me about that. Whether I thought you'd care to see her.

I don't know, he said. Why ask me that now?

He looked almost pained, as if someone had requested he consider the unthinkable.

I can understand why it would be difficult for you to see her. On the other hand, it's been so many years, Vincent. And she's so sick.

Well, that's true, he said. I could see him softening, as if I had pulled the plug on his fear.

I know I don't need your permission to do the favor she's asked, but I wouldn't do it if it made you unhappy, I said.

No, it wouldn't make me unhappy. He lifted his glasses and pinched the bridge of his nose like he did when he was thinking about something. If she wants to do it, if it's important to her and you're okay with it, I guess you should do that for her . . . don't you think?

Yes, I said. That's exactly what I think.

When does she want to go?

Soon. Next week, after her last treatment.

He was calm now. The shock was over. I could see him adjusting to the facts I'd laid out before him, and I knew intuitively he still cared for her as much as I did. Maybe more, for all I knew. Just because someone breaks your heart doesn't mean you stop loving them. It was as Flaubert had said—our feelings never simply disappear. Every one of them is preserved. Every one. They become those mummies in your heart, which never fall into dust, but peer back at you with their open unmoving eyes whenever you glance down the long shaft that leads to their resting place.

I CALLED Jolene the next morning and told her the good news. I would make the trip with her. There were a few things to work out before we left, and we agreed to meet at her house the following day.

It turned out the house she had rented in Silver Lake was a place I knew from driving past it occasionally. I'd always admired this house. It was the sort of place I'd love to live in. Not grand, just beautiful. A lovely old Spanish revival, the walkway bordered by lavender gardens with orange and fig and grapefruit trees growing out front. It sat above the street, with a balcony that had a perfect view of the Hollywood sign and the Griffith Park Observatory.

She met me at the front door, wearing loose gray pants and a pink sweater. No cap today. The thin pale fuzz covering her scalp had the texture of boiled wool. She seemed brighter, more energetic than she had at the restaurant, perhaps because it was earlier in the day, and walked without needing a cane. I had brought a map with me and we sat at a table outside, on a little deck overlooking the garden, near a long narrow pool shaded by leafy plants, and I spread the map out before us. It was a map of the western states. I explained that I had made many driving trips to Utah with Vincent over the years. When we were first married we had gone there once or twice a year but after my parents died, passing within a few months of each other, we began going less often. Our last trip had been over five years ago, and we had not been back together since, although I had once flown home on my own for a cousin's funeral.

I told her there were a number of different routes one could take, but our favorite involved driving through rural Nevada, straight across the heart of the Great Basin, taking two-lane roads all the way and avoiding freeways. I described the beauty of the landscape, how wild it was, how unpopulated, a huge empty country where there were only a few towns separated by very long stretches of lonely roads.

That sounds just perfect! she said.

I traced the route for her with my finger, showing her how we'd head out to the desert town of Mojave, ninety miles from L.A., then cut north to Bishop, making our way along the eastern slope of the Sierras. I knew of a small café in Independence, owned by a Frenchman and his Algerian wife, where we could stop for a decent lunch. At Bishop we'd turn inland and cross into Nevada on Route 6 and spend the night in the old mining town of Tonopah. The Mizpah Hotel, built in the early 1900s, had been renovated and the rooms there were rather old-fashioned and charming given how rustic and remote the town was. In the morning we'd continue on to Ely, a three-hour drive through some of the most beautiful basin-and-range country. This was my favorite part of the drive, I told her. You hardly passed another car on this section of the road, and the land was so empty of inhabitants you could believe you were the first to see it. I often glimpsed wild horses in this area, and also antelope and deer and the occasional lone coyote. From Ely we'd continue north to Wells, a truck-stop and casino town known for its legal bordellos, and at Wells we'd turn east and drive across the Salt Flats to Salt Lake City. From there, as she knew, it would be only an hour or less until we were home.

The trip would take two days—two long days of driving. Maybe seven hours the first day, and nine the next. I hoped she could spend that much time in the car, though of course we could stop often and get out and stretch our legs. And there was no hurry. If we needed to take more time we could spend another night somewhere along the way. For me the important thing was that she should be comfortable. I'd see that we had a cooler and food for the road. Fruit and nuts. Some bread and cheese. And of course plenty of water. We'd recently had the car worked on, I said, and I felt confident we wouldn't have any problems.

She studied the map of the western states that I'd laid out before her and traced her finger along the route I had outlined in red. And then she looked up at me and smiled.

This looks so perfect, Verna. Absolutely right.

Good then, we're set.

What can I bring? Maybe some wine?

If you'd like. It's hard to get good wine on the road.

Yes, of course I can do that.

She hesitated for a moment and looked slightly troubled before asking, How did Vincent take the news I've come back to L.A.? Is he okay with us making this trip?

Yes, he's fine with it, I said.

And the fact I'm back?

It might take him some time to adjust to the idea that you'll be living here now—

Assuming I actually go on living, she said, and laughed.

All right, assuming that. But why not be optimistic?

You haven't changed. Always the optimistic one.

Actually, I think I have changed. A lot has become different over the years. But you're right. I still try to be positive, why not?

I told her I would be very surprised if Vincent didn't want to see her eventually. When we returned we could see about that.

Not before we leave?

No, not before we leave. That would not be a good idea. Better to give him some time, I said.

INA CAME outside then and brought us glasses of iced tea. She sat down and began asking questions about the trip, wanting to know more about the route, where we would stay, how long it would take us. She was interested in everything. She said she had always wanted to see the American West. She had an easy manner, and I found myself drawn to her—she was both open and reserved, a quietly sophisticated woman. So *European,* I thought. She wore no makeup. She didn't need it. Her skin radiated good health. Everything about her so unstudied and real. I could sense how close she and Jolene were.

After a while I said I should be going. We agreed that I would pick her up the following Sunday around nine o'clock.

Can I keep the map? Jolene asked. I just want to look at it.

Yes, of course. Just remember to bring it when you pack.

IN THE week that followed Vincent and I hardly discussed Jolene. She came up only in passing. He helped me prepare the car. Saw that the seats were arranged to allow her to lie back. She'll be able to rest better that way, he said. He didn't use her name. Not once. Whenever he did mention her, she became just *she.* He avoided talking about her except in relation to making travel arrangements.

He got out the cooler and cleaned it, made sure that we had flashlights and flares. Put two gallons of water where it would be easy to get at to refill our drinking bottles. He reminded me how to use the jack in case we had a flat. He was thorough, mechanical, businesslike in seeing that everything was ready. He became his super-serious self. This was done, I knew, out of love masquerading as strict concern.

I felt his complete lack of jealousy or envy over the fact I was making this trip with Jolene. He was untroubled by the idea we were heading off together. I tried to imagine myself in his place. Bidding him farewell as he took off on a long driving trip with my ex-husband, whom I had not seen in thirty years. But there was no correlation. His feelings were unique. They were not mine. They were less conspiratorial. Purer.

THE DAY before we were to leave, high winds struck the city. We did nothing for an entire afternoon but sit in the living room, quietly reading and listening to the ferocious sound of the wind. Inside a preternatural stillness, outside a shuddering and shaking world. From my place on the couch next to the window I could study the vigorously swaying treetops, sweeping wildly across a vivid sky of variegated blue. We said nothing to each other for long periods. Hours went by. The brass chime hanging from the eaves of the porch clanged urgently. The wind spoke in voluminous and violent gusts. New books had come in the mail that day, a collection of Chekhov's short stories for me, and a book on Mallarmé for him.

Do you think we could ever leave the city? I asked him later when we were sitting at twilight, having a drink.

For what?

Life in the country maybe?

No, he said, laughing. I don't think we could ever do that.

I knew he meant he thought he could never do that. But I knew I could.

HE WANTED to take me to dinner—somewhere nice, he said, on the last night before Jolene and I left on our journey. We chose a small, family-run Italian restaurant on Melrose where the food was simple and authentic, based on—if the owner was to be believed—his own mother's recipes. We came home from the restaurant and made love and lay in the candlelit darkness, not saying anything, just holding hands beneath the covers, our breath rising and falling in almost imperceptible union.

In the morning he stood in the alley with me as I finished packing the car. And then, when I was ready, he held me, but just for a few quick seconds.

Be careful, he said, as he released me.

I promised him I would.

13

I remember once, not long after we were married, sitting on the living room floor in the apartment reading the Sunday paper, wearing a green dress with yellow butterflies on it and no underwear, my knees raised up and making a little tent out of the fabric, while Vincent sat across from me in his Eames chair, alternating between looking at me and examining a new camera he'd just acquired. At one point he raised the camera up and took a picture of me, with my privates exposed, and also caught the expression on my face, which was one of pure complicity and trust. We have that picture still, in the box of slides we keep for ourselves. All those early pictures of us being in love. Really nothing happened on that gray afternoon in April. Except I opened myself up to him even more. I wanted him to look, and I wanted not to fear his looking. My wish, perhaps, to abandon bodily shame and throw off the prudery of my past.

Later, very much later, after she was gone from our lives, I brought up this picture he'd taken of me and told him how it had made me feel that day when he took it. I asked him, Do you think maybe that was what she felt when she made her art? That by exposing the most private parts of her body the way she did in her work she was casting off the shame of women, the shame of our bodies, our sex, instilled over many centuries, and he replied, Well, that may have been part of it, but I don't think it's the whole shebang.

The whole shebang.

The she-bang he spoke of that day, and the way he divided the word syllabically to give it a special emphasis—seemed appropriate to the discussion. But it really wasn't a discussion: it never had a chance to become that because, as with so many others things that caused him discomfort, he simply quit the idea, changed the subject, and thus gained the safe high ground of silence around a topic he didn't wish to discuss.

WHAT WAS it then, the whole *shebang* of her work? Now that she is gone I find myself thinking about this. What, in the end, did it mean? Why had she done it? Could anyone have predicted what happened? Perhaps. Perhaps I should have. She had given me plenty of clues during that long drive we took together.

AS IT turned out, we had to delay leaving on our trip by a day. The morning we were to set out, the garden in the front of the building caught fire. Some boys walking by on the sidewalk threw fireworks into the foliage, which had become very dry in the absence of the weekly visits from Luis, the gardener. The fire took off quickly, charred the bottoms of the palms and yucca and burnt the bougainvillea and lantana to the ground, leaving everything razed and blackened. The good news was the firemen were able to put out the fire before the flames burned farther up the hill and reached the building.

Still it was very disturbing, and I could not bring myself to drive away that morning, even once the fire was out. Vincent and I stood on the steps above the street and watched the firemen extinguish the last of the flames. The water from the fire hoses mixed with all the ash had turned into a thick black slurry on the sidewalk and stairs—a mess of sodden remains. The garden was gone. Nothing left but charred ground and blackened trees and plants.

We had not yet learned the cause of the fire, and as we stood there looking down at the devastation my first thought was that once again, as with the leaky gas line, a dangerous incident had occurred and I wondered if the fire could have been intentionally set in order to frighten us into moving. Vincent found this idea absurd. No one would intentionally set a fire that might burn down a building they were hoping to sell, he said.

Unless, I countered, they planned on destroying the building anyway to build something much bigger. Then it would make sense.

I think you're taking it too far, he said.

As it turned out, he was right. By the end of the day it had been confirmed that the boys with their firecrackers had started the fire. There was no grand scheme. No nefarious plot by Ingenious. I *had* been taking the thing too far. And yet nothing about that stance contradicted my general state of mind.

I texted Jolene and told her what had happened. She replied it would be fine to postpone our departure until the next day.

LATER THAT night I went outside and stood at the top of the steps looking down at the devastation. The same steps I had climbed thirty years earlier to rent the apartment were now an impassable mess of charred foliage and mud. Who would clean it up? There seemed to be no one taking care of things any longer. It gave me a strange feeling to see the garden in blackened ruins, as if this place where I had lived for so long was descending into darkened chaos. When I looked up at the building I saw there were no lights on in any of the windows in the apartments. There never were these days. The elderly tenants lived much of the time in their bedrooms, which faced the back of the building, leaving their living rooms dark. I knew that looking up at the apartments from the street not one light would have been visible. Was it any wonder the kids and the homeless hung out in the dark on the steps that were now rarely used?

I realized that out of all the people I'd known over the years who had lived here in this complex, none had really ever had any visitors. No friends or family stopping by. Not Lee, who played the piano at weddings and funerals and roamed his apartment naked, and not Hector, the retired nurse who limped now from bad feet. Not Shirley, the madwoman in the attic, nor the English couple the Beals—she who had managed the candy and cigarette concession at the old Bradbury Building, where he was the maintenance man—or Caroline, the retired phone company worker who had lived in one of the duplexes when I first moved in. She had eventually become so obese she stopped leaving her apartment, yet she was a kind woman, very sweet, and Vincent had taken pity on her and done her grocery shopping once a week for many years, patiently gathering the items on the list she scrawled in pencil: *bag of marshmallows, chocolate chip cookies, Pringle potato chips, ice cream, Cheez Whiz, freeze dried soups, 2 bananas, 2 yams, Tootsie Rolls.* . . . I had once given her a haircut, after she had no longer been able to raise her arms and brush her hair for a very long time and a great tangled oily mass had formed atop her head. One day I asked if she'd like me to help her by cutting it off, and she said yes, and with scissors I removed the thick matted nest, cutting it away in one piece and trimming off the stringy gray strands hanging down, and then I helped her stand at her bathroom sink while I washed her head, scrubbing away the dirt and scales. I gave you the Gertrude Stein haircut, I said to her afterward as she stood looking at her new self in the mirror, and though of course she didn't know who I meant, she smiled at herself and said, *It feels very nice, thank you.*

No one had ever visited Billy Ray, our sweet landlord whom we had liked so much, a flaneur who spent his days walking the city, or Harold, who had died alone in his apartment next door, leaving an extensive record collection of organ music. No one had ever visited Margaret, our elderly neighbor who had once worked as a cleaning lady in an office building downtown and who occasionally would treat herself to an overnight bus trip to Las Vegas to play the penny slots. A tiny, feisty woman, no more than four and a half feet tall with a small mousy face, Margaret seemed to have no friends at all, not even acquaintances, only a daughter who lived in Florida with whom she had quarreled long ago and from whom she remained estranged. For a while when I had first moved into the apartment, Margaret and I had taken very early morning walks together, always stopping at Maggie's Donuts across from the Big 6 Market for a coffee and a shared chocolate-glazed doughnut until something happened—I never knew what—and she stopped speaking to me.

No one ever visited Mark, the eccentric middle-aged bachelor doctor who worked at an urgent care facility and lived amidst terrible clutter, and who had moved into Caroline's old apartment after she died, or Justin, the youngest and newest of the tenants, a sweet gay man who taught fencing to children out in the Valley. No one visited Mike, the former plumber, who suffered from heart disease and now rarely left his apartment.

They had all been and still were solitary people. They lived such modest lives, surviving on very little money. Most of the tenants took buses because they didn't own a car and couldn't have afforded one. Some, like Margaret and Caroline, didn't have phones for the same reason. They hauled their groceries home from Jon's Market on Third Street in small bags, light enough so they could be carried on the Number 16 bus and up the steep alley. They did a little shopping every day, a little ritual that helped them pass the time in their solitary lives. They had tiny refrigerators in their diminutive kitchens, along with economy-sized stoves on which they cooked their modest meals, which they invariably ate alone. They were the sorts of nearly invisible urban dwellers who could easily be ignored by the city's more vigorous inhabitants—and for years they had been.

Somehow I had never considered this before—how isolated all of our neighbors had been over the years. How friendless, how without any social lives, how unusually *solitary* they had all been. Standing on the wide porch, with the cracked concrete balustrades and disintegrating wooden flower boxes, I looked out toward the cold blue lights of downtown, and it seemed to me the city itself was complicit in their isolation. What had Chandler said about L.A.? "Real cities have something else, some individual bony structure under the muck. L.A. has Hollywood and hates it. It ought to be grateful. Without that it would be a mail order city: everything in the catalogue you could get better some place else."

These people didn't have Hollywood, so why would they be grateful? Hollywood did nothing for them. They were forgotten, lonely people, sequestered in the shadowy lives they conducted in elderly seclusion. Their deaths, their illnesses, their wants and needs remained unseen, except by the occasional county health worker or the van driver who arrived to transport them to medical appointments. There was nothing remarkable about these lives. Nothing to distinguish them. Often not even one person to note their passing. When Margaret, at the age of ninety-one, had fallen on the concrete steps and I found her and called an ambulance, I couldn't locate any-one to notify except her estranged daughter in Florida, who had no interest in hearing anything about her mother once she learned there was no money to inherit. It fell to Vincent and me to locate a nursing home in West Hollywood that would take care of Margaret after she was released from the hospital. In the years before she died, we would visit her there occasionally. By then she had forgiven me for whatever transgression had caused her to stop speaking to me years earlier: we were the only people who ever stopped by to see her as she sat in her wheelchair, clutching her teddy bear and Bible.

I was overcome with a powerful feeling: we *must* leave this place, I thought, and we must do it soon, before it runs to complete ruin, before it depresses our lives even further and we somehow end up as estranged as everyone else. I resolved that when I returned from the trip with Jolene I would have a serious talk with Vincent. We had to find a new place to live, and we had to do it very very quickly.

I PICKED Jolene up the next morning, and we set out under a curdled gray sky. The freeway was slow going through Hollywood, yet once we reached Highway 14 we sailed along past Vasquez Rocks and the dry canyons where the gridded clumps of subdivisions spilled over the golden treeless hills.

She said little to begin with. Just looked out the window. I felt a relaxed silence fall between us whenever the conversation stopped, like when the furnace suddenly goes off in winter and you're fully aware of how quiet it has become. Such an abrupt silence can feel welcome, as if the natural stillness of the world has been reborn. Our pauses were like that. There was nothing disturbing about them. I was glad for this. We had a long way to go, and I was uncertain how this trip would unfold.

We stopped in Mojave at the local McDonald's and used the bath-room, getting to-go cups of coffee for the road. She really shouldn't be drinking coffee, she said, but what did it matter? In fact, she said, she'd like some French fries as well. French fries and black coffee: one of her favorite meals. She was going to eat whatever she wanted on this trip. She saw no reason to hold back. Except on sugar. Cancer loved sugar, she said. It was a good thing she'd never much cared for sweets.

Also, she said, I don't intend to stay in touch with people during our trip, except Ina if she needs to reach me. I brought my phone along, but I won't be checking it except for texts from her. I'd rather simply forget everything else for a while, if that's okay, so you needn't try to bring me any news of the world.

That's fine, I said. I actually prefer that as well.

And so we were agreed: We'd unplug for a while. Just the two of us. On the road, leaving the world to do what it wanted without us.

YOU HAD to get very far from L.A. before you really felt you were away from the engulfing footprint of the metropolis. I knew this from all the trips Vincent and I had made, driving this route to see my parents. Not until you left Mojave—a hundred miles from L.A.—and headed north on a two-lane road did you begin to feel you'd escaped the sense of being caught in the sprawling web of cities.

Then suddenly one left it all behind. The country opened up into a dry desert landscape dotted with Joshua trees—the tree that had gotten its name from the Mormon pioneers who thought its shape resembled a prophet raising his arms to heaven. On either side of the road the land stretched out, uninhabited, save for the occasional abandoned roadside café or derelict farmhouse.

Her thin pale fingers lifted the French fries delicately, one by one, from the cardboard container that sat between us, and she ate slowly, as if relishing each bite. She wore gray slacks and a red sweater—I remembered now that red had always been her favorite color. The same gray leopard print cashmere cap covered her head. Were it not for her thinness you wouldn't have believed she was sick. Except for the way her chest seemed to rise in a slightly labored way each time she took a breath.

We passed the turnoff for California City. The pale humps of distant hills began to appear on the left, the start of the Sierra Nevada mountains.

Maybe we could have some music, I said. I slipped a CD into the player. Bach began filling the car. Cantata no. 78.

It was a few minutes before I realized she had begun quietly crying.

Sorry, but could you put on something else, please, she said.

Maybe you could look through the box of CDs, I suggested. Anything you'd like?

She picked out a recording of Turkish folk music that Vincent had bought in Istanbul when he took me there for my sixtieth birthday. The lively music sounded jarring, excessively loud. But she soon turned it down so she could speak.

I'm not going to dwell on this, she said, in fact we don't need to talk about it again, but I was told after my most recent scan last week that the chemo seems to be working—only in the sense that it's holding the line. The cancer isn't spreading. For the first time my doctor actually had something to smile about. He said with continuing chemo it's possible I could have two or three more years. It's remarkable how two or three years can sound so expansive when as recently as last year the thought would have distressed me mightily. I was informed in January that given my recurrence things could go very fast, and I knew there was no way of knowing how much time I had left. So last week, after talking to my doctor and hearing the good news that I might have two, even three more years, my horizon suddenly moved again, and with the hope for breaks from chemo I'm delighted to think of the books I can still read, the visits with friends, nature to experience, paintings to relish. I don't believe I'll make any more significant work beyond this last piece I'm planning, but I feel suddenly my life is rich again. I'm allowing myself the guilty pleasure of enjoying more than one glass of wine, wearing my Missoni, making modest plans for the future. I want you to know all this so you understand where I am with my illness. I feel now that I haven't drawn the shortest of straws after all. In any case, when we return to L.A., I'll have a break from the chemo to see how things go. For now, I can't tell you how wonder-

ful it feels to be out here, driving through the world with you. And
now that I've said this, we don't have to discuss my health again. And
you don't need to say anything.

Okay, I said.

Not even okay.

Okay, I said, and we laughed.

The news that she might have more time made me happy, and I
told her so, and then added, but I'll say no more. That's it.

That's it?

Yes, definitely, that's it . . . for now, at least.

You're sure?

Yes, I'm absolutely sure.

You better be, she said with mock sternness. I don't want to hear
another word from you about it.

THE ROAD began to climb, and the landscape ahead of us narrowed:
we entered a canyon with red rock walls. The rocks were pleated and
folded, layered into stunning forms, slanted and running horizontally
in beautiful patterns. The color changed from red to pink, purple,
and mauve, seams and striations of marvelous hues blazing from the
canyon walls. Amazing, she said, gazing out the window. Just look at
that.

A lake appeared on the right-hand side of the road. Ducks were
floating on the water, and the wind caused the surface to run with
ripples. She grew tired of the Turkish folk music and switched to the
radio. A man was speaking, telling a story about a village in Japan,
just north of Tokyo, where he had once been posted as a soldier. When
the Americans troops entered the town at the end of World War II
they had forced all the people to come out of their houses and kneel
down. They were ordered to first take their clothes off, and then kneel
down and turn around and watch as their houses were burned to the
ground. The man said, This is not a story most Americans have heard.
I am not proud of what we did. It's haunted me all my life, the sight
of the villagers naked, kneeling in the snow and shivering, watching
their houses burn. Their faces were so stoic, not one person cried. I

don't know why we forced them to take their clothes off. It was so cold outside. I guess we wanted to just make them feel even more miserable.

She turned the radio off.

I can't bear it, she said. Flaubert was right. What an awful thing life is. It's like soup with lots of hairs floating on the surface. You have to eat it anyway.

Some lives are harder than others, I said. Mine has been okay. The soup hasn't been so unpleasing.

But what do you do about all the terrible things human beings are doing to one another? All these shitty little proxy wars. The poverty and violence. Racism. The crazy-ass leaders now running things? How do you accept this?

I said I tended to agree with Nabokov, who said writers should occupy themselves only with their own meaningless, innocent intoxications. *I am writing my novel,* he said, *I do not read the papers.* I know it's chicken of me, I added, but I often simply don't read the papers. Or watch the news. We tend to avoid it much of the time.

Well, she said, that's one way to bear it I suppose. But I don't approve. Artists and writers must remain engaged. It's no use just switching things off.

You were the one who just turned the radio off, I said, poking her arm gently.

She shook her head and rolled her eyes. Okay, okay. Touché.

Look how quickly I let the world leak in, she added, even when I don't want it to.

SHE ASKED me how long it had been since I'd been home, and by "home," of course, she meant the town where we'd been raised.

I mentioned it had been several years. My cousin Joan had died, and I'd gone back for her funeral. I said that over the years it seemed as if with each trip home I had encountered fresh losses, new agonies among the aging members of my clan. My father had died of heart failure after a long illness, my mother from the same malady not long after. My oldest brother had succumbed to cancer. Cousins and uncles and aunts had suffered debilitating problems, and inevitably they appeared further diminished with each successive visit. Yet everyone always appeared so pleased to see me and welcomed me as if my visit was a happy event for them. Still, it seemed that the cheerful and kind greetings I was met with were always tinged with the accounts of diabetes and heart-valve replacements, cataracts, hysterectomies, prostate troubles—an endless litany of ailments. It had been difficult to go back for Joan's funeral because her death occurred in winter and I had to make the trip alone. Vincent hated the cold and never liked Utah in the winter. Maybe left over from his feelings about all those bad experiences of winters in Switzerland. I had always loved winters— the landscape after a snowfall turned to a lunar stillness. But he said he sensed a *satanic stillness* in such a buried, icebound world. The little houses lining the frozen streets. The stoves and furnaces blowing heat and smoke, the stuffy rooms redolent of a long winter entrapment. Dwellings that felt to him as if they were waiting for a doom that would cover them silently in the night. He was loath to return. So I had gone to Joan's funeral alone. Of course I had flown.

Ah, Vincent, she said. So strange how rigid he always was— probably still is. I can't see him changing. During our years together he would only do what he felt like doing, no matter what you might want. Is he still this way? He was so *intractable*. So set in his ways. It used to drive me crazy.

I was afraid she was going to say more and our conversation would now turn to Vincent, and I didn't want that. I hadn't meant to tell such a revealing story—all she had asked was, when had I last been home? Why had I even mentioned him?

She said she couldn't really blame him for not wanting to go home with me. Such a conservative place, she said, filled with such provincial people. How had we survived our years there in that town? she asked. How had we done that?

There was one other question she had for me: Had I perhaps seen Jeannie Wokersein during any of my visits?

I said I hadn't. I didn't know if she even lived there anymore.

She seemed to mull this information over quietly, and said nothing more.

———

AT OLANCHA I stopped at the Ranchhouse Cafe to give her a chance to get out and stretch her legs. She emerged from the passenger seat very slowly, taking her time, cautiously standing up by clasping the door and steadying herself. I wondered if she might want to walk around a bit. Stretch her legs. But she said no, she didn't. She stood for just a moment, holding on to the car door and looking around at the old ranch implements scattered around outside the café. There was a cool wind blowing through the big cottonwoods at the far edge of the parking lot. Small American flags had been attached to each picket on the low fence. Dozens of little flags flapping in the stiff wind, making a loud snapping noise.

So patriotic, she said, looking at them. A bunch of faded little cheap flags. I guess that's how you tell the real Americans from the rest of us. What is this place anyway?

She looked tired and sounded cranky. We'd only been on the road a few hours, and I wondered how she could possibly endure eight hundred more miles of driving—and how I could endure them with her. My concern must have shown because she looked at me and said, Don't imagine I'm going to drop dead. I look weaker than I feel. And I'll try not to be so surly.

WE PUSHED on. She laid the seat back and closed her eyes. The Sierras now loomed on our left, the high basins between the tall peaks still covered with deep snow even this late in the spring. To the east the sky was a vivid blue against low colorless hills. A white dust arose from the dry lake bed. Toxic alkali blowing up on the wind. There were black shadows on the pale hills from the clouds overhead. We passed irrigation canals full with spring runoff, the banks lined with mauve and purple and chartreuse willows. Black crows settled on the roadside, their wings shellacked with sunlight.

She began speaking without opening her eyes.

Do you know the story of how I met Vincent?

I knew this was coming. That there would inevitably be that

moment when she would want to discuss him. I dreaded this, yet I didn't see how I could ask her to quit the subject without appearing to be afraid of her past with him, and so I said nonchalantly, Yes I know. He told me how you met at a park in Brooklyn at some art event.

I didn't mention the part about her wearing black leather on a hot day and the dangerous-looking boots with spiked studs.

He was so good-looking in those days, she said, not that he isn't now. I went after him. I don't think he really wanted a girlfriend, but he knew it was expected of him and that sooner or later he'd hook up with somebody and I think his attitude was, why not her?

She hesitated a moment to see if I was going to say anything, and when I didn't she went on.

Not long after we met he invited me to his apartment for dinner. I found that charming. I mean, that he wanted to cook for me rather than take me out, because he didn't seem at all domestic. It took me a long time to find his place, it was in a part of Brooklyn I'd never been to before. I climbed the steps and knocked on the door, and he immediately opened it as if he'd been standing just inside waiting for me. I walked into a room that was so sparsely furnished it looked like a monk's cell. There was one chair—a leather Eames chair and an ottoman—and that was it. There was nothing on the walls. Everything was white. A small pleated paper lamp stood in a corner. The chair, the lamp, the white walls—nothing else. Please come in, he said in that formal way he has of speaking, and he pointed to his one chair and added, Have a seat and I'll get us some wine.

I sat in the Eames chair and he sat on the hassock, and we talked for a while and drank a glass of wine—very good wine, by the way, he's always been able to judge a bottle—and then we went into the kitchen and he served dinner. He'd made some sort of eggplant dish, I remember, and rice and a salad—even then he was a vegetarian. The more I talked to him over dinner, the more I realized how well read he was. Much better read than I was, and in such a wide variety of subjects—not just his field of music, but art and philosophy and literature. He knew more about art history than I did. He seemed to me one of the most intelligent and erudite men I'd ever met—and also in some strange way the most serious. A combination of brainy eccentric and polymath musician. There was a gravitas to him that made him seem older than the other guys I'd dated during those days. The kitchen was just as spare as the living room, and after a while I asked him, Don't you have any books? Because he was obviously so literate, and yet there wasn't a book in sight. Oh yes, he said, and stood up and opened the built-in kitchen drawers and showed me how they were filled with hardcovers. You keep your books in drawers? I said. Oh yes, he replied, it keeps the dust off them. Later—not that night but when we'd begun sleeping together—I saw his bedroom. It was just as spare as the rest of the apartment. There was a futon that he could fold up during the day. A low set of drawers. A small desk where he worked. Again, nothing on the walls. It all felt rather Japanese to me. When I looked in his closet I saw that he had just a few shirts, all black linen with Nehru collars, and maybe two or three pairs of pants. That was his entire wardrobe! Five or six things. And yet when I looked at the labels I realized the shirts had been made for him by a tailor on Fifth Avenue. In those days he used to wear round tortoiseshell glasses and his hair was jet black, and he looked great in his custom-made black Nehru shirts. He looked so perfect in his clothes and glasses, everything so elegant and neat. He's always been one of those men who wear clothes very well. In those days he had this habit of smoothing one eyebrow with his pinky finger when he was listening to you speak. That gesture looked so *highbrow* to me, like something an aristocratic person would do. When one of my friends first met him she said, Oh, he seems so much more European than American. And I thought, *She's right*. It made him even more attractive to me. Maybe it was all that time he'd spent in Switzerland. Or those stiff manners he'd acquired at boarding school.

SHE HAD been telling this story with her eyes closed, reclined in her seat, but now she flipped a lever and sat up and looked at me. She was laughing.

Still, I'd never met anyone like him, she said, shaking her head.

I stared straight ahead at the road and said nothing. I could feel the blood pulsing in my back resting against the seat, my heart rhythmic and loud and running fast.

She went on, seemingly unaware she might be causing me discomfort. Not just rousing jealousy but protectiveness. A proprietary feeling, perhaps? I didn't want her to know him better than I did, to have known him *way back when* . . . but then she said something that threw me off this line of thinking.

The problem was, she said, the more I got to know him the less I felt I knew him. In his case familiarity didn't breed contempt, as the old saying goes, it just bred puzzlement. He would fixate on the oddest things, and yet he seemed to think it was perfectly normal. There was a tree he loved, for instance, growing in his neighborhood. It was a nice tree, I mean, a really beautiful tree actually, though I don't even know what kind it was, but every time we would pass that tree on a walk he would grow eager with anticipation and then say, There it is, and he would slow down and stand in front of it and admire it for a while. It was so predictable, so repetitive. It started to drive me crazy, and I began making sarcastic comments in response. I'd say things like, Yes, wow, imagine that, it's still there. But he didn't get sarcasm at all. He thought I was serious, and he'd say, Yes, wonderful, still there.

SHE LAUGHED. I gazed at the gigantic RV just ahead of us with the words *Leisure Seeker* written across the back, wondering if it was safe to pass. I didn't like the way it blocked my view of the road. I wanted to get by it, but I couldn't see the oncoming traffic clearly. I must have been scowling because she said, You look upset. You don't mind me talking about Vincent, do you?

Would it matter if I did?

You shouldn't mind. After all you're the one who ended up with him while I felt the loss for a very long time, even though it was my decision to leave him. Later I felt that was the biggest mistake of my life. It was the moment things became chaotic. I don't feel that way anymore, all these years later. But it was a shock when I learned from friends that he'd begun seeing you a few months after I left. And that later you two had gotten married. That really felt like a betrayal.

It wasn't—

Of course it wasn't. I was the one who had the affair, who was unfaithful to him and ended up leaving. And yet it was still very difficult to think of the two of you together. To tell you the truth, to this day I can't quite picture it. How two such different people could have fallen in love and made a life together. But you *are* happy, aren't you? And he is too?

Well, you would have to ask him to get a truthful answer, I mean in terms of how he feels. But yes, I have been happy, at least for the most part. He changed my life.

He's such an odd mixture of qualities and quirks and behaviors though, isn't he? I was never really able to understand him.

I wanted to change the subject, and I saw my opportunity. I asked her if she was hungry and told her the small town of Independence was coming up and I knew of a good place there to have lunch, and she agreed she'd like to stop.

THE STILL LIFE CAFE got its name from the dozens of little paintings that covered the walls, some rather crude, some more accomplished, all hung side by side salon-style in two small rooms. It was a charming spot where Vincent and I had often stopped—not only did we like the food, but the owner, Michel, always had good jazz playing and he offered nice wines. Michel greeted us and gave us a table in the corner. When Jolene heard his accent she began speaking to him in French, and in no time she had charmed him. Soon they were laughing together, about what I didn't know.

He went away and came back with two glasses of wine, and after he recited the daily specials we ordered the same thing, the coq au vin. When he'd left I asked her what they'd been laughing about and she said, I was complimenting him on his choice of music, and he quoted John Cage to me, saying, "The function of music is to sober and quiet the mind." How incredible to find someone who can speak French *and* quote John Cage in such a remote place. *To quiet and sober the mind.* Isn't that wonderful?

I wanted to tell her it really wasn't so remote but on a busy highway used daily by thousands of Angelenos heading north to the ski resorts and hiking trails in the Sierra Nevada mountains, but of course it must have seemed like a complete backwater to her.

SHE BEGAN talking about her time in Paris and once more brought up Lucien.

How did I make such a mistake? she said. That a woman like me, in the fullness of her career and at the height of her creativity, would be consumed by a mad love and allow herself to be transformed from happy to furious? I mean, I wasn't blind. I wasn't twenty years old. And yet what can I say? The need for love is the central experience of our existence. It's true of all humans. We drag this feeling around with us day and night, everywhere we go. I used to joke that I married him for his apartment, and I'm ashamed to admit it was partially true. I was seduced by the glamour. I have to confess my cupidity got the best of me. Still you should have seen that apartment! Out of another era. The dinners we had were amazing. He knew everyone, the most interesting people—and of course some of these people had collected my work, which was very flattering—but mostly he liked to socialize with the old monied people from families like his, who of course thought all Americans were barbarians, me included. And do you know what—they were right. We *are* a crass lot. Always so preoccupied with money and consumption—and always *talking* about it, which is the worst part. I knew it wasn't going to work out with Lucien long before I admitted it to myself. I had to wait until love had disfigured me, until I felt eviscerated emotionally and psychologically before I could leave, and then of course it was too late. I found out I was sick, and it didn't surprise me. With Lucien I finally awoke to my masochistic sexuality and learned a hard truth, that I am a small fallible container for a primary force beyond my understanding. And I had chosen a sadist for a companion. Like a key fitting a lock, we were a perfect match.

She took a sip of her wine and shook her head. It occurs to me that, in remembering things this way, I'm attempting to orchestrate lies, strictly speaking, in order to tell the truth. It sounds so wretched, doesn't it? I often tell wretched stories and I wonder why. I assume the outside description of a life can somehow capture the inner reality when all we do is create narratives about how, and not so much *why*, things have happened to us the way they have. The stories of our lives are always performances. I keep thinking of Nietzsche, who took for his motto a phrase of Pindar's: *Become what you are*. I think this has been the thrust of my whole life, an attempt to discover who I was. Who I am. It was at college I felt I found the answer. I am a radical feminist performance artist who has never given up painting. But the more I thought about Nietzsche I wondered, what did he mean? How did you *become* what you already *are*? You know what I mean?

Yes, I suppose, I said.

I'm boring you, aren't I?

No, you're not.

I'm talking too much.

I'm listening, believe me.

I really don't mean to go on about myself. I've gotten worse since I've had to contemplate the ending. I'm often racked now by contradictory feelings, imaginary slights, old wounds erupting in fresh anguished feeling, the miscellaneous crowd of things in the head, the debris in the muddy waters of the brain, the feeling I'm always verging on being offensive or bathetic. I'll stop now. And just in time, here comes Monsieur with the food.

SHE ATE as if she hadn't really eaten in a long while. Oh my god this is good, she kept saying, mopping up the juices from the coq au vin with bread. Every time Michel appeared they gabbled on in French, and I stared at my plate or smiled abstractedly, at nothing in particular. I was happy for her because she seemed so energized. It was as if being able to speak French for a while with an actual Frenchman, even if he was only the owner of a modest café on a backwater highway, had given a great lift to her spirits.

When we left, Michel kissed us and made Jolene promise to return, and in her most droll voice she said, this time in English so I'd catch her meaning, I'd *die* to come back here.

All I have done, she said, when we were once more back on the road, is talk about myself this whole damned morning. Now I'm going to shut up and rest.

She leaned her seat back and drifted off almost immediately. I could tell by the way her body went suddenly slack that she had fallen asleep.

I HAD felt the sting of jealousy when she'd talked the way she had about Vincent but also been fascinated by what she had to say. Of course he had puzzled her, as he had me for so long, and yet I knew I would never tell her what I had discovered. It would feel too much like a betrayal to reveal what I knew without his consent, and especially to her. I also couldn't deny that keeping this secret gave me something she would never have, and that is an understanding of him she could not possess.

It called to mind something I had read that Elizabeth Hardwick said about Robert Lowell, to whom she had been married for over twenty years until he left her for another woman. Hardwick had certainly suffered in the marriage, she'd been the one who'd had to deal daily with Lowell's severe manic depression and multiple hospitalizations, and also with the affairs he inevitably got caught up in as the bouts of mania came on. And yet she had later written, long after he'd left her, of the rewards she felt that had come from her relationship with him: *I knew the possibility of his illness when I married him, and I have always felt that the joy of his "normal" periods, the lovely time we had, all I've learned from him, the immeasurable things I've derived from our marriage made up for the bad periods. I consider it a gain of the most precious kind.*

The immeasurable things I've derived . . . all I have learned from him. Vincent had also been a gain of the most precious kind. Perhaps

Jolene had realized something similar after she'd left him and that's why she'd admitted to feeling such a deep loss. I knew that by revealing this to me she had made herself more vulnerable, and of course she must have understood this as well.

SHE SLEPT through the next little town we passed, and the one after that. She didn't even wake when I stopped in Bishop to gas up. Her face in sleep looked rather morbid, but it was only her thinness and the pale ashy color of her skin and the way her mouth fell slightly open that gave this effect. I had the feeling she was now lost to me, and in the best way.

Just north of Bishop I turned onto the two-lane highway that led into Nevada, and we began climbing up a steady grade, rising higher above the valley floor with the tall gray mountains looming on the right.

It was the moment I knew I was finally leaving California behind, not just the vast reticular cities that bled one into another, spreading their tentacles out so far, but any human domination of the landscape. The emptiness of the Great Basin began to announce itself—the openness, the grandeur and solitude of the huge bowled spaces separated by the towering mountain ranges. This was a world to which I felt intimately connected, and I could sense a feeling of the sublime entering me, offering a rush of happiness.

WHEN I was young I often used to wake before dawn and sit outside in my pajamas in a treehouse my father had built in the backyard and wait for the night to change to day. I loved witnessing the way the morning light came on all soft and liquid, reflecting off the lake. The night rolling back in a great upthrusting, a warm luminous glow issuing from an invisible side of the world. Later on, when I worked for a while as a wrangler on a dude ranch, part of my job was gathering up the horses from the big pasture where they had been turned out at night. I'd set out on my horse before dawn, while it was still dark, riding up the steep slopes and into ravines, gathering the horses one by one until I had formed a herd I could drive back to the barn just as the sun began to come up. To see the dawn break that way, day after day. To watch the sun rise from the back of a horse while riding over the hills. Unforgettable.

I thought of these mornings now as I looked out the window. I sensed the whole of nature, and it seemed kindly and pensive on this calm afternoon. I was flooded with a great love for the land, a sense of return to the landscape that meant so much to me and for which I felt such deep affection. I wanted to call Vincent, and yet I knew I wouldn't. I'd wait until later when I was alone in my hotel room.

WE PASSED over the Nevada state line and continued to climb until we crested Montgomery Summit and came to the burned remnants of an old casino and the adjacent motel, a cluster of decaying structures. I pulled over, thinking I would slip out and quietly relieve myself in a stand of trees, but as soon as I'd stopped the car she woke up.

Where are we? she said.

Nevada. I just need to stop and pee.

Ah, she said, me too.

We walked up a dirt trail a little ways and entered a thicket of cedars and relieved ourselves, squatting some distance away from each other, and then we strode slowly back to the derelict motel, which had graffiti painted on the side that said BUCK RELOVES LUCINDA.

Ha! Jolene said when she saw it. Isn't that rather unlikely, to relove someone? Or am I just kidding myself?

I shrugged, thinking I might quote Flaubert to her about the mummies in our hearts that never disappear, but I quickly gave up on that idea.

Instead I told her about the burnt-down building and old motel we'd parked in front of, how it had once been a casino and bordello. The abandoned motel was where the prostitutes had taken their customers. Prostitution was legal in Nevada, and there were a number of these little bordellos on the two-lane roads that wound through rural areas. Most of the business came from long-distance truckers. Once Vincent and I had stopped at one of the abandoned places and walked through the rooms—a very creepy experience. Old plastic hot tubs, purple shag carpet climbing up the walls beneath mirrored ceilings. A deflated waterbed. You wondered how women could do it, I said, become prostitutes and allow themselves to be used that way, and in such depressing surroundings with such a gnarly clientele.

They do it because they are poor, she said, or addicted, or uneducated and abused, or because they have otherwise been shafted by an unhappy life and don't see alternatives. And who knows, some might even enjoy sex work. We want to blame them, ask how they could possibly make such a bad choice. But what about the men who use them? Who take advantage of their poverty, their addiction, their abuse? You shouldn't wonder how the women can do it, or why they might choose such a life. Because it really isn't a big mystery. And in any case, they have the right to use their bodies any way they wish.

And by the way, she added, you shouldn't really call them *prostitutes*. They prefer the term *sex workers*.

I FELT slightly rebuked and chose not to say anything. Instead I got out an orange and peeled it, and we sat in the car sharing it with a bright breeze blowing through the windows. Jolene began speaking, picking up the subject again.

The thing about *prostitution,* she said, staring out at the derelict motel, is the word is derived from the same Greek root as *exhibition*. I explored this in a piece I did a few years back at the Venice Biennale. I hired twelve sex workers to greet people and interact with them. That was it. The entire work, though I did have some text on the wall. It was really a piece about Venice and its history. For many years the city had been so powerful and rich, it controlled much of the commerce in the world, until other nations created larger and more powerful navies and its influence diminished. Then Venice had to reinvent itself. It became the city of pleasure. The Las Vegas, so to speak, of the Mediterranean. During the height of this period one in every twelve citizens of Venice was a prostitute—or as we would now say, a sex worker. I felt excited when I discovered this statistic. When you think about the way art is presented—the way it is *exhibited*—it often feels as if the work has been prostituted. Something that can look so vibrant and alive in the artist's studio becomes something else when affixed to the walls of a gallery or museum, in a sanitized and blatantly commercialized space. It becomes deracinated, commodified, extirpated—and above all co-opted by forces that are actually antithetical to the creation of art.

I didn't quite know what to say, so again I said nothing. As was the case from the very beginning of our friendship, she had the power to make me feel she was much smarter than I was. That she had some kind of deeper understanding of the world and of many different subjects, and this was never truer than when she began to talk about art.

WE SET out again. It was a perfect temperature outside, and we left the windows down and let the fresh air flow over us. She lifted the last orange segment from the napkin and slipped it into my mouth, grazing my lips with her fingers. The piece of orange burst in an eruption of sunny liquid. Out of the blue she asked if I had ever read Mary McCarthy's novel *The Group*. I said I hadn't. She'd been thinking about it lately, she said.

She described the plot: It's about a group of seven women, she said, all of whom attend a college presumed to be Vassar, the college McCarthy herself had gone to as well as her friend Elizabeth Bishop, on whom a character is based. One of the women, Kay, is from Utah, the daughter of a doctor, just like me, she said. She is the only one of the group to have come from the West—all the others are easterners from wealthy families. Kay is a woman who insists on *playing the truth,* as McCarthy puts it, ranking her friends, intruding on others unannounced, offering the awkward but honest comment, and yet somehow these qualities are made to seem bold and admirable. Even though Kay doesn't seem to realize the little social nuances, there's something about her that you know McCarthy is drawn to—it's the quality sometimes attributed to westerners, of seeming to rise from the soil, having frank opinions and not being averse to sharing them. The book opens with the women having just graduated and now gathering for the hasty and poorly planned wedding of Kay, the first of the group to get married. Each of the women is described in the opening scene: They're all rich, a privileged bunch of prattling snobs. Kay alone is the truth teller, the taker of risks, the figure who will come to represent the tragedy of unmet desires and betrayal. The story seems rather dated now, and it was hard to imagine how shocking the novel was when it was published in the 1930s, how it dared to feature women openly discussing sex and orgasms and—most upsetting of all to the censors of the time—their use of contraceptive devices. Still, Jolene said she found it to be an interesting read, and she couldn't help identifying with Kay. At the end of the book, after her husband betrays her and has her briefly committed to a mental institution, Kay kills herself by jumping from a window in the Vassar Club in New York City in an act of self-obliteration. Thus the book opens with her wedding and ends with her death.

Lately I've wondered, Jolene said in a quietly subdued voice, if I am not that figure of Kay, the doctor's daughter from Utah who went east to attend Bryn Mawr, only to find herself set on a tragic course. And now that my life has taken a decidedly bad turn, I find myself affected by a pitiable and almost impenetrable loneliness. I often have suicidal thoughts. Isn't that pathetic, to admit to such a thing? I spend so much time thinking about myself—about what *was,* the mistakes, the wrong turns I may have taken. Everything I have learned assures me that there is nothing new of value that is not filtered through some reflection of the past. But there are also moments when it's necessary to let go of all that has gone before, or when it lets go of you. That's what I'm hoping will happen by going home. I want to be *let go of* now. I want there to be only the present, to be in the moment as it unfolds around me, to fully live every day left to me. And yet here I am, removing myself from the present by talking to you the way I am. You must forgive me. I should just be looking out the window and admiring the world out there, not boring you to death with these bathetic thoughts.

There's nothing to forgive, I said.

She took my hand and kissed it and then pressed it to her cheek, a gesture I found so intimate and loving it frightened me a little. There was so little flesh on her face. Her cheekbone felt like the hard, curved tine of a fork. Her skin was cold. And papery dry.

I shook my head, looking straight ahead because I couldn't bear to meet her eyes, and said, I like listening to you talk. Though I don't like to think of you having suicidal thoughts.

WE DROVE on. She laid the seat back and, propping the pillow up against the window, let me know she intended to rest again. Before closing her eyes she looked up at the sky and murmured, Such beautiful clouds. And then she fell asleep once more.

The stratus clouds spread out above us in a blanket of horizontal white, filtering the sun so that the light fell in striated rays, what I thought of as biblical light, like the light coming from the heavens in the pictures of Jesus I had seen as a child—divergent rays divided into separate streaks like the spokes of a wheel, fanning out like a special blessing on the land. I thought of lines from a Wallace Stevens poem: *I was the world in which I walked, and what I saw / or heard or felt came not but from myself; / And there I found myself more truly and more strange.*

Who was it that said our wish to be understood is our most violent form of nostalgia? I felt that was what she wanted from me now, to be understood, and to be desired for herself, for what she had become as well as what she had always been. I believed it was why she had asked me to take her on this journey. The wish to revisit her origins was secondary. Above all she wanted to explain herself to someone, someone who shared her past. She wanted for one person to see her as she truly existed, to see what she had become, what occupied her mind now that she knew her time was growing short. I had agreed to be that person. And I still did not know if I was up to the task.

Would the revelations she seemed intent on making—her wish above all to be *seen*—make it impossible for her to go on seeing me when the trip ended?

14

The weather changed suddenly and a wind arose in the afternoon and great clouds of white alkali blew up from the earth, partially obscuring the road ahead of us before we passed through the whiteouts and everything cleared again. It looked like a storm was gathering over the mountains just ahead.

We came to the area where Vincent and I had often glimpsed small herds of wild horses. There were signs along the road indicating the places where they frequently crossed, advising motorists to slow down. These were not the noble free animals people liked to imagine when they thought of mustangs but shaggy thin creatures with ragged coats and long hooves, ribbed out and often trudging along single file with their heads hanging low, trailing each other in search of a watering place, searching for the meager scraps of grass in this desiccated landscape where winter had just ended and the spring growth had yet to come up. There were no wild horses around today, just the piñon-covered hills below a serrated horizon. The hills had the texture and color of yellowcake, denuded here and there and marked by runnels and rivulets and dotted with sparse rabbitbrush and sage. The scars and ruined hilltops, the conical skirts of golden earth, indicated where mining had occurred. And it had taken place everywhere. Piles of slag spilled down the slopes, and the coral-colored slashes of mining roads zigzagged across the faces of steep mountains in the distance. Soon a light rain began to fall, and the drops on the windshield made little *puck-puck* sounds and left bright spots in the layers of dust on the glass.

———

IT WAS late afternoon when we reached Tonopah. The town was positioned high in the distance, between two hills that rose on the horizon. From the first time I had glimpsed the place many years ago I felt it looked like the city of Oz floating in the golden light. There was something surreal about it. The yellow and red earth uncovered by the mining of the surrounding hills gave it an unnatural glow. It seemed to shimmer in the desert light, especially at the end of day, and float free of the landscape. The whole area had been heavily mined, the hills were nude, gouged into bare golden knolls rising up from the edge of town. Small weathered wooden houses lined the steep narrow streets, and the town itself was suffused with a feeling of decay. Great fortunes had been made before the gold and silver was played out and the mines were largely abandoned. Now the town relied on a trickle of tourists passing through and the workers' wages from nearby government installations, places far out in the desert that housed a secret project—the Stealth Bomber, which had been built and used in the first Gulf War. These remote governmental and military outposts in Nevada were like small towns in themselves where housing and cafés were provided for the workers in an effort to make their lonely, isolated existence more palatable. The last time Vincent and I had passed through Tonopah the clerk in the motel told us that the government had converted the facilities used to build the secret Stealth into command headquarters for much of the military drone activity worldwide. This had been done at a cost of fifty billion dollars, she said. It had seemed astonishing to us that men and women sitting in buildings located in a dry desert basin in Nevada were pushing buttons to anonymously drop bombs on the other side of the world. But, the clerk added, who knows what really goes on out there? It's all hush-hush. All I know is, I've seen a lot of black helicopters flying around. And suddenly we've got more people coming into town to do business.

I PULLED into the parking lot of the Mizpah, the old hotel where I'd reserved us rooms. A stone structure rising seven stories, once the highest building in Nevada, it stood in the center of town on a main street lined with similar stone buildings, many now vacant. Jolene was still sleeping, and as I touched her shoulder she came suddenly awake.

Where are we? she asked.

Tonopah, I said. The hotel where we're spending the night. Don't worry about taking anything in now. I'll bring our bags in later.

A few years earlier, the Mizpah had gone through a renovation after being bought by a wine-making family from Napa who had invested a lot of money in the place, and still it always felt empty to me, like an old western ghost hotel, as if it were waiting for customers from another boom that had not yet arrived, and once again it seemed that way when we walked inside. The place was largely empty. An attempt had been made to give the lobby an authentic turn-of-the-century feel, with flocked wallpaper and antique chandeliers, but the decor slid into cowboy kitsch—mannequins dressed as dance-hall girls and mustachioed outlaws, antique slot machines, and heavy old settees and chairs covered in faded red velvet and crowned with steer horns. I saw Jolene gazing around with a bemused look as I filled out the registration forms, and I thought to myself, *She must find this place so corny.*

What kind of name is Mizpah? she asked as we rode the elevator to the fourth floor. Native American or something?

I told her what I knew, that according to the history of the hotel printed on the menus in the dining room the word *mizpah* had been engraved inside the wedding ring that Jim Butler, the mining baron who'd founded the town in 1900, had given to his wife, Belle. Supposedly it had some biblical reference meaning "to come back together with those you love."

Really? she said. And then she raised her eyebrows and shook her head and looked amused. She said nothing more, but in truth I think we were both thinking the same thing.

WE FOUND our rooms, located next to each other. It was only five-thirty in the afternoon. We decided we would rest and meet in the bar downstairs in a couple of hours.

The rooms were small but not without charm—a brass bed, an antique dresser, and, hanging on the walls, old black-and-white photographs from the town's boom days. From my window there was a nice view of the golden hills and a little cemetery with a grid of white wooden crosses. I went back downstairs and retrieved our bags from the car and delivered Jolene's to her room, and then I stretched out on the bed, feeling exhausted from the long drive, and called Vincent.

From the moment I heard his voice I knew something was wrong.

WITHOUT BOTHERING to ask how I was or what the drive had been like, he launched into an account of what had happened that day. He'd discovered the apartment building had been sold. The new landlord had shown up unannounced, he said, and he was a very rude man. When Vincent heard someone knock and opened the door, Max and Barney had been startled and bolted out. The new landlord, who was standing there, introduced himself quickly as the new owner of the building and then immediately said, Are those cats yours? Because if they are, I'm not going to allow animals here anymore. You'll have to get rid of them.

Vincent said he was so shocked he hadn't known what to say. The landlord, a middle-aged, paunchy guy, unshaven and badly dressed, had then said, without any preamble, that he would offer twenty thousand dollars if we left the apartment voluntarily. It could save you guys a lot of money in legal fees if you don't fight this, he'd told Vincent. You're paying nothing in rent. And one way or another I'll get you out or make your lives so miserable you'll want to leave. Trust me. You'd be smart to accept this offer now, because I won't make it again.

VINCENT SOUNDED very shaky as he repeated what the new landlord had told him. I knew I needed to say something to calm him down, but I found my own heart was racing. Get rid of our cats? How could we do this? As if pets were disposable items one could simply cast aside.

What did you tell him when he offered you the money? I asked.

I told him we wanted to stay in the apartment.

But perhaps we *don't* want to stay in the apartment, I said as gently as I could, knowing he might not want this option pointed out to him yet again.

I think it's time to leave. Especially if he's going to make our lives miserable.

I don't know, Vincent said, I just don't *know*. His voice rose on that last word, as if it contained the equivalent of a hand-wringing gesture.

How can he make us get rid of the cats! he cried. He can't do that. He just can't.

No he can't, I said. We won't let that happen.

I REALIZED I needed to help him calm down. I could tell his feelings were launching toward some precipice.

Listen, I said. It's going to be okay. We're going to find another place to live—

But I don't *want* another place, he said. This is our home.

It's *been* our home, but it doesn't mean we can't find another. It must have been a terrible day for you. The new landlord sounds like a horrible man. But for now try to forget about him. We'll figure it out. Put some music on. Make yourself some dinner. Have you eaten today? Are the cats inside with you now?

That's the thing. I don't know where Max is, he said. He hasn't been here all day, not since the landlord left. What if he does something to the cats? What if he tries to poison them or something?

That's not going to happen, I said. You know it's not. You're taking things too far—remember that's what you told me about the fire? And the leaky gas line? That I was taking things too far? We're just frightened. It's easy to imagine things. It's hard to be apart when something like this happens. I wish I'd been there today to help you deal with it.

I wish you were here too, he said. His voice sounded calm but very sad.

So do I, I replied, I really do.

———

WE TALKED for a while, and I could feel him settling down. I told him about the drive, how it had gone that day. I didn't mention Jolene specifically, just the nice lunch we'd had at the Still Life Cafe and how beautiful the mountains had looked coming up over Montgomery Summit. I asked him what else he had done that day. He told me about the new Robert Lowell book he'd ordered, which had finally arrived, and we began to have a more normal conversation. He said he'd spent much of the afternoon, after the landlord had left, reading the new book, which was called *Robert Lowell: Interviews and Memoirs*.

Tell me about it, I said, hoping to draw him out, keep him on the phone. Often it wasn't easy to do. He usually wasn't one for staying on the line, having lengthy conversations. But now I had his interest, and he began telling me a story.

HE LIKED the book, he said, this anthology, but he thought some of the shorter personal remembrances were more interesting than the other essays. One he had particularly liked was written by a woman friend of Lowell's. It described his final years.

You probably don't know this, he said, but Lowell died in the back seat of a taxi on his way home from the airport.

He told me that Lowell had flown to Ireland to see his son, the child he'd had with the English writer Caroline Blackwood, for whom he had left Elizabeth Hardwick. That marriage had been a disaster, and after four years of strife and unmanageable manic episodes he found he missed America and was so unhappy with his new wife that he left her and came home and asked Elizabeth Hardwick to take him back, which she did, now more as a devoted friend than lover, but always a *wife*. A short while later he'd flown to Ireland to visit his young son, and on his return, in the taxi from the airport, he'd had a heart attack and died. He'd been on his way to Hardwick's apartment, and the taxi driver had called her from the street and she'd gone down to find Lowell dead in the back seat. He'd been bringing back a portrait of Caroline Blackwood, painted by her former husband, Lucian Freud. Returning to one wife, carrying a portrait of the other.

He was only sixty, Vincent said. The same age as both of his parents when they died of heart attacks.

I didn't know that, I said, I mean how he died. That's very sad. To die all alone in a taxi. The saddest part to me, of course, was that he'd just recently reunited with Elizabeth Hardwick, who had cared for him so deeply and so well over the many years they were together and was committed to doing so again.

There's another piece in the book I liked, he said, from Mailer's *Armies of the Night*.

He then began describing that excerpt, and looking out the window at the scudding clouds, I thought how so like Vincent this was. One moment he was panicked, working himself up to a fine state of anguish over the confrontation with the landlord, worrying about the cats, and the next he was happily lost in the world of a poet he loved, recounting a story that amused him.

HE SAID Mailer had described a dinner both he and Lowell attended in the late sixties. It was during the height of the Vietnam War protests, which of course they had both participated in, with Lowell famously refusing an invitation from President Johnson to attend a garden party at the White House because he so objected to the war. In his account of the evening, Mailer referred to Lowell and himself as the only two men of remotely similar status at the dinner even though there were other distinguished writers present that night.

That's just like Mailer, don't you think? Vincent said. To be so arrogant.

Both men had been invited to read from their work at this gathering to raise money for the antiwar cause. It's funny, Vincent said, because this whole long piece from Mailer's book is about the competition he felt with Lowell, about who was the better writer, even though it was like comparing apples and oranges because they worked in totally different mediums.

Anyway, he said, Mailer had introduced Lowell at this reading, and Lowell, even before he started to read, got a huge applause, which

irked Mailer. He didn't like being upstaged. Mailer, in an attempt to
be entertaining, felt he had been fatally vulgar because he resorted
to hucksterism in his introduction, but even worse he had made a big
deal about how Lowell came from the upper class, pointing out what
an unusual thing this was for a poet. Mailer felt depressed because
clearly Lowell wasn't pleased he'd done this, and in trying to embar-
rass him this way he'd only embarrassed himself with his graceless
comments. In contrast, Lowell was naturally elegant and when he
began reading he made no effort to win the audience by seducing or
bullying them or employing vaudeville-like clown antics, as Mailer
felt he had done. He just stood and read his poems, and even though
he wasn't actually a very good reader of his own work it didn't matter:
the audience was mesmerized. Mailer wrote that the audience adored
Lowell—for his talent, his modesty, his superiority, his melancholy,
his petulance, his weakness, his painful almost stammering shyness,
and not least his noble strength. Mailer discovered he was deeply jealous of Lowell. Not of his talent, because even though Lowell's talent
was very large, Mailer was a bulldog when it came to the value of his
own talent. No, Mailer was jealous because he had worked for this
audience, cranking up his vaudeville act in the introduction, and Lowell without effort had stolen them away from him. Mailer wrote that
he felt a hot anger at how Lowell was loved and he was not. And he
listened with bitterness as Lowell read from a poem called "Waking
Early Sunday Morning."

Do you want to hear a bit of that poem? Vincent asked.

Yes, of course, I said—and I thought: Lines of poetry read to me
while I lay in bed in Tonopah, Nevada, at the conclusion of a conversation that began with him being so distraught. Here was a man who
could change moods in very little time, and wasn't this a good thing?

He began reading, in his beautiful, cadenced voice, which surely
Lowell would have envied:

> *Pity the planet, all joy gone*
> *from this sweet volcanic cone;*
> *peace to our children when they fall*
> *in small war on the heels of small*

war—until the end of time
to police the earth, a ghost
orbiting forever lost
in our monotonous sublime

Wonderful, I said. Thank you.

Call me before you go to sleep, he said.

I told him I would. And then I asked him to text me the lines of the poem so I could read them again later.

I'll go out and call Max now, he said. I hope he'll come.

Yes, I said. Go call Maxie. And fix yourself something to eat.

JOLENE DID not feel she could eat anything that night. She called my room not long after I hung up from speaking with Vincent. She was tired, she said, and her stomach felt upset. It was the big lunch she'd eaten. Too rich. The coq au vin and all the bread. She should have known. She hadn't eaten a big meal like that in a while. It had simply tasted so good. She hoped she'd feel better in the morning. She refused my offer to bring her something and, before hanging up, thanked me for what she said had been a wonderful day.

I ORDERED a sandwich from the restaurant downstairs and spent the evening in the room, reading from the book I'd brought with me, the copy of Chekhov's stories that had arrived just before I left.

When I began to feel sleepy I called Vincent to say good night. He sounded worried because Max hadn't yet returned. I reminded him that sometimes Max was gone all day and didn't come in until the middle of the night. I said I was sure he'd come back. And still I couldn't reassure him: I heard the fear in his voice as he said good night and—no doubt by mistake—hung up in the middle of my telling him that I loved him.

I GOT up early and took a walk through town, climbing the narrow streets lined with empty trailers and dilapidated houses, circling back to the hotel past the old stone buildings on Main, their chiseled rocks so perfectly fitted. I passed a mural of the Stealth Bomber painted on the side of one of the old buildings and it looked like a Marvel comics flying machine, a futuristic blade flung against the fake blue sky. By the time I returned, Jolene was sitting in the lobby with her suitcase beside her. She didn't smile when she saw me and stood up shakily, holding on to the back of the chair. She looked as if she had passed a bad night. The dark circles under her eyes had become deep hollows. When I asked her how she felt she simply waved me off and said, Fine, fine. I'm okay—don't worry. I really didn't sleep, but I'll catch up with naps in the car.

I asked her what she thought she'd like for breakfast. She said she didn't think she could eat much, but perhaps she could get some tea and toast. She was wearing all black, a black knit cap, a black turtleneck and jeans, but around her neck she had a luminescent red scarf. Her jeans were cinched with a silver belt. She looked impossibly thin. And also very chic. Her thinness was the thinness of starved-down models who stride runways, boosting fashion on their skinny frames, and like them she looked very beautiful and elegant in her clothes. I remembered the Levi skirt she had made in high school and thought, *She's always had great style, she was born with it, and look at her, even now. Like she stepped out of a fashion shoot.*

THE RESTAURANT in the Mizpah, just off the lobby, was a place where Vincent and I had eaten many times, a small room with etched-glass windows showing mining scenes and featuring booths along one wall and tables in the middle.

We sat at a booth, with Jolene facing away from the light as I now knew she would always want to do. A waitress I had seen before brought us our menus. She was an earnest, overweight young woman, rustic and pink fleshed, and I knew from what she had said on earlier visits that she had two kids she was raising on her own and had lived in Alabama before she moved to Tonopah. She liked to talk. She had once given me her recipe for a terrible-sounding Jell-o pie when we were discussing dessert. But she didn't recognize me now as someone she had waited on before.

You gals want coffee? she asked.

I said I did. Jolene ordered tea, Earl Grey, she said, and the waitress said she'd bring her a basket of tea bags to choose from.

Gals? Jolene said, wrinkling her nose, after the waitress had left. And a basket to *choose* from? Couldn't I have just Earl Grey? Which is what I want. What I asked for. Is that too difficult?

She put on her dark glasses. I knew it was because she wanted to conceal how tired she looked this morning, or maybe it really was just easier on her eyes to filter the light and that's why I almost never saw her without them, even inside. Her hands shook slightly as she studied the menu.

When we'd ordered she looked at me and said, Can you tell how short of breath I am?

Not really. I don't notice anything.

Are you just being polite? Or honest?

Honest, I said.

Some days I feel it more than others. This morning every breath feels a little labored. It makes me wonder. Has it spread to my lungs?

What could I say to this? I nodded, as if I understood the anxiety of a disease perhaps quietly colonizing her body even as we sat there, though of course this was something I could not really imagine.

Maybe you're just tired from the long drive yesterday, I said, plus it doesn't sound like you slept much.

I'm not looking forward to seeing my mother, she said. It's making me anxious. Perhaps that's why I'm feeling short of breath. I don't think she'll even recognize me. According to my cousin, she doesn't recognize anyone anymore. I like to think she won't know who I am. It would make it easier.

You could always decide to not visit her, I said. I mean if you feel it's going to be too upsetting.

No, I'll see her. I have to. It's difficult to explain, so I won't even try.

It's a terrible thing to admit, she said after a pause, but growing up

I felt that in her presence all joy went out of existence—there wasn't even a little corner left that I could fill up with affection or humor or respect. I don't know what I'll feel when I see her again now, after all these years. But it's got me feeling anxious.

OVER BREAKFAST she told me a story about her mother. It involved Vincent. She said that not long after they'd gotten married she'd taken him home to meet her mother. Her father by then had remarried and retired to Hawaii, and her mother was living in the old house alone. She had decided to surprise them when they arrived by throwing one of her elaborate cocktail parties to introduce her friends to her new son-in-law. Everything had gone wrong.

You know how private he is about his music—how he doesn't like it when anyone asks him to play. Well, in the middle of the party my mother decided to bring everything to a halt by banging on a glass with a knife and making a big deal about introducing Vincent. She wanted everyone to know her new son-in-law was a brilliant composer and musician. She made the mistake of asking him to play something, taking hold of his arm, trying to lead him over to the piano-—saying, Please, play anything you'd like, darling, though I hope the piano isn't too out of tune, no one has played it for years. Well, Vincent just stood there, resisting any attempt to move him. He went blank, like he can. He wasn't going to play and I knew it, but finally he let my mother lead him to the piano because he couldn't stop her. Everyone was watching him now, waiting for him to sit down, but instead, very politely, he said, I'm sorry but I don't wish to play, then backing away from her he returned to his drink. But she wouldn't give up. She tried to take hold of him again, telling him he shouldn't be so shy, and this time he said, Please, I'd prefer not to, and when she still wouldn't give up he turned away suddenly and abruptly left the room and went upstairs. My mother looked out over the room, at her friends staring back at her. It was such an awkward moment, but I couldn't blame Vincent for what he'd done. Still I could see how embarrassed and angry she was, but she laughed and shook her head and said, Well, to hell with that. Let's have another drink.

I went upstairs and found Vincent sitting on the bed in my old room, just looking out the window. She shouldn't have asked me, was all he said. I told him I didn't blame him, he shouldn't worry about that, but then I realized that he wasn't worried at all. He was just fine. I had wanted to make sure he was okay, but in fact he seemed quite unfazed by what had just happened. I knew that all he wanted now was for me not to mention it again. That's all. It was one of those moments when I realized how much he didn't like to talk about anything upsetting. It was already history to him. For him it was over. Done. And not to be discussed. I knew that when he saw my mother again in the morning he would treat her exactly as he'd done the morning before, with politeness and good manners. It would be as if nothing had happened. You couldn't hurt him that way, or throw him off.

Anyway we never went back to Utah, except for one time and that was to attend my grandfather's funeral. By then Vincent knew what to expect from my mother, and so did I. She'd never forgiven him for not entertaining her friends that night. She treated him like a leper. At the reception at my cousin's house after the funeral I overheard her talking with someone who'd asked about Vincent, who, as usual, was standing off by himself. *I don't know why she married him,* my mother said to this woman, *but I guess you have to belong somewhere after a while.* It's funny, but I remember thinking, *She's absolutely right.* I mean about having to belong somewhere after a while, not about marrying a loser, which is how she viewed him. I never thought of Vincent that way. I just never understood him.

She waited for a minute to see if I would say anything. I didn't.

You don't want me to talk about him, do you? she said.

I shrugged. And then I lied, because it was the easiest thing to do. I really don't care, I said. It's fine.

THE WAITRESS came to see if we were finished with our meal. You still working on that? she said to Jolene, indicating her half-eaten toast and cup of fruit.

I was never really *working* on it, Jolene said sharply, but yes I'm finished. The waitress looked momentarily confused and then gave a little nervous laugh, picked up the plate, and walked away.

I don't think she deserves a tip, Jolene said. She took so long to bring our food. And no hot water refill for my tea until I asked for it twice. We don't need to leave anything.

That's not nice, I said. Not to leave a tip.

Nice isn't my specialty.

Well, I'll leave a tip then, not to worry.

The last thing I'm going to do is worry about a tip, she said, and began to gather up her bag and jacket from the seat beside her.

People either deserve tips or they don't, she said. This waitress doesn't. What upsets me is that employers don't pay a living wage here in this country, so we're all expected to make up for that. It's not that way in Europe, where you're not expected to leave big tips. You're not forced to feel guilty for not subsidizing some fat capital-ist who's skimping on his employees' wages or pretend you've gotten good service when you haven't. It's not really about rewarding service any longer anyway, is it? It's about capitalizing on profits for business owners at the expense of both workers and customers. And I think it's a humiliating practice that exploits everyone and lets the owners off the hook.

I said, You mean it lets you off the hook, not to have to leave a tip for someone who probably really needs it.

Ha. Who wouldn't want to be freed from *that* kind of guilt? Having to tote up a tip at the end of every meal. You talk about the poor. But tipping is really a scam perpetrated by the rich at the expense of the poor. Bad service or good, it doesn't matter. You can pay your employ-ees less because you rely on the public to make up the difference.

Is everything a polemic with you? I said.

She looked at me as if I were stupid. Of course it is, she said. That goes without saying. I'm a walking opinion, a bleeding controversial-ist. And what bad luck for you to get stuck with me on a long trip.

She smiled, and I smiled back at her, and then she got up, saying she'd meet me in the lobby, she needed to use the restroom. I paid the bill and left the tip, still mulling over what she'd said.

15

We picked up our bags from the front desk and checked out of the hotel and after filling the car up with gas set out on the two-lane road for the long journey ahead of us. The road between Tonopah and Ely was one of my favorite parts of the drive. Route 50 had long ago earned the name "The Loneliest Highway in America." And it seemed true. One could go for a very long time and not pass another car. A sign just outside town said NEXT GAS STATION 173 MILES. There was really nothing to distract from the pure, solitary beauty of the landscape. The road ran across immense sloping valleys that stretched between high mountain ranges. Up and down, and up and down again, over basin and range. There were several high passes to be crossed during the drive, summits that could be dangerous in the winter but which now, in spring, were mostly clear of snow. It felt like a perfect day to be traveling. Cool weather. Great formations of dense white clouds. The air vibrating with pointillist light.

A GREAT empty expanse opened up as soon as we'd left town. Not for everyone, I thought, this largely treeless, vacant world. But for me the landscape offered a curative desolateness.

I was thinking about your mother this morning, Jolene said. The comment came out of the blue and surprised me. I never remembered Jolene having much to say about either one of my parents.

Your mother was such a naturally sweet person, wasn't she?

Yes, I said, she was.

I always liked coming to your house when your father wasn't around because he seemed to change a feeling when he entered a room—and she also seemed to change. Without him I felt your mother could be herself. I remember coming over and finding her sitting around a quilting frame with her friends, how they were always laughing, telling stories. When women are alone they talk to each other differently than when they're with men, don't they?

I said I thought this was true. I had discovered this early on by listening in on my mother's conversations. She had been skilled at the home arts—canning and pickling and preserving, quilting and sewing. I remember her darning our socks, sitting on the sofa in the evening, repairing a hole. When she'd finished she'd examine the lovely crosshatched stitches. Who would think of darning a sock now? Did they still even make wooden darning eggs?

Who was it that said all heroism lies in endurance? Jolene said. I would say that describes your mother's life. It can't have been easy raising eight kids on your father's salary.

She enjoyed homemaking, I said. She loved having kids. There was nothing else she wanted to do with her life except make a good home for her family. She considered it a challenge to do so on very little money. She felt proud she could do that.

Lucky her, Jolene said. To know what makes you happy.

I don't know that she was so happy. But I also don't know that she worried much about whether she was happy. I think she came to think that part of becoming an adult is learning to disappear and hide your feelings almost to the point of vanishing. That's what my mother did. That's what many women of her generation did. *It's what many women still do,* I thought.

I could never do that, Jolene said, in which case perhaps I'm fated. I think all my relationships have largely been based on the allure of the feeling of being admired by someone more important than me. I don't know why it excited me so. It always excited me, even though you could say I didn't get anything out of it. Now the repeated failure of relationships over the years has left me convinced of the limitations of intimacy. Now I realize none of that matters anymore.

I didn't think she was telling the truth that she didn't care about intimacy anymore, but I didn't say anything—and who knew what she meant by the *limitations of intimacy*. She seemed to know I was doubting her words.

What you say about family emotions, she said, their durability, perhaps that's true, but it's not the kind of intimacy in this country that seems to last. Families are different here—I know that's a generalization, but it's not like it is for many Europeans. Here family relations seem no more that the relations between birds—parents feeding the little greedy, open beaks of their children, teaching them to fly, then they do not recognize you nor you them in the treetops a few weeks later. I think the older cultures in Europe are not as careless as we are. Not as screwed up about child raising. Family matters very much to them. It doesn't rely on this constant upheaval of feeling, or perhaps they have a better way of dealing with it. It's different.

What could I say to this? I knew nothing about how Europeans viewed their family relations. She seemed to think everything Europeans did was somehow better than our inferior ways. I didn't think what she was saying made sense. How could she talk in such sweeping generalities about whole cultures? About how people raised their children when she had none of her own? Her entire view of the subject had been formed by the corrupted relationship with her own parents.

I fell silent, and so did she, as if neither one of us really believed very much in what we were saying, so why bother adding anything more or trying to defend it?

WE CAME up over a summit and began a steep descent into a broad valley where pale hills rose from the middle of an immense basin— lilac-colored mounds with pink tips surrounded by scant scrub brush. The road was lined with tasseled cheat grass—a noxious plant no one would ever consider beautiful—and yet it looked rich and lushly green, nourished from the previous day's rain. A mirage appeared on our left, what looked to be a silvery lake formed against the base of the far mountains, water reflecting sunlight. Nothing more than an illusion but such a convincing one.

———

SHE BEGAN speaking about her work and how it had been to be a woman in the art world at the time she began making her first pieces. She said that early on in her career she had been rejected by feminists for using images from pornography in ways they felt objectified the female body.

Yeah, well they were wrong, she said. My side won. In those days people felt there was a proscribed way of being feminist, but my side won. There is no proscribed way, as we've discovered. Everything is subject to change and the forces of history and human agency. The sense of limitless freedom that I, as a radical woman artist, sometimes felt was a new kind of being. It was a period when some very iconic work was being made by some very fearless women artists. Ana Mendieta's performance called *Rape Scene,* for instance. Imagine this, being one of her fellow art-school students and being invited to a performance in her apartment in 1973. You arrive to find the door slightly ajar, and inside there is Ana, stripped from the waist down and bent over a table. Blood is smeared over and drips down her buttocks, thighs, and calves, and a pool of it is partially visible on the dark floor beside her feet. Her head and her arms, which are tied to the table, are not visible in the low light, and broken dishes and bloodied clothes are strewn around the floor. She doesn't speak, leaving the students and the few others who have been invited to sit there in the room and discuss what they are seeing among themselves, and this goes on for about an hour. And then it's over. Everybody who was there that day knew they had seen something they would never forget. When I discovered that performance, I began using my own body as the armature for my work. I simply could not have existed as I am in any other time or place. My own art was made possible because of the fearless women artists who showed me the way. That piece of Ana's, by the way, was based on an actual rape scene—the murder of a fellow student—and restaged by her as a protest. And in Ames, Iowa, by the way. I mean, *Iowa.* They had never seen anything like this.

———

SHE TALKED on. Mostly I listened without commenting, attempting to pay attention even when I found what she was saying upsetting or confusing, or when I didn't exactly understand her, as was occasionally the case if it involved some complicated idea. The idea of *Rape Scene* disturbed me deeply, what to make of someone being able to do that. But I hardly had time to think about it, as she continued speaking.

She said the old patriarchal morality of proper behavior had long ago robbed women of something much more ancient—their connection to the worship of nature, the worship of the body, a pleasure in sensuousness. That's part of what those radical women artists were fighting against, she said, and she went on to describe other disturbing works of the time that had greatly influenced her. Many of these women had been disrespected and criticized for their work at the time, and only now—now that they were old, in most cases after years of neglect—were they finally being given their due. Their work was being rediscovered and shown.

I continued to gaze out over the landscape. We were passing through a wide valley. The sky was like a cataract over a blue eye, hazy and whitish. The road a straight black line, running down one side of the broad basin and up the other side, coming to a fine point like a stylus before disappearing again into the far hills. How far away were those hills? Twenty, thirty miles? To the south the basin opened up and offered an immense unobstructed view, range after range of mountains fading in color and height to the farthest horizon. I wondered if she was even aware of this world we were passing through.

SHE SAID she had known right from the beginning that she would meet resistance to her work. In art school she had seen the future. Performances. Events. Happenings. *Circumstances.* She said she had felt then like she needed to blow up her life. Attune her senses differently. She realized her body had a natural perfection, a great beauty. She could say this now without sounding vain. This was important at that time because it made it easier to accept what she was doing, the fact she was attractive and looked so appealing without her clothes on. Unfortunate, but true, that this should have made such a difference to the way her work was received, but she thought it was the case. By using her body in action she could represent multiple levels of meaning built of multiple references. But her first works were met with derision by her male professors. They had said to her, If you are going to represent physicality and carnality we cannot give you intellectual authority. It was just too silly, she said. A mind-body split she wouldn't accept.

By then she had become an intellectual, and she felt they couldn't diminish that. She'd become a passionate reader and enthusiastic student of art history and philosophy. She also studied the picture plane fractured into phrases of larger rhythms and contributing details. This is where Cézanne had been useful.

Even now, she said, she considered herself primarily a painter. Most critics didn't get this. How even when you use the body as your primary canvas the body still has to enter perception visually. Many artists who saw her early pieces thought she was just doing something incredibly perplexing. Many of the men seemed to consider her as someone to be fucked or suppressed. It was hard for her, hard for men to think a woman who takes her clothes off doesn't want to be fucked. How could she be so vulgar as to expose herself and not want that, even unconsciously? How could she expose her pussy and not feel shame?

She said she felt her unique contribution to the art world at that time had been to literally draw the eye back to the body that sees, in everything she did, whether performance or painting. What is seen is a scene wrapped around the body. Eventually, in certain pieces, she knew she was asking these questions: Is sex still the domain of men? And is that why it is so problematic for women?

WHEN SHE began staging her first performance pieces she decided to make a Super 8 film of her having sex with her boyfriend, Marcus. She filmed a number of hours of them engaged in various love-making acts. Marcus had been a wonderful partner, they had lived together several years, and they'd always had great sex. The Super 8 film she made entirely herself, with Marcus's willing participation. This was a very unique thing at the time, an outrageous idea—for a female artist to film herself in the sex act, to just set the camera up on a tripod and to make it look as if a neutral entity was the observer. She had really wanted to see what *the fuck* was, as she put it, and locate that in terms of a lived sense of equity. What would it look like, she had wondered? Most people, particularly women, had no idea what they looked like while having sex. Women at that time didn't even have any conception of what their genitals looked like—the vulva, the vagina, the clitoris, the labia—the parts of themselves they couldn't easily see but that male artists had been looking at and representing forever. Just think of Courbet's *The Origin of the World,* she said, that remarkable painting of a woman lying back against a white twisted sheet with her legs spread wide open, a work that doesn't even bother showing the woman's head, just the gorgeous details of her voluptuously ripe sex. She felt in her work she could reference a suppressed history of the sacred erotic. She could explore free expression, open sexuality. She could rupture, in her film, the idea of pornography by making her own erotic vision. She wanted to penetrate the culture's suppressions with her own body. That's what she had been doing with that film. And most people simply hadn't gotten it.

When the film was shown at various screenings, mostly private galleries and a few festivals, she said women would come up to her afterward and thank her. Sometimes they would start crying and say, *Thank you, thank you, this is the first time I've seen female genitalia and I'm going to be able to look at my own body now! I'm going to look at my vulva!*

I laughed at how enthusiastically she had cried out those last words, *my vulva!*

I know, she said. Wild. Look at the good I did for those young women.

I MENTIONED a rest stop was coming up and wondered if she needed to take a break, get out and walk around a bit. I said that on long drives it was good to stop every couple of hours and take even a short walk in order to keep blood clots from forming in the legs.

I definitely don't want blood clots, she said, now that I've been given a bit longer to live. Yes, let's do stop.

The rest stop was a bleak affair—bleak in that particular way a Nevada rest stop can be. Portable toilets—turquoise plastic shells standing at the edge of a gravel parking lot, with an overflowing trash can nearby. A couple of thin leafless trees rose from the pebbled ground next to a metal picnic table chained to a concrete slab, and all around a great yawning immensity with no sign of life. The wind gusted in voluminous, sudden bursts and carried a chill. It began to rain as we pulled up, a fine light drizzle.

She got out of the car first and drew her coat around her and walked off a ways and then stopped and stood still, staring into the vast distance. The coat had a fur-trimmed hood, and the wind blew the fur around her face so it looked like a little animal frantically circling her head. I got a hat from the back seat—an old weathered Stetson that had once belonged to my Aunt Marie, who had given it to me before she died. I could see the first drops were beginning to fall. I was aware of the way Jolene turned and looked at me when I got out of the car and started to walk over to where she was standing.

You shouldn't wear that hat, she said as I came up to her. It makes you look like a mistaken sheriff. Like a misbegotten sheriff.

Really? What sort of hat do you think I should wear? I was standing near her. Smiling my crooked smile. The one I had perfected when I needed to pretend I wasn't taking offense.

A beret, I think, she said.

Oh, a beret.

Yeah. It would suit you.

I don't have a beret—not with me right now, anyway, so I guess I'll just keep wearing this hat. I didn't own a beret, of course, but I wanted to continue messing with her.

Well, I do. I brought a beret with me. A red one. And just the right color of red by the way, you have to be careful with that. I'll lend it to you.

Okay, I said.

I've got hats coming out my ears. Or rather covering them. I can't tell you how disturbingly naked one feels without hair.

I smiled at her and shook my head. She shrugged, as if to say, *So it is now. So it is. That's life without hair.* I liked the fact she was taking me away from my earnest self, helping me become more ironic. I'd never learned how to be ironic.

WE DREW our coats around us and began to walk toward the edge of the asphalt where it met the dirt. The drops of rain were coming down a little harder now. She wouldn't use the portable toilets, she said. She found the idea disgusting. They gave off a terrible smell even from a distance. Instead she walked out into the sagebrush and squatted, and I followed her. I tried not to look at her while she peed, but I saw that her legs were too weak for her to lower herself very close to the ground. She was holding on to a branch of sage to steady herself, and the piss was splashing up against her pant legs.

There was a dead rabbit lying in the dirt behind one of the trash cans, but we didn't notice it until we walked back to the car. The rain was coming down steadily now. Soft rain. Pleasant, in a refreshing way, especially after the closeness of the car. The rabbit was nothing more than tufts of fur and a set of tiny teeth and paws. The smell of the rain on the dry earth filled the air with the odor of petrichor as the organic compounds in the ground released their scent with the moisture. A fresh, rich smell in a very dry world. *Petrichor.* I'd always loved the word ever since I'd discovered it. It didn't sound like what it described but something much harder and coarser. It was the smell of the West. Rain on a dry landscape. The odor of wet sage.

She stood for a while in the quiet drizzle and gazed around. Without looking at me she said, It's amazing you would do this for me. This trip, I mean. It's as good as I've felt in a while. Doubly wonderful being with you. Aren't you the good egg?

She turned and smiled at me.

I smiled back at her but could not think of what to say. We simply got back into the car and drove away, with the rain falling harder, making a staticky sound against the roof of the car.

———

IT WAS as if her confession of gratitude had lingered in a need for silence. We drove for miles without talking. I was very aware of how she was looking at the landscape now. It was as if she had suddenly noticed where we were. Every once in a while she would make a comment. Look at the color of that hill, she would say. Oh my god. And those willows! Pink and purple and mauve—and chartreuse!—such luscious color!

We crested another summit, and a great wide view suddenly opened up. A vast basin, and the road dropping precipitously before us in a series of switchbacks, another mammoth range on the other side, the mountains beyond floating like great gray ships in the distance. Coming up over the summit—and then the vertiginous feeling of a steep world dropping away so fast it took one's breath away to look out over such suddenly falling space. I could sense how it hit her, this feeling of the sublime, magnified by the thrilling height and the great distance that had opened up before us, and how it caused her to sit up straight very suddenly. My god, she said, would you look at that.

She asked me to pull over, and I found a place where the road widened into a flat graveled pullout. The mountains rising before us, on the other side of the vast basin, were lilac at the base, shading to dark purple near the ridges, and streaked with slashes of orange earth and golden slag where mine tailings spilled down slopes in great slabs of vibrant hues. She took out a notebook and began drawing. The colors, she kept saying. These amazing colors.

SHE SAID she felt a little nauseated. Also her chest felt tight. Was she getting a cold? She hoped not. But there was that feeling, the one she had started to get in her chest at breakfast when her breathing became more difficult. Was there anywhere, she asked, where we could stop for a cup of hot tea?

I had to tell her there was nowhere we could stop. There wasn't another town for a hundred and twenty miles, not until Ely, more than two hours away. We'd stop there, I said. Could she make it? I offered her some water and she said, Thanks. She'd be okay, she could wait for the tea, she said. But I noticed how her hand shook when she took the water bottle.

SHE FINISHED her drawing, and we set off again as she picked up the conversation from earlier, talking again about her work, this time referencing the piece she wanted to do in MacArthur Park. Something that would deal with General MacArthur himself, she said—and guns, armaments—all relating, of course, to the idea of war and her own family history.

She had been trying to figure out how to connect this final work to the family business. The guns her mother's family was famous for manufacturing for over 150 years, from the first innovative rifles made for hunting in the nineteenth century to the arms they supplied to the military as far back as World War I. Their guns had been used in many wars around the world, in different eras. World War II. Korea and Vietnam—in fact the company was still supplying arms to the military right up to the present. They were being used by the American military in the Middle East.

She had been raised on money made from guns. Guns had paid for her education. Guns had furnished her with a trust fund so she'd never have to work. They continued to make everything possible, enabling the lifestyle she had enjoyed for so many years. She hadn't had to struggle like so many other artists. Guns paid for the apartments and houses in the various cities she'd lived in, and for the travel she'd relished, not to mention the excellent health care she had received when she most needed it. The money from guns had funded her artwork. Guns had given her freedom to pretty much do whatever she wanted. She had lived off the profit from guns, and now she wondered, how could she deal with this in some interesting way in a final performance piece about war—this highly personal connection to weaponry and armaments?

She found it shocking, she said, to think of America being the world's major arms supplier. Billions of dollars made from selling increasingly sophisticated weaponry to other nations, many with terrible records of human rights. And then to pretend we're so high and mighty, such an example of how to organize a democratic society with respect for human life—how do we justify this crime? Shocking, too, that in this way fortunes were being made by some very nasty people. Some very immoral and bad players. People who would sell anything to anyone and not care how it was used.

Did I know, she said, turning to look at me, that in its entire 242-year history America has enjoyed only sixteen years of peace, making it the most warlike nation in the history of the world? Think of that, she said. A mere sixteen years of peace. Since 2001 the United States has spent six trillion dollars on military operations and war. Imagine, she said, what might have been done with that money. How it might have been spent to improve lives.

She felt it would be different if women were in charge of things. I mean, name me one female arms dealer, she said. Just one.

I laughed. What do you mean? I couldn't name a male one.

Women make war too, I added. I know this is boring, but think of Thatcher and—those islands in South America. I couldn't remember their names, and then it came to me.

She invaded the Falklands, didn't she? And wasn't that rather stupid?

I'm not sure that counts as a major war.

It seemed to her, she said, that what could be definitely thought of as *major* war making had become the defining activity of our age—and no, she did not think it had ever been thus. Wars were perpetual now, never-ending states of constant combat—wars never formally declared. And they were nasty wars, wars in which there was no compunction about killing civilians and destroying their towns and dwellings, making life impossible to resume, destroying cultural sites. Drones dropping bombs and killing innocents. Bombs that killed children during school outings, or families at weddings, targeting hospitals and clinics. It wasn't always thus, she said. You can't say it was always this way.

War was no longer the exception but the rule, she said. Making war drained the wealth of some nations, made fortunes for others, and made daily life brutal and unbearable for massive numbers of people

just trying to go about their lives. War was the cruel disrupter, producing dubious losers and victors. The world was awash in wars and
weaponry of all kinds thanks in large part to American arms sales.
She thought war was, and always had been, male-driven, no matter
what I might try to say to the contrary. War required testosterone.
Aggression. A will to dominate. War required angry, proud males
looking to consolidate their power, swinging their dicks around. Forget Thatcher. She was a blip. Men were the problem. War-making
men. Her family's company had always been run by men, ever since
her great-grandfather started it in the late 1800s. The women in the
family were never allowed to hold any positions. Her mother had
never cared. Just send the checks, she said.

And yet all the research she had done into her own family history had convinced her that her great-grandfather was a genius,
someone to be proud of. The guns he invented had originally made it
easier for people to put food on the table, defend their livestock and
homesteads—guns with a purpose primarily of making the settlement
of the West easier. Of course therein was another problem, no? The
guns her family had manufactured, the patents sold to Remington,
were used to make rifles that displaced the native people from their
lands. They were used to kill millions of buffalo, often shot for sport
or to deprive Indians of their food source. How to reconcile this? The
respect she had for the genius of her ancestor with the carnage every
generation of more sophisticated weapons caused?

If women had as much power as men they would be less inclined
to make war. She believed this fervently. War was men's business. But
this was obvious, wasn't it: The point was, what could she say about
war that wasn't obvious? That hadn't already been said? In America
war simply didn't touch most people. War was voluntary and distant,
waged by enlistees, with no fear of forced conscription. War was
mostly fought by the poor. War was an opportunity for an education, a VA loan, a job—and, as it turned out, a regrettably fraught
future of missing limbs, haunted memories, and shattered brains.
But above all war was big money. Huge returns for investors in the
business of military machinery and providing privatized support to
armed services. The commodification of war had become rampant

over the years; it was exactly what Eisenhower had warned us about. The military-industrial complex. Think about that term, she said. The *military-industrial complex*. War was very big business. War was a capitalist's dream, you got great bang for your buck. For generations war had been very good for her family business. Guns had fueled their prosperity. To think of this troubled her. It caused her to feel she had blood on her hands.

GENERAL MACARTHUR. She saw him as a perfect emblem of fraudulent American heroism, she said. A human manifestation of our warmongering national arrogance, a man with such a huge ego and lust for victory that he ended up unnecessarily prolonging the Korean War by years, only to end up back where he started. Millions had died because he refused to stop his northern offensive fifty miles from the Chinese border, which might have ended the war two years earlier. But MacArthur couldn't back down. He had a Roman idea of conquest, of bringing China to heel, and through his indecision, vacillation, and faulty judgment an opportunity was lost. All this she'd learned by doing research on him, she said. These were things she'd never known, and she didn't think most other people knew about them either. There was a reason it was called *the forgotten war*. There was so much talk now about the Korean Peninsula, so much fear North Korea might lob a nuclear bomb at us, yet no one really discussed how MacArthur had fucked things up. We didn't have to end up as we have. MacArthur was disconnected from reality, she said, and no one would stand up to him and his need for "victory." Is this sounding familiar, she asked? MacArthur's tactics in Korea ended in failure, though he denied it, laid blame on others, and was eventually fired by Truman for his blunders. But by then it was too late. All those thousands and thousands of soldiers and civilians had died unnecessarily, not to mention millions of Koreans and Chinese. Talk about blood on your hands.

You don't know any of this, do you? she said. Any of what I'm telling you?

No, not really, I said. I don't.

That's what I mean. More people should know more about what MacArthur did. The mistakes he made. Because it changed a lot.

MacArthur, she said, represented the view, supported by some people, that war is a cataclysmic event intended to effect the complete destruction of an enemy, but Truman defined war as an extension of national policy—carried out only to achieve specific limited ends of the state. There was the big difference. MacArthur was an autocrat and egomaniac, and that's why he made the mistake he did and the war lasted so long. He was an arrogant bully. And yet he was much more popular than Truman. After he was fired by Truman for his arrogance and summoned back to the States, crowds lined the streets to welcome him home—cheering in San Francisco, a ticker-tape parade in New York City. And then he gave that famous speech on the Senate floor about how there was no substitute in war for victory. Well, where is the victory now in all these shitty wars that go on and on? Who were the good guys in all this endless war making? You couldn't tell anymore.

SHE HAD been talking and talking, steadily becoming more and more agitated. Of course it was important what she was saying. But she had been talking since we left L.A. Talking about art and her career, her past with Vincent, about Lucien and her general disillusionment, the final work she hoped to make, and now General MacArthur and the Korean War. I needed a rest. I wanted her to look out the window at the world we were passing through. I needed her to shut up for a while.

So I keep saying to myself, she went on, what can I do? What sort of performance makes sense? To immolate myself in front of the statue of MacArthur, in reference to all the Buddhist monks who had set themselves on fire to protest the Vietnam War? I know you'll find that idea pathetic, but the more I've thought about this I felt I could do it. I could make a profound statement—a *blazing* statement—and since my days are numbered anyway, why not exit with passion in an act of self-sacrifice enfolded into a final message? But then I got the news I might have another year or two. And I thought, would I really want to sacrifice those years?

You're upsetting me now with this kind of talk, I said. I looked over at her and shook my head. I thought of what my Aunt Marie had said all those years ago—*that girl isn't right in the head.*

Please don't set yourself on fire, I said. It's a terrible idea. You mustn't do that. Promise me you won't.

She didn't promise. Instead she simply shook her head and went on.

Perhaps you heard about the man in Brooklyn who set himself on fire recently. An environmental activist. Early one morning, when no one was around, he immolated himself in a public park. He believed in living morally, had devoted himself to all these environmental causes, collecting scraps from restaurants and supermarkets and creating a community composting site. He planted trees and flowers, organized recycling efforts, became a passionate activist. But he grew increasingly depressed thinking about climate change and the dead zones in the ocean, and he would occasionally talk to his partner about the self-immolation of monks. He thought those were very courageous acts. He did not see them as suicides. He had studied Buddhism and felt self-immolation could be a kind of communication. He quoted a Vietnam-era antiwar activist who said, "To burn oneself by fire is to prove that what one is saying is of the utmost importance." He felt that the monks who set themselves on fire did so because no other action can so meaningfully address the harm they see.

I can't believe that, I said. There are other meaningful actions that don't require torching yourself. What are you thinking? You *can't* do that. I can't even believe we're having this conversation.

I think, Jolene said, that this person saw his self-immolation as an incandescent act of speech, just as I might see it as incandescent work of art. I've always used my body as speech, as an tableau, as canvas. The difficulty with war—like the challenge with climate change—is that the problem is so large it can't be grasped. What can be grasped is that a man who lived an almost saintlike life of helping others and tried to do good in the world, who cared passionately about saving the planet, died alone in a very painful way in a public park, abruptly reducing his unique living body to black ash because he felt it was worth it. All I'm saying is I can understand that. I've thought of doing the same.

I can't bear to hear you talk this way, I said. It would be such a violent way to die, a horrible and painful death. You can't even think of doing that to yourself.

THE CONVERSATION had become very disturbing to me. Because I could see Jolene taking her life in such a manner. Hadn't she always gone to extremes? Even when we were young?

I'm not saying I'm going to self-immolate, she said. Only that I've thought about it. The thing about this man's death is, even though what he did was reported widely and lit up the Internet for a day or two, it made no difference to anyone except his close friends. His death by fire hardly caused a ripple in people's consciousness. Not even burning yourself to death can generate more than a passing notice these days. I don't know that his death seemed real to people because there were no pictures and no one was there to witness it. These days we can't imagine things without seeing a picture. In the end no one seemed to care.

Well, that's all the more reason to not even consider setting yourself on fire. If it makes no difference to anyone that this guy killed himself this way, why should it make any difference if you do the same?

Because I'm more famous, she said. I hate to sound so arrogant but it's true. My death by fire would get a lot more attention than his did. And I'd make sure to have pictures.

I couldn't even think of how to respond to this.

You don't want me to talk this way, I know, but that's only because in my own way I'm becoming less afraid. I can see many ways of dying, including by fire. I'm already in a way on fire. According to the Buddha we are all burning from eleven kinds of physical pain and mental agony . . . we are burning from lust, hatred, illusion, sickness, decay, death, worry, lamentation, pain, melancholy, and grief. Think of this list as our burning interiors. Our familiars, every one.

I lifted up the water bottle and offered it to her. Don't you want a drink of water, just to try and cool off?

Ha ha. The Bible is full of burning bodies—like in Jeremiah:

Cleanse your minds and hearts, not just your bodies, or else my anger will burn you to a crisp because of all your sins. That's God speaking, by the way. What I'm talking about is the extraordinary symbolic power of fire. Like the tradition of *sati*—widows throwing themselves on their husbands' funeral pyres in India. Burning a witch alive. Burning heretics as a kind of ultimate punishment. But can it be used to stop wars? To change thinking, as happened with the Arab Spring, which as you remember started with a Tunisian street vendor self-immolating? Holy men have gone into the fire to teach us to stop using war to solve our conflicts, to stop our harmful ways. To do this today we'd have to stop the grotesque amount of armaments flooding the world. Stop the wholesale traffic in armaments. Stop *profiting from death machines.* Here is where it gets interesting for me. Where the family business comes in.

Suddenly she stopped talking. She stared straight ahead and grew quiet. When I glanced at her I saw how her face looked very white. She had placed her hand over her mouth. She propped up one of the pillows against the window and said, Perhaps that's part of the piece I'm trying to put together. Now I'm tired. I just want to shut up and sleep for a while. This news must come as a big relief to you. Don't even try to deny it.

16

She slept for a very long time. We passed the turnoff for Lunar Crater National Park and the signs for the old abandoned mining towns of Golden Arrow and Silver Bow and the Tybo military outpost, where the motel owner said she had seen all those black helicopters. It looked sinister even without the helicopters. Now and then a dirt two-track led off the main highway and ran up one of the narrow canyons and into the hills, leading into a vast unpopulated world. I thought when I looked at these roads of how I'd like to ride a horse into that country and see where I'd end up. The rain had turned to sleet, and patches of white were beginning to build up on the ground, lying in thin layers between the rabbitbrush and sage like soiled little rags. I liked the quiet that had descended in the car. I found myself thinking about what Jolene had just said. About self-immolation. My grandmother, who was very religious, had a piece of needlework hanging in her living room, beautifully done, with flowers and flames surrounding the words THE LORD OUR GOD IS A PURIFYING FIRE. A saintly-looking woman rose up amidst the flames, eyes cast toward heaven. I had to believe she wouldn't do it. That nonsense about an incandescent act being incandescent art. As someone said about Robert Lowell, *Here is a man who devours himself.* Hadn't she always done the same? Her personality burning away far too bright?

WE PASSED oil refineries, with the thick white steam rising from the stacks dispersing into the low clouds and the derricks pumping ceaselessly out on the flat land. I thought of the term *extraction industries*. The digging and scraping and drilling and blasting of stuff out of the earth that had long ago replaced ranching as the state's main money-making business. In Railroad Valley dozens of deer were standing in the alfalfa fields. One had been hit by a car and left a bright streak of blood running across the black asphalt to where the deer's body lay torn open at the side of the road. A coyote was feeding on it. The live animal standing there over the dead one startled me. I stared briefly into the coyote's yellow eyes as I passed and felt a thrill as he returned my gaze and held it.

Snow still clung to the north faces on the mountains, and I could see how fresh snow had fallen on the lower slopes in a straight line. It looked much colder outside, and I noticed the gauge on the dashboard said it was below freezing. I remembered a chicken that Marie had once saved after its foot froze to the ground and came off. She bandaged the stump and let the hen live in her laundry room until spring, when it rejoined the flock and kept producing eggs for her.

WE CRESTED Black Rock Summit, over seven thousand feet, and dropped into a valley and came to an old stage stop with a rotting log cabin and dugouts carved into hills, the vestiges of a settlement from the nineteenth century. An old corral was made of boulders and rocks that had been stacked into a large circle. No trees out here to make a post-and-rail corral. The road became curvy, winding beside a river with cliffs like black claws casting jagged shadows over ravines. White patches of ice lay against the banks of the river. I thought she might wake up as I braked and turned and the car swayed around the sharp curves, but she slept on. I felt sorrow when I gazed at her. Not pity, which she never would have wanted. Just sorrow. She looked so frail.

I passed more animals that had been killed on the road. And there were lots of them, especially rabbits, all lying in various states of decay. Black clutches of crows fed on the kills, pulling at the carrion with their fierce beaks and waiting until the last minute to fly up and out of the path of the car.

We passed Duckwater, nothing more than a falling-down old

motel and a few abandoned buildings. The motel looked like many
of the places where I had stayed with my family on drives through
the West. Motels with carports so you could park right next to your
room, like the motels Humbert Humbert had stayed in with Lolita on
their drive through the West. These were the kind of motels Nabokov
and his wife had rented while he was writing the novel and that he had
loved. He once said that the principal invention of the American West
was the motel. Now many of them were abandoned or had become
run-down places that rented rooms by the month to workers in the
extraction industries. The once festive neon signs had gone dark, the
clever names a reminder of another time.

The goldenrod lining the road looked lush from all the water running off the asphalt. It was a world of such contrasts. Hard and soft,
pale and bright, sloping banks of soft-bottomed clouds laying gently
on the sharp ridges. Every once in a while we passed a cluster of ranch
buildings huddled in a stand of old limbed-out cottonwoods where a
few horses, still shaggy with their winter coats, stood in dilapidated
corrals. It was a hardscrabble world: few rural families had the money
to spend on the upkeep of a place. A line of white-faced cows trailed
beside a barbed-wire fence, one behind the other, plodding along, rain
glistening on their backs. I turned the wipers on high as we passed
through a sudden heavy cloudburst.

I BEGAN thinking about the apartment. The idea the building had now
been sold and we had a new landlord was certainly a new twist. Someone who wasn't nice, not at all like Billy Ray, who had been so good to
us over the years. What could we do now that reality had descended
except leave, and do it quickly, as soon as we could find another place
to live?

I thought of my former neighbor Margaret for some reason. My
first friend in L.A. aside from Jolene and Vincent. An elderly woman
who never complained, even though she lived alone with no one ever
coming to visit her. Working her jigsaw puzzles. Growing old in her
solitary surroundings. Watching her favorite religious *Hour of Power*
TV program and sitting for hours before the window in her kitchen

that looked down on the alley. She used to talk to me about how that had become her daily habit, sitting at the window and spying on the alley, though she'd never have called it spying. She just liked to watch what was going on, she said. The kids returning from school, the dope dealers and car strippers, the Mexican women hauling their laundry and groceries home, and the older men stopping for a piss against a telephone pole—she often observed this, she said laughing, without them ever knowing she was watching them. Everyone used the alley—the vegetable truck, the man selling tamales out of the trunk of his car, the Good Humor man, the homeless with their carts rattling down the brick as they stopped to check the garbage bins. She watched it all. People who never imagined they were being observed. She once said to me, *You wouldn't believe what I see, you just would never believe it, what people do when they think no one's looking.* After she passed away, when Vincent and I were cleaning out her apartment, I lifted the plastic cover from the table where she had sat all those years and found dozens of tiny notes she had written to herself, scrawled in pencil on scraps of paper: *Pills behind napkins; peanut butter in pot in-the-cabinet; noodles-and-sun-flower seeds in the blue pan; spices in tin can; clippers behind toaster; tuna-sandwich in the ice box; string in drawer behind spoons and forks; hour of power church 10 on Sunday; rain cap in clothes closet on a hanger; safety pins in chain purse; playing cards behind radio.*

I had come to see how a certain fustiness had crept into our own lives, a feeling of isolation, and that must change, I thought, or I could end up like Margaret, sitting at a table, watching the alley all day, scribbling little notes to myself.

AS WE got closer to Ely the landscape changed, and we entered the Humboldt-Toiyabe National Forest, where the piñons and cedars were so thick you couldn't see between them. I had to pay attention to the road now. The wind had risen, and it buffeted the car so it bucked suddenly from side to side like a shying horse. The rain came even harder, and I put the wipers on the fastest speed. Oncoming trucks threw up blinding amounts of water as they passed. All the noise and commotion caused her to wake up.

Where are we? she asked, drawing herself upright.

Almost to Ely, I said.

Can we stop there?

Yes, I know a place where we can get a cup of tea or coffee.

I mean can we stop for the night? I'm sorry, but I just don't think I can go on. I'm not feeling well.

I had not planned on this, but of course I told her we could stop. How could I say anything different, even though I'd hoped to make it to Wells or possibly even Wendover for the night. Her hand was covering her mouth again. She said she felt sick. I asked her if she wanted me to pull over and she said no, just keep driving. But please get me someplace where I can lie down soon.

I STOPPED at the motel where Vincent and I always stayed—a clean place with an okay Chinese restaurant next door. She asked if we could get one room. She said didn't want to sleep alone.

I went inside the motel and asked for a room with two beds. The woman behind the counter wasn't anyone I'd seen before, not the same receptionist. She said she only had one room left and it was a deluxe with two queen beds and a kitchenette. I told her we'd take it and signed some forms saying we didn't have pets with us, we wouldn't smoke, and if any towels or items went missing after I checked out my card would be charged an extra two hundred dollars.

I had to help Jolene into the room. While she used the bathroom I brought in our suitcases and pillows and the throws I'd brought along in case we needed extra blankets. I adjusted the heat—it felt cold in the room—and then I went back to the car and got the bag with the wine and travel food. I opened a bottle of white wine and poured us two glasses even though it was only midafternoon. I didn't care about that. I put some almonds on a plate and cut an apple into sections. She was taking a long time in the bathroom. I asked if she was okay in there, if she needed any help, and she said, I'll be out in a minute.

I chose the bed nearer the window, leaving her the one closer to the bathroom. I thought, I should open the curtains a little and let some light in but decided I liked it the way it was. It felt calmer with the low light. I picked up the remote and turned on the TV but hit the mute in case the noise might bother her. She still hadn't come out of the bathroom. On the wall across from my bed there was a cheap print showing a forest scene with a bear grabbing a big fish out of a river.

After a while I got up and opened my suitcase and hung up a few things. I hadn't really brought much that needed hanging, but it was something to do. I put my cosmetic bag on the counter next to the sink and looked at myself in the mirror. The light was bad. I thought I looked old. But other than that not too bad.

I lay back down on the bed and hopped through some channels, but there wasn't anything on TV except afternoon soap operas and Fox News, so I turned it off, though if I'd been alone or with Vincent I might have watched some news just to see what people were saying. I didn't think Jolene was the kind of person who would want to watch Fox News in the middle of the afternoon—or any time, for that matter.

I took a sip of my wine and felt a little guilty and then I thought, *What for?* I deserved everything and anything for doing what I was doing. It wasn't that I wasn't enjoying myself—I never got tired of driving through the Great Basin—I just couldn't figure out what was coming next with her. Not like traveling with Vincent.

I wished I could call him. I'd wait, though, until I saw how she was doing. Maybe I could go fill up the car with gas, find a place to park where I could be alone to talk with him. I don't know why it seemed so impossible to talk to him with her in the room, but it did.

WHEN SHE came out of the bathroom she had both hands on her stomach.

Would you mind turning down the bed for me? And getting my nightgown out of my suitcase? In fact, never mind the nightgown. Just help me with my shoes and socks, please. It's hard to bend over.

She sat on the edge of the bed, and I knelt down and took her sneakers and socks off. Then she stood up and undid her jeans and said, Can you help me with these, indicating I should pull them down, which I did. She had on bright turquoise underwear, and her legs were very very thin. Her thighs, especially, had so little flesh on them. I helped her get under the covers and put another pillow behind her head as she asked me to. She closed her eyes and breathed out slowly and said, Thank you so much, Verna. I'm just going to rest now.

Don't you want to take your hat off? I asked, and she said, oh yes, but she didn't make any move to do it, and I realized she wanted me to do that for her too, so I slipped off the black cap and tossed it on my bed. Her thin fuzz looked flattened down and patchy. I don't know why, but I rubbed her head a little and then I raked my nails gently across her scalp, spreading the thin growth over the bare spots, and she said, Oh my god that feels good, please keep doing that for a minute, and I did until I began to feel I should stop. Thank you, she said again, without opening her eyes, and I felt she didn't want to be disturbed anymore.

I told her I was going outside for a while and would probably take the car and fill it up with gas. I drove out to the edge of town near the freeway ramp where the gas was cheaper. I filled the tank and checked the oil and the tire pressure, all of which was okay. As I did this I felt very competent, the way I did when I realized I didn't need men to do men things for me. There was a small espresso place around the corner from the gas station where Vincent and I always got coffee, and I decided to go there. A group of women were sitting in the back in the little gift shop, and they stopped talking when I walked in and stared at me. I saw that they were painting flat rocks with different sayings. One of them got up and came to wait on me. The others stayed silent as if they couldn't talk now that I was there. I got a cappuccino, and then I went outside and sat in the car with the heater on and called Vincent.

HE WASN'T answering his phone. Maybe he was at school, I thought, though I knew this wasn't one of his teaching days. I left him a message telling him what was going on, that Jolene wasn't feeling well and we'd only gotten as far as Ely, where we were going to spend the night. I asked him to call me when he could.

I sat in the car and drank my cappuccino. It was a gray day, and the town looked more dismal than usual. It wasn't a very nice town to begin with. There was a museum in the old railroad station. That was about it for tourist attractions aside from the casinos. Some sort of massive mining operation sat high above town against a mountainside that had been torn open and sculpted into great salmon-colored tiers of tailings, like gigantic steps ascending an ancient pyramid. The tall concrete stacks at the base belched a dark smoke.

Slubs of dirty snow had been pushed up at the edge of the street in front of the coffee shop. I finished my cappuccino and decided to drive to the old downtown area where there were some casinos that had been there a long time. They were okay, they had an old-timey flavor, but once I left that area there wasn't much to see, just a lot of empty buildings lining the wide street that led back to the motel. I passed a few businesses—a dog-grooming place and a beauty parlor, a market and liquor store, the liquor store far bigger than the market— and a thrift store where Vincent and I had once stopped on one of our drives. Cold day, the owner said when we walked in. She was an older lady with a droll attitude. Well, at least there isn't any wind today, I said. She looked up without smiling and said, Day's not over yet.

Day's not over yet.

Vincent and I laughed about that one. It became something we said to each other now and then when we wanted to forestall any premature optimism.

WHEN I got back to the motel Jolene was propped up in bed watching TV. She had put lipstick on and was wearing a pretty nightgown and robe. I thought she looked as if she might be feeling better.

Where were you? she asked.

I filled up the car. Got a cappuccino and drove around town a bit.

I didn't know where you went, she said. You just disappeared.

I didn't bother saying I told her I was leaving. But maybe she hadn't heard me. She was watching a cooking show on TV. The chef was pushing a magic pan that could cook hotdogs in under a minute.

Are you hungry? I asked.

I think I could eat a little something, she said. But what I don't know.

Do you want to go out? Or I can get takeout?

I couldn't possibly go out, she said. But I don't know what I could eat.

Would you like some soup? A sandwich? Maybe some Chinese food from next door?

It's crazy, but Chinese food sounds good. Do you think they might have sizzling rice soup? Or maybe wonton soup?

I'll see.

Don't go yet. Let's wait awhile. I'm not that hungry. But maybe I'll have more wine.

I don't think they open until five o'clock anyway, I said. I hadn't even noticed that she'd finished the glass of wine I'd left for her. I looked at the clock on the night table: it was 4:20.

I POURED us more wine and then got the Chekhov stories out of my bag and stretched out on my bed, thinking I would read for a while. I pulled the flannel throw over myself and put one more pillow behind my head. From this low angle I could see myself in the mirror on the wall next to the TV, and I could also see her. I could tell she was watching every move I made. I let myself be observed.

What are you reading? she asked.

I held the book up.

Oh, Chekhov. Lovely. The thing about Chekhov as opposed to some of the other Russian writers is he was such a humanist, unlike those moralists and political or religious thinkers like Tolstoy who always wanted to bring God into it. Chekhov had such a deep appreciation of the moral complexities of life. It's as if he said, Let's put God and all these grand progressive ideas to one side and be kind and attentive to the human. Let's begin with respect, compassion, and love for the individual. His stories are so full of feeling for ordinary mortals, I think.

Listening to her speak this way, I thought of what she said earlier about how she had become an intellectual during her university years.

But hadn't she always been that way? She could still say things that surprised me and revealed such a sublime intellect, such learning. She was the one who'd gotten the education. I felt we would never be on the same level—I could not claim to have her knowledge—still it pleased me that we now loved so many of the same authors and could talk about them as we never could have before. Flaubert, Chekhov, Faulkner. I also realized at that moment something I hadn't thought of before—that we were probably fond of the same authors because they had been some of Vincent's favorites and he had no doubt influenced her reading habits, just as he had mine. He was our common influencer.

WE DISCUSSED Chekhov for a while longer, and then she began talking about the two authors she loved so much who had in part been responsible for her wanting to move to France. One was Colette, whose writing she was mad for, but she also admired the way she had lived her life with such freedom. Had I ever read her novels? *Cheri,* or *The Vagabond?* Maybe *Break of Day?* I said I had not.

The other writer who made her want to move to France was Janet Flanner, who left the Midwest for Paris in the 1920s and started writing a bimonthly column for *The New Yorker,* then a brand-new magazine. For almost fifty years she had written her Letter from Paris column for *The New Yorker* under the pen name of Genêt, right up to the 1970s, when she died. Nothing escaped her interest. She wrote about art and music and theater, Parisian culture, books and authors, fashion and flowers and gardening. She interviewed politicians and celebrities, she wrote about war. She knew everyone—Gertrude Stein and Hemingway, even Colette. Every two weeks she had to come up with a column for *The New Yorker,* describing life in Paris. She had lived in hotels, including, for a while, in the Ritz, writing late into the night, holding court in the bar in the afternoon. She never had an apartment of her own, never learned to cook or keep house. She loved good food and wine and stylish clothes, especially the mannish suits she had made by her favorite Parisian designers, and she had a particular passion for shoes. A diminutive woman and chain-smoker with a husky voice and shock of white hair, she was witty and brilliantly entertaining. Everyone wanted to know her. In that sense she was like Colette, who had reigned supreme over Parisian society in her day. I should read Colette, she said. I *had* to read her. She thought there were actually some similarities between my writing and hers—between my life and hers, in the sense we were both provincials who met sophisticated men who tutored them and turned them into writers.

Is that what you think? I asked, interrupting her. That Vincent "tutored" me?

I thought you wouldn't mind that description.

You once said you felt I gave him too much credit.

Did I say that?

Yes you did. When you were leaving after our lunch in Beverly Hills. You said we aggrandize the men in our lives to our own detriment. Isn't it aggrandizing Vincent to say he *tutored* me? Giving him too much credit? I mean I did in part find my own way.

You would never have become a writer without him, would you? He brought you into a *milieu*—that's what I'm saying, and encouraged you, and that's what happened with Colette and Willy, her older lover, the cad who took credit for her first novels. He didn't *make* her a writer. He just created the circumstances where it might be possible for her to become one. Somehow I thought you might be more offended by my calling you a provincial.

What do you even mean by that? A provincial? Am I *a provincial*? I looked over at her. I tried to assume a look that might be neutral, but my face felt stiff, as if I'd just washed it with too much soap and it had dried into a tight mask.

Well, you *were* a provincial, believe me, and don't take it as an offensive term. When you arrived in Beverly Hills with that truck and horse trailer—when I saw you after all those years, yes, it would not have been wrong to say you were a provincial arriving in the city.

Okay. I get your point.

Then you shouldn't take that term as something bad.

Okay, I won't.

I can tell you're miffed, but don't be.

I'm not miffed. I just didn't know what you meant.

Colette would never have minded being described as a provincial who became a woman of the world because she never lost her love of the countryside and she was also crazy for animals—especially cats. Don't you think you're like that too?

Yes, I am like that.

Well, there you have it.

Anyway, she said, both Colette and Janet Flanner were gay—or in Colette's case bisexual—not that this has a lot to do with anything, but it probably did lend them both a certain aura and allow them to lead freer, more unconventional lives. Colette had many affairs with both men and women and was married three times. But Flanner was a different case: she had a very long-lasting relationship with one lover, an Italian woman named Natalia Danesi Murray, a publisher and editor who divided her time between Rome and New York. From time to time they lived together for short periods and always arranged to take several vacations with each other every year, as well as spend time at Natalia's beach house on Fire Island, but much of their relationship was conducted long distance, via letters. Still they'd had the most beautiful life together. They were both such smart, chic, worldly women with superb taste and cultural sophistication. Theirs had been a great romantic love. After Janet's death Natalia published a collection of the letters Flanner had written to her over four decades, called *Darlinghissima: Letters to a Friend.* "Darlinghissima" was how Janet always addressed her letters to Natalia.

It was the most beautiful correspondence, Jolene said. Reading these letters made her realize what great love meant, how it could express itself with such tenderness and intelligence. Flanner also painted such a vibrant portrait of her life in Paris. What she was thinking about various subjects and current events, who she was seeing for drinks and dinner, what she really thought of the plays and concerts and art exhibitions she was writing about—and the writers and politicians she entertained and amused. Who wrote letters like that now? Who wrote *any* letters at all? Do you ever write letters anymore? she asked.

I said that I didn't, unfortunately. I don't know why I added *unfortunately,* since I'd never been one to write many letters.

It's a great loss, she said, the way we've abandoned letter writing for these banal little emails we now exchange. I'll never be able to understand why whenever something new is invented we rush to give up the things that came before, even when those things are so rich and meaningful, like taking the time to write a real letter. In the future we won't have any of these beautiful collections of letters that say so much about a time and place and an author's personality. That's tragic. You know what Emily Dickinson said about receiving a letter? That it was a pleasure denied the gods. Now it's one denied even us mortals.

Did Vincent ever write you any letters? she asked.

No, I said. I guess we were always together.

He didn't write me any either. Well, maybe one or two over the years. But you know Vincent. How matter-of-fact he is. How unromantic. He never even remembered our anniversary or Valentine's Day. Of course it would be beyond him to write a really romantic letter, wouldn't it?

I didn't say anything. But then I knew I wouldn't need to. She'd keep talking for me. Or rather *at* me.

I closed my eyes. It helped when listening to her speak about Vincent if I didn't have to make eye contact. I felt like she was telling me bedtime stories, even though it wasn't my bedtime and I didn't really want to hear them.

When you read a collection like *Darlinghissima* you realize how people are starting to forget how to even express romantic feelings with words, she said. Maybe our feelings are becoming stunted and we'd be embarrassed to profess affection in such open and sentimental terms. Flanner would end her letters with these beautiful endearments, like *I long for you. I miss you with my heart and soul. You are not absent a minute from my thoughts. We will have happiness when we are reunited again. . . . I love you I love you, we shall be together soon my love.* Well, no one in my whole life has ever written a letter to me that said things like that, let alone an email. I think email has probably stunted our ability to express deep feeling in favor of the idea of expediency.

MY PHONE suddenly rang. I knew it was Vincent before I even looked at it.

Excuse me, I said to her.

I shut myself in the bathroom and turned on the light, which was connected to a fan that made a terrible racket. I had to raise my voice to be heard over the background noise.

Hi, honey, I said.

Hi. So you're in Ely?

Yeah. She needed to stop. She wasn't feeling well, though she seems better now. I tried to speak softly, yet loud enough to be heard over the fan.

How are you?

There was a long silence, and then I heard him sigh. Well, not so good. Max hasn't come back. I was out looking for him when you called. I've been walking the neighborhood. Calling him. Asking people if they'd seen him. No one has.

Oh. That's not good. But you know cats sometimes just take off for a while.

Not Max. He's never done this.

But it's only been one day.

Two days, actually—yesterday and today—and one night. I thought he'd come back last night and he didn't. Now I'm beginning to really worry. He's never been gone overnight before. Maybe I should put some signs up around the neighborhood.

Or give it one more day.

I could do that, I guess. I just have to find a picture of him and make some flyers.

It shouldn't be too hard to find a picture, I said. Whenever I looked at the pictures on my phone they were mostly of the cats. It was the same with him. Somehow we never seemed to have enough photographs of them. It was crazy, but who cared?

Try not to worry, I said. I think he'll come back. He's a pretty smart guy. He'll get hungry sooner or later.

Maybe somebody thinks he's a stray and is feeding him, he said.

Max is too shy to let anybody near him. I don't think he's out making new friends. He probably got scared by the new landlord.

I got scared by the new landlord, he said.

———

I WANTED to change the subject, I didn't want to even think about the landlord, so I asked, What else have you been doing since I've been gone?

Listening to music. Reading. It's quiet here without you. I don't like having you gone. Do you have any idea when you'll be back?

Not yet. But I'll talk about it with her. We could make it home in a couple of days, I said. If I take the freeway down through Utah and Vegas it'll be a much quicker trip. My impression is she only wants to see her mother and visit the house, not hang around too long. So maybe only a few more days until I'm back?

I realized when we spoke about her she was still *she: She* made it seem like she could almost be anybody.

I'm going to go out again now, he said, and see if I can see Max. Call me before you go to sleep tonight, okay?

HOW'S VINCENT? she asked when I emerged from the bathroom. I wondered how she was so sure I'd been speaking to him and not someone else, but that was pretty obvious.

He's worried, I said. Our cat Max didn't come home last night. The new landlord showed up yesterday and probably scared him off. Vincent's been out walking around the neighborhood, and he sounds pretty worried.

So he's still crazy about cats, huh? At one point we had three, but that was before we moved to the West Coast, when we were still living in my small apartment in the Village. I never particularly liked cats, so don't ask how that went. I find litter boxes disgusting. And with three cats that can't go outside? Well, all I can say is the smell got to me. We used to have fights because I felt he wasn't cleaning the boxes often enough and I certainly wasn't going to do it. Rather I had a fight because you know how it is with Vincent. One person yells, and the other doesn't say anything. Guess who the screamer was. I used to get so angry with him when we fought about something that I'd just lose control. I would lash out at him because he didn't seem vulnerable.

Everybody's vulnerable, I said.

I'm not so sure. I felt he didn't have a vulnerable personality. I felt like he might be pathologically indifferent to criticism and you just couldn't get to him.

Well, he's not. He's just . . . quiet. He has an even nature. He never gets too high, and he never gets too low, and he rarely gets upset. He doesn't like to fight. I could have added *plus he has a brain that works in a very different way from other people's,* but I didn't.

One time I kicked a hole in the bedroom door, she said, when he wouldn't come out and talk to me. I had to live with that hole for years. Every time I looked at it I'd feel embarrassed and remember that fight. I was the one who always looked like a jerk in the end, acting out and getting so angry and saying wild things while he maintained his aloof silence and came out unsullied. I could say almost anything to him and he wouldn't get upset. Fighting was impossible because he wouldn't argue. He never said anything. And then afterward, after I calmed down, it was as if nothing had happened. He was always so forgiving and pleasant. I would end up despising him for being so pathetically passive, but it was me I really came to loathe for acting so hysterical and losing control.

I knew she was watching me, looking in my direction, but I kept my eyes closed and didn't move. I had always understood the ferocious and frightening power she had over other people, and I could imagine how she must have scared Vincent—any sort of emotional outburst caused him to shut down. You'd think she would have figured that out. I'd never been afraid of her, but I knew other people who had. Kids in high school who would never dare cross her because she could be so cutting and ruthless in the way she'd treat you if you fell out of favor with her. I knew she expected me to say something now, and I felt a certain kind of power by denying her wish. One thing Vincent had taught me was you didn't have to talk if you didn't want to.

Are you falling asleep over there? I can't tell if you're listening to me or not.

I smiled, just to indulge her, and then said, Um, I'm feeling sort of hungry now since we didn't really have any lunch. I think if it's okay I'll go next door and get us some food. Do you mind eating early?

You're like him, she said. So adept at changing a conversation you don't like. But that's okay. We're all like family now, aren't we?

I PUT my coat on without saying anything and walked over to the restaurant, thinking, *family?* Really? Is that what we were like? In some ways it seemed true. Weren't we all intertwined by the sort of tensions that get played out in families? The jealousies and resentments and history and affection. The hurts and unmet desires. The sullen withdrawals, which was rather what I was feeling right then. I really wished she'd stop talking about Vincent. I felt a fierce need to protect him. From whatever. Her gossipy talk. The claim her memories made on the past. Stop being such a jealous nerd, I thought. But I didn't quite know how to do that.

It was cold and windy outside, and the restaurant felt pleasantly warm and filled with the intense aroma of cooking. Vincent and I had eaten here so often we knew the menu well though we'd never ordered soup, so I wasn't sure about that. It was a family-run place— parents in the kitchen with their teenage son and daughter waiting tables. We had often looked at these kids and wondered what it would be like to grow up Chinese in Ely, Nevada, and spend all your spare time working in your parents' restaurant. Neither the girl nor the boy spoke much; they seemed shy and were always businesslike and somber when they took your order or delivered the dishes. The girl had a pretty face. I placed my order with the girl and told her it was takeout, and then I sat at a counter next to a humming Coke machine and waited.

WHEN I got back to the room Jolene was on the phone. She was laughing and I heard her say, *She just came back with the food.* I placed the bag on the table and took out the containers—a round one with the soup for Jolene, a flat one with the stir-fry for me. *I will,* she kept repeating into the phone, *I will.* And then she hung up.

That was Ina, she said. She sends her regards. I can tell she wishes she were making this trip with us. But selfishly I didn't want her to come along. I wanted it to be just us.

And here we are, I quipped, two long-lost pals together again. I was trying to be light, but I realized it didn't sound very amusing.

Are you upset with me? she asked.

No. I'm tired from driving. I just want to relax and eat something.

I think you're not telling me the truth. I could tell you didn't like it when I said Vincent tutored you or that you were provincial.

Well, you're not completely wrong about either of those things, I said, placing the soup next to her on the nightstand. No sizzling rice, I said, but they did have wonton. Do you want more wine?

Yes, please. You're too nice to me.

Unlike you, niceness is my specialty.

That's because you were raised in a culture that valued niceness in women above everything else. It trained girls how to be if we wanted to be wanted.

There are worse things than being nice.

Name one.

Being mean, like you.

I'm not mean. I'm truthful.

So you say. But I think I'd need outside confirmation of that. Maybe three character witnesses.

I felt like I was trying to loosen up with her, but it wasn't working: I knew that beneath every word I uttered there was a little sharpness, a prickly edge of truth sticking out. I didn't know where this was coming from.

Just so you know, I felt I was tutored by men too, that's the way it went in those days. You didn't find women teaching in art schools, nor were they being shown much in galleries. They were the consorts, even the great female artists like Lee Krasner or Carl Andre's girl-friend Ana Mendieta—the artist who made that shocking rape piece and who Andre may or may not have pushed out the window to her death. Personally I think he did it because she was getting more atten-tion for her work than he was at that time and they were arguing about that. I suppose that's one way to get rid of the competition, but my point is, these women artists were all standing in the shadow of their male artist lovers. I don't remember one female art professor. But there was, memorably, one male professor I had an affair with—an older artist who ended up stuck in academia, but he still exuded such irresistible charm. He thought I was brilliantly talented, so how could I not fall in love with him? He called me his protégé. He sought to furnish my mind, as his *protégé,* you know, with all sorts of ideas. He wanted to groom my taste, show me the world—not simply make me a better artist but a better human being. I came to hate his fickle, tortured, proprietary attitude just as I came to really dislike the look of him without his clothes on. I saw how he was spreading his attention around, how riveted the other female students were simply to be in his presence—such a big important artist even if his reputation was beginning to wane. I believed he was only having sex with me and that the others were simply getting mental infusions from his glorious manhood, but it turned out I was wrong about this. I found out he was sleeping with other students too. We all hoped it might help our careers. In those days, you know, it happened a lot. It wasn't such a big crime then, there were a lot of professors who slept with students as if it was their right. Later, I discovered the kinds of rewards awaiting us as we experienced a slatternly letting go with guys our own age. Once we embraced our sloshy natures the whole art-school experience got a lot better.

I looked at her then and shook my head.

This is all so foreign to me, I said. While you were going to graduate school and making your art and having affairs with professors, I was still in Utah, married to a cowboy and taking all kinds of jobs, from managing a dude string to waitressing in a snack bar. You've never asked me about that time. About what my marriage to Leon was like or whether it had been hard to make that move to California. Not a word about that part of my life. Not one question, ever.

I'm a self-centered bitch, what can I say?

Well there's that, I said.

I started to cry then, which was a terrible thing to have happen.

Oh shit, she said. I was just joking. But I've really hurt you, haven't I?

No, you haven't, I said. I'm just thinking about a lot of different things.

Like what an ass I can be? And how you're now stuck with me on this trip?

She pulled the covers back and swung her legs out of bed and stood up. I saw that she planned on getting in bed with me, and I thought, oh no, not that.

Move over, she said.

I set the cardboard container from which I'd been eating on the nightstand and moved over. She got into bed next to me and put her arms around me.

I kept crying. I just couldn't stop. I felt like my thoughts were growing dim, so I couldn't make out anything anymore. My mind a swamp of dusky emotion. A gurgling mess. Why *was* I crying? I couldn't find anything to grab on to in all that murkiness. I just couldn't stop the tears from coming, and it caused me to feel weak and helpless in front of her and I hated that feeling.

She pressed my face against her chest with one hand and stroked my hair. Her arm felt uncomfortable behind my neck. Everything so awkward.

I'm okay, I said, hoping that would make her go away, just get back into her own bed and leave me alone.

She kissed the top of my head. Oh, Verna, she murmured. You were always the good one.

The *nice* one, I said. I made the word sound as icky as I could, but she didn't take the bait.

Yes, the nice one. Truly, honestly nice.

I can't breathe, I said. You have to let me go.

She pulled away from me. But she didn't leave the bed and kept her arm around my shoulder.

We're so very different, aren't we? she said. She was looking down at me. I refused to look at her.

Yeah *very*, I said. It was such an understatement it annoyed me. Being annoyed helped me get a grip on my feelings, and I stopped crying just as suddenly as I started.

You know I'm jealous of you? she said.

No. I don't.

Well I am.

I didn't even want to ask why but I couldn't help myself.

What would you be jealous of?

What do you think? More than anything the fact that you ended up with Vincent. He was supposed to be mine.

The comic reality, she went on, is that we spend our lives as conduits for forces we don't understand. I thought I wanted to leave him, and I did. But almost immediately I had regrets. He was the most solid thing in my life. The *truest* man I ever met. I just couldn't understand him.

What do you mean by *truest*? I asked. I wanted to know, why this word?

He's a man without artifice. He couldn't say something he didn't mean. Nor affect a feeling he didn't really have. I never saw him be cruel to anyone, or try to exert unwarranted power. He could be very blunt in what he said but not mean. If someone wronged him, he let it go. He couldn't hold a grudge if he tried to. He always had this clarity about what he felt or thought, and I really envied that. What he liked, or didn't like, he just knew what that was and never had to stop and think. He didn't say things just to please people. He had such a strong moral center—I don't know how else to put it. I always admired that. He could spend vast amounts of time alone and never seemed to mind. Of course it annoyed me that he could be so strange sometimes. So opaque. So distant and at the same time so self-involved that you might think he would never even miss you when you were gone, but I guess what I'm saying is, he was always so true, so natural and calm, while I was so urgently needy and in constant turmoil, especially at that point in my life. I thought he didn't love me because I felt he wouldn't give me what I needed to prove this was true, and I was always harping on him. But later I realized he gave me what his idea of loving meant. We just had different ideas of how you showed love for another person. If I had been able to understand this at the time, things might have turned out differently.

You had a big career, I said. You got a lot of what you wanted, didn't you? You've received so much attention for your work, and I assume you've met really interesting people along the way, including the men you lived with over the years—maybe not Lucien, but they can't have all been bad, there had to be something good about other relationships. You've told me more than once you couldn't have stayed with Vincent. So you left. I don't see how you can complain.

Complaining is never a condition one has to earn the right to, she said, and laughed. It doesn't arise out of some idea of fairness. You don't have to remind me I've had a lot of luck in life. I've been given a lot of breaks.

She was silent for a moment. I could see our reflection in the mirror opposite the bed. I looked like a child cradled in her long arms, my face pressed against her flat chest. She appeared sexless in her pale robe. She could have been an angular version of either gender. Her face looked so colorless now that the bright lipstick had worn off. I didn't know exactly why I had felt like crying, but now it was over and the embarrassment had passed. I felt calm. I didn't mind she was holding me.

SHE BEGAN speaking again. She said, Maybe it's right that I ended up with a man like Lucien who was so innately dishonest, so completely untrue with me, to teach me a lesson. I've always cared more about money than I should. Money and appearances. Success and recognition and all that—well, you know better than most that this is true. My terrible *cupidity*. I've always wanted nice things. Expensive things. All the things you think matter or might make you feel good. I remember the first time Lucien took me to his parents' Paris apartment. I was dazzled. It was twice the size of his, and much grander. The dim light of those high-ceilinged rooms in their Left Bank mansion, the leaded-glass windows, massive banisters, the ornate woodwork and studded leather armchairs in his father's library. I'd never been inside such a beautiful apartment. Lucien was both an aristocrat and a rebel and I loved that he had these two parts to him. They seemed so complementary, and I thought maybe by attaching myself to him I could possibly end up being both myself in some oddly conceived way. I thought coming from the background I did would matter to him and his family, make it easier for me to be accepted in those *aristocratic* circles. But his mother saw things much more clearly. She could never understand why he married me. Perhaps you have repressed plebeian instincts, she used to tell him, a comment he enjoyed repeating to me. It's possible I got what I finally deserved with Lucien, for going for all that was so superficially lovely about him. I'm telling you this so you'll understand that compared to you I'm pretentious. I've led a pretentious life.

It sounds as if Lucien was a bad choice, that's all, and I don't know that you have to make any more out of it than that.

I wanted to sit up now and pull away, to separate myself from her so she could go back to her bed, but because she began talking again I stayed where I was.

I wanted to use Lucien as some kind of magical mirror, I think. I've always used relationships that way. As a means to reflect the elusive wholeness of a fractured self. It was during this period that I reread Colette. She reminded me that to boldly embrace one's sexual nature was essential to liberating the self. And yet we mustn't kid ourselves that women aren't always alone in our desires: men never give us what we need, the solutions to our solitariness. Men exhaust women, use them up, but not Colette, she could always renew herself in another relationship. And when her relationships failed, Colette could always find comfort in returning to nature, by going back to the land and the village where the divine solitude of nature and her love of animals restored her happiness. But me? I don't even like the idea of pets, and I've never really known the country life. I wouldn't know how to live that way, I've always been such an urban creature. Still I feel such longing now for some peace—some solace. I feel irremediably consigned to my solitariness. That's why I am jealous. I always thought Vincent would be a good person to grow old with, that he's the sort of person who would take very good care of you if you really needed it. I get the feeling you've had a very good life with him. You have made each other happy. Am I right?

You're not wrong.

I didn't think so, so you can see why I'd be, if not jealous, then at least envious. I could never settle for just happiness. It all had to be special. Everything had to be so special, especially at that point in my life—when I made the decision to leave him. It had to be more and more about me, while for him it had to be more and more about him, so it had to collapse, I guess.

I was moved by the way she confessed these feelings. But I knew what my life had been like with Vincent, and *happy* was not the first word I'd have used. The pain I'd experienced all those years when I had not understood why he behaved as he did—but I would not reveal any of this to her. Instead, I said that maybe happiness, like niceness, wasn't the best measure of anything, including a marriage.

What is, then? she said. How do you judge your life if not by considering whether you've known happiness? I've missed happiness. I used to know it. But not for many years now, I'm afraid. The more success I've had, the harder it's been for me to settle into any real relationship. It's like there was never time. Never the right person. And then Lucien came along. I leapt at the bait. What a fucking mistake.

She covered her face with one hand. I couldn't tell whether she was crying or not, but I didn't think so.

What I know is this, she said, removing her hand from her face and looking down at me as she spoke. It didn't take me long to realize I'd made a mistake by leaving Vincent—not a *total* mistake, but nonetheless for a while it felt like a pretty big one—because he was the force that had encouraged my seriousness about who I was and what I wanted to do. He had always shown me through his total commitment to his own work what I need to do with my art, and afterward I felt jostled and sparked by conflicting needs and ideas. He had *grounded* me, and after I left him I was like a loose wire, dangerous to the touch. I entered a period where, in terms of my relationships, I experienced nothing but incinerated romances, like a series of bad theater pieces. Men chosen for the wrong reason, or just the wrong men. Vincent was my last serious commitment to another human being. The rest have ended up as conveniences in one way or another: I have used them, or they have used me. I left Vincent because I felt he could only offer that kind of tight asphyxiating sincerity and rigidness, with all his strangeness and claustrophobic behavior, and I wanted to breathe—so I went out for air. And when I looked up again, thinking I might reconsider, I learned he was living with you.

I sat up, pulling away from her. Her pink satin nightgown was damp from where my tears had left a wet spot on the front.

The food is getting cold, I said. We should eat.

Food, she said, as if the thought disgusted her.

Don't you want your soup?

I stood up and moved aside so she could leave my bed.

I really exhaust you with my talk, don't I? she said.

I didn't answer that. I didn't think she expected me to. I just looked at her and slowly shook my head and allowed a very small smile to form on my lips, a look that I knew she could interpret in different ways, in any way she wanted to.

SHE GOT back into her own bed. We returned to our food. Or rather I did. She held the container of soup in her hands, resting it on a towel on her lap but she didn't eat anything.

Can I just say a bit more about Colette? she said after a while. I won't speak any more about Vincent if you don't want me to.

It's all right. Say whatever you want. I'm here to listen.

She laughed. Oh, I like that. Oh, hear my confession, Holy Mother.

Go on, child, I'm ready. I said this in a deep, fake voice of heavy religious authority, just to stay with the joke. But, oddly, I felt suddenly freed of the awkwardness of the scene that had just taken place, able to play the role I think she had really wanted me to assume from the very beginning—that of the listener, the one to whom she could confide. And I saw how it might be a relief to go ahead and act it out under the guise of a farce and be her mother confessor. But there was nothing farcical about what she began to say next: it was clear she was speaking intimately, so I turned toward her so that she would know she had my attention.

I'VE ALWAYS had such a profoundly strong sexual nature, she said, from very early on. Drawing and masturbation were the first sacred experiences I remember. I was four years old when I began masturbating. I remember my mother used to come into my room and catch me at it and try to shame me, but her words had no effect. I would be lying there on the bed, lost in the warmth and perspiration, in absolute ecstasy. I realized the exquisite sensations I could produce. As another friend once told me—she had also been a compulsive masturbator as a child—*I thought my genitals were where God lived.* That's how I felt. I thought what I felt was some kind of holy experience. To be able to produce these kinds of sensations.

My father, as a physician, took care of bodies, as you know—and as you also know, not just any bodies but women's bodies, women with *female trouble.* Women who couldn't get pregnant. Women who needed hysterectomies, whose fallopian tubes were blocked or who didn't ovulate or suffered from a variety of other reproductive ailments. He saw women through their pregnancies and helped them give birth. All day he stared at women's genitals. My mother liked to walk around the house naked, and I used to feel she was trying to compete with all those women he saw without their clothes on every day. But of course that's another subject, isn't it? Maybe in part as a result of all this exposure I grew up with, I felt I had the right to indulge my sexuality any way I wished—to explore my body—and later of course it became a part of my art in very explicit ways. I was never afraid of letting it play out in my life in a rather bold fashion. It had to do with a desperate desire to capture the passionate things of life. To revel in the sensuous malice of the dangerous female body— the body that is so celebrated, and so feared. When I began making art I realized the potentiality of the destabilizing powers of the female body in my own hands.

And then as I grew older—I mean much older—I couldn't use my body in the same way anymore, and I didn't want to. I had already done that, and I was ready to give it up. But Colette helped me understand that despite misogynistic laws and traditions, French culture ultimately prizes and respects sexual appetite and daring in women and, as these women age, values their prowess and wisdom. Even their aging bodies are thought to have beauty. That's one reason why Colette could have affairs with men half her age. She remained *desirable,* with a full appetite for sex. The French do not see older women as spent old crones or dried-up matrons, and it must be said that French women don't allow themselves to age that way either—not if they can help it. They never quite give up on caring for themselves as attractive, vibrant creatures, and they do it in a rather natural and effortless way. They don't have the ridiculous preoccupation with youth that you find in this country. They find older women can still be very sexy, and very desirable, and also very wise. They value their appeal. And yet—and yet—there is a point, of course, when the aging woman does become repellent.

Do you really care so much about still being desirable? I asked.

I wish I could say it isn't important, but it's not an easy thing to give up. Even with my ravaged body I feel vain. It's always been one of my greatest sins, my vanity.

As your mother confessor I must advise you *not* to give it up. Why should you? You've always been so beautiful. So chic. It comes naturally to you, and it always has. Think of how well your body has served you all these years. I say continue to adorn it, make it lovely as you always have. That's Mother Confessor's advice.

I felt pompous making this little speech, even disguised as an act, but I believed it was true. She was now and always had been so beautiful, and part of the beauty was how effortlessly she had accepted and worn it. I had been trying to reassure her, yet I noticed that she had now begun to cry.

I didn't try to say anything. After a while she stopped crying and assumed a calm, almost beatific look. She turned and stared at me, looked right into my eyes for what felt like a long time, and I met her gaze with steadiness and calm. I didn't wonder why she was looking at me this way. Or why she had begun crying. I told her that she looked lovely right then. And it was true. Her face had softened, the crying had brought color to her skin, and I could tell it made her happy when I told her this.

Look at us, she said, turning from me and gazing into the mirror on the opposite wall, where we were both reflected. Isn't it extraordinary we've known each other as long as we have?

I made a noise like *Mmmnnn,* as if to say, *Well there you have it.*

———

FOR THE rest of the evening we watched TV. We caught most of the movie *The Last Picture Show* on a cable channel, and it was as good as I remembered. That wind-blown little Texas town. Cloris Leachman as the lonely middle-aged housewife who takes a high school student for a lover, infusing her life temporarily with such feeling and tender hope before she is crushed when he rejects her, leaving her to feel undesired once again, spent and old and alone. Cybill Shepherd, in her role as the sexy teenage vixen from the wealthy family who becomes a magnet for all the boys in town, just like Jolene had been.

When the movie ended we got ready for bed even though it was still early. She moved slowly around the room, as if walking were difficult. She made such a long lean elegant column in her pink robe. A figure of exquisite gracefulness.

I went into the bathroom to change into my nightgown, shy to undress in front of her, and then made a call to Vincent while sitting on the edge of the tub with the door closed. Max still hadn't come home. I could tell Vincent didn't want to talk, and when he didn't want to talk he simply couldn't make the effort. He sounded tense and unhappy from the moment he answered the phone. I knew he wanted to simply end the call. He said he'd text me in the night if Max showed up.

I GOT into bed and turned my light off.

In the dark she asked if she might come into my bed for a while, just to lie next to me. She said she had missed the contact of another human body. This had been one of the hardest things for her since her breakup with Lucien. This feeling of the warmth of another body next to her at night. That's all I want, she said, I just wanted to be near you for a while.

I said okay. I moved over, and she climbed under the covers and immediately turned her back toward me. I turned toward her, and we lay in the dark awkwardly, our bodies spooned together, facing the same way. After a while I relaxed a little and it didn't feel so strange for her to be there. I wrapped my arms around her with her back against me. She fell asleep that way, with my arms around her. My hands holding on to her forearms. Her body was astonishingly cold, especially her feet. I placed my feet against hers to warm them up as we had done during sleepovers in our youth. I knew she was telling the truth that she only wanted to be close. To be held. Nothing more. And I was fine with that.

In the morning when I woke she was gone from my bed. I could hear her in the bathroom taking a shower. After a while she came back into the room. She was naked, holding a towel in one hand. I wanted you to see, was all she said, what has become of this body. She stood before me, her lips formed into a faint smile, and I gazed at her. At the scars. The various scars. The bones protruding from her hips, her sharp ribs and shoulders and emaciated arms. I didn't say anything. I didn't need to. Instead I simply said, Yes, I see, and knew I would never forget.

17

We left the motel in Ely early, stopping only to pick up coffee and scones at the espresso place. I had not heard from Vincent in the night, so I knew Max hadn't returned.

We headed north, passing through McGill, the small town nestled below the massive mining operation high on the mountain. Miners' housing lined either side of the road that ran through town, little wooden cottages, each surrounded by a chain-link fence. The sky was overcast with low-hanging clouds. We had a long drive ahead of us to the next town of Wells. A two-hour journey, with nothing in between but isolated ranches. I planned on stopping in Wells to get something to eat and gas up again.

I asked her if she minded if I played some music. I put on a Sam Cooke CD. She said, That's good. I like that.

She seemed better this morning. Calmer. She was wearing a gray cardigan over black jeans and a white T-shirt. The same cap on her head.

Before we left the room she'd taken out the red beret and insisted I wear it. Indulge me, she said, and I let her arrange it, tilting it at just the right angle as I stood in front of the mirror. I liked it, but it was made of wool and it was beginning to bother me now, causing my forehead to itch. I didn't take it off, however. I thought I could stand wearing it a bit longer, just to please her.

I was always pleasing people, I thought, even if it made me uncomfortable.

———

WE DIDN'T talk. It was as though we had talked ourselves out the night before and now we only wanted to listen to music and look out the window. There was some sense that perhaps too much had been said, and we had pulled back so as not to exhaust ourselves. A purple haze clung to the base of the mountains on the left, and the landscape had a muted, pleasantly sedate quality. The emptiness around us translated into a feeling of sublime silence. Mile after mile of sagebrush and barbed-wire fences. The rocky pleated scarps tipping toward the rims of the high basins still filled with snow. An occasional cluster of black cows kicked up dust as they scuffed through the sage. No high passes before us now to climb over as yesterday when we were heading west to east and crossing over the summits, but rather a long straight road stretching due north. The alluvial fans spread out at the base of clefts in the mountains, forming little skirts of pale yellow, and the blocky snow-covered peaks looked like patriarchs in their white robes.

At the rest stop that marked the site of the old pony express trail we stopped and got out and stretched our legs. The air held an icy freshness: patches of thin snow still lay on the ground from the storm the previous day. I wandered over to where a display explained how the riders for the pony express had traveled this route year-round, changing horses every twenty miles, setting off on a fresh mount and riding over a hundred miles at a stretch through all kinds of weather. They'd used sturdy mustangs crossed with military mounts. There was a display showing a rider tossing a mail sack over a saddle as he attempted to mount a fractious horse, ready to set off on another leg of the journey. My great-grandfather had been among the original pony express riders who traveled this route when he was a boy of only sixteen. You had to be young and strong to endure those rides. The love of horses ran deep in my family. I liked to imagine the courage and skill of those riders and the magnificent strength of horses that could gallop for twenty miles at a time, even through a snowy landscape, and the boys and men who could ride a hundred miles at a stretch. When Jolene wandered over to the display I pointed to the picture and explained that my great-grandfather had been one of the original riders, and she said, Oh, that's interesting, but she said it in a way that let me know she didn't find it interesting at all.

IT WAS almost noon when we reached Wells. We stopped at a café called Bella's, owned by the people who ran the bordello of the same name just a few blocks away. Sitting on shelves when you walked into the restaurant were cups and T-shirts with pictures of scantily clad women, but if you didn't know the other Bella's existed you wouldn't get it. Vincent and I had eaten here often because it was a convenient place to stop and they sold delicious pastries.

The waiter was an overweight young man I had seen before. He had such bad acne it was hard to look at him when you placed your order. I could feel sorry for him and still have trouble thinking of food while looking at the raw weeping pustules that covered his face.

The restaurant was so busy it took a while for the boy to bring us our tea and coffee and even longer to get our sandwiches. Looking around, I saw that almost everyone in the restaurant was badly over-weight. Couples so obese they had trouble fitting themselves into the booths or on the wooden chairs pulled up to the tables. Like many overweight people, a couple sitting near us looked not just fat but *sadly fat,* as if burdened by their immense bodies. It could seem nor-mal now, especially in these little rural communities, to be so heavy because everyone around you looked the same way. I knew Jolene was aware of all the overweight people sitting around us. I saw the way she was looking at the couple seated near us.

She shook her head. I don't get it, she said, staring at the couple, how did America get so fat? Don't these people care about what they look like? Don't they worry about their health?

I thought she was going to tell me how thin people in Europe were and how great they looked compared to Americans, but in fact she said it was becoming a problem in France as well. People were getting fatter there, too, especially children. For generations the French had eaten butter and cream to their hearts' content and managed somehow to survive, but now, after just a couple of decades of fast food, all that was changing. Still it was much worse here.

It's one of the biggest differences I've noticed since returning to America after being away for a long time—how fat people are, she said. That and all the homeless. Weird how one reflects having too much, the other too little. These two things say so much about America. What a cruel fucking country we've become.

You're on a roll again, aren't you?

What? You're not supposed to notice people are so fat now? That the whole country is ballooning in size—like over forty percent of Americans not just fat but *obese*. I mean, c'mon. Don't you think this sounds rather crazy? We all end up paying for that kind of unhealthiness. And yet you're not supposed to *fat shame* people. I'd never heard that term until I returned to the States. One would think that you wouldn't have to fat shame people, that they would feel shame themselves about their extremely unhealthy state. But that gets us back to corporations, doesn't it? And the subject of predatory capitalism— creating products you know will be unhealthy and get people addicted: sugary drinks for children, the fat-salt-fried craving in adults, cheap fast food for poor neighborhoods that don't even have grocery stores anymore, so you have this massively overweight population that feels shitty about themselves and gets depressed . . . and then you can sell them lots of drugs to help them feel better!

Please, I said. You're doing it again.

Doing what?

Going off the deep end.

I don't consider it a deep end. I consider it something we should all be discussing and trying to do something about.

Okay, but not now. Besides you're talking so loud people can hear you. And that's rude, since you're talking about them.

She stared at me, silent, looking into my eyes for a long time. I wasn't sure why she was looking at me this way. Because I'd drawn the line? Because I'd challenged her? Because I didn't want more of her rants?

Then, slowly, she smiled at me and said, Okay, Verna. Actually,

I think you're right. I can be rude. Someone needs to yank my chain once in a while and lead me back to my cage.

Thank you, I said. And we went back to eating.

IT WAS early afternoon when we left Wells, heading west on the interstate. The atmosphere in the car was much quieter then. Things seemed to hang unspoken between us, but I wasn't sure what those things were. We were headed toward the town of Wendover, which straddled the Nevada-Utah line. Half the town in one state, half in the other in what I'd always considered a schizophrenic arrangement. The Nevada side had casinos, bordellos, and liquor stores: the Utah side had a Mormon church, funky motels, and an old military installation that was now largely abandoned, including an airfield and hangar where the *Enola Gay,* the plane that had dropped the A-bomb on Hiroshima, had been stored after the war. I'd always found this creepy. That people made pilgrimages to the site just to stand and look at that plane that had caused so much death and suffering.

Dense cedars covered the low hills on either side of the freeway, and thick white cumulus clouds cast deep shadows over the distant mountains. There were a lot of RVs on the road with names like Outlaw, Vagabond, and Maverick—all driven by older people. Did it make them feel like outlaws and mavericks or vagabonds, that they could simply take off in a massive carapace and hit the road, go anywhere they wanted, and still drag along a simulacrum of home? I could see the appeal. When old people traveled this way I thought it was for relief from a life that they had gotten to know too well and that bored them, yet ironically they felt compelled to bring everything along with them.

I put on the original cast recording of *Oklahoma!* from the 1943 production, music that inevitably made me feel happy. Jolene said, Oh my god, *Oklahoma!* Now we're really getting into the corn.

I'm not changing it, I said, and I don't care what you say.

That's fine. It sort of goes with the landscape.

Not really, I said, looking out at the dry desert. This is hardly corn country.

That depends on what kind of corn you're talking about, she replied, and laughed.

I ignored her and began singing along with "Oh, What a Beautiful Morning." An amazing song. A song to set any day right. A song I loved to sing.

I'd forgotten what an incredibly beautiful voice you have, Jolene said when the song ended. I think Vincent loved that about you when he first met you. That you were so musical, unlike me. Do you sing a lot for him?

Sometimes, I said. He plays and I sing. But not so much anymore as we once did.

What do you sing?

Lieder, I said, Schubert's songs mostly. Sometimes he'll ask me to try out something he's working on, just to hear it.

Ah, she said. Well, that sounds just lovely, doesn't it? I can't think of another couple I know who make music together.

I'm sure there are many, I said.

Still, I'm envious. I've always wanted there to be more music in my life. I've always felt it would be a gift to be able to play an instrument. Any instrument. I used to love it when Vincent played the piano.

Why don't you get a ukulele? I said. They're easy to learn to play.

A ukelele? she said.

Yeah. A ukelele.

She laughed, and said, I just might do that. If I get a ukulele and learn to play, will you sing along?

Sure, I said. But only if you learn to play "Over the Rainbow."

WE PASSED a prison area and a sign that said picking up hitchhikers was prohibited. There were other signs for ranch exits with no services. The burned-out cab of a semi sat at the edge of the freeway, like some kind of apocalyptic warning. There were signs for deer crossings and a game tunnel under construction, and a billboard advertising "Adult Distractions," just ahead in Wendover.

What do you suppose "adult distractions" are? Jolene asked.

Sex, booze, and gambling, I said. It's a trucker town, Wendover.

A lot of long-distance haulers stop there, looking for a few hours of relief from the loneliness. A few hours of—uh, *adult distractions.*

The sun was dropping now, and I wondered if we could actually make it home by nightfall. We were only four or five hours away. Her energy seemed to be holding today, but I understood now how quickly that could change for her. The road ran through rock cuts that had been covered with screening to keep boulders from tumbling down onto passing traffic. We stopped on top of Pequop Summit and looked out over the chaotically beautiful landscape—the stained scarps and buttes, the ridges and mesas and peaks, the coulees and basins and braided ravines, denuded slopes sporting slag remnants: we could see a very long ways, range after range visible beyond a broad dry swath of desert, a landscape so otherworldly it looked like *Forbidden Planet.* A gouged mountain came into view, one side completely removed by machines, and the bright orange earth stood out as a sharp ragged shape against the deep green of the cedar-covered slopes. Such big views, she said, taking in the grand vista that had opened up before us. Such distance, she added. Far ahead of us, we could see the beginning of the Salt Flats, the vast stretch of whiteness looming on the horizon.

The clouds had turned to mares' tails, long dark wisps twisting down from the sky in ropey skeins. By the time we reached Wendover it had started to rain. Casinos lined the main road coming into town—fake Italianate and mock western structures, massive places with largely empty parking lots on a weekday afternoon save for the lines of big semi trucks and the RVs parked in rows. We passed the Red Garter Casino, advertising *All You Can Eat Pasta, All You Can Drink Wine $10.99,* and a couple of strip clubs and an enormous liquor store. In the middle of town a white line had been painted across the road, marking the point where the state lines met, and a big sign said WELCOME TO UTAH.

Ah, Utah, Jolene said, reading the sign slowly, the word coming out like an exhalation: *u-taahhhh.*

I TURNED off Main Street and headed down a rutted road that led to the abandoned airfield. I told Jolene I had something to show her, but I didn't say what. We passed an old stone church that had been turned into funky apartments and continued on until we came to the edge of the derelict air base and drove past rows of run-down wooden barracks, each the same size, originally built to house airmen. On the right were several large hangars with windows broken out. At a gravel pullout near one of the hangars I stopped in front of a display that showed pictures of an atomic bomb being loaded on the *Enola Gay*.

We got out of the car and stood reading the sign that explained how thousands of airmen had trained here during World War II before heading overseas to Europe and the Pacific Theater. The *Enola Gay* had been only one of hundreds of planes based at the airfield. After the war the *Enola Gay* was retired and kept in its own special hangar. The hangar was now a memorial site. The airfield was no longer used except as a private airport and for emergency military needs. Everywhere you looked you saw how seedy everything had become. How run-down and decayed. Even the roads were broken up by deep potholes and difficult to navigate. The dead air base had the aura of a spent past.

My god, Jolene said, studying the *Enola Gay* display. She shook her head and turned away and stood looking out over the scene—the empty hangars, and rows of wooden barracks where the airmen had lived, many now with doors or windows missing, and some with walls or roofs caved in.

Fat Man, she said. *Fat Man.* I wonder who named that bomb? And Little Boy, the second bomb. Fat Man and Little Boy. Perfect names to describe a certain kind of American male.

WE GOT back in the car and drove along the rutted asphalt, circling the perimeter of the base. You could see how a few of the sturdier barracks were still being used: one had been repurposed as a tire repair shop with mounds of old tires and abandoned car parts stacked around it. Another had become a Pentecostal church and thrift store. I was looking for the old complex of barracks where Vincent and I had once stopped that housed the Center for Land Use Study, an artist and environmental collective that offered a do-it-yourself tour of an exhibit detailing the way the areas around Wendover had been used over the years. I knew Jolene would find it as interesting as I had the first time I saw these graphs and charts and photographs that lined the interior of one of the buildings. And it turned out I was right. Once inside the exhibit she moved slowly through the displays, taking notes, making drawings in a little book, and occasionally calling me over to look at something.

This whole area, she said, has been blasted and poisoned to hell! It's nothing more than a massive bombing range and hazardous waste site.

A map she pointed to showed the Salt Flats and the surrounding muds of the ancient Pleistocene era in all their pristine beauty, the miles and miles of the surrounding dry desert that for eons had created such an inhospitable and forbidding landscape of purity and agelessness—like an alien planet with no trace of humans—that had been converted into a vast military test range and toxic dumping ground. She stopped in front of a large display with pictures and text that explained how in the middle of the twentieth century the military began using over three million acres in the region for bombing and training activities. There were still a thousand square miles of unexploded bombs left out on the desert. Each day squads went out and attempted to locate the bombs and dispose of them, but the task was endless. Rocket engines and explosives and propellants were manufactured at two large industrial sites in the region, and settling ponds and tailing mounds as well as hazardous waste disposal facilities dotted the landscape. Other areas were devoted to the storage of chemical and nuclear waste and the testing of biological weapons. Toxic and radioactive detritus came from far away and was entombed in shallow troughs, closing parts of the landscape off to humans for thousands of years. The whole region was a no-man's-land, millions of acres off limits to all but authorized workers.

Jolene read parts of the text out loud to me:

This vast portion of the American West had become an *anthropic landscape*—a landscape refashioned and formed by men, a place to test bombs and store contaminated detritus.

A large wall map showed the Salt Flats and western Utah desert identified by areas of military, industrial, and commercial activity, and she read the list of businesses and installations that humans had created over the years in the vast unpopulated areas spanning the restricted areas, pointing out where each was located: The Clive Incineration Facility, Envirocare Radioactive Waste Disposal Facility, Aptus Hazardous Waste Incinerator, Grassy Mountain Hazardous Waste Site, Magnesium Chloride Plant, Tekoi Test Range, Dugway Proving Ground, Intrepid Potash, Tooele Army Depot, Pilot Peak Target Area, Utah Test and Training Range, Aragonite Hazardous Waste Incinerator, Energy Solutions Waste Disposal Facility.

There were nine hundred munition storage igloos scattered across the Utah desert and over two million square feet of secured storage for armaments, and every day blasts occurred at these sites to destroy unstable weapons, either at the Little Mountain Test Annex or Bacchus Works, a large explosive complex. Hill Air Force Base, located some miles away, was the nation's primary provider of maintenance and logistics for intercontinental ballistic missiles, keeping up with the task of taking care of the nuclear warheads and military ranges. Both above- and belowground nuclear tests were detonated at test sites farther to the south—Yucca Flats and Area 53. An aerial view showed the massive subsidence craters, enormous depressions in the earth where the land had been sucked into vast craters by an atomic bomb detonation thousands of feet below the surface. Between 1951 and 1992 there were almost a thousand nuclear detonations at these test sites. Subcritical tests continued right up to the present in order to establish that a stockpile of an estimated 6,550 nuclear weapons was at all times ready to use.

Six thousand five hundred and fifty nuclear weapons! she repeated. Six thousand five hundred and fifty . . .

IT'S ALMOST too much to take in, she said after we had left the barrack with the displays and were driving away. She had no idea that so much of Utah was given over to toxic chemical and nuclear waste.

And bombing ranges, she said—millions of acres bombed over the decades! What about all the animals out there? she said. What about the people exposed to that radioactive stuff?

Do you remember, I said, when we were in elementary school and they were doing aboveground atomic testing in southern Nevada? More than once a toxic cloud drifted over our area, distributing radiation fallout.

She shook her head. No. I knew tests were happening, but I don't remember radiation clouds near us.

I remember, I said. Because I looked at the picture on the front page of the newspaper one day just after a toxic cloud had passed over and I saw all these white boulders in a big field, and then I realized they weren't boulders, they were dead sheep, killed by the fallout. Hundreds of sheep died from just that one test. I always wondered what it did to the humans—to *us*, I mean. I know a lot of people got sick later, especially in southern Utah where the radiation fallout was the worst. People ended up with thyroid and other cancers. Later the government started paying people if they could prove their cancer might be linked to those tests.

We were the *downwinders,* I added. The people living in the path of the worst of the fallout.

Ah, she said. Ah. I hadn't thought of that. How very disturbing.

She fell silent. A deeply serious look crossed her face. I hadn't meant to suggest her cancer might have resulted from those tests so long ago, but I knew that was what she was thinking. And so was I.

WE DROVE around awhile longer, through the sad and run-down neighborhoods at the edge of town. Streets lined with trailers or mobile homes in poor condition. Many were abandoned, block after block of derelict dwellings with broken windows and gaping holes in the outer walls through which you could see old bathroom fixtures and broken furniture, the detritus of abandoned lives.

Jolene said she wouldn't mind stopping somewhere for a beer— she thought it might help settle her stomach, which was feeling a little upset again. Signs for Carmen's Black and White Bar led us to an old

double-wide converted into a bar, but it was closed until five p.m. The
Salt Flats Cafe was open, however, and we stopped there and found a
cavernous place with folding chairs pulled up to a dozen small tables.

It was empty at four in the afternoon, but the tacos we ordered
were good although Jolene ate very little. She seemed more interested
in the beer. She drank two glasses—the first quickly, the second more
slowly. I could see she was tired. The dark circles under her eyes had
taken on a kind of bruised quality. I realized that this was the moment
in the day when she lost energy very quickly. She not only looked tired
but a little tipsy now from the beer. She clung to my arm to steady
herself as we walked back to the car. I thought, *Maybe she will sleep as
we drive across the Salt Flats.* It was less than two hours to Salt Lake City.
Another hour beyond that and we'd be home.

SHE DID not sleep, however, as we crossed the Salt Flats. She gazed out
the window, studying the immense stretch of whiteness bounded by
distant jagged mountains, only occasionally offering a comment about
the eerie landscape we were passing through.

Another time she wondered aloud if there wasn't something in
humans that desired conflict and change. You wouldn't imagine this
would be the case, she said, but I think it's true. We must love war as a
species to spend so much money and time on it. Look what we've done
with our treasure. Think of what we've done to the desert out there.
All that land bombed and poisoned, test sites with huge underground
radioactive caverns. *Subsidence craters.* That's a new term for me. Never
heard that one before. The earth just sucked down into itself, leaving
those gigantic depressions as a result of underground atomic bomb
blasts. They looked like—like what? Huge pox scars on the landscape.
Empty eye sockets. A diseased landscape. Such violence and damage
to the earth.

She talked about death. She quoted a thinker named Eve Kosofsky
Sedgwick who believed that after her demise she would be "differently extant." Jolene felt this was an interesting way to put it: differently extant. Here, but not here. Extant, but different. What would
that difference be? Jolene had her own theories, mostly aligned with

Buddhist thinking about reincarnation, but she didn't actually like the word. To her, being *differently extant* was a much more open idea. Why imagine you might come back as a bird or a tree when your energy, your molecules, your *whatever* might just as easily be more generally mutable, distributed across a wide and shifting spectrum of nature?

She had read a number of books on Buddhism over the years, beginning with Suzuki, the first to bring Buddhist teachings to the Western world. She told me that as he lay dying, his last words were *Don't worry! Thank you, thank you.*

If only she could be that brave, she said. That *grateful.* But she was frightened. That was the truth. She was frightened not so much of death per se, but of just how bad the end might be. She didn't want to suffer. But who did?

There are so many more things I'd still like to do, she said wistfully. So many that I won't.

WE WERE now driving through the middle of the Salt Flats. For as far as you could see outside the window, a landscape so evenly flat and white—a rather dirty granular white when you really looked at it. It was hard to believe this was all a natural landscape, it seemed somehow man-made. All that flat whiteness, a level plain of pale salty earth. In places people had arranged dark rocks on the whiteness, spelling out words in hearts. The lone skeleton of a radio tower and a line of abandoned railroad tracks were the only other features breaking the monotony.

Ghostly tall mountains began to appear as the distant Wasatch Range came into view. The whitewashed sky, the flat white earth, meeting at an uneven horizon with the white peaks standing out so starkly. We passed the turnoff for Iosepa, the isolated colony the Church had established in the nineteenth century for Hawaiian converts when leprosy was discovered among them and they had been dispatched to this forbidden world. I had once visited the abandoned town site, where I could feel such haunted sorrow.

AFTER A while she began talking about her work again.

She said, I realized some time ago that I have made of myself a fetishized subject in part because of the art I chose to make, which was so directly *there,* I mean *right in front of you,* and because it always involved my body and that was inescapable. Now I simply wish to disappear. To let go of this body. I want to go with dignity, not be completely ravaged by disease. This last piece will be a work of separation, that much is clear. But I am not ready to vanish just yet. Though I do love the title of that Louise Bourgeois illustrated book *He Disappeared into Complete Silence.* This would be the way to go.

I told her I was glad she didn't want to vanish just yet, but she didn't respond. She only reached over and laid her hand on my forearm—the skeletal pale hand that looked so fragile yet so elegant—and kept talking.

She said, I realized early on people have made the big mistake of saying my work is about sex when it's really about the nostalgia of the body.

I had no idea what she meant by *nostalgia of the body* and I didn't have time to ask, though what she said next was very easy to understand.

After I left Vincent I lived for a while with a much younger guy named Marco, he was also an artist, a very good one. I never in my life was with anyone the way I was with him. I'm not saying I didn't have good times before, but with him I could be so lighthearted and free. He was the opposite of Vincent, who had such a difficult time breaking out of his seriousness. But with Marco—no one was ever so carefree, so light and easy to be with and just ready to play and live. We used to go up on the roof of the building where we both had studios and fuck on moonlit nights, howling together. Yet we really cared about what was happening in the world—and you know how little interest or tolerance Vincent has for that stuff. He was always so cocooned in his own world. One of our friends said of him at the time, *There's no shadow on him.* I knew what he meant. He always steered clear of the darkness.

She removed her hand from my arm and lay back and closed her eyes, tilting her face away from me toward the window. I couldn't tell whether she wanted to rest now or if she was gathering her thoughts to go on, but for the next little while she didn't stir and then it became clear she had dozed off once more.

THE LANDSCAPE changed. No longer were we crossing the Salt Flats. Exits for small towns began to appear. We passed the off-ramp for Magna, the mining town where my mother was born and where my grandfather had worked in the mines until black lung ended his life. The long blue throw of the lake was now visible, with the pale islands rising from the water. I took the freeway exit, skirting Salt Lake City, and turned north past the big oil refinery, with orange flames spewing from the tall stacks. Not until we were driving into town a half hour later did she finally wake up.

Where are we? she asked.

Home, I said.

She sat up slowly and looked around. And then she shook her head and said, I hardly recognize it.

18

It's true the town had changed, even since I had last been home.

The street near the old train station, once lined with bars and secondhand stores, had been transformed into a trendy area. Now there were sushi places and organic cafés and coffee shops, and a little boutique hotel in an old building that had formerly been a bank, and this is where Jolene had booked us a room before leaving L.A. As she checked us in I overheard her telling the clerk, *Yes, a suite with two beds, that's what I reserved,* and I knew we would once again be sharing a room. I also realized that this had been her plan from the very beginning. It had always been her intention to have me with her all the time, even at night when she slept.

As soon as we had unpacked she called her cousin Aimee to tell her we'd arrived, and Aimee invited us to come over for a drink. I didn't know who Aimee was. I couldn't remember ever having met her, but after Jolene hung up she explained that Aimee was the relative who'd been helping to care for her mother. Her cousin's daughter, whom she had always liked. She had bought the Tomb when her mother was no longer able to live there alone. It was Aimee who'd found the upscale care facility where her mother had spent the last few years and where Aimee visited her every week. She's a godsend, Jolene said, the way she takes care of everything. As you know, it's not something I could have ever done, even if I hadn't been living in Paris. She also happens to be a really lovely person, and I can't say that about many of my relatives.

———

WHILE JOLENE took a bath and changed her clothes, I went down-stairs and called Vincent. His voice sounded remote and sad when he answered. He told me that Max still hadn't shown up. He said he didn't know what to do. It had now been three days, and Max had never been gone so long. I asked him if he'd put signs up and he said he had. He'd put them up in many places and also offered a five-hundred-dollar reward. Again he said he didn't know what to do. He felt Max might be gone forever.

I told him he shouldn't give up, but he interrupted me.

Also the new landlord was here again yesterday, just snooping around, looking at everything. I heard him ask Hector about the cats. He asked if they were strays. He wondered if they actually belonged to anyone. Hector told him there were a number of stray cats in the neighborhood who came around and he didn't know who they belonged to, but I also heard him say the two black and white ones were ours. The landlord replied he was going to board up the area underneath the building so none of the cats could get under there any-more. He was also going to trap any cats hanging around, no matter who they belonged to. They were a menace, he said. I saw him unload a wire trap from his car and set it up. He baited it with tuna fish and left it out by the front steps.

Oh my god, I said. He *is* evil, isn't he?

What if Max is hiding down there under the building? What if he boards it up and Max gets trapped?

You'd hear him meowing. You'd have to find a way to let him out.

What if he goes for the tuna in the trap and—

He won't do that, I said. I really don't think he will.

The tuna could be laced with something, you know, poisoned and—

Max doesn't like tuna. I've never been able to get him to eat it, and I don't think he'll start now.

I can't take this, he said. When are you coming home? It's terrible being here alone with all this going on. Please come back, he said, just come home.

———

I RODE the elevator back up to the room, thinking I must talk to Jolene and tell her we had to leave after she visited her mother the next day. She needed to see her mother and get that over with so we could head back to L.A. We could take the freeway home, heading down through southern Utah and Las Vegas. If I drove straight through, we'd be home in ten or eleven hours, if Jolene could take being in the car that long. If not we'd stop. But I needed to get back. It wasn't fair to leave Vincent to deal with such a difficult situation alone.

When I returned to the room, however, Jolene seemed too nervous to bring up anything with her then. She was anxious to get to Aimee's, she said, and demanded to know where had I been. She didn't like it when I just disappeared. I knew she was tired, so I let this go. I decided I would talk to her later, over dinner perhaps when we could relax and make a plan.

JOLENE'S COUSIN Aimee was waiting for us in the courtyard of the old house, a thin woman in her forties, with a kind face and straight blond hair cut blunt. She was wearing a brown sleeveless dress and heavy sandals with blue socks, an outfit that made her look sort of Scandinavian. On the way over Jolene told me Aimee had never married and that she volunteered at a raptor recovery center where injured birds were treated. She had gotten her degree in veterinary science years before but never actually gone to work as a vet. She could do as she pleased, as one of the heirs to the family fortune, and it pleased her to volunteer her time caring for injured birds.

I might not have recognized the house, it had been so transformed, or perhaps my memory of it had radically changed over the years. It was smaller than I remembered, and still it was an imposing old place, three stories tall, surrounded by beautiful landscaping and winding stone paths.

Aimee wanted to give us a tour of the house so we could see the changes she'd made, starting with the kitchen, which she'd completely redone and which had a beautiful orange cast-iron stove. She'd changed the feel of the living room with its massive stone fireplace and heavy beams by painting the walls white and installing minimal furniture. The house, she said, had become so run-down over the years and been so permeated by the smell of cigarette smoke that the realtor the family had hired had despaired of ever selling it, and that's when she'd stepped in and decided to buy it. In fact it had taken a lot of time and much more money than she'd imagined to make it livable again.

She took us upstairs, to the second floor, and showed us how she had converted the maid's room into a library. Jolene's old room on the third floor was now the guest room, and her parents' bedroom and an adjoining room had been combined to give Aimee a large bedroom suite with a sun-filled sitting room and windows that overlooked the garden and swimming pool. Everything had been done with great taste. Gone were the garish colors on the walls and the heavy dark furniture, replaced by pale colors and fine pieces of mid-century furniture.

We stood together at the window looking down at the pool.

Unfortunately, Aimee said, a boy had drowned there a few years back. Jolene's mother, who by then had all the symptoms of advanced Alzheimer's and was often found roaming the neighborhood disoriented, had left the gate open and a three-year-old boy who'd been visiting his grandparents in the house next door had wandered off and later been found in the pool. It was at this moment Aimee decided she had to take charge, and she had convinced Jolene's mother it was time to move to a care facility.

You never told me about the child, Jolene said.

It was a terrible thing to have happen. And afterward no one wanted to talk about it. I felt you were so far away, why should we trouble you with such hard news?

JOLENE TURNED away from the window and crossed the room and sat down in one of the large chintz-covered armchairs. If you don't mind, she said, I'll just sit here for a moment. I'm feeling a little shaky after the long drive.

Aimee and I sat down in chairs opposite her, and for a while no one said anything. The light in the room was lovely, and it felt pleasant just sitting there. Then Aimee asked, Would you like me to fix a drink for you and bring it up here? Or would you prefer to go downstairs?

Here would be fine, Jolene said, I like this room. A glass of white wine if you have it.

I said I would take the same, and Aimee left to get the drinks.

SHE'S VERY nice, I said, after she had gone.

I shouldn't have left her to deal with everything. So cowardly of me.

I wouldn't say that.

Well you're not me, she said sharply.

I shook my head. Don't be that way, I said.

What way?

Mean, I said. Don't be mean. Not to me, not to yourself.

If I had come back and dealt with things earlier, perhaps that boy wouldn't have died. I knew how bad my mother was. Aimee kept telling me in the letters she sent. She was gaga, completely incapable of living alone, and yet she refused to leave the house. I let it go on too long. And look what happened.

I knew there was no point in telling her again she shouldn't blame herself. The truth was she was selfish. Always had been. And it was also true that family had never mattered much to her. She'd left them behind long ago.

AT THAT moment a cat wandered into the room. A beautiful gray cat with short hair and a large round head. It crossed to Jolene and rubbed against her legs.

Oh my god, she said, drawing away from it. Doesn't that thing know I don't like cats?

How can you not like cats? I said, and stretched out my hand toward it. Slowly it turned and came to me and sniffed my fingers. Lovely cat, I said, stroking its head. What a beautiful thing you are. Lovely little *pudder*.

I can't get over how seemingly adult people instantly go childlike when they start talking to animals, she said, it's like they suddenly feel compelled to revert to using their little baby voice.

So what? I said, laughing. What harm is there in that?

It sounds ridiculous.

Well, I don't mind being ridiculous, I said, and laughed some more just to let her know I wasn't going to let her get to me. It truly was a handsome cat, and so friendly. I wished Vincent could see it. Its short fur was as velvety as a plush toy. I could feel its body vibrate with purring as I stroked it. It had lovely emerald eyes.

I could never get over the way Vincent treated cats, she said. He could be so rough with them. He'd pat them hard and I'd think, They must hate that. But no, they'd arch their backs with pleasure, and the harder he patted them the more they seemed to enjoy it. He'd pull their tails as they passed by—sometimes even lift them up by their tail a little, or pull them backward across the floor—and I'd think, That is *so* cruel. I'd yell at him to stop it—stop torturing the cats, I'd say. But I guess it wasn't torture because they always came back for more. He'd swipe at them with his hand and they'd swipe back with their paws, and this would go on for some time until he got scratched and started bleeding or they ran away. I never understood it. This kind of rough treatment. It upset me, the way he acted with the cats. One of them turned into a mean little thing that sometimes attacked friends when they came over, and I felt it was his fault. And yet they loved him, that was clear. It's as if he and the cats were somehow on the same wavelength, fellow creatures. I mean it's crazy stuff to me, what people do with their animals. How much money they spend on them now—teeth cleaning and haircuts and all that stuff. It's like animals have become the substitute for . . . what?

I wanted to plug my ears. And still she droned on.

Pets are like *what* to humans now? What are they substituting for? Why are people spending billions every year in this country to make sure their animals get the very best care while they walk past homeless sprawled out on sidewalks every day without even giving them a glancing notice? You know what I think it is? It's that people are bored and lonely. It's like something I read recently that said, They've been freed from a lot of the drudgery of daily labor and they live so separate from nature and this has increased focus on their need for love, their craving to be loved by someone, by anything, so it's the new duty of animals to love us and make this loneliest of times feel a little less lonely.

I was glad at that point Aimee came back with our drinks. Seeing the cat there, Aimee said, Oh Eddie, I see you've come out to greet our guests. Eddie was a stray your mother had been feeding, she said to Jolene, but she never allowed him to come into the house. Once she was gone he moved right in with me, and it turns out he's the nicest fellow. He's been a great companion for me these past few years. I'd be so lonely without him.

Jolene looked at me and raised her eyebrows, as if to say, *See? Just what I said.*

THE TALK turned to Jolene's mother. At ninety-three, she was in surprisingly good health, Aimee said, especially considering her dementia had progressed to the point where she had been robbed of any real quality of life. She appeared semicatatonic much of the time, but at other moments she could become animated. She was being well taken care of, there was no question about that, as Jolene would see for herself. She doubted very much her mother would even know her: she had long ago stopped recognizing Aimee. Still she made a point of visiting her twice a week if only to monitor the situation and make sure she was receiving the correct care. Other members of the family also saw her occasionally, including Aimee's mother, Jolene's aunt and her mother's long-estranged sister. She went to visit Jolene's mother every few weeks, even though the sisters had quarreled years ago and stopped talking to each other. They had never really made up and now it was too late, but it didn't matter. In the end, family was family, wasn't it? Aimee said. You had to let go of old grudges.

She described the care facility for Jolene, a place that had embraced the idea of trying to create a feeling for the patients that they still lived in their own house. The large central room was designed to look like an old-fashioned town square. There was a small fountain surrounded by plants, a "main street" with lampposts and benches with signs for a bus stop. The carpet was patterned to look like green grass, and along the walls were facades of what looked like little white wooden houses with "porches" and rocking chairs. Each patient's room was really a little faux house with a front door that opened onto the fake street where there were signs for grocery stores and a library, an ice cream parlor, and a movie theater. The skylights in the ceiling gave the effect of sunshine falling on the scene, and at the end of day the skylights were rigged to begin shutting down and an artificial dusk was induced. Then the unit began to look like a small-town street at night. The whole thing was like the nostalgic set from a bygone American life.

Your mother particularly enjoys sitting on the bench waiting for the bus, Aimee said, even though of course no bus ever comes. She doesn't seem to mind. I don't think time is something that passes in the same way for her as it does for us. It's where I often find her, on the bus-stop bench. Sometimes she'll ask me, When do you think the next bus is coming? And I've learned to say, Before long, I think. That seems to make her happy.

It sounds rather ridiculous, Jolene said. Why trick those people into thinking they still live out in the real world? Waiting for non-existent buses? Besides the fact I don't think my mother ever took a bus in her entire life.

It seems to work for some people, Aimee said. She said that she had been coached by the nursing staff on how to interact with Jolene's mother. The important thing was not to try and correct someone when they asked an inappropriate question, for instance why their husband hadn't gotten home from work yet. It didn't matter that the husband was dead. If you simply went along with them and said, Oh, he'll be home soon, it worked out better. They stayed calmer. It was cruel to remind them their husband was dead, because they seemed to experience grief all over again, as if that death had just happened and they were only then learning about it.

What does she do all day long? Jolene asked.

The staff tries to keep the residents busy. They play hangman and bingo and beanbag toss, and they have a stretching class every morning. Your mother attends Bible study and gets a manicure each week.

Bible study? Jolene said. My mother goes to *Bible* study?

One of the things I don't quite approve of is they've given some of the residents these very lifelike vinyl baby dolls, along with diapers, bottles, and clothes. Some residents become so attached to their dolls they seem to believe they are real babies. I'm afraid this has happened to your mother. She never goes anywhere without her doll. She seems visibly calmer when she has it with her. She spends a lot of time caring for it. Changing its clothes and feeding it with the little bottle, though of course the bottle has nothing in it. I thought I should warn you in any case. You'll see how attached she is to it.

My god, Jolene said. She could never really mother me and now she's mothering a vinyl doll instead? Don't you find that somewhat demeaning, the notion that it's infantilizing a person, an adult person— I mean a woman in her *nineties,* for God's sake—by getting them to cuddle a toy baby? And then let them believe it's real?

Nothing's real in their world, Aimee said gently. Or perhaps everything's all too real. And that's why they need to be protected like children. And I don't think there's anything wrong with that. After all, what's more important at this point in their lives, dignity or happiness? Their memories often take them way back to childhood, when having a doll to play with was a very natural thing. It's just sometimes disconcerting to see how very attached she is to it. How much she appears to *love* it.

Jolene folded forward slightly, resting one arm across her midriff and holding her forehead with her other hand.

I can't even begin to know what to make of all this, she said wearily.

WE STAYED awhile longer upstairs. Jolene commented on how much she liked the room where we were sitting. Nothing about the house felt the same to her, she said. It was as if Aimee had dispelled the darkness and gloom, all the residual sadness she had felt as a child. It seemed so peaceful to her now. So filled with light and serenity. She could see herself staying here, she said. Just moving in and never leaving. Maybe it's appropriate, she said, that the place I used to call the Tomb suddenly feels like the place where I could end my days.

I was surprised to hear her say this. But there was no question she was sincere: I knew her well enough to know that she meant what she'd just said. I could never have imagined her wanting to live here again—not in this house, and not in this town. But I believed at the moment she was actually contemplating such a thing, even if it turned out to only be a passing notion.

Aimee responded quickly by telling her there would always be a place for her here. She could have her old room back anytime she wished, and she could stay as long as she wanted. She could have the bedroom suite where we were sitting if she so desired. Any part of the house could be hers. In truth, she said, the place was really too big for just one person—she would be grateful for her company.

That's only because you have no idea what lousy company I can be, Jolene said. She just doesn't know, does she, Verna? But you can tell her.

Oh yes, I said to Aimee, she can be quite dreadful. I'm not sure I could give her a recommendation in the good company department.

I could tell Aimee was watching the way Jolene and I were looking at each other, and I knew she didn't quite know what to make of what I'd just said, because no one was laughing, or even smiling, and in that look we were exchanging was something completely unreadable.

JOLENE WANTED to see the garden, and we took our drinks out back. The light was fading, and the tall sycamore trees ringing the yard were silhouetted against the deep purple sky and the mountains lit by the setting sun—such tall mountains, and so close by, the peaks and highest basins still covered in snow. Aimee talked about the brilliant landscape architect who had helped her lay out the new garden when she moved in. You could sense the care and thought that went into the work. Gone was the expanse of lawn with the old pergola, and in its place was a variety of drought-resistant plants and a circular stone fountain. A beautiful bronze sculpture of a nude woman with her arms outstretched had been placed in a reflecting pool in the middle of the fountain. The woman's hands were uplifted and held sculpted birds. Aimee mentioned she was not yet finished with the garden. In the area adjacent to the pool she planned on putting in raised beds to grow vegetables. I thought it was one of the most beautiful gardens I'd ever seen.

We stayed outside awhile longer before wandering back through the kitchen and out to the driveway where we'd left my car. I looked down the street at the grand houses and the large trees casting shade in the little pocket park in the middle of the road. It all looked so perfect, so enchanted, each house more graceful, more beautiful than the next. All the old houses in the neighborhood had been restored, and the gardens were well kept and lush. It had to be the nicest street in town. Nicer, even, than when Jolene had lived here growing up.

Before we parted, Aimee and Jolene made a plan to meet the next day to visit her mother. Aimee said she would pick her up at the hotel at ten o'clock. They invited me to come along, but I said I planned on spending the day alone. There were things I wanted to do, I said.

WE RETURNED to the hotel and gave the car to the attendant and then walked across the street to a Japanese restaurant for dinner. She ordered nothing but a few pieces of sashimi and a large saki. I told her she needed to eat more. She said I shouldn't tell her what she needed to do, she knew her own body. I ordered shrimp and vegetable tempura and a beer and she said, You know how unhealthy that is, right? I mean that deep-fried stuff. So fattening.

I looked at her and wondered what I should say. I was tired of her rudeness. All evening the tension between us had been rising. But I let her comment pass. Instead I told her about the situation at home with the landlord and the cat, how upset Vincent was by it all. I said I needed to get back to the apartment to help him deal with things. I wanted to leave right after she visited her mother the next day, if that was all right. I hoped we could drive straight through—I knew I could do that without any problem, I'd made much longer drives alone. We could take the freeway home, which would make the trip much faster. But if she found herself getting too tired, of course we could always stop somewhere along the way and get a motel.

She looked at me and shook her head. So we just got here tonight, and you want to leave tomorrow? Because a *cat* is missing for a couple of days and Vincent just can't deal with it by himself?

That's right, I said. I kept my voice even.

There's something you're not telling me, she said.

I thought I just explained the situation pretty well.

No, there's something you're not telling me about you and Vincent. Isn't there? There's something going on that you don't want me to know about.

What's going on is a cat we love very much has gone missing. What's going on is we're facing a crisis with our apartment and we're being forced to leave and we don't want to do that and it's causing a lot of stress for both of us.

What else is going on in your relationship?

I don't think that's the point here.

I don't think you're telling me the truth.

Maybe I don't think it's any of your business.

Or maybe you want to pretend you haven't suffered in your relationship with him all these years, because you understand I know him very well. I knew him before you did. I know he's an exceedingly self-involved man and that he almost has to be forced to think of others. I couldn't do it. And I wonder how you have.

I thought you said leaving him was the biggest mistake of your life.

Did I say that?

Yes, you did.

Well, maybe those two things aren't so contradictory. I felt I couldn't stay with him. And it was perhaps a mistake to leave. Had I been more mature and less egotistical myself I might have made a different decision.

I see. You'd like to have it both ways. As usual.

As usual?

Look, I've driven a long way. I agreed to this trip to try and help you. But you're not helping me by being so rude. I don't understand how you think you can treat people this way and expect them to go on caring for you.

I don't expect anyone to care for me anymore.

That's not true and you know it.

Look, I'm dying. I've come to *the end*. It's a lonely business. The thing about death is, you do it alone. And I'm scared. Very scared. I'm also not a very nice person. That much has become pretty clear to me. I don't always like how I act, but I don't seem to be able to do anything about it. I've always been this way. People don't change so easily, especially when they're running out of time.

She stared hard at me then. I had to look away. I wanted to tell her, If you're dying and you know it, wouldn't that make you want to finally open up your heart, let the borders dissolve?

If you want to leave tomorrow we'll leave, she said. But I'd like to see how I feel after I see my mother.

That would be fine, I said. We can stay another night if needed.

THE DINNER was awful. We found little to say to each other after this horrible exchange. She paid the bill, and we walked back to the hotel. We took turns using the bathroom and got into our beds even though it was only nine o'clock. Exhaustion had overtaken me, and I could feel how tired my body was when I finally lay back against the pillow. All that driving. All the intense conversation. I turned out the bedside light and everything grew very, very still.

In the darkness every sound was magnified. Her breathing. The noise of the traffic moving along the street below. Voices drifting up. People in the hallway passing by our door.

I had just begun to finally relax when I heard her get up. She lifted the covers on my bed and slid in beside me. *Not again,* I thought.

I'm sorry, Verna, she said. I'm very, very sorry.

She laid her cheek against my shoulder. It was wet with tears.

I'm so afraid, she said. I don't know what to do.

I touched her head and let my hand rest against her woolly scalp.

It's okay, I said. I understand.

Her body shook. She was trembling all over, as if she'd caught a chill and just couldn't get warm now.

Let me stay with you tonight.

Of course, I said.

She turned her back to me, and once again I held her, as I had the night before. After a while she stopped shaking. Her breathing grew regular. She fell asleep. But I did not. I lay awake much of the night, thinking the sorts of thoughts I knew I'd never tell anyone.

IN THE morning she acted subdued. She put on a loose gray dress and some pretty yellow flats and tied a yellow scarf around her head in an attractive way and asked if I thought she looked okay. I said she looked lovely. She held me close to her for a few seconds before leaving the room, and then she picked up her bag and turned and went downstairs to meet Aimee.

I stayed in the room awhile. I tried calling Vincent, but he wasn't answering.

After some time I got up and dressed and went downstairs and asked the front desk to have the valet bring my car from the garage. It was one of those mornings utterly distorted by the night's dreams, only I couldn't remember the dreams, which made it even worse. I left the hotel with a disturbed feeling, a vague intimation that something was wrong.

I DROVE to the part of town where I'd grown up and turned onto the street where I'd lived with my family in a small wooden house. The house was still there but the neighborhood had changed, and so had the house itself.

My father had taken pride in keeping up a place, as he put it. How you kept up your place was a reflection of who you were, he said—just as he used to say, *Never do anything that would bring shame on our family name.* The name of a family was important. It had to be protected and revered as if it was part of your wealth. And the way a house and yard looked announced what sort of person you were.

Everything about the house now looked derelict. It appeared so small, dwarfed perhaps by the vision of Jolene's house the day before. I tried to imagine how my parents had raised eight children in such a small place, but I knew how they'd done it. With love and bunk beds. Two sets of bunk beds in two rooms meant beds for eight kids, though later, when we got older, the boys had to make space for three bunk beds in their room because it wasn't right to sleep in the same room with their two sisters.

The ditch flowing between the house and street was still full of clear flowing water, but the cement in the driveway was badly cracked and an old truck had been parked in front of the garage for so long it had a flat tire and was covered with dead leaves. The metal railings on the front porch were rusted, and it looked like someone was using sheets for curtains. It didn't appear anyone was home, so I got out of the car and quietly walked down the driveway and into the backyard.

The neglect was even more evident here. The weeds had grown high around a worn dirt path. Gone was the big expanse of lawn where we used to play late into the evenings on summer nights. The fruit trees had grown to an immense size, but they had not been cared for. The plums and peaches and apricots had been allowed to fall, and the rot lay strewn on the ground in layers of dark pulp. A broken chain saw sat on an old picnic table near a stack of rusted metal chairs. It would be easy to think no one lived here anymore. But I felt sure they did.

Once there had been a large sandbox and rabbit hutches, gooseberry bushes, a huge vegetable garden, and a great stand of raspberries—all gone. I walked back under the trees and overgrown weeds, making my way to the rear of the yard. I found the old chicken coop still standing, but barely. I could see through gaps in the fence to where our neighbor, Mr. Bagley, used to raise his chinchillas in long rows of wooden pens. I'd been fascinated by his chinchillas. Occasionally I'd been allowed to take one out and hold it like we did our rabbits. The chinchillas had the softest fur of any animal I'd ever touched. Once Mr. Bagley accused my younger brother James and me of turning the chinchillas loose. We hadn't done it. But we spent the afternoon trying to help him find them anyway and put them all back, and later he apologized when he realized a clasp on the cage was broken and they'd let themselves out. He told us that chinchillas mate for life, a fact that deeply impressed me. The chinchilla pens were now gone. In their place someone had parked a row of dead cars and left an old wooden rowboat tipped on its side.

It was too much. How could so much have changed in the years since I'd last been back here? My parents had sold the house in their later years and moved to a small condo where I had visited them regularly until they died, but I'd never bothered to come back to the house. I was rather sorry I had now.

I walked back to the car and drove around the block. I saw a lot of Mexican kids playing in yards. At the end of the street stood the old sandstone church where I had been baptized in a large font in the basement when I was eight and where a great part of my childhood had been lived out. Now it was owned by a Pentecostal congregation, and all the signs were in Spanish. Long ago I realized I had been raised in not just a religion but a culture—a *tribe* as it were—and that there would be no denying this. Like the Jews, we were a religion that became a people, and you don't leave your people so easily.

I HEADED up the canyon. It felt like a good day to be out driving around with no agenda. Nothing in particular to do. No one I felt I needed to see. It was the landscape I wanted to revisit—the places I'd loved growing up. It had been a long time since I'd been up the canyon, a beautiful drive on a narrow, windy road that ran alongside a river rushing between steep rock walls. In several places waterfalls dropped from the tops of the cliffs into the turbulent river, which was separated from the road by a low wall made of local rock. The road led to a high mountain valley and Pine View Dam, a large reservoir that was used for boating and recreation. This is where Jolene and I had spent many summer afternoons sunbathing on the sandy beaches. This high valley is where her ancestors had settled and her great-grandfather had built his first innovative gun in a primitive workshop.

The valley was known for the stone fruit that came from the old orchards. Many of the houses were from the pioneer era, and there were still a lot of small farms dotting the valley. I slowed down each time I saw a group of horses standing in a corral or field so I could look at them. I could never have really explained to anyone the deep pleasure I took from just seeing these animals. Or the way I longed to ride one again.

I DROVE to a parking lot at the north end of the reservoir and walked down to the water and lay on my back in the sand, looking up at the white clouds with their soft scumbled margins. My brothers had taught me to water-ski here on this lake. Now two of them were gone, one taken by cancer, the other by AIDS, and the rest of my siblings had moved to another part of the state, where they all lived near one another. I didn't see them often. Family had never been important to Vincent, just as it never had meant much to Jolene. They'd both wanted to escape their pasts. Gradually, over the years of being married to him, I'd more or less adopted his attitude, especially after my parents died and the ties that bound us seemed to naturally begin to loosen. Time passed, and before I knew it I had become an outsider within my own clan.

What I understood was how many of his ways and attitudes I had adopted over the years as a means of adapting to life with him, and it felt as if this had been brought into harsher relief over the last few days. I'd been thinking about how much I'd given up to find a measure of tranquility, just as I had in the months after the therapist had given me the hard news. He would likely never change, he would always be living largely in his own world, captivated primarily by his music and books. That hard-earned tranquility felt disturbed by the time I'd spent with Jolene and also by the return to the world I had come from. I was reminded of who I had once been. And what I had lost. Only I hadn't lost it. I'd left it.

You have to wait and see how things turn out, I told myself, because no one knows anything for sure, not even what they do or decide or see or suffer—each moment sooner or later dissolves, everything traveling toward its own end with the passing of days. We don't understand the immensity surrounding every single moment, or the infinite possibilities.

I knew that Jolene felt there were things I couldn't or wouldn't tell her about Vincent and our relationship. I realized it puzzled her. And I didn't care.

I had not forgotten what she told me years ago, how the deepest art comes out of not being afraid to stick one's finger into the wound—and not just stick it in but wiggle it in an attempt to activate the pain and discover the source of the wound. At the time the image had disturbed me. Why would anyone *do* that? I wondered. But that was before I became a writer. Before I understood that's what novelists do. Each of us narrates our life as it suits us, but novelists tell stories with the bandages pulled off.

Neither she nor I would ever really *have* him. His mind was beyond colonizing. He existed outside the reach of any one person.

Just accept me the way I am. That's what he'd always told me— as Flaubert had said to his mistress, *Ask me to do nothing and I'll do everything*—and that's what I had done. Or tried to do. What I was still doing.

Maybe you want to pretend you haven't suffered in your relationship with him all these years, she said last night, *because you understand I know him very well. I knew him before you did. I know he's an exceedingly self-involved man and that he almost has to be forced to think of others. I couldn't do it. And I wonder how you have.*

I FOUND I didn't really want to stick the finger in the wound anymore. Just as I didn't wish to discuss Vincent with her. I didn't care to disturb what tranquility I had. I wanted to return to L.A. and write *Cookbook for Idiots.* Find a new place to live. Continue to tell myself the stories that suited my needs. We all lived inside a great fiction. The trick was to keep an acceptable version going.

Do you realize, a friend once asked me, that by writing the novels you have inserted yourself into other people's lives?

To what degree, I wondered?

And to what end?

I wanted to believe this had been done in a *good* way. That whatever I had offered a reader, beyond the bones of a story, might have affirmed certain things that I imagined might matter. I knew these things were possibly antiquated ideas I had carried forward from my childhood. I was an earnest person. Often I wished I weren't. I'd never had the cool, wry temperament of Jolene, sincerity being my natural default. It wasn't something I felt I could change—just as Vincent couldn't change who he was.

I wanted to keep on nodding terms with the person I used to be, as Didion suggested—the woman who had married at seventeen and then spent the next twenty years working odd jobs, gossiping with cowboys at a bowling alley and wrangling horses before she became something else. I was no longer that person, but sometimes I became nostalgic to know her again. That was what I was feeling right then, lying on the sand as the waves sucked noisily at the shore and then fell back with watery little slaps.

HUNGER FOR contact underlies our human perversity, I thought. I had always longed for a *real* connection with Vincent, what I thought of as a *normal* life, and the fear I wouldn't ever have that had never really gone away though I often pretended it had. I saw that I bore responsibility for what I'd chosen. It felt too late to change. And hadn't we made our peace? Fashioned a life that suited us? Nobody ever got all of anything, I had to remind myself. And look at the life we'd managed to make. The joy it contained, the illumination and, yes, the intimacy. *All I've learned from him, the immeasurable things I've derived, a gain of the most precious kind.* I knew that what we had created was a great love. That's what Elizabeth Hardwick had understood. That's what she'd known with Lowell.

I HEADED back toward town, out to the north end of the valley where my cousin owned a small farm on a rise overlooking the Great Salt Lake. The chickens were loose and pecking at the dirt in the driveway as I pulled up in front of the house. My cousin's wife, Alma, came out onto the porch, and when she saw who it was in the car she let out a whoop.

I came inside and sat at her kitchen table. Everything in the room looked cluttered and disorganized and none too clean, but freshly washed eggs were lined up carefully on a towel on a counter. Beautiful eggs—turquoise and white, buff and brown, of different sizes. She asked if I wanted a cup of coffee, and I said no. She was a big woman with a loose gray bun and patches of white scalp showing where her hair had thinned out. She looked hurt that I didn't want coffee. I asked if they still kept horses, and she said, Just the two old ones left. They're out in the corral, she added. I told her I'd like to take a short ride, just around the fields, and she said, Help yourself. The tack's in the shed.

I walked out to the corral. Some of the rails were broken and held in place by baling twine. The corral hadn't been cleaned out in a while, and the horses were standing in muck. I recognized the gray mare in the corral. Once, years ago, I had come by to take a ride and the gray mare was standing in the pasture, and because she was so easy to catch I slipped a halter over her head and led her to a fence and climbed on bareback. I intended to just take a quick ride, down to where the property ended at the marshes near the lake shore. But as I circled the pasture I noticed something shiny and black lying in the grass. It turned out to be the gray mare's stillborn foal—she'd dropped it earlier that morning. Given birth to a dead foal and no one had even noticed. The thing that struck me was she seemed fine, just the same as she might on any other day. I had climbed on her without realizing what had happened. When I understood I slid off her right away and walked her back to the corral. Afterward, I'd spent a long time stroking her neck, looking into her eyes, wondering what she felt about such a great loss.

I NOTICED her feet now needed attention. One front hoof had begun to split and break up, and the other was so long I could see it was causing her to put too much weight on her fetlock. She saw me standing at the railing and began to walk toward me, clomping through the muck with her long hooves, and the old bay horse followed. I found a bin of oats in the tack shed and put some in a bucket and fed both horses slowly by hand, first the one, and then the other, their rubbery lips picking up the last morsels from my flattened palm. I found I didn't want to ride the mare after all, not with her feet looking so poor, and the old brown gelding was past riding. Instead I climbed through the rails and stood with my arm around the mare's neck, pulling knots out of her tangled mane and talking to her, looking into the dark eye that reflected my own, rubbing under her forelock to get the winter hair off. She dropped her head and yawned. Let me know how relaxed she was. How much she enjoyed the attention. I wanted to give my cousin Will the money to get her feet trimmed. He was tight that way. Didn't spend money on his animals like he should, especially if they weren't much use to him anymore. But you shouldn't let a horse's feet go. Because if the feet go, well, the horse can go.

I got a brush and curry comb out of the tack room and slicked off both horses, wearing some old boots I'd found in the shed. The clumps of winter hair dropped on the ground in great big rounds. I could tell no one had paid any attention to these horses for a long time. I scratched the mare's belly with the curry comb, and she stretched her neck out and drew her top lip back in delight. *Do you think we could ever live in the country?* I'd asked Vincent. He'd laughed at that and said, *No, I don't think so.*

To be human is finally to be a loser. In the end everyone lost their precious life. I'd heard it said that you have to think about death every day in order to be ready for when it comes for you. Nobody I knew did this.

Except perhaps Jolene.

I imagined she thought of death every day now.

I LOOKED out over the tin-colored water to the very far distance. The Great Salt Lake stretched to the far horizon and shimmered with tiny scallops of juddering light. A lake so inhospitable it had successfully resisted all attempts by man to put it to any constructive use whatsoever, from the day men first laid eyes on it right up to the now.

I had the feeling I was missing something, and regret bubbled up in me, a sour, sad emotion. I felt squeezed through the tiny conduit of a personality that I had learned to make small so that I might live in a strictly regimented world. It wasn't so different from the mores of this small town. Geographically I had leapt into the world, moved to L.A., married Vincent, written books. And yet? Why did my life now often feel so much smaller?

Whatever else you were, you were a sensitive girl acutely attuned to the emotional world, Jolene had said to me when we were discussing Colette and the similarities she found in our writing.

A sensitive girl.

Acutely attuned to the emotional world.

Didn't that also make me a perfect conduit? And wasn't it ironic I had ended up married to someone rather insulated from feeling? I thought I could hide myself in my writing and the wound would lie undisturbed, but it hadn't worked. Because to write truthfully, as I had discovered, you actually do have to take the bandages off.

I LEFT the horses standing in the corral. The mare nickered as I turned and walked away from her. I left the boots where I had found them, and put the bucket back with the oats in the tack room. My hands were dirty and I smelled of horses. I went into the house and washed my hands at the kitchen sink. My cousin's wife offered me a glass of cold water. She asked if something was wrong. She said I looked *stricken.* That was the word she used. I said I'd driven up from L.A. with a friend who was very sick, and I needed to get back to the hotel where we were staying to see how she was doing.

Well, that certainly was a short horseback ride, she said.

Yes, very short.

I went out to the car and got my wallet and then went back in and laid some money on the table.

Tell Willy to get those horses' hooves trimmed. It's my gift to them.

I don't believe you look well, she said when I left. You take care.

———

BACK AT the hotel I gave the car to the attendant and rode the elevator up to our floor. She was already in the room. Lying on the bed with her eyes closed. She had taken off the scarf covering her head but was still wearing her dress and shoes. Her face looked ashen.

Come sit by me, she said without stirring.

I sat down on the edge of the bed. She opened her eyes.

She asked me if I'd had a good day, and I told her what I'd done. I didn't mention that I'd stopped by my old house. I didn't want to talk about that. I just said that I'd driven up the canyon and spent a little time at the dam, then stopped by my cousin's farm.

It sounds like you had a better day than I did.

Was it hard seeing your mother?

Not so much hard as strange. She looks good, she's still very trim. She looks like an aristocratic old lady and dresses the part. She always did buy nice clothes and wore them well. Funny but in some ways it's the best I've ever seen her. The most natural looking. Her cheeks are ruddy and her eyes are still bright, and her gray hair is caught in a loose bun—she looked so healthy and natural to me, as if she'd just come in from a walk across a windy moor. Like she'd been out with Heathcliff. We found her on her bus-stop bench, holding her doll. Every so often she'd try to stand up to see if the bus was coming, and then she'd throw open her arms wide as if in utter bewilderment. What's going on? she'd say. Does anybody know anything? What's happening? Then she'd grow calm and just sit back down again.

Did she recognize you?

I don't think so. But it's hard to say. She kept looking at me and saying, Why are you here? What are you doing here? Do I know you? Aimee explained to her that I was her daughter but it didn't seem to produce any reaction other than a blank stare. I guess many people with dementia grow angry and difficult, but the thing is, my mother seems to have grown nicer. Maybe the dementia has taken her back to a period when she actually *was* happier. All her prickliness is gone. All her shrillness. She seems like a daffy old woman who just wants to wait for a bus and take care of her doll. The staff spoke to me about their method for keeping a person safely inside their world, how it was necessary to figure out the boundaries and contents of that world. One of the rules was never contradict anything a patient said, no matter how distant from reality, in order to spare them a distressing confrontation with their own decline. Try to identify what keeps the person happy by figuring out the roles that were important to them. For some reason she has adopted the role of a bus rider—and mother of a vinyl baby—which I find hysterical. Also maybe a little touching. A large part of every day is spent waiting to board a bus that never comes in order to take a trip to nowhere with a fake child. I think Beckett would have approved.

SHE CLOSED her eyes and grew quiet. She had begun to tremble. I could feel her shaking next to me—shaking rather violently now, tremors that convulsed her body. Her face was very pale.

Are you okay? I asked. Can I get you a blanket? I took her hand and held it loosely between my own.

I'm not feeling well, Verna, she said softly. I don't think I can leave for L.A. I feel like it would be very difficult to even stand up, much less to move from this bed.

It's okay, I said. We don't have to leave today. It wouldn't be a good idea to set out now anyway. It's too late. It would mean driving after dark. But do you think you might be able to head home tomorrow?

Yes, she said. Yes, I'll do that.

But only if you feel like it. We can take as much time as you need.

I know you want to get back to Vincent.

It's really the cat, I said. The fact that Max is missing. Otherwise he wouldn't care. But he's just so upset because Max hasn't come home, and he thinks he's gone for good.

I thought maybe he was missing you.

I shook my head. He's fine without me. It's the cat.

The . . . cat . . . she said slowly. Her words were slurred. She closed her eyes again.

Have you eaten today? I asked.

Not really. Aimee wanted to stop for lunch, but I told her I didn't feel like it. I think she was a little hurt. I know she wanted to spend more time together, but I had to get back here as soon as I could and lie down.

Why don't you undress and get under the covers. I'm going to go out and find us something to eat and bring it back. Maybe you'd like to take a warm bath. I can feel you're trembling still. Are you cold?

No, not cold, she said. I shake when I get tired. And I'm very tired. I think a bath would only sap what little energy I have. Just help me undress.

I helped her stand up and put on her nightgown and found a sweater to put over that, and then I helped her back to bed. I brought her a glass of water and made her drink some even though she didn't want to, and then I left her there and went out to find something for us to eat, regretting that she'd managed to book a hotel that didn't have room service.

FOR THE rest of that afternoon and evening we lay side by side in bed, watching TV, grazing on the Japanese food I brought back from the restaurant across the street. We managed to drink a bottle of wine before it even got dark. When she asked me if I'd mind going out for another, I did as she asked.

We watched an old episode of *Curb Your Enthusiasm* and it made us laugh, then we watched another, and another, and for a while it felt as if the laughter made us happy and childlike with each other, the way we'd been so long ago. I felt a little high from the wine, and I know she did too. Vincent called while we were watching the third episode. I didn't bother taking the phone into the bathroom, just lay next to her and spoke to him. When I told him what we were doing, watching TV and eating in bed, he didn't say much. Max still hadn't shown up. That was mostly what he wanted to let me know. He understood Jolene was there next to me in the room, and it felt to me as if he'd decided to keep things brief because of this.

As it was, the conversation was pretty stiff. I said he shouldn't give up on Max coming back, but in response there was a long silence on the line. Finally I told him we were going to try and leave early in the morning. This seemed to be all he really wanted to hear, and not long after that we said good night and hung up.

WE STAYED awake only a little while longer. When we finally turned out the lights it was a given she would sleep with me. I didn't mind. I believed her when she said this had been one of the hardest parts for her, sleeping alone, missing the feeling of another person next to her in bed. But again I didn't get much sleep. During the night my mind ran through a number of different scenarios. I'd get home and discover that Max had shown up, and we'd be elated and relieved. Or Max wouldn't come back and we'd be heartbroken, and it would add to the stress of having to leave the apartment. I imagined us moving to a house with a nice yard. I could see us having friends over for dinner again. Jolene would come to visit. But would we really end up seeing much of her, even if she decided to stay in L.A.? How would Vincent feel about that? Or—and this was the hardest thing to think of—would all this be irrelevant . . . because she would no longer be with us?

I hoped we would continue to see each other. I couldn't explain this need for her. This wish to be close now that we had come together again. It was the trip, of course, that had revived this feeling. She had brought live greetings from a distant past. She *knew* me in a way others didn't, just as I *knew* her. And if I needed her, for whatever reason, didn't she also need me, now more than ever? Would Vincent understand this? Yes, I thought, he would. It was the way he was made. His ability to let bygones be bygones. Perhaps he could manage to do this even with Jolene.

In the morning we woke early and packed up and left the room just as the sun was rising over the mountains. By seven we were on the road, driving south on the freeway, stopping only for coffee and breakfast. All morning we drove under a sky that was heavily overcast, laden with a thick gray pall, as if forest fires were burning somewhere. But there were no forest fires: it was only the early mist hanging over an inclement spring day. The fire season had not yet begun.

PART THREE

MacArthur Park

19

Female honor, she once said, *is having survived your experiences without being destroyed by them.* She was quoting someone, but she couldn't remember who. She had so many thoughts about women. About our bodies. Our relationships. Why we do what we do. How we end up so often with the short end of the stick. On that long drive home I remember her talking about how there is an easy sharing among women that doesn't exist between men. We swap not only our secrets but our anxieties, our thoughts and histories, our troubles, complaints, and desires, and all this passes so loosely back and forth it amounts to a kind of promiscuity of emotion. That's what I'd felt on our trip, only she had done most of the talking, and I had been the compliant listener, her navigator and driver—her Charon ferrying her, if a bit prematurely, across the River Styx.

Is this a good thing or bad, the way we women talk among ourselves? That's what she wondered, she said. She called such behavior an emotional gynaeceum, this urge we feel to spill so much. But do we really give that much away? Isn't a great deal of this easy exchange really performative? It's quite possible that we're never doing much more than trying to make our own lives seem better or worse—but usually better—which means what we're really doing is erecting a buttress of deception, with ourselves as the most deceived. I can't say why she revealed as much as she did during that drive, but I still believe more than anything she simply wished to be *seen.* And most of all to be seen by me.

———

SHE WANTED to stage a piece about war. That's what she'd said. Something to protest the perpetual states of conflict now plaguing the globe and the obscene amount of weaponry the United States was supplying to the world. So why not use MacArthur, she said? General Douglas MacArthur. America's greatest warrior and greatest buffoon, the man who screwed up the Korean War so badly we are all still living with the consequences. Why not set her performance in front of that statue of him in the park that bears his name, the park forever memorialized by a song whose lyrics no one really understands? Whose cake was it, after all, that was left out in the rain? And what was that recipe we'll never have again?

ON THE drive back to L.A. she had Googled "MacArthur Park lyrics," and we sang along on YouTube with Richard Harris, the version, she said, that made her fall in love with the song in the first place. Our voices sounded loud and exuberant in the enclosed space of the car, and I realized once more what a strange and beautiful lyric it was— not just the cake left out in the rain but the *spring never waiting for us, girl* and *the yellow cotton dress foaming like a wave, the sweet green icing flowing down, the birds like tender babies in your hands. After all the loves of my life,* we sang, *oh, after all the loves of my life I'll be thinking of you—and wondering why.* We gave the song everything, the full-volume treatment for the full seven minutes it lasted, vocalizing together, growing especially loud when we came to the part that repeated the long mournful wail OH NO! *Oh noooo,* we cried, *o-oh no-ooooo! We'll never have that recipe again OH NO-OOOO-ohOOO!*

I felt this moment marked a high point of the trip, not just because of the way we loosened up with each other but because it felt so sincere somehow, the way we sang. It felt so beautiful. To cut loose on that song. Sincerely cut loose. Nothing held back. Afterward everything grew very quiet in the car, and I felt that feeling like a furnace going off in winter, a sudden deep silence. Then she broke the quiet and said, For all the pain in that song, it feels so wonderful to sing it, doesn't it? Really sing it and feel it. It's such a gorgeous song, it gives you the chills. And you're not even quite sure why.

SOMETHING ELSE she said on that long drive home from Utah: The thing about taking your own life, she suggested, is you can see the end, determine it, prepare in any way you wish, and if that means devoting hours, days, even months to your library of favorite books before you go, what better way to say goodbye to the earthly pleasures? The only thing in question now, she said, was whether she'd have the courage to go the way she'd planned.

I DIDN'T hear from her for a long time after we returned. She simply went silent. There was no response to the texts or emails I sent, and she didn't answer her phone when I tried calling.

It didn't surprise me, this silence. Nothing she did ever surprised me. But it did hurt. She had thanked me when I dropped her off late that night after the long drive back to L.A. We were both tired as we said our goodbyes. I left her with Ina, who had come outside to help her with her things. We stood in the narrow street in the dark, watching out in case a car should suddenly appear. She kissed me and said, Thank you, Verna, thank you very very much. And without looking at me again she walked away, leaning on Ina's arm. I had expected her to stay in touch, really thought I would hear from her again right away, and it caused me pain when I didn't. I thought she could have done that much, after what I had just done for her. But she didn't stay in touch. I guess she just couldn't.

I HAD begun to think that she had slipped from our lives again when a couple of months after we'd returned from our trip there was a knock on the apartment door, and I opened it to find her standing on the porch.

Vincent was sitting behind me, in his chair in the living room, reading.

May I come in? she said. I hope it's not a bad time.

It's fine, I said, come in. It's good to see you, I added, feeling a bit dazed to find her standing there.

I stepped aside and glanced at Vincent, as if to say, *Look who's here.* I saw him raise his eyes. A look of confusion passed across his face, as if he wasn't quite sure of who he was seeing. It had been so long. And she was so changed.

Leaning heavily on a cane she made her way slowly into the center of the room and then paused. She appeared out of breath. She stood there quietly for a moment. She wore a red sweater over a black dress and the same leopard-print cap on her head. Large dark sunglasses hid her face as usual. I could see how he might not recognize her.

Those front steps, she said finally. Quite a challenge.

I glanced at Vincent, waiting for him to greet her, but he appeared frozen in his chair. She took off her glasses and looked at him—really looked at him and smiled and said, Hello there, Vincent, and at that moment I saw he knew her.

He put his book aside and stood up slowly.

Tell me if I'm interrupting, please, she said, gazing at each of us in turn, but I'm going to leave town soon and I wanted to see you before I went. She seemed nervous. Vincent wasn't making it easier for her by saying nothing. Finally, as if slowly emerging from a fog, he greeted her with a studied politeness.

He said, Oh, hello, and that was all, as if he had just seen her recently and there was no need to make a fuss.

She sensed his discomfort, of course, knowing him so well, and tried to put him at ease by telling him how good it was to see him and how well he looked. You never age, do you? she said. He never changes does he? she added, looking at me.

Sit down, was all he said in response, and pointed to the couch as if instructing a wayward pet.

THERE WERE half-filled boxes of books sitting around the living room. She eyed them and asked, Are you moving soon?

I saw the look that crossed Vincent's face, a look that pleaded with me to please *not* tell her everything that was going on. The look that said, Don't mention the *quit premises* notice we found posted on our door a few weeks ago. Don't tell her how the new landlord lied about not receiving our rent checks as a means of forcing us out. How he had just torn them up and claimed we'd never sent them. And *please* don't tell her about the incompetent lawyer we hired who failed to get court paperwork in on time, thus leaving us open to eviction. *Don't tell her anything,* his look pleaded. And I didn't.

I said only that we were starting to pack up, but that yes, we would be moving soon. She wanted to know where we'd be moving to and I said that hadn't yet been settled.

Ah, she said. Well, I hope you find something that's right for you. I can see how nice it is here, she added, looking around. It's a lovely apartment. I understand why you've stayed here so long. Great light . . . with these tall windows. The arched doorways. It's got a feeling of old Hollywood, doesn't it? Like the set of a Thin Man movie, with you two like Nick and Nora Charles. All you need is that little dog—what was its name? Asta? Yeah that's it. Asta.

I ASKED her if she'd like some tea, and she said she would, and I left her with Vincent in the living room. As I waited in the kitchen for the water to boil I could hear them talking, though it was mostly her keeping up the conversation. She mentioned she had read somewhere that he had recently gotten a Guggenheim Fellowship, and she congratulated him on that. How many times did you have to apply? she asked. I can't remember, he said, but too many. She had gotten one years ago, she said, and described her project—something about the invasion of Iraq and a video she'd made entitled *Yellow Cake*. She asked about his project—what had he proposed to the Guggenheim?—and I could hear him describing it in detail. He went on at great length as he did whenever someone asked about his work. Safe ground for them both, I thought.

———

WHEN I returned with the tea, Vincent appeared more relaxed. His hands were no longer balled into fists pressed into his lap. He and Jolene were still talking about their work.

Do you remember, she said, when we first met and I sat down across from you that day in the park? She turned toward me and continued talking, as if he were no longer in the room.

I said to him, I'm at the Brooklyn Academy of Art, and he said, I'm at the Juilliard School of Music. I said, I'm an artist and I treat space as if it was time. And he said, I'm a musician and I treat time as if it was space.

Do you remember that? she said, turning back to him.

I don't actually, he said. I mean I don't remember saying that.

Now I'm trying to treat time as if it weren't running out, and I could care less about space, except I don't have enough of it to accommodate all the stuff I've amassed over the years. It all needs to go somewhere. I'm trying to put things in order, giving stuff away, attempting to place my archive with an institution—there's some interest in that. It's time to arrange a dispersal, that sort of thing. In fact there's something I want to give you, she said to me. I'll send you a text with a picture of several things I have in mind. Or I'll simply choose something I think is right, if you don't mind.

Of course I don't mind, I said. And I'd rather you choose.

She looked at Vincent and said, You? I haven't figured out what I'm leaving you yet. I'm still thinking on it. You're a bit harder.

She said she had recently made out a new will, leaving some money—quite a lot of money actually—to a group fighting climate change. This was the issue for our time, wasn't it? An issue, she'd decided, even greater than that of war, though of course the two were inextricably linked and would become even more so in the time to come. And yet people continued to have children as if they believed these kids might have some kind of future. But they have no future, these children, not in the sense their grandparents or people of our generation had a future, she said.

I could see Vincent's attention drift, as if she'd now lost him as surely she knew she would by bringing up such a serious subject. But she seemed not to notice or care.

Not long ago, she said, Ina and I went to the beach in Santa Monica. I wanted to just sit in the sun and watch the waves. We took a short walk along the sand. There was a family we passed—a husband and wife with their two small children—and we ended up spreading our blanket not far away from them and just resting for a while. The children were very beautiful, and the parents made such a handsome couple. I couldn't stop looking at them. I saw a vision of something I'd never had—these people were living in their moment, with their beautiful children, and they seemed so content living in this moment. I was living outside it. Which was more real, I wondered? Sometimes now when I see a woman with a new baby, or a couple with small children, I think, How could you? What sort of future do you think you're going to be able to provide for these beautiful children in the face of looming environmental collapse? But that's the point. They are in the moment, caring for their children, suffused with love for them, while I'm already living in the immolated future. Which is more real? Living in the moment? Living outside it?

Vincent shook his head, paused only for a beat, and then said, So, do you plan on leaving L.A. then?

YES, SHE said. She had decided to leave L.A. The city had never really been a good fit for her anyway. She was going back to Utah, as strange as that may sound to us. She was taking Aimee up on her invitation to come back and live in the old house. As we probably knew, the Huntsman Cancer Institute in Salt Lake City was a terrific place, and she'd found a doctor there who was willing to try a new therapy. Very experimental, her expectations weren't that high, but why not try? Ina would continue to work for her though she had no wish to live in Utah. She would be overseeing everything from abroad, but of course she'd be visiting her whenever she needed her. They had given up the lease on the house in Silver Lake. She was leaving for Utah in a few days. Flying back with Ina—and this really would be her last plane trip, she said. The very, very last.

I'm surprised you didn't decide to go back to New York, Vincent said. I mean, all the friends you have there.

Precisely, she said. All the people who would feel sorry for me. Who would look at me and see only this sick old bag about to croak. But listen to me! So full of self-pity, eh? Self-pity is just sadness in the pejorative. Who said that?

She laughed. I shook my head and smiled at her, as if to say, *Oh stop.* Vincent looked away and said nothing. I was aware of how he hadn't been able to make any comment about her illness. But she didn't appear to mind. Because she knew him. She knew what to expect.

I think it was Renata Adler. She's the one who said self-pity is just sadness in the pejorative, in her novel *Speedboat.* Did you ever read that? she asked me.

I said no.

I know you read it, she said to Vincent, because you bought it when it first came out and read it before I did. You gave it to me. I can even remember what you said at the time—*you'll be wanting to read this.*

I don't remember much of it, he said.

What are you reading now? she asked him, pointing to the book he'd put down when he first saw her.

He turned it over and held it up so she could read the title.

Ah, *Bovary,* she said. I remember it was one of your favorite novels. How many times have you read that by now?

Many, he said, and smiled lovingly at the book.

She said, I keep thinking of that line about *her dreams falling into the mud like wounded swallows.* Did you know the first English translation of *Madame Bovary* was made in 1886 by Eleanor Marx Aveling, a daughter of Karl Marx, who later committed suicide in much the same manner as Emma?

He said he did not, and I said I didn't either.

SHE DIDN'T stay much longer. She finished her tea and then began gathering up her things, including the cane she had laid next to her on the couch that she now used to help steady herself as she stood up. As she prepared to leave she turned to Vincent and said, What about your cat? Did your cat come back?

I was sorry she had asked this question. It was a terrible subject to raise at that moment, just when she was leaving. I knew Vincent wouldn't want to answer her, so I did. I told her Max hadn't returned, unfortunately. And since it had been more than two months now that he'd been gone we didn't have a lot of hope he ever would.

She nodded. I'm sorry, she said. I hoped he'd turned up.

When she got ready to leave, Vincent walked with us to the door, though he stood back as she and I embraced.

Please stay in touch, I said. I wanted to add *You owe this much to me,* but I didn't.

She turned to Vincent.

Come here, you, she said. It wasn't a request but a demand.

He moved closer, with a stiffness, and when he reached her side she put her arms around him quickly, taking him by surprise. He returned her embrace briefly and then let his arms hang and tried to back away. But she wouldn't let him go. She said something to him as she held him close, speaking to him in a voice I couldn't hear. Whatever she said, it was done quickly, and then she released him and smiled—first at him, then me, and then she stepped outside and began to leave, one hand holding on to the wall. She appeared rather unsteady on her feet and I wanted to reach out and hold her arm, but I didn't. At the last minute I asked if she would like me to walk down the steps with her, and she said, no, she would be fine. Ina was waiting for her in the car.

Take care of each other, she said, before turning and walking away.

When she'd gone we were silent. We went back inside and sat down opposite each other and didn't say anything for a while. After some time I said I was glad she had come to see us before she left. I was happy about that. But Vincent only made a noise like *un-huh,* and then he simply sat in his chair, his head tilted back with his eyes closed. And he stayed that way for a long time.

20

It was several months after she had come to visit us at the apartment that I got the first letter from her. The envelope was a little work of art. She had made a drawing of herself on the back, one hand raised in a wave, standing against a background of mountains I immediately recognized as the Wasatch Range.

Inside I found a long letter, written on cream-colored paper and dated September 21, 2014:

Darlinghissima,

Do you mind if I call you that? I hope not. While we don't have the sort of relationship that Janet Flanner had with her beloved Natalia it's not for lack of desire on my part. You must have known that I've been attracted to you ever since we were in school, starting in Mrs. Terry's class in sixth grade. Do you remember that time in the high school bathroom when I kissed you? It wasn't out of any confusion of feeling. By that point in my life I realized I was interested in both girls and boys but it wasn't something I cared to talk about. When it became clear that you were totally straight, I gave up. But I never gave up loving you.

When I was younger, I had affairs with both men and women. Women were ripe for the picking at Bryn Mawr and I enjoyed that time very much. But at some point I decided I was more interested in men. Women, it seemed, couldn't stop talking about their *feelings* and in the end it bored me

to death. I'd get a sharp rap on the knuckles from feminists
for saying this but it's true. I wanted to have sex and they
wanted to gabble on about their fathers and all the pain
they'd suffered growing up. After a while I got sick of all
that emotional excavation. I pivoted toward men, and for
better or worse that stayed my orientation. I have to admit
I simply liked the company of men better. I think it was
my weakness. I always wanted to be more like them. Less
emotional. More decisive. I certainly wanted their power.
The kind of power that's been denied women forever and
which men simply take as their birthright.

Most people are in fact blinded by their emotions. They
think feelings are facts. I've made an effort over the years to
tone mine down, and in doing so grew rather tough myself.
Obviously one can never really tame the emotions, and as
it turns out what I've been left with is little more than a
clear plastic shell through which you can still see the blood
sloshing.

I have to admit I have suffered from a melancholic longing
my whole life, for what I don't know, something I can't quite
put my finger on.

Everything was always so clear and clean in Vincent's
mind. That's what I envied him more than anything else, and
I could tell when I stopped by to visit you that his mind is as
calm and clear as ever—was there ever a more centered man
(or should I say self-centered, which may be the same thing)?

What did I envy you? Your kindness, I think. I'm afraid I
never learned how to do kind. This was brought into sharp
relief during our trip when I acted so prickly but of course
it's something I've always known about myself.

I'm writing to you from the upper level of the Tomb,
where I have taken the suite of rooms Aimee insisted should
be mine because she knew I coveted it—the bedroom and
sitting room that overlook the pool and garden. This used to
be my parents' bedroom (I try *not* to imagine them fucking
in here but I don't imagine they did that much of that, not

with each other anyway). Who would have believed it, that
I could have ended up back here? I was so convinced I never
would. Life has so many little surprises in store, doesn't it?

In the end I chose Colette's solution: I took the path
she suggested in the Claudine novels: her cure for
disillusionment, to seek refuge from the world's hurt by
going home to her village where "the divine solitude, the
restful foliage, the wise blue nights, and the peace of wild
animals" could restore one's balance. There are no wild
animals here, at least not on Eccles Avenue, but I find no
shortage of wise blue nights. I had forgotten what nights
really looked like. Skies so full of stars. The moon exploding
in silence.

I brought only my clothes and many boxes of books with
me. My library of favorite art books, in fact, all those I've
collected over the years and carried with me from place
to place, now whittled down to only the most treasured
volumes. Each morning I devote several hours to looking
at one book. Just one each morning. I look at it for as long
as I want, sitting in that little room just off the bedroom
overlooking the garden, in a big overstuffed chair—one of
the few things Aimee kept from my mother's time—and in
this way I am making my way through my library, shifting
the stacks from one side of the room to the other, book by
book. My favorites I keep next to the bed.

Books snare so much of what is happiness in life, don't
they? This morning I looked at a small volume of Manet's
pastel drawings of flowers, the last work he made before
dying. Vincent gave me this book long ago. *The Last Flowers of
Manet.* He bought it for me when I was recovering from an
appendectomy. I remember the morning he walked into the
bedroom and handed it to me, saying, *This will make you feel
better.* And it did. I like looking at the page where he signed
it to me—*To J, with endless love, V.* I could almost believe he
might still feel this way if I hadn't seen him before I left L.A.
I realized that day when I stopped to see you that he had lost

his feelings for me. And why shouldn't he have? Still, I wish
you would tell him I am looking at the Manet book again.
And thank him for me. It has given me so much pleasure.

Ina helped me get settled here, but I told her she didn't
need to stay. I don't think she quite understands why I've
chosen to come back. All I want is quiet now, a good view,
peace. Aimee, who is so lovely to help me, for company. I've
pretty much stopped responding to emails from anyone but
close friends (and of course my medical team). If I do have
to communicate with anyone I usually do it by letter, as I am
now doing with you.

Will you agree to correspond with me this way, at least for
as long as I am able? I don't mean you have to write to me all
the time, just now and then in response to the letters I might
send you. As I told you during our trip (here I go again) I
find the disappearance of the written letter disturbing, for
what it signifies: the very record of human conversation
and intimate thought is being lost. History will be harder
to parse without the letters of the artists and writers and
thinkers. I have come to regard the shunning of my iPhone
and the writing of letters as two of the most radical acts I
can imagine during my final days.

And there is no question things are coming to an end, as if
it were a tale that has now been told.

I wanted to come and see you and Vincent before I left
town but I was also afraid, and you must have been able to
tell how nervous I was when I showed up unannounced.
But I couldn't ask beforehand. I was afraid Vincent wouldn't
want to see me. I was also a bit afraid to see the two of you
together, enjoying an intimacy I could never really establish.
And yet I decided to come anyway.

For a long time after I left him I felt our relationship
wasn't finished. If I never saw him again I could cling to
that feeling—that something else was still ahead for us (it's
a bit like his inscription in the Manet book, I'm afraid—
that *endless love* he professed). Perhaps this is something like

what Maria Callas must have felt when Onassis flipped her
for Jackie: she could never quite let go of him. That's a bad
analogy so forget it, after all it was I who *flipped* Vincent,
so to speak, and Onassis did end up coming back to Callas
though by then he was very sick. The truth is, I didn't think
I could bear to see the two of you together, living happily.
And you are happy, aren't you? You didn't answer that
question the first time I asked you on our drive, so I don't
expect you to answer it now. I think, however, I know more
than you give me credit for. I do *get* it, Darlinghissima, if
you understand what I mean. The idea didn't occur to me
until quite recently but Vincent is on the autism spectrum,
isn't he? People didn't talk about those things so much
during the years I spent with him. I simply thought he was
eccentric. But now I see it differently. I wonder if I'm right.
If so, I'd like you to tell me please. It would help explain a
lot. All those deficits in social-emotional reciprocity I never
understood.

I'm not inclined to give you a report on my own health
since the subject is so boring. Suffice it to say I've been put
on the experimental immunology regimen I've been hoping
for, the outcome of which is decidedly undecided. But I do
like the new oncologist I'm seeing at the Huntsman Cancer
Center. His name is Dr. Brilliant. I can't go wrong.

I find Aimee the most congenial of roommates. She's such
an intelligent and kind person. She takes me to my medical
appointments and in every other way cares for me in a
manner beyond anything I deserve. She never makes a fuss
and is so quietly cheerful and smart, and because she has
spent her whole life here she thinks of nice places to take
me occasionally on a little outing. The other day she drove
me out to the lake to see Robert Smithson's Spiral Jetty. A
lovely experience. The water has gone down and you can
see it again, the rocks extending out into the pinkish water,
making such a beautiful dark swirl. It's extraordinary to me

to think I had never seen it before now. Where have I been all my life?

Of my mother I have nothing much to say. For some perverse reason I find myself visiting her more often than I care to admit. And the weird thing is, I enjoy it. Just watching her act out her role of a loving mother is such a riot.

I'll end this now—as my friend Peter likes to say, my rickshaw has arrived and I must go. But I did want to ask, what are you working on these days? I'm making little drawings and watercolors, taking my inspiration from Goya, who never let old age or sickness stop him from working every day: *I'm Still Learning* is the title of one of his late drawings, showing a stooped old man, bearded and fragile, leaning heavily on a cane but looking out at the viewer with an indisputably strong gaze. *I'm still learning.* When he made this drawing he was nearly blind, and mostly deaf and crippled, but still making art each and every day. I will do the same.

I adore you, my dearest V., and always have: you are the truest of friends.

All my love,
Jolene

P.S. May I ask another favor? Since I don't believe I will ever return to MacArthur Park, will you write to me from there and tell me how everything looks now? I spent so many happy days there, sitting on the benches, feeding the ducks and geese, looking at the colorful garbage floating in the water and the homeless scratching their lice, all the while dreaming about my last performance—it was such a *real* place to me, so bereft of the privilege and gentrification you see in so many other neighborhoods in L.A. and somehow much richer for it, at least to me. I like to believe that I, too, am still learning. And don't think I have forgotten about the gift I want to give you. I finally thought of something for Vincent as well, something I'd like to send to him. Expect a package soon.

I wrote back to her the next day.

September 22, 2014

Dear Jolene:

I'm happy to hear from you and glad to think the Colette cure is working out. I like to think of you returned to the peacefulness of that landscape where we both started out. I do find it ironic that you, the cosmopolite, have gone back to the village while I, the one who feels most at home in the country, am now more or less permanently moored in this city you've come to so dislike.

We have settled into a new house, not that far from our old place on Carondelet. It's in a mixed neighborhood—a lot of Hispanic families, mostly Guatemalan. The area hasn't yet been gentrified though I see more and more young couples on the street pushing strollers. It's still one area of the city where a family starting out might be able to afford something. Ironically, the house is on Bonnie Brae, the same street where Chandler lived when he moved to L.A. in 1912.

When we first looked at this house, the realtor selling the place asked if we were searching for a starter home for our grandchildren. I don't think he could imagine that people our age would be buying their first house in this city. Especially such a modest one.

It's small but charming, a classic California bungalow. There's a deep shaded porch and a big backyard with citrus and avocado trees, all enclosed by a high hedge which gives a feeling of privacy. We sit out back in the evenings, have a glass of wine, and watch the antics of the two new kittens we got from the shelter, Ava and Anton (after Gardner and Chekhov). I'm afraid our old cat Barney recently passed. We're starting over with these two—a brother and sister.

You asked what I am working on: well it might give you a laugh to know it's the idea you ridiculed. Yes, *Cookbook for Idiots* is coming along nicely. I'm working my way through Cissy's recipes. Last night I made her "Eggplant Cissy" for Vincent, and because I know *just how much* you'd appreciate having this recipe I'm including it here, verbatim:

Peel and slice an eggplant. Saute slices in butter until they soften, then put in layers in a casserole with minced onion and bell pepper and ripe olives, then grated cheese. Cover with Spanish tomato sauce on top. Cook 1¼ hours in 350 degree oven. Take from oven and leave a little while to cool slightly so that the casserole may be placed on the table with an asbestos pad underneath.

It's a sort of poor man's Eggplant Parmesan which you can spruce up considerably with good cheese and a homemade "Spanish" tomato sauce, and really it wasn't bad even if I feel very deeply the olives didn't belong. We had to take a punt on the asbestos pad because of course they've become a little outré.

There isn't a great deal more I can add to this letter, except to say two things:

One, I never realized you were attracted to me, I mean sexually or physically or however you want to put it, and at this point what difference can that make?

You must know by now how much I care for you. I'm grateful you've come back into my life—I wanted to say *our* lives, but I understand why that may never happen, and I'm certain you do as well. You are not wrong in your suspicions. He is, in fact, on the spectrum: he was diagnosed for the first time about ten years ago, so you see I, too, was in the dark for a very long time. But I don't think we need say anything more about this, do we? At least I don't care to, as I feel that it's really his story to tell.

I'll leave it to my next letter to give you a report from the park. This is more than enough for now.
    With all my love,
    Verna

And so the correspondence began.

SOMETIMES SHE wrote very long letters, sometimes just a brief note, but her letters arrived frequently, sometimes two or more a week although later when she grew weaker they came less often. The shorter notes seemed to contain a kind of compressed emotion as if she'd felt an urgency to get something down immediately and send it off.

SHE THANKED me for confirming what she suspected about Vincent.

I CAN now see my own past more clearly, she wrote, and it helps to explain so much.

He was always so *sense-sensitive,* if you know what I mean, and that should have been the first clue. He could hear noises I couldn't—water running in pipes, something clanging outside—little noises that upset him until he could discern their location and cause. He always reacted so strongly to smell—he never liked me to wear perfume and I couldn't understand that. And then there was his aversion to touch, and to any dirt. If I happened to accidentally brush his pant leg with the toe of my shoe while crossing my legs he would immediately begin brushing off the fabric as furiously as if I'd left a great smear of mud there instead of a tiny bit of dust. It also of course helps explain his self-absorption, which I always mistook for a sidebar to his genius. Now I simply realize his exceptionalism is all of a package, and the organizing principles of his mind have apparently helped to

foster this brilliance. I can only say that the most difficult
part for me, as I'm sure it has been for you as well, was his
disinclination to respond to feelings in any "normal" way,
or express his own readily, but given my attitude about the
excess of emotions driving contemporary events, how can I
really call this a limitation? Besides, there was so much to be
charmed by—his love of that particular tree, for instance. I
keep thinking of that—that tree he used to stop and swoon
over on our walks. How could you not love someone who
could become so besotted with a *tree*? That, of course, was
part of his visual acuity, his close reading of the world. Now
I get it. Everything makes sense. And I'll say no more, out of
respect for your feelings (and his).

OCCASIONALLY SHE sent a postcard. These were always carefully
chosen with an image that might reflect the message she'd written
on the back. One portrayed a reproduction of a 1910 painting by Max
Pechstein showing a colorful horse fair, with a message that simply
said, *Are you still wearing your misbegotten sheriff hat?* Another card pic-
tured a Blackfeet buckskin shirt from 1890 with the words *Short Face*
wore this shirt, decorated with weasel tails and lazy-stitched beadwork, as per-
sonal medicine.
    I could use a little of that myself right now, she'd written.

I DIDN'T discuss the letters with Vincent, and I don't know if he
read her postcards if he was the first to pick up the mail. I suspect he
didn't. He was rather correct in that way. He never actually made
any comment at all on the fact we'd begun corresponding, except to
ask, after the first letter from her arrived, So did she move back to
Utah after all? He continued to avoid using her name when he spoke
of her. It was as if the very word *Jolene* contained too much intimacy
for him.

———

THE PACKAGE she said we should look for finally did arrive, but not until weeks after she said to expect it. Two packages came. One for him. One for me.

We opened them on the afternoon they came, sitting out in the garden.

In mine I found a blue velvet box, containing a pale stone pendant in the shape of a heart, with an intricate little jeweled crown hanging on a gold chain. *For V.,* she had written on a plain white card. *From Scotland, 19th Century, yellow Citrine. A special stone to the Scots, and now to you. Think of me, love, J.*

I put it on, clasping the chain around my neck, and felt the stone settle on my breast lightly, but with a solid weight. A yellow heart, so translucent with light that when I held it up to the sun it fairly glowed.

Isn't it beautiful, I said. He agreed.

Then he opened his package.

Inside was an object wrapped in a batik cloth. When he unrolled it, it revealed a carved wooden head. A black figure he could hold in one hand. It appeared to be very old. Rather plain in its crudeness. A face that was more a suggestion than a face. A primitive object, but from where? He gazed at it, smiling, holding it aloft and turning it. Wow, he said. Wow. It was the sort of minimal figure I knew he liked. She had found him the perfect gift. On a card she had written, *Vincent, Don't let this go to your head, but I send this with much love. It's Brazilian. Balsa wood. Old, very old. That alone should remind you of me! Adieu, Jolene.*

We put the carved balsa wood head in our cabinet of curiosities, next to the figure of the Guatemalan saint with the tin hat. I began wearing the citrine pendant. Both objects became daily reminders of her continuing presence in our lives, little talismanic prompts. Just as I knew she hoped they'd be.

AT ONE point she delighted me by sending a drawing along with a short note that simply said,

> To my great surprise, I have formed a deep attachment to
> Eddie the cat and, not knowing of all my flaws as a human

being, he has boldly decided to reciprocate my affection. He spends long hours with me, sitting on my lap in that great big overstuffed chair, or resting with me, curled up on my bed. How could I have been so immune to the charms of these animals for so long? When he comes up onto my chest and I feel the thrum of his purr against my own beating heart I imagine we are momentarily joined in the mutual pleasure we take in each other's company. How remarkable this makes me feel, how intimate with another living creature, and how I've missed that. Colette would approve of my awakening, don't you think? And so must you. I'm sending you a little drawing of Eddie which I made this morning when he was curled at the foot of my bed: I hope it captures his beauty—and he really is a beauty, isn't he? Plus, he ACTUALLY LIKES ME!

I KEPT a photo of us on my desk in my new study. A picture from high school. We're sitting in Liberty Park, in front of a stone fountain. I'm in front and she's sitting slightly behind me with her arms wrapped around me, her hands clasped over my chest. I'm leaning back against her. She's wearing a scarf tied around her head with long earrings dangling to her shoulders, and I have a flower pinned in my hair. We look like gypsy women. Beautiful gypsy girls. The way we gaze out so directly at the camera would make you think there was nothing in the world we were afraid of. And nothing we couldn't do. Or hadn't already done.

THE RECOGNITION for her work seemed to increase during this time, even though she'd more or less withdrawn from public life by moving back to Utah. Like many older women artists of her generation she was having a certain *moment*. Occasionally, in a letter, she would mention that this or that was happening with her work, at some museum or gallery, and it appeared to amuse and please her.

AS THE letters continued over the winter, her handwriting began to change. The penmanship grew shakier, and the lines became uneven, sloping upwards at a slant the way my mother's writing used to do when she grew old. I thought it meant she could no longer sit at a desk and must be writing from bed. There were other clues her health was deteriorating. She mentioned in one letter that she had gotten five liters of blood in one week, and in another that she was receiving a series of potassium drips. But most of the time the reference to her condition was limited to a wry comment here and there.

Her letters were often filled with beautiful descriptions of the garden, the weather, and of course Eddie, as well as Aimee's cleverness: Aimee is very *crafty,* she wrote, and then wondered how the word went from meaning cunning, deceitful, and sly and instead had become a term for a person highly skilled at turning flattened bottle caps into trivets.

There was almost always a little drawing at the top of the letters— like Manet at the end of his life, she said, she wanted to illustrate her world. He had often embellished his correspondence with drawings from his surroundings after he had been forced to leave Paris for the suburbs on account of his health. She enjoyed doing the same. He had missed his old comrades as she also missed hers, and an illustrated letter was a way of reaching out to them and offering a little gift.

MY ART-MAKING has become a very private affair, she wrote, I no longer feel in need of an audience. A daily drawing or watercolor or a little illustration at the top of a letter quite satisfies me—with you, very often, as the only audience I have in mind.

IN SPITE of the tender drawings and the front she tried to keep up in terms of her health, often a new edge of despair now crept into her letters. She found the conditions in the world so depressing. Her mood grew darker during this time and so did her letters. She expressed her despair over the rise of nationalistic tendencies. The slaughter happening in Syria and the waves of refugees. The use of chemical weapons on children. The long winter was now causing her to feel housebound, she said, not that she really had anyplace to go. She visited her mother much less frequently, mostly because it was becoming challenging for her to go anywhere except doctor's appointments.

The truth is, she wrote, my mother is happier greeting one of those panting therapy dogs they drag around to rest homes these days than she is to see me. And yet for reasons I don't understand, when I do visit her I feel more affection for her than I ever have. Maybe it's because I know she can no longer wound me.

AS SPRING came on, the atmosphere in the country increasingly disturbed her and she often mentioned her anxieties in her letters. Things took a bad turn in early summer. *When I saw that idiot coming down the escalator to announce his candidacy I thought, Nah, it can't happen. But now I have to admit it is happening, isn't it? Tell me I'll be dead before the election, just in case.*

And then a letter arrived in August, laying out her situation in very frank terms:

> Darlinghissima:
>   The news, I'm afraid, is not good. Tumors have been found in four other places in my body, including several large ones in my liver, so it appears the immunotherapy is not working and we are stopping all treatments as of this week. There are no options left. I asked the doctor to be honest. He said, We are looking at a matter of months. He suggested I get my affairs in order—but it's been so long since I've had affairs I told him that should be very easy. He didn't laugh.
>   There was, however, some good news: It hasn't spread to my brain. This was my greatest fear, that I would lose my mind first. Now I am accorded the plausibility of being mentally competent to the very end.
>   The End. How shall it go?
>   I'm sorry I wasn't able to mount that one last performance piece in the park before I shuffled off, something to express

my outrage that America has become the biggest weapons
pusher in the world, rewarding tyrants and dictators with
the means to be even more lethal while turning a blind eye
to the massive civilian deaths and the evil we cause. My
heart breaks for Yemen. It's a fool's errand, of course, to try
and say anything about a situation everyone is already aware
of. We have made of the world one gigantic killing field with
our excellent weapons. It's left every American with blood
on our hands though of course we're too busy buying stupid
things we don't really need and getting massively fat to see
anything beyond the next purchase or Happy Meal. (I have
the right to say Americans are fat because they are, just as
tipping is still *my* option, so please don't lecture me.)

I have accepted I'll hardly ever leave the house again
and have visited my mother for the last time, not that she
understood this when I said goodbye to her (I couldn't help
feeling a bit cheated right at that moment, knowing she was
going to outlast me, that she gets to go on even in her wasted
state when I would have made such good use of more time—
but then it all seemed rather amusing to me and I kissed the
old bag goodbye and she patted my hand, and for a moment
it felt the perfect conclusion). I can only stand for a very
short time. I need a walker to even make it to the bathroom,
and then it takes me forever. You can imagine what stairs do
to me. Getting in and out of cars.

I can no longer sleep without sleeping pills, and they rarely
do the trick. I lie about the house all day, and lay about my
bed all night, awake and restless. I stare into the dark and
beg sleep to come but it never does. It isn't easy to read,
but I still try to look at my books each day. I keep the large
volume of Goya's late work next to my bed and look at it
often—oh those black paintings! How they can catch my
mood, such ecstatic fear and mystery, the feelings that come
with nearness of death—those monstrous creatures haunting
these works, that endearing little yellow dog looking over
the edge of the abyss. Sometimes I wake in the morning to

find I've left Goya next to me all night, weighing down the mattress beside me like my absent lover, with the round face of the Countess Maria de Puga on the cover gazing back at me with her placid expression. I don't have the concentration I once did but the tenets of Buddhism still interest me, as they did John Cage right up to the end. By the way, that Cage quote the owner of the little French restaurant tossed off when we stopped there for lunch? How *the function of music is to quiet and sober the mind*? It's only half the quote. This is how it really goes: *The function of music is to quiet and sober the mind, thus making it susceptible to divine influences.*

These divine influences. They do make themselves felt. Particularly when I look at my mountains.

I have lost all desire to eat and drink, though I still take a glass or two of wine in the evening mostly out of habit (and because I'm a lush). My weight has dropped to 98 pounds though my height remains as it always was—5'9". Without a sense of taste anymore, that coq au vin I ate at the Still Life Cafe is one of the meals I most enjoy going over in memory. My sense of smell has become acute but who cares about that? I can smell food in the kitchen even when Aimee isn't cooking.

All I've wanted to do is fall asleep and wake up when it's all over.

Why am I telling you all this? I don't know. It must be disturbing to you. I suppose I want your company—not literally of course. I know it upsets you I won't allow you to come see me but I won't relent on that. I much prefer that our intimacy be played out in our letters than for you to see me the way I am. Don't think of this as mere vanity. Though much of it is.

I want you to know everything. To help me through this time: I need my best friend to be with me now. Do you remember how I used to call you that in school? My *best* friend. I could see how it pleased you to no end. What a manipulating and sly little egoist I was (and still am).

I take pills for pain. They leave me dopey. I struggle out of bed to open the curtains, then struggle to get out and close them again. The sun hurts my eyes, yet I can't do without light. I wait for Aimee to bring me tea and the bits of things she keeps urging me to eat even though eating has lost its appeal: it's the ritual of her arrival I value. When able I get up and sit for a while each day, often with Eddie on my lap. From my top-floor window I observe the household routines, the coming and going of gardeners and the cleaning lady, the electricians and repairmen, Aimee's departures and arrivals. I try to shower each day though I don't always feel like it. I've discouraged Ina from visiting. I don't want her to see me. She's very good at taking care of everything related to my work so I don't have to think about that.

I went to the bathroom this morning and looked at the scarecrow in the mirror and cawed at myself. *Caw caw caw!* Sometimes I have dreams about running a brush through my nonexistent hair.

Ah, I see the rickshaw has pulled up again and just in time as I fear I was about to spark a spasm of jealousy in you by saying something about Vincent. Don't think I didn't notice your reaction every time I brought up his name on our drive. I knew it was perverse of me. But art itself is inherently subversive, and having spent a lifetime in that world I'm afraid I've ended up as a very subversive woman.

May I point out that you haven't sent me a report from the park in some time. Can you do that please? I'd particularly like to know how the birds are doing. Use all your powers of description. And don't forget to add a little note about the General. I can still see the graffiti scrawled across his body. You have to admit the man did know how to dress.

Your devoted friend, forever—as long as this particular forever lasts.

J.

IN MY next letter I went to some lengths to give her a detailed report on the birds of MacArthur Park. It was one of the last letters I wrote to her, almost a year to the day after we first began our correspondence.

September 12, 2015

Dearest Jolene:

It's a gray day in the park. The air feels cool and fresh this morning. I'm sitting on the bench near the concrete boat ramp where the birds always gather. The seagulls rise in a great flock from the surface of the lake and wheel above the water while below the mallards and pigeons peck at greenish clumps of—what? Lettuce, maybe, that's been dumped on the cement. People leave the strangest assortment of things for the birds. Little red balls are bobbing at the edge of the water, and I see now they are radishes that have been left for the birds who I do not think will ever be inclined to eat radishes. People think these birds will eat anything, but they aren't that desperate. Instead much of what's left simply rots in the sun, lending a distinct odor to the air.

The mallards are pruning, nibbling at their own feathers, fluffing, shaking, while the black mud hens drift by in an orderly flotilla. No sight of my favorite pair of geese this morning, the white drake and—what is the word for female goose? I suppose it's gander, though that sounds so male. This pair are never apart. And neither are the coupled mallards, the female with her speckled brown feathers, the male with his glorious crown of iridescent green. There are brown seagulls, and white and gray seagulls, and one lone seagull with a speckled head. He stands on one leg and stretches the other behind him, then lifts his clawed foot and shakes it vigorously to one side. A few well-dressed Korean ladies circle the lake in pairs, taking their morning exercise. Elderly Mexican men in straw cowboy hats occupy the benches near the place where the boathouse once stood. Sometimes they bring guitars and serenade the passersby.

More and more people have begun to walk in the park. I sense the neighborhood slowly changing and still one sees mostly the ragged and ravaged, the poor, and the newly arrived. Every tree in the park has a homeless person beneath it, a body that has taken shelter. At least the trees befriend them, offering homelike refuge. Without shade, the days must be unbearable.

Let me move on to the General.

He's looking worse than ever. Someone has taken off a bit of his nose. One can hardly read the text on his peacemaker side for all the graffiti, while his soldierly words are much more legible (wouldn't you know?). I'm still wondering what he meant by this *spiritual* aspect of war he refers to. The reflecting pool at his feet has no water, and therefore reflects nothing. It's an expanse of dull gray cement with irregular blue lumps, a dried-up ocean where the crumbling islands of the Philippines grow smaller every day.

I wanted to walk by the statue this morning, but it's become the roughest area of the park. I can't describe, really, the desperate-looking group of homeless men who have made their camp in front of the General, they are some of the roughest men I have ever seen here in the park. It would be impossible for me to walk past them without feeling worried. Many more single men now live in the park. So many men, dressed so poorly, huddled together, throwing dice, playing cards—but mostly just looking lost and bored and forlorn. Where are the women? Nowhere to be seen.

I am frightened and attempting to avoid the subject of your health. Your last letter caused me to feel so worried and sad, and I don't know what to say. I would still like to come see you if only you would let me. But you won't let me, will you?

What will you let me do?

I could be there by tomorrow. And stay for as long as needed. Please let me come.

All my love,

Verna

———

SHE DID not let me come.

Instead I received what would be the last letter from her.

September 19, 2015

Darlinghissima:

You are not to think, under any circumstance, of coming
here. In any case, by the time you receive this letter I will be
gone. I wouldn't call it a final performance exactly, but I have
thought things out carefully and I've decided to go now rather
than wait for this illness to further ravage me. Don't think I'll
suffer: I've hoarded pills and I'll have taken those long before
the flames reach me. You might say that I will die, and then
simply self-cremate. Think of the money that will save on
funerary costs!

At dawn, on the morning of my choosing, sometime very
soon, I'll take my life.

I like to think it might be a gentle death. I've done my pharm
research, believe me, and it should be over rather quickly.

Of course Aimee has no idea what I have in mind. Nor
does anyone else.

Except now you of course.

The burning will only happen in my mind, as it has been
happening for a very long time. Where could I possibly
"perform" such a ritual as self-immolation now? In Aimee's
backyard? Leaving her to find my charred remains? It's
enough that I had to ask her the other day, Will you be okay
if you wake one morning and find me dead in my bed? She
simply looked at me, her eyes filling with tears. Of course I
knew her answer.

No, Darlinghissima, there'll be no burning of this body,
what's left of it, much as I might have once imagined that as a
possibility.

This morning I spent an hour or two with a volume of Kiki

Smith's work. I was delighted by the reproduction of her
pen-and-ink drawing *Woman on the Pyre,* which is just what it
says—a naked woman kneeling atop a stack of logs, yet to be
lit, with her arms outstretched as if in prayer or supplication.
I wish I could discuss it with her—what was she thinking
when she made this drawing which so closely resembles my
own idea? Had she, too, imagined self-immolation? Are we
women naturally prone to such dark thoughts? After all it is
the wives who commit sati, throwing themselves on their
husbands' funeral pyres, not the other way around.

Fire will be the first absolute power, said Prometheus, the fire
bringer. *It will be the last to rule. I am burning in my own fire.* So
it will be.

I feel it's time to go now, and not wait for more suffering.
I'm forever tired because I no longer sleep and am in
considerable pain. I mean pain I really can't manage
anymore. I lie awake in the dark. Something is causing night
sweats. That doesn't help. I wait for morning to come. The
inky light, the change from black to blue and then the reds
and oranges. Ah, I think, ah, I live another day. But the days
are becoming too hard.

Fatigue at this level is paralyzing. I spend a lot of time lying
on the bed with Eddie, looking out toward the mountains.
That is my spiritual peace. I can picture myself outside,
walking up a trail, hear the crunch of pebbles underfoot.
I also imagine my body flying through the air up to the
very highest ridges. At night, when I can't sleep, I lie in
the dark and visit cities I've loved. I walk certain streets in
Paris I know so well, revisit them, take a long stroll and
visualize the places where I once shopped, the cafés I loved,
the favorite pâtisserie. I can do the same with streets in
London and Rome where I've spent a lot of time. I find this
very enjoyable, revisiting these beloved places, taking my
imaginary walks along familiar streets.

Aimee's sister and her mother come by once in a while,
they're very nice women, as are her sister's kids. Other

relatives sometimes stop by. But being in company takes a lot
and conversation is demanding because my voice has become
rather weak. It's one of the reasons I really don't wish to
have a phone call with you. What we have to say to each
other, in so many ways, we have already said. I can hear your
voice without really needing to hear it again.

There's something that is more difficult for the friend of the
dying person, knowing what to say, but really we don't want
words of wisdom, we just want love, gestures of affection. My
old New York friends Lynda and Carolee came to visit a few
weeks ago—I didn't encourage this visit, by the way, but they
came anyway, all the way from the East Coast, so how could
I turn them away? Carolee came into my room one afternoon
when I was having a very hard day and she just lay down on the
bed with me. I was having some chills and had a heating pad
but it wasn't helping, I still couldn't stop the shakes. Carolee
put her arms around me and hugged me very tight. I told her
that she made me feel loved, and she replied she could never
make me feel loved enough. That's what we want to hear.

I've had the most amazing life, Darlinghissima.

Now I plan on having an amazing death. I have the right to
do that, don't I?

Strangely I'm not afraid. All the things I have occasionally
despised in myself over the years . . . being a moral coward,
being a liar, being indiscreet about myself and others, acting
harshly toward people, being aggressive and above all my
insipid longing for nice things—my awful *cupidity,* if you
will. I feel I can expunge and leave these things behind by
bravely facing the end. And really, truly, I am not afraid.

I don't know how to end this letter. So I will simply say, as
the great poet W. S. Merwin wrote, *And when we have gone,*
they say we are with them forever.

Goodbye, dear friend—my very *best* friend. I have loved
you truly, if perhaps not so terribly well. Maybe I'll get
another crack at it when I shall be differently extant.

J.

21

She died on the first day of fall, the autumnal equinox, the moment of perfect balance between night and day. I'm sure she thought it an auspicious time to go. The memorial was held two weeks later—nobody wept and a lot of the talk over the afternoon was humorous and upbeat. There were so many beautiful children and a lot of older relatives, so many people I hadn't met, including a few of her closest friends from the art world, all gathered in Aimee's beautiful garden on a golden fall day. It felt more like a big family picnic than a wake. She was right about her mother's family being a large clan. If they were doubly grieved by her suicide—and why not just call it that?—they didn't show it or perhaps they didn't really know. Some probably had an idea of what had actually happened, but most spoke of it as a natural death brought on by her illness. I overheard people remark how it was too bad the cancer took her so young, and since a good number of people who came were very old, sixty-seven must have seemed young to them.

AIMEE KEPT saying to me, why would she do it? It was such an unexpected thing for her to do. If you could have seen her room. All the books she'd left open around her on the bed. And more books open on the floor. The drawings with women and children in bombed-out buildings, refugees, scenes of people fleeing, the paintings that she'd tacked up everywhere on the walls, showing boats capsizing and drowning figures, pictures that were so disturbing and tragic, all hav-

ing to do with war and refugees. Aimee said that music had been playing when she came into the room—"MacArthur Park." That's what
woke her up at dawn and caused her to finally come upstairs to check
on Jolene. She heard music somewhere and thought perhaps the CD
player in the living room had started up on its own, as it sometimes
did, but then she realized it was coming from Jolene's room, from a
computer Jolene had left open on her desk. When she went to shut it
off she had discovered the pictures of the monks on the screen. And
then she had discovered Jolene. She looked very peaceful, she said. At
first she hadn't realized she was gone.

No one was actually there to see what really happened at the end,
except Eddie. Eddie was on the bed with her, curled up near her head.
I just didn't know what to think when I found her, Aimee told me.
And then I saw the empty pill bottles. And I just knew.

She had left a letter, thanking Aimee for everything she had done
for her, and asking her to leave everything in the room as it was. This
was the last installation piece, her last performance, and she had written to Ina, leaving her instructions, asking her to come and photograph the room later so that perhaps the scene might be reassembled
for an exhibition—including the open books, the drawings of war,
the video loop of the monks self-immolating, the background music
of "MacArthur Park." Her final work.

VINCENT COULD not bring himself to come to the celebration of life
with me, and I didn't press him. I flew home the day after the service,
arriving back in L.A. in the early evening. He picked me up, and once
we had left the chaos of the airport he asked, How was it?

His voice was cool. I couldn't really tell what he was thinking, but
I knew he was upset. He was clearly sad. The thing about finally coming to accept someone without reserve is that you see all the things
you once felt were hidden. You come to an unfettered place. I gave
him the short account of the wake. I don't know why, but I felt reluctant to say more. It wasn't about him not coming back with me for the
memorial. I really didn't care about that. In some ways it was easier
that he hadn't been there. I didn't say more to him because there were

things I wanted to hold close for a while rather than discuss them. I also understood he really didn't care for the full report, and I was ready to leave it at that, as I was sure he would be, but he surprised me by speaking up again.

Do you think she suffered a lot at the end? he asked. I mean right at the end? I don't want to think she did.

He was looking straight ahead as he said this, staring through the windshield at the traffic ahead, waiting for a light to change, and it felt almost as though he was speaking to himself, finally saying what he'd been afraid to ask.

I think it could have been much worse, I said.

I wanted to protect him right then by telling him that, I was so moved by what he'd asked. There was no reason for him to know how hard it had actually been for her during her final days. I felt such closeness to him at that moment, that he could have even asked that, allowed himself to feel what I knew he had always felt. I told him that I thought she knew when to leave, and added that she had gone in her own way, the way she wanted to go, and that was the good part.

He nodded, just barely, more a quick downward jut of his chin, and continued to look ahead. And then I decided to tell him one more thing, knowing it would be the last thing that I would say to him about it.

She did love you, I said.

He reached up and pinched the flesh between his eyebrows with his thumb and forefinger for a just a moment and looked down in his lap, and I knew that he had closed his eyes, though I couldn't see them behind his sunglasses. He said nothing, not needing to. His quiet and the quick intake of breath let me know that he knew that, and felt it, and then the light changed, and we drove on and said nothing more.

SHE WAS right when she had suggested in an early letter that people might say some unflattering things about her once she was gone.

Jolene Carver was interested in being morally pure, one old acquaintance said in an interview, but at the same time she was one of the most immoral people I ever knew. Pathologically so. Treacherous, I would say.

I loved her, another person said, but I didn't much like her. She had a way of managing to offend you even when she was trying for a compliment. She thought she was being honest. I found her completely tactless.

One of her former colleagues, a gallery owner who had known her when she'd lived in Paris, said she felt Jolene was a person more to be pitied than envied. She had a hard life, she said, in the sense that a lot of people didn't understand what she was doing with her art, and by the time they did, the kind of work she was making was going out of fashion. "Not everybody loved the idea of feminist body art," she said. "Jolene developed a chip on her shoulder over the years, daring you to disagree with her. You have to admit she was a groundbreaking artist. Absolutely fearless. I still think one of her best pieces was *Meat,* her protest against the Gulf War. It had the character of both an erotic rite and an illustration of the true carnage."

One person claimed that until Jolene Carver came on the scene the culture was starved in terms of sensuousness because sensuality was always confused with pornography and objectification. There's no question that she, along with several other women artists of her era, changed that perception completely. The author emphasized what I had heard Jolene herself say on our trip, that she had challenged the old patriarchal morality of proper behavior and improper behavior and showed that the power of women's sensuality could be related to something much more ancient—the worship of nature, worship of the body, a pleasure in sensuousness.

IN SOME articles, she was quoted heavily, comments taken from previous interviews where she'd talked about her physician father and homemaker mother.

"I remember looking at all of my father's anatomy books," she told one interviewer. "He was happy that I would prowl around and look at things that I wasn't supposed to see. I was very lucky to end up at

Bryn Mawr. It was before the era of women's self-determination had really taken off, but I felt surrounded by such extraordinary women. Still I remember one of my teachers saying, You're very talented but don't set your heart on art. You're only a girl. Well, really, I thought. It only made me more determined to succeed."

HER ATTITUDE toward her mother—and the whole idea of family— changed a great deal at the end of her life. In one letter, written just before her last visit to see her mother, she said she felt a great sympathy for her:

> You'll remember me saying how you can never get rid of the past, that even when you cut it off it continues to grow on you, like fingernails or hair. I've come to see that's the beauty of it. You absolutely need fingernails and hair. I am lucky not to have ended up alone, as I very well could have. I have been so well taken care of here. I've felt such love from my relatives, and enjoyed their company. I now think, by all means stay with the family if you can.

IN THE same letter she mentioned she'd done some thinking about Jeannie Wokersein.

> I finally figured out what I think drove us to do what we did—I mean what drove me and Clare, not necessarily you (you simply got drawn into our mischief). I think both Clare and I were working out our lesbian tendencies around that time, and because we were tough girls, we didn't yet understand that we didn't have to act like horny boys and overpower a girl or attack her sexually. I can't speak for Clare, and guess I shouldn't try, but I also think I was reacting out of a sublimated hate for what I saw as female weakness. Jeannie was weak and she repulsed me. I wanted

to punish her for being so stupid. But I was punishing her for
something she was not and couldn't ever be. I think Clare
was just naturally mean. And you simply got caught up in it.

MONTHS HAVE now passed since Jolene's death. The house on Bonnie
Brae feels more and more like home, and the question of how to live
seems to have been largely settled. I feel much like Hardwick when
she wrote to Lowell shortly after he'd left her, *If you need me I'll always
be there, and if you don't need me I'll always not be there.* This might sound
like a pathetic thing for a person to say, especially a woman, and yet I
understand it so well. It's both the lock, and the key to freedom.

Sometimes I wonder, what was it that Jolene whispered to Vincent that day when she was leaving the apartment—the last time we
actually saw her? But I've never asked. And I never will.

Of course we miss Max. The loss of him was made so much worse
by the chaos that was unleashed when we were forced to leave the
apartment so suddenly. The way everything got so frantic at the end.
With the notice from the sheriff's department saying we had until the
next Monday morning to quit the premises, leaving us one week to
pack up. I think we felt somehow we could have kept Max from disappearing if only things had been different. If only the landlord hadn't
been such a monster and lied and cheated the way he did, forcing us
out.

Occasionally I've returned to Carondelet, hoping I'd catch a
glimpse of Max. I've imagined him wandering the neighborhood,
fantasized about perhaps even finding him waiting for us on our old
porch. But of course he's never there.

The last time I stopped by I walked up the front steps and sat
down on the landing for a while, just looking out over the familiar
scene and the tall buildings of downtown. I found a piece of paper
that had been left on the steps, some kind of official form that said
"Transfer of the Non-Exempt Former Home by an Institutionalized
Individual." I wondered who had been institutionalized. And to whom
the former home had been transferred. We knew that two of the older

tenants had ended up on the street after they'd been evicted. Single men who had relied on the low rent for years to make ends meet and now had nowhere else to go. All around the city people were losing their homes, being forced out of their apartments by unscrupulous landlords who wished to raise the rents and maximize their investments. The streets in so many neighborhoods now lined with tents and crude shacks. An epidemic of sorts. An indication of the ruthless times. How cruel it has all become.

The building hasn't yet been torn down, but all the units are now empty, except for Shirley's apartment. Because of her age and infirmities (and because she has always known how to fight, using every trick in the book to get her way) they can't evict her, and she refuses to leave voluntarily. The developers are waiting for her to die, and so is the building, and meanwhile she has become the last tenant, hanging on in her desecrated rooms, an old crone lodged in solitude. The pale light emanating from her top-floor bedroom window is the only sign of life left in the building at night. We always joked she was indestructible, that she'd be the last one left standing, the madwoman in the attic, and how ironic that it has turned out to be true. I can almost hear her laughing: *heh heh heh.*

A c k n o w l e d g m e n t s

Every book is an assemblage of ideas and influences, an accretion of thought from multiple sources, gathered over many years. I would like to thank the writers and artists who have contributed to my thinking as I was working on this novel, foremost among them the late iconic feminist performance artists Carolee Schneemann and Ana Mendieta, and the Austrian artist Valie Export. I drew inspiration from the volume *Carolee Schneemann: Imaging Her Erotics* to create my fictional artist, and I am grateful for the ideas and performative actions I discovered in Schneemann's brave and brilliant work and wish to give her credit.

The late photographer-artist Allan Sekula, a much-admired friend, staged a performance action, *Meat Mass* (very much like Jolene's *Meat* piece), by tossing stolen cuts of meat onto the San Diego freeway in 1972 and photographing the results. Sekula was an artist of very high consciousness whose work, like Jolene's, was social and political in nature.

I wish to pay tribute to the environmental activist David Buckel, who self-immolated in Prospect Park in Brooklyn in 2018, and to the writer Jesse Barron, whose piece in *The New York Times Magazine* in 2018 celebrated Buckel's great moral courage and his "incandescent act of speech," an urgent call to arms, a plea to protect our fragile planet.

The late Dan Frank, who shepherded many of my books through the labyrinth of a literary life, was every writer's dream of an editor. Enthralled by good writing, knowledgeable and curious about so many subjects, he possessed the genius editor's mind, skills that inevitably not only enabled him to make a book immeasurably better but inspired you to dream on. He could always point to what mattered in a story, and in this way led you to the marvelous, wondrous discoveries. *MacArthur Park* is our fifth book together, completed in the months before Dan died. For all that he gave me, year after year, not only the conversations and brilliant editing from which my books so profited, but for the sweetness I found in the friendship of a truly genial and lovely man, I'll always be so grateful. Dan's close friend and colleague, and my long-time agent, Joy Harris, once again offered such wisdom and faith and steadiness as I worked on this book during difficult times. From the beginning of our relationship thirty-five years ago, I have counted it among my greatest blessings and good luck to know and work with Joy.

To A.H., I can only say, I am so profoundly grateful for your love and boundless generosity, never more deeply felt. Though a novelist works in isolation, there are those whose love and guiding spirit are always with me, none more so than my son, Todd Thorn, who passed away as I was writing this book. I finished it for him, with the example of his lifelong courage always before me.

A NOTE ABOUT THE AUTHOR

Judith Freeman is the author of the novels *Red Water, The Chinchilla Farm, Set for Life,* and *A Desert of Pure Feeling; Family Attractions,* a collection of stories; and *The Long Embrace,* a biography of Raymond Chandler, as well as a memoir, *The Latter Days.* She lives in California and Idaho.

A NOTE ON THE TYPE

The text of this book was set in a typeface named Perpetua, designed by the British artist Eric Gill (1882–1940) and cut by the Monotype Corporation of London in 1928–30. Perpetua is a contemporary letter of original design, without any direct historical antecedents. The shapes of the roman letters basically derive from stonecutting, a form of lettering in which Gill was eminent. The italic is essentially an inclined roman. The general effect of the typeface in reading sizes is one of lightness and grace. The larger display sizes of the type are extremely elegant and form what is probably the most distinguished series of inscriptional letters cut in the present century.

Typeset by Scribe, Philadelphia, Pennsylvania

Printed and bound by Berryville Graphics, Berryville, Virginia

Designed by Maria Carella